Praise for *The Dead Girl in 2A*

"One of those books you devour in a single sitting. *The Dead Girl in 2A* promises a lot from the start and delivers in spades."

—Alex Marwood, author of *The Wicked Girls*

"Will grip you from the first chapter and never let go. A lightning-paced thriller reminiscent of Dean Koontz. I couldn't turn the pages fast enough!"

—Liv Constantine, international bestselling author of *The Last Mrs. Parrish*

"Readers will stay up all night with Carter Wilson's latest psychological thriller. With a story as riveting as it is mysterious, Wilson's *The Dead Girl in 2A* is a terrifying plunge into the depths of a childhood trauma rising back into the light. Wilson's characters are as deep as the mystery that surrounds them, and the fast-paced plot doesn't disappoint. This is not to be missed."

—R. H. Herron, international bestselling author of *Stolen Things*

"Carter Wilson's novels slip under your skin with the elegance and devastation of a surgeon's scalpel. In his latest book, Wilson weaves a gripping tale in which the present can die in a single careless moment, and the past is as unknowable as the future. *The Dead Girl in 2A* is a high-wire act, exquisitely balanced between shattering suspense and the sudden opening of our hearts. I couldn't put this book down. Bravo!"

—Barbara Nickless, author of the award-winning Sydney Parnell series

Also by Carter Wilson

Mister Tender's Girl

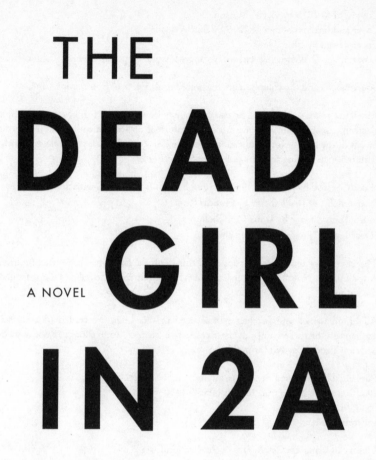

THE
DEAD
GIRL
A NOVEL
IN 2A

CARTER WILSON

Poisoned Pen
PRESS

Published by Poisoned Pen Press, an imprint of Sourcebooks
P.O. Box 4410, Naperville, Illinois 60567-4410
(630) 961-3900
sourcebooks.com

Library of Congress Cataloging-in-Publication Data

Names: Wilson, Carter (Novelist), author.
Title: Dead girl in 2A / Carter Wilson.
Description: Naperville, Illinois : Sourcebooks Landmark, [2019]
Identifiers: LCCN 2019000366 | (trade pbk. : alk. paper)
Subjects: | GSAFD: Psychological fiction.
Classification: LCC PS3623.I57787 D43 2019 | DDC 813/.6--dc23 LC record available at https://lccn.loc.gov/2019000366

Printed and bound in Canada.
MBP 10 9 8 7 6 5 4 3

For Jessica

Shake my body, release my soul.

Punish my senses, lose control.

This body's young but my spirit's old.

Scatter my ashes and let these feelings grow.

—JAMES, "LOSE CONTROL"

PART I

ONE

The Day Of

JAKE BUCHANNAN PLACED HIS palm on his eight-year-old daughter's cheek, hooked a strand of chestnut hair behind her ear, and wished again that he could change the past. Em lay on top of her bed in her room, beneath a ceiling light needing two of its three bulbs replaced, and Jake thought her scar seemed a deeper shade of purple than usual.

Thirty-seven stitches. That was how many it had taken to sew his little girl up again. The scar wound from just above her right eye across her temple, then up over her ear, looking like a millipede forever crawling on her face.

I'm sorry, Jake thought. His therapist had told him to stop apologizing out loud, because it wasn't helping his own healing process. Apparently, he had to learn to forgive himself first, and though Jake said he understood this, he didn't really. Or didn't want to. He wasn't ready for forgiveness. Not from himself, or anyone else.

"I gotta go now, honey," he said.

"For how long?"

"Just a few days."

"I wish you didn't have to." Em's words were better, but not perfect. The word *didn't* came out slurred, as if she were just coming out of anesthesia.

"I know, me too. But this is a good job. Good money."

"How much?"

More than it should be, Jake thought.

"A lot," he said.

"Enough?" she asked.

That one word caught Jake off guard. There was only one way his young daughter could have an understanding of how much money was "enough," and that was because she'd overheard the arguments. Arguments about the accident, arguments about the medical costs, and…god…arguments over whether their little girl had permanent cognitive damage. Em had certainly overheard things neither Jake nor his wife wanted her to hear.

They had argued less since Jake moved out a month ago.

"Let me worry about money, and you take care of your homework," he said.

"Okay."

He reached down and kissed her forehead, and his lips could feel the tight, rippled skin along her scar. "I love you to the moon," he said.

"I love you to Mars."

"I love you to Jupiter," he said.

Jake knew what was coming next.

"I love you to Ur-*anus*." Em burst out giggling, which always ended in the most wonderful snort.

He leaned in, smiling, and she wrapped her arms around his neck. "Come home soon."

Come home.

"I will, love. I'll call you from Denver. Now finish your homework."

"Okay."

One last kiss, then Jake stood and left her bedroom, stealing a final glance of Em as he passed into the hallway. He instinctively began to head to the master bedroom to finish packing—until he remembered he was already packed and his clothes no longer existed in that bedroom anyway. His bag was in his car, outside.

Another memory fog. Perhaps this one was excusable… He and Abby hadn't been separated long. But his memories *were* slipping, and whenever it happened, it filled his stomach with ice. He'd always been unable to recall his early childhood, but now his mind fuzzed over recent things. Conversations he had only days before, or appointments he was supposed to attend and simply forgot. At thirty-five, Jake knew he was too young for these memory slips to be occurring as frequently as they were, so whenever this happened, he'd stop himself and force a memory to the surface, as if to retrain the muscle inside his skull.

Yesterday's outfit? he asked himself. A few seconds passed, then it came to the surface. *Jeans, Ecco loafers, blue oxford shirt.*

His therapist had suggested the memory loss could be stress related, or due to his poor sleep habits, adding he should see a special-ist if he was truly concerned. Jake never did. He knew he could only get answers if he told the specialist *everything* that was happening in his life. This would mean Jake would have to admit it wasn't just the memory loss that was different.

There were other things. Mood swings. Heightened emotions. Even…moments of enlightenment.

He wasn't ready to tell anyone those things.

Jake had secrets.

He continued into the kitchen. Abby was there, her back to him, intentionally or not. She wasn't quite his wife at the moment, and she wasn't his ex-wife. She was, he supposed, just Abby.

"I'm taking off," he said.

She turned to face him. That helped.

"Okay. Have a safe trip."

He tried to read her and struggled. *Ironic*, he thought. *Suddenly I can read the emotions of strangers, but Abby is a brick wall.*

"Thanks."

They locked gazes, and a thousand words died unspoken between them.

Jake walked over and gave her a hug. She squeezed back, but not as hard as he wanted.

He let go, left the house, and drove to the airport as the first few drops of rain spittled from the Massachusetts sky.

Jake had to accept he was a different man now. Different for so many reasons, and still changing every day. He might not be able to forgive himself, but he was starting to learn to accept.

I'm going to make things better, baby. I promise.

Inside the airport terminal, a sea of people swirled around him, and for a moment, Jake fought against breaking down and crying. He managed to keep it together.

Still, one tear escaped.

TWO
Jake

Wednesday, October 10
Boston, Massachusetts

GODDAMN IF IT ISN'T happening again.

Right here in the airport terminal, a sudden burst of emotion, coming from nowhere. I have no idea what triggers it, if anything at all, but here it is, spidering up my chest and flushing my face. A wave of heat, and a moment, always just a moment, where I have to force back tears. A single tear snakes down my cheek, and I wipe it away.

I rarely used to cry. Maybe once a year? And now…I'm a mess.

The thing is, it's not even sadness. Not exactly. It's more like a sudden, profound understanding of something, a sense the universe just contracted a fraction smaller around me, and in the process, I become larger within it and have more of a sense of place. Of purpose.

I remember taking a Psych 101 class in college and learning about Maslow's hierarchy of needs. We learned the ultimate goal, the greatest need, was self-actualization. Its definition always resonated with me: *The realization or fulfillment of one's talents and potentiali-ties.* I remember thinking for so long, how is it possible to completely fulfill all of your potential? How would you even know?

But now, in the moments where sudden emotion threatens to buckle my legs, it's exactly how I feel. As if I'm reaching my potential, even when I can't point to anything that's changed about me. Like I'm standing at the podium, having a gold medal hung around my neck as the anthem plays, but I haven't even gotten up off the couch.

Steady yourself, Jake.

I board the 757, giving the outside of the plane a light tap as I pass through the doorway. Superstition of mine. Touch the plane gently, pay a little respect, and she'll get me to my destination in one piece.

Today, that destination is Denver.

The flight attendant at the front of the plane nods and smiles, but there's exhaustion behind her well-worn smile, desperation just behind her blazing, sea-blue eyes. She's in some kind of struggle. I don't know what it is, of course. But I know it as certain as I'm breathing.

Last year, I wouldn't have noticed anything about the woman beyond the half second she smiled at me.

A lot has changed in the last year.

First class, seat 2B. I haven't flown first class in years, but my client insisted. I didn't argue.

I place my leather bag in the overhead bin, slide it to the left, then reach for my noise-canceling Bose headphones. After slipping them on, I take my seat.

I thumb on the headphones, and the ambient sound around me is sucked away, as if I've just been dropped inside a snow globe. Then I navigate my phone to a playlist containing only the recordings of thunderstorms. I know each track and can almost predict the violent thunderclaps as easily as the hook from a song. My go-to is a tropical storm, where nestled within the hiss of a rain-forest downpour are the metronomic calls of some exotic, lonely bird. In my mind, the bird is telling his mate to find shelter because the rain is exceptionally fierce and unrelenting.

The pang of emotion has subsided, but I know it sits close to the surface. I wait for it as I would a hiccup, in anxious anticipation. Nothing comes. Breathe in, hold, breathe out, then glance around me. Passengers file in, and each who passes leaves a trace of energy behind, like a dust mote of dried skin, clinging to me. Collecting. This woman is pleased with something. That man is frustrated. A child is scared.

All this emotional noise. I can't escape it.

Last year, I wouldn't have noticed a thing.

A sudden flash of Em's face in my mind. Strange, in my mind, I don't see the scar.

Thunder rumbles deep in my ears. The sound of a steady, digital downpour. I look out the window at the tarmac, where actual lighter rain falls. Cold, steady drizzle. Not common for Boston in October.

I give myself another memory test. *What was the weather yesterday?* I close my eyes and think about it, feeling the tendrils of panic swipe at me as my brain freezes. Then it comes. *Cloudy. Maybe sixty degrees.* Okay, good.

The accident with Em isn't the main reason Abby and I separated, though the stress of her continuing recovery finally broke us. No, the real issue is I'm losing my goddamn mind, yet a part of me embraces the process. Abby's been trying to help, but I keep her at a distance. She's worried about my memory loss and my mood swings. I'm too young for a midlife crisis, she says, and too old for puberty. She Googles my symptoms, reporting back to me dismal potential diagnoses like *early-onset Alzheimer's*, or even *borderline personality disorder*.

Abby thinks the accident caused my behavior change, but the accident was in January. She knows this all started happening a good month before that. Besides, the accident barely hurt me, just a bloody nose from the impact of the airbag. It was my little girl who took the brunt of the damage.

She shouldn't have been in the front seat, Jake.

I know. I know.

What were you thinking? What's wrong with you?

I don't know.

She could be dead, Jake. Dead.

Goddamn it, don't you think I know that?

No, the accident isn't the cause of the things happening to me.

I look down, aware that I'm doing it again, sliding my wedding band back and forth along my finger. What'll happen if there's no longer a ring there? Maybe it will be like a phantom limb, something I've lost but can still feel. An itch of regret.

A woman standing in the aisle is talking to me. I lift the left cup of my headphones.

"Hi, that's me," she says.

My seatmate. 2A. She smiles and points to the open seat. She seems nervous.

"Of course."

I stand and let her in, and as she passes within inches of me, I catch her scent, thin traces of flowers layered within something I cannot at first identify. It's distinct, and it takes me a moment to place the other smell, and while I'm not positive, I think it smells like mosquito repellent. But it's not the actual smell that jolts me. It's the *memory* of the smell, fleeting but visceral, a déjà vu so powerful, I could be in a waking dream. I try to hold on to it, explore it until I can pinpoint the memory, but it washes away within seconds.

Isn't that something they say? Smell triggers memory more than any other sense?

As she sits, I try to look at her without staring. About my age, I'm guessing, midthirties. Perhaps younger. Kinked red-brown hair, which falls well past her shoulders. Slim and rather pale. She seems out of time, as if her looks would be better suited for a character in *Les Misérables*.

I return to my seat, buckle in, then edge up the volume on my headphones. The rumbling thunderstorms drown out the safety demonstration and the roar of the engines as we take off, but my attention is focused on 2A the entire time. I don't talk to her; she doesn't talk to me. I order whiskey; she gets water.

I reach for my drink as I remove my headphones, no longer wanting to hear the rain or anything else. The cabin lights are dimmed. My seatmate and I both have our reading lights on.

She's writing in a journal. Left-handed. I steal sideways glances from two feet away. She seems unaware of her audience.

The sense of memory slams into me a second time, more powerfully than before. This is especially jolting because memories have been sliding away rather than appearing lately.

I look at my arm, which is suddenly washed in goose bumps.

Jesus, what is happening?

There's something else I never would have done a year ago, and that's start a conversation with the person on the plane next to me. But the familiarity of this woman is so intense that I'm barely aware I'm speaking before I actually hear the words coming out my mouth.

"Excuse me, do I know you?"

THREE

The Book of Clara
10/10/2018

Dear Reader, Page One. The Book of Clara.

You have found this book, so I like to think you have a responsibility to read it. It's all I ask. I want someone to know me.

I'll be working backward, starting from the present moment and moving into my past, year after year, until I get to my very first memories, which don't really begin until very late, maybe around when I was eight. Moreover, lately, I've been forgetting swaths of my adulthood, so forgive me if my writing is scattered.

When I hold the journal to my face, the blank pages have the faintest scent of chemicals, but the black leather cover smells of raw, beautiful flesh. A worn saddle from two hundred years ago, hung to dry in a dusty barn. I close my eyes and imagine a life back then, but the moment doesn't last. That's been happening. My mind fizzles. I think my brain is a battery that has reached the end of its useful life, no longer able to hold a charge.

Which is one reason for this journey, and this journal entry. I want you to know some of what I've seen, of what I've experienced. The sum of the parts that add up to the existence of Clara Stowe. You will likely judge me for what I've done in the past year. Say to yourself, *Why would she make those decisions?* And you will likely be right in asking. Strange things have been happening. Strange and beautiful, leading me to make a decision I surely won't be able to explain here through words. But I'm at least going to try.

What kind of strange things?

I don't even have to reach back in time for an example. There's one right next to me.

This is the longest I've been surrounded by people in some time, yet I'm much calmer than expected. Perhaps my sense of purpose is more powerful than my unease with the world at large. Still, I cannot escape the craving to be back in my apartment, surrounded by books and blankets, cozy, cocooned, and removed from society.

The airplane smells strangely of sawdust and sweat, broken-down people and, I think, fear. Maybe it's a fear I've never noticed before, a collective worry we'll crash, sending our bits and pieces scattering somewhere over a tiny stamp of America. I don't have this fear, or at least it's far down on my list, because just being in the outside world is horrifying enough. A plane crash would be a terrible way to die, surely, but the real shame is no one would ever read these words. They'd incinerate along with luggage and bones and hair.

We've been flying for about twenty minutes, and I've been able to sneak enough glances at the man sitting next to me to form the distinct sense I know him. But that's not possible, is it? First class on a 757, seats 2A and 2B, departing from Boston Logan, bound for Denver. I'm not even supposed to be in first class, but when I checked in, my seat had been upgraded. But yet there it is. That energy of familiarity about this man, crackling and popping. Perhaps even his scent is familiar. His cologne, maybe.

He could be my age, give or take a couple years in either direction. His face has a thin layer of stubble that looks less stylish and more a concession. Close-cropped hair, brown. Blue oxford shirt, sleeves rolled up over forearms that are grooved by muscles, telling me he's no stranger to the gym. Jeans. Black sneakers, clean.

On his left ring finger is a simple gold wedding band, which this man slides up and down over the knuckle with his right hand. Back and forth, as if it might burn through his skin if it settled too long in one spot.

I can't discern anything concrete about why he's so familiar, and whenever I dare glance over, I have only his profile to observe and his energy to feel. There's a toughened sadness to him, like a cop pushing past his emotions to continue working a brutal crime scene.

There's nothing specific that tells me why I should know this man, other than the primal sense that I do, but I no longer trust my hunches. Reality has become a river for me, part of it deep and permanent, other areas dangerously shallow and in high risk of drying out.

We share a drink rest between us, his side occupied by a whiskey, mine by water. He turns on his light, and I risk another glance. As I do, I meet his gaze.

My god.

I know these eyes. No. Not quite the eyes, but the way he looks at me. Unique as a fingerprint.

I think I might—

FOUR
Jake

SHIT. I'VE STARTLED HER, I can see it. I scramble.

"Sorry, I'm not trying to be weird, I promise. But…it's just that I have this strange sense I know you."

The tip of her pen hovers over a journal page half-filled with perfect, flowing script, and when she looks at me, I see her eyes for the first time. Coffee-brown, flecks of cinnamon. The familiarity deepens even more.

I'm now certain I've fucked this all up. I don't know this person. I just had another misfired synapse, and now I've freaked this poor woman out at the start of a long flight.

"I'm sorry," I manage to stammer. "I just—"

"That *is* strange," she says. Her voice is soft, almost meek. "I was thinking the same thing. You look familiar."

She just threw me a lifeline. Maybe I'm not crazy. Yet.

She squints and shakes her head. "No, no, that's not quite right. You *seem* familiar, but I can't say you *look* familiar."

"I'm Jake Buchannan."

I pivot in my seat to face her more directly, then reach out my right hand. She gives it a light shake. Her fingers are cold.

"Clara Stowe."

"I don't recognize your name."

"Me either. Do you live in Boston?"

"No," I say. "Just outside. Arlington."

"I don't ever get out there," she says, adding cryptically, "or anywhere, really. I live in the city. North End."

"Maybe we know each other professionally?" It's worth a shot. "What do you do?"

"I used to be a teacher. But I'm not working anymore. You?"

"I'm a writer. Mostly freelance. Men's magazines, an article here or there with the *Globe*. Ghostwriting work pays the bills. I also have an incomplete novel sitting on my hard drive."

"A novel," she says, her eyes widening. "What's it about?"

I used to be uncertain. The book, started years ago, was about a man who struggled to find how he fit in the world, but the plot— if there was one—was vague at best. I would think about it from time to time, occasionally write a thousand words, then delete half of them and move on to a writing project with a deadline and a check attached. And though I haven't touched the manuscript in some time, the entire plot revealed itself to me recently, in a moment as powerful and uncontrollable as my waves of emotion. The *entire* plot, start to finish, chapter by chapter, all in my head, as clear as if it were a work by another writer that I'd studied for years. This moment occurred six months ago, and it was as close to an epiphany as I've ever had.

Self-actualization.

I haven't written it out yet, and am almost afraid to, as if it might not be the book I think it is. And though I'm losing more of my short-term memories, the details of the book root deeper in my brain, every detail, not one element lost in the fog of my mind.

"It's about nostalgia," I answer. I vow to myself in this moment to finish writing it as soon as my current assignment is finished. It's time.

"Nostalgia." Clara softly shakes her head, seemingly sucked in by that word. I break the ensuing silence.

"So we don't know each other professionally. What else could it be?"

"I don't know."

"It's probably something simple."

"Maybe," she says. "Maybe it doesn't matter at all."

I'm getting the sense she doesn't want to talk anymore, and my impulse is to leave her alone. God knows, I don't want to come off as a creep, but she *did* say I was familiar to her. I give it one last effort. "But...aren't you curious?"

Clara now turns more fully toward me, loosening her seat belt in the process. She takes a deep, meditative breath, slowly lets it out, then locks her gaze directly on me. She's about to say something, then holds back.

She softly shakes her head at me, as if wishing me away, and then goes back to writing in her journal.

FIVE

The Book of Clara
10/10/2018

I made the decision last week, not too long after the repressed memory surfaced. I'd never felt so certain about anything before. Things were suddenly so much clearer, more so than in years, fresh smells and bursting colors. Affirmation of an inevitable decision. I knew where to go.

The Maroon Bells. Those humbling twin peaks in the Elk Mountains of Colorado. I've only seen pictures, but I have a connection with them beyond their beauty. I don't think I've ever been to Colorado—if I have, I would have been just a child—but I've had the sense if I ever visited the Maroon Bells, I'd feel like I was coming home.

Most of the money I have comes from my adoptive parents. They don't understand my situation, but they've been kind in their support. I had enough for a plane ticket.

The airline workers were curious with me at the airport. A one-way ticket to Denver. No bag to check. I'm sure I looked suspicious—I was nervous enough already, being this far outside the womb of my apartment. I was even pulled aside at the security point and asked some extra questions. A gnomish little TSA agent asked why I was going to Colorado, and I was tempted to tell him the truth. But that would have just complicated things, so I simply said I was visiting a friend and didn't know how long I was going to stay.

He scrunched his face a few times before letting me go on my way.

Then everything was fine. In fact, for no reason at all, the gate agent called my name out, then upgraded me to first class. Me. A woman with no status in the world, much less with this airline. Definitely a message from the universe. Confirmation.

Everything was clear. I had complete and total purpose, perhaps for the first time in my life.

Then the man on the plane started talking to me.

SIX
Jake

TIME SLOWS. THE SILENCE grows thick, and with each moment that bleeds out, I'm become more obsessed about how I know this woman. I order another drink, which probably isn't the best idea. There's been too much drinking lately.

Dinner is served and cleared without another word between us. I keep my headphones off, tired of storms. I just sit here, sipping whiskey, giving myself memory tests, and trying to ignore what seems almost like a supernatural presence next to me.

That's it, I think, vaguely pleased with myself. Clara's a ghost. I'm probably the only one who can see her.

Just as this thought exits my mind, she breaks the long silence.

"I haven't flown in years," she says. "In fact, I barely leave my apartment. I'm a bit of a recluse."

Okay, she wants to talk. Good.

"You barely ever leave your apartment, yet here you are flying first class to Denver? Must be a special occasion."

"It is," she says, offering nothing more.

I tread lightly.

"How does it feel to be flying?"

She thinks about this. "Unsettling."

"Are you afraid of planes?"

"I'm afraid of the world."

There's a lot to unpack in that one sentence, and I don't ask her to do it.

A few moments pass, and she adds, "Listen, Jake, it's just that… Well, I *am* curious about you. It's just that I'm really focused on something, and I don't know if it's good for me to be distracted from that."

"I get it," I say, not really getting it. "But we *are* here, and we've got a little time left in the flight. Maybe we treat it like a game to pass the time…you know, Twenty Questions. We'll figure out how we know each other and then go our separate ways in Denver."

She looks at me, *really* looks at me, with a slight tilt of the head. A few seconds later, she closes the journal, lays the pen on top, and straightens into a small stretch. She wears the thinnest trace of a smile.

"Twenty Questions," she says. "Well, okay, I suppose we don't really need to keep count. I'll start. So, Jake Buchannan, why are you going to Denver?"

"I'm meeting a client. He hired me to ghostwrite his memoirs."

"His memoirs? What does he do that he has a book's worth of memories?"

"Honestly, I don't really know. But I suppose I'll find out."

A guy named Alexander Eaton contacted me two weeks ago looking to hire me, then insisted on flying me immediately out to Denver. Once in a while, I'll get a cold call for a memoir job, someone who's seen my website or otherwise found me online. These almost never go well. They're either shocked at the fee, which starts at $20,000 for a slimmer volume and goes up from there, or I meet with them and realize they have nothing to say aside from one interesting story that might fill one chapter. Then I end up blamed for a thin volume about a dull life.

I initially told him I wasn't interested. I definitely needed the income, but something seemed a little off with the guy, and I pictured myself spinning my wheels and not getting paid. It's happened before. But this Alexander Eaton refused to take no for an answer, telling me to name a price. I literally laughed at the clichéd line, but he politely waited for an answer on the other end of the line. I thought about it a moment, then said $75,000 for three hundred pages, with a $10,000 nonrefundable retainer. I said I had the right to stop work for any reason after fifty pages, no questions asked.

He immediately agreed, then told me to book first-class airfare on this specific flight, and he'd arrange a room at the Four Seasons in Denver.

That was unexpected. And, to be honest, a godsend.

I asked him what he did for a living, but he declined to answer, telling me he preferred to talk in person. This was strange, since most ghostwriting subjects will talk about themselves ad nauseam any opportunity they're afforded, so I spent a little time Googling his name. I found information about a few different Alexander Eatons, but couldn't connect any of them to Denver.

True to his word, the retainer hit my bank account a few days later. Everything just fell into my lap, and the money came at a time we needed it most. Em's medical bills from the accident seem endless, and the insurance company had just denied coverage for a series of doctor-recommended occupational-therapy sessions. Whoever Alexander Eaton truly is, I'm grateful to him. He's helping me take care of my little girl, which matters most right now.

"How long have you been in Boston?" I ask.

"Seven years. You?"

"In the area, nearly twenty. What kind of teaching did you do before…before you left?"

"I was a middle-school teacher," Clara says. "Do you have kids?"

"One," I say. "A daughter. She's eight. That can't be the connection."

"Do you work in the city?"

I think of the office in the house I occupied until a month ago. My single-dad apartment lacks one, though I didn't make that a priority when finding a new place. I hopefully won't be there long. "About half the time. I lease a small space on Exeter Street. But I don't think that's the connection either. What *is* it?"

We exchange more bits of our lives. I tell her I'm married, but don't tell her I'm separated. I tell her about my daughter, Em, but don't tell her about the accident. I suppose I'm avoiding talking about my shame. Shame that I was the one who lost control of the car. Shame that my daughter might have permanent impairment as a result of the crash. Shame that my marriage is now crumbling, and that I'm struggling to be the provider I've always thought I needed to be.

Everything is just a goddamn shame.

Clara tells me her history, summarized in pithy detail, holding back, I'm guessing, enough to stay a bit in her shell. She's thirty-four, a year younger than me. Grew up in Maine, college in upstate New York, moved back to Maine and worked as a middle-school teacher before getting a better job in Boston. Unmarried, no kids. Never been outside of the northeastern United States. This is in stark contrast to me, though in all my travels, I can't overlap any of her geographical and chronological history with mine.

"So you were a teacher. First in Maine and then in Boston?"

"That's right," she says. "Ten years."

"Middle school. I think that would be a tough age to teach. You must really love it."

"I did, yes."

"Will you go back to it?"

There isn't the slightest hesitation. "No."

"So…so you said you've been living as a bit of a recluse," I say.

"Yes."

"Can I ask why?"

The plane suddenly drops, not severely, but enough to elicit a group gasp. Clara rides it with an expression of wonder on her face, like a child on a roller coaster.

She thinks about my question but then shakes her head. "It's long, complicated, and I'm not even sure I can answer that. I'll just tell you I've been lost for a while, but now I have focus. Purpose."

Then it happens again, the feeling of the universe shrinking around me. My understanding of the world grows a few inches, and with it, a certainty I'm supposed to know this woman for a reason. Still, nothing about her *looks* familiar. Now that I know about her reclusion, I see signs of it. Hair a bit unkempt, skin a bit pale. What I first registered as thin now seems closer to scrawny.

"Well, that's good, then. Does this purpose have something to do with why you're headed to Denver?"

"Yes, actually. Though I'm not going to Denver. I'm headed up to Aspen. To the Maroon Bells."

This sounds familiar, but I can't place it.

"What are the Maroon Bells?"

"Two mountains. Maroon Peak and North Maroon Peak. Just southwest of Aspen."

"I see. So this is a vacation, then?" I ask.

"No, not exactly."

"So what, then?"

Clara looks at me as if I've just asked her the meaning of life. She's thinking, and thinking hard. I realize she's not mulling how to explain something complicated, but rather deciding if she wants to tell me at all.

And then she does, saying simply:

"I'm going there to die."

SEVEN

I HAVE NO FUCKING idea what to say to this.

"You're the first person I've told," she says. "Imagine that."

She must be sick. Incurable cancer, something like that. I look away from her, because now it feels as if my eyes are scanning her for disease. I grab for my drink, wishing there were more of it left.

"I'm sorry," I manage. It sounds weak.

"I don't have any real family left," she says. "I never socialized with anyone at work. And now I've literally closed myself off. I didn't expect to tell anyone what's happening to me, mostly because I'm not really sure myself. I was telling my story here." She taps her pen on the journal in her lap.

"What is that?"

"I call it the Book of Clara. I'm writing memories of my life, starting from right now and working back. It's fitting you're in the first chapter. The stranger on the plane who wasn't really a stranger."

"So, a memoir."

"A suicide note."

My stomach tightens. *Suicide.* So, an incurable disease, and she'd rather take her own life than suffer. Maybe Colorado has legalized assisted suicide?

I don't ask what's wrong with her. I don't want to be like the people looking at Em and asking what happened to her face.

Instead, I ask, "Who's going to read the Book of Clara?"

"Well, whomever finds it, I suppose. I just..." She looks down and studies the finely crafted words on the vanilla pages. "I just want someone else to know me."

"That's a big project. It's going to take some time." I look at the book, the vast number of unfilled pages. "Maybe by that time you'll..."

"Change my mind?"

"Yes."

"No, I don't think so. I'm not going to cover my entire life, just the things I remember most. Which isn't that much these days."

I instinctively open my mouth to commiserate but shut it again. Talking about my memory loss only makes it seem more real, more threatening. "You're writing a memoir," I say.

"Yes, a memoir." She smiles. "I like to think a part of me will still exist through my book. That someone will understand my decision. My absolute *need* for death."

"Need?"

"Yes. Need."

"So...so you're not sick?" I ask. "I assumed maybe a degenerative condition, or—"

"No. I'm perfectly healthy."

"I don't even know what to say to that."

"I don't need you to say anything. I'm just telling you."

"But you're having trouble remembering things?" I ask.

"Yes," she says. "And it's getting worse. So maybe I have some kind of dementia. But that's part of the reason for the Book of Clara. I want to see how far back I can remember. A lot of my memories are fragments, especially those of childhood. Pieces of a mosaic. Scattered."

Part of me wishes Clara had never sat down in seat 2A. What was once an intriguing connection is suddenly feeling like a vortex I'm getting sucked into. But if I couldn't let this go before hearing of her impending death, I'm really dug in now.

I take a deep breath. "Do you ever look at old photos of yourself and can't remember the moment the picture was taken?"

"There are very few old photos of me," she says. "But yes. It's like looking at a child actress playing me."

"Right." I don't *feel* years of my past are gone. They *are* gone, as lost and irretrievable as a deep, dreamless sleep.

"So you have the same thing?" she asks.

I don't want to admit the truth, because then I become her. I don't want to be her, a person with an unwavering desire to die.

"Maybe that's another way we're connected," Clara says. "We're both losing our past."

She becomes more inquisitive as I feel myself wanting to retreat into my shell.

"Are your parents alive?" she asks.

"What?"

"It's just something that occurred to me. Are your parents alive?"

My breathing quickens. "That depends on who you're talking about," I say. "I'm adopted. And yes, my adoptive parents are still alive. They live in California."

I know what she's going to ask next, and the thought of it scares the shit out of me. There will be some other thread between us, something else making this more surreal than it already is. Before she does, the flight attendant leans in and asks if we want more drinks. I jump at the offer, ordering my third. We don't talk as the attendant retrieves another mini-bottle of whiskey for me, and after she moves down the aisle with the cart, I pour but don't speak. If Clara wants to ask, she can ask.

And she does.

"What about your biological parents?"

I bring the glass back to my mouth and keep it there, letting the alcohol slowly breach my lower lip and trickle onto my gums, numbing them. For a moment, I have a flashback. A vague memory, sometime after my parents died. My adoptive parents had a large bathtub in their bedroom, and I used it often. I think, perhaps, it was a cocoon for me, a safe place to disappear. The water was always just a bit warmer than my own body heat, cloaking me like a soft blanket at bedtime. After soaping up, I would often lean back, take a deep breath, and go under the surface. Mouth closed, breath held, eyes open. I'd see the wavy, shimmering bathroom light through the water. It felt so right under the surface, so comforting. I would hold my breath until it became a struggle, and then, if I really focused and pushed all thoughts out of my mind, I'd break through to the other side, where it was no longer hard to resist. Where all I felt was peace, brilliant comfort, and a heavy pull toward sleep. I'd never give in to the pull, though sometimes I wanted to.

Every now and then, in the water, in that in-between place bridging consciousness and the deep black, I'd have a flash. A snippet of a memory. Of me as a younger child, happy, curious. Wondrous. A pureness, whole and still. In those moments, I became convinced death was simply a state of complete innocence.

"They were killed when I was eight," I say.

"How?"

I suck in a deep breath. "Drunk driver. They were coming home from a restaurant. I was having a sleepover at a friend's house."

This is not something I talk about much, partly because it doesn't exist in my mind. Occasionally, I'll have a glimmer of my parents, but when I think about it, the images I see in my mind are from photos I still keep, not actual remembrances. At least I'm lucky not to remember the moment I was told their lives had been snatched away, quick as the wings pulled off a moth.

Clara doesn't tell me how sorry she is. Her face doesn't register shock.

"You're an only child," she says.

"How did you know that?"

She doesn't answer.

"Let me guess," I say.

"You don't have to guess," she says. "You already know."

"You lost your parents as well."

"Yes."

"How?" I ask.

"Also a car accident. They went out to the movies, slid on ice. I was with a sitter."

"And you're an only child?"

"Yes."

"So we were both adopted."

She nods. "I was seven."

Clara is a dream. A dream, a ghost, or a hallucination. The people behind me must be wondering why the man in 2B is talking to himself. He must be crazy or drunk. Probably both.

"Do you remember any of your childhood before you were adopted?" Clara asks.

Whatever is happening, I'm deciding right now to go along with it. Real or not. Sane or not. This is the weirdest flight of my life, and I'm both scared and fascinated to find out what happens next. Hell, maybe this is like *Lost* and the plane crashed on takeoff.

I smell the alcohol on my breath as I speak.

"No. No, Clara, I don't. I don't recall a single damn thing."

EIGHT

The Book of Clara
10/10/2018

To know me, you have to understand the last year of my life. I feel like I should have a name for this time period—the Troubles, or some such thing—but I can't think of any way to tie it all up nicely in a choice description.

I took a sick day last December. I was feeling fine physically, but I remember an overwhelming need to stay inside. Perhaps the biting Boston cold had something to do with it, but more than seeking coziness, I simply wanted to avoid the outside world. That's okay, I thought. We all need to escape inside to our little worlds every now and then. I called in sick to school, hoping they could find a sub on short notice.

I spent the day doing all the things one would seek during a sick day—watched a little TV, read for a while, lay under a fleece blanket on my couch, web-surfed. Even made myself some hot cocoa. But none of it felt quite right. Nothing I did addressed this nagging sense that the world outside the walls of my apartment was suddenly scarier than I had ever realized. There was just...too much going on out there. Too many moving pieces, too much chaos, and if I went back out there, I'd get swept up by some current and dashed away forever. My apartment was the anchor keeping me safe and grounded.

One day off turned into two. The second day was a Friday, and I've always wondered what would have happened if my second day off had been a Tuesday. If so, perhaps I would have felt just normal enough to go back to work on Wednesday, and that one day back would have been enough for me to "shake it off." But it wasn't. It was a Friday, and then I had the whole weekend to stay inside. And those two extra days cemented my path. By Sunday evening, the idea of going back outside terrified me.

I tried. Monday morning came; I dressed and got as far as about twenty feet outside my apartment building's front door. The wind was stinging cold, and I remember wrapping my scarf around my face, then having the feeling of wishing it was long enough to disappear completely within. Mummify myself with wool. It's a seventeen-minute walk from my apartment to the middle school where I used to teach, but that day, it might as well have been a three-week trek. It wasn't going to happen. Outside, on the sidewalk, people weaving in and out of one another's paths, cars whooshing by, horns blasting, buildings casting dooming shadows on dirty streets, garbage bags piled in heaps. The sickening sense that I could get swallowed by some creature at any moment was so powerful, it nearly buckled my legs.

I went back inside, heart pounding, struggling for breath, stripping naked and crawling under my sheets. I yanked the covers over my head as a child does, following the illogic of "If I can't see the monster, it can't see me." In that moment, I knew something was wrong with me, permanently wrong, and it was real and unfixable.

I never went back to my job again.

Funny how easy it is to become a recluse. As long as you pay the bills, no one really cares. My expenses were relatively modest and my savings enough for at least a year, at which point I assumed I'd have some kind of answer as to what to do next. Yes, there were people concerned for me, but I have little family to speak of, and my social circles were very limited, even back then. My adoptive parents sent me some funds and suggested therapy, but otherwise seemed to care little about my erratic behavior. We'd never been very close.

Some fellow teachers sent concerned emails, as did a few women from the yoga class I used to attend regularly. I assured them I just needed to unplug for a bit. I disconnected my internet service and turned the ringer off my landline so no one could reach me except by coming to my apartment. A few of them did, and I'd open the door and politely tell them I just wanted to be alone. A couple of them pushed back, insisting I must be crazy and in need of psychiatric help. In the end, they too went away. A handful came back a second time, but none of them attempted a third. After time, I was completely and totally alone. Just me and my sweet, comforting books.

My period of isolation all began two months after I went to see a man.

He's the reason I decided to kill myself.

NINE
Jake

SHE'S WRITING AGAIN, JUST like that. Suddenly, and with a sense of urgency.

I'm tempted to reach over and touch her arm, just to make sure she's real. I don't.

She's focused, her words flowing from her pen with speed and precision.

"What part of your life are you writing now?" I ask.

Her pen stops. "Sometimes I have a memory. I just had a snippet of one, and I wanted to write it down."

"What's the memory?"

The buzz of alcohol is making me dizzy.

"There's a man," she says. "It's the only time I've had the same sense of knowing someone. Though it's much stronger with you."

"Okay."

"Wait," she says. She goes back to writing, filling a page. I'm tempted to read over her shoulder, but I restrain myself. Minutes pass.

Then she stops writing and turns her head to me. "Have you ever lost something, Jake? Something you were sure was gone forever? You searched and searched everywhere for it. Frantically. Then, after you've completely resigned yourself to it being gone forever, it appears, and it does so in a place you are absolutely certain you already checked? It's like magic. Yet you don't question it. You don't try to explain it. You just let that magic exist in the world, and your day goes on."

Immediately I think of a watch. Not a watch I remember, but one I have a photo of. A Mickey Mouse watch bought for me by my biological father for my sixth birthday. I have no memory of either my father or the watch, but I do have a photo showing both, a boy and his dad, the boy proudly showing off his favorite birthday gift, all captured on fading photo paper, bleeding saturation. Like all things from my youth, the watch was barely more than a photo memory, and I always wondered what became of it.

"I'm not sure where you're going with this."

Pen down. A strand of kinked hair falls over her left eye.

"When I asked you about your parents, I was thinking about a man I went to visit in Boston a couple months before I locked myself away in my little apartment. I wanted to write about the day I met him before my memory of it went soft."

Soft memories. I know about those. Clouds of the mind, which cannot be held or contained.

"Who was the man?"

She looks poised to say something, then shakes her head.

"You can tell me," I add.

"No, Jake. I don't think I want to say any more."

"Why?"

"I don't know why we were put here together. On this plane, at this moment in time. I think you're something I lost, perhaps a long time ago. Now that I've found you, I'm not going to question it and I'm not going to explore it any further. I'm just going to let this magic exist in the world."

"What are you talking about?"

She smiles, and it's the gentlest thing I've ever seen.

"I need to do this. I'm going to the mountains, and I'm never coming back. That's how it's supposed to end."

She returns to her journal. Clara says nothing more to me for the remainder of the flight.

TEN

AIRPLANE WHEELS BUMP AND squeal on the Denver airport tarmac, and Clara still remains silent. She's been writing in her journal without pause since she stopped talking. I've snuck a few peeks and have been able to catch a few words (*book, aroma, alone*), but not much more than that.

My hands are slick with a film of sweat, and there's a noticeable spike in my heart rate. Clara and I have a connection that's deeper than just seeming familiar to each other, and in a way, I feel like I'm seeing my future self in her. What if my memory issues make me start thinking like her? I shudder at the thought of considering death the only option.

I can't just let this end here. It's not that I feel I have to save her. More like I need her to save me.

I unbuckle as other passengers rise and start opening overhead compartments. We'll be walking off this plane in less than a minute.

"This isn't magic, Clara," I say. "This is purposeful. We need to understand what's happening."

She shakes her head. "Jake, I—"

"Maybe you're not really supposed to kill yourself. Maybe the real reason for you to take this trip was to meet me. I can't just let you get off this plane and never see you again."

"It's not for you to decide these things." She nods at the aisle. It's my turn to deplane, and I've never been less ready to do that in my life. I hesitate, feeling the impatient glares of the others behind us.

I take a step back into the aisle and let Clara out. She carries only her purse and a small overnight bag. I follow her off the plane, walking directly behind her, a sense of quiet panic welling inside me.

When I was fifteen, I went on a school trip to France, where I met another American girl from a different school. We fell in love for ten days, the kind of obsessive, soul-shattering love that only exists at that age. The day we had to leave each other, she boarded a bus for the airport, and I walked on with her just to say goodbye. That *moment*—that singular second when I had to actively choose to walk away from her, to leave her on that bus—that moment is now. Shortened breath, painfully beating heart, the sense no decision has ever been more wrong. But I'm not a teenager anymore. I'm an adult, well versed in the pains and pleasures of life, my feelings forged and rubbed smooth over time, leaving me emotionally fortified against most vulnerabilities.

But as I watch Clara walk in front of me—hair lightly bouncing, shoulders squared with purpose—I have never felt so convinced that letting someone disappear would be a life-alteringly bad decision.

I follow her. To the train, to the main concourse, weaving in and out among dozens of people.

She heads straight to the door leading outside. I panic, finally race up and stand in front of her, forcing her to stop.

She looks at me for only a moment before dropping her gaze to the ground.

"My daughter," I say. "Em. Back in January, she…*we* were in a car accident. It was my fault. I was driving."

"I'm sorry to hear that."

"I was fine. Of course I was. Not even a burn mark from the airbag. I came away with no more than a bloody nose, but my daughter was severely injured."

"Why are you telling me this?"

"Because since then, I've been losing control. And it's happening again," I say. "Right here. Now."

"I can't help you with that."

"I think you can. I need to know how we're connected. It's important," I add, not saying the one fear pulsing through my brain. *Because I don't want to end up like you.*

"I'm sorry, Jake. I need to go."

Out of desperation, I rummage in my bag and snatch a business card. For a moment, I think she won't take it, but she slowly reaches her hand up and plucks it from my fingers.

"My cell-phone number is on there," I say. "Just…just don't throw it out. Call me if you need me."

"I don't—"

"Clara, just *call* if you need me."

She nods. "Okay. If I need you, I'll call."

Clara skirts around me and I don't stop her, too numb to move. The airport doors whoosh open, and she steps into the afternoon air, into the swarm of taxis and shuttles, of buses taking people far away from others. A few steps later, her illuminated figure dissolves and fades into black.

For a moment, I am fifteen again.

And the girl is gone.

ELEVEN

The Book of Clara
10/10/2018

The man who came into my life and started me on a road to death went by one name: Landis.

One year ago, a crisp October Friday. I walked into a small office building near the Boston Public Garden. My scheduled appointment time was 1:00 p.m.

I'd seen the flyer in my apartment building lobby for two weeks prior. Cluttered among announcements for lost pets and guitar lessons, this one simply said:

MEMORY ISSUES?
Revolutionary Medical Breakthrough:
Volunteers Needed for Clinical Trial

The only other items on the glossy white flyer were a

phone number and a picture. The picture was odd and alluring—a sketch of a boy and an old man walking through the woods, as forest creatures watched. The sketch itself was rendered from thousands of tiny ink marks, and I couldn't comprehend how long it must have taken the artist to create the image. Nor did I have any idea what the picture itself had to do with memory issues, but I do know the image captivated me. I passed the flyer daily, and each day, I became more taken in. After a week, I couldn't stop staring at it, and I even went so far as to remove the flyer and take it up to the apartment with me. A replacement appeared the following day.

It wasn't just the picture that absorbed me. I've always struggled with my memory, as if a piece of my brain has just dried up and crumbled to dust. I don't recall anything prior to the age of eight, not my biological parents, my childhood home, nor the black-and-white cat named Inkspot. These things all existed, because I have photos. But I don't remember anything. I have a theory that the tragic deaths of my biological parents shocked my brain into a data purge, but I suppose it doesn't really matter. I simply *don't remember*.

Were it not for the image on that flyer, I probably never would have called. But the picture comforted me, like slipping on the softest fuzzy socks on a bitter January day. Perhaps it was somehow hypnotizing me, but I developed an urge to remember. I wanted to know about my childhood more than ever, and my thirst for my past led me to that appointment one year ago.

I walked into a small, plain office, perfectly professional if not a little sparse. A few plants added a splash of color to the otherwise bland setting, and copies of *Psychology Today* and *People* sat perfectly aligned on a glass table, looking to have never been as much as jostled. A black leather love seat appeared completely free from use. The logo on the wall read *Arete Memory Research* and had a little jagged line crossing through the tops of the letters. I supposed the line was either a mountain range or an EKG readout.

There was no receptionist, but moments after I entered, a man hustled from a back office to greet me. He wore a wool overcoat and a gray fedora. I hadn't seen anyone wearing a fedora in a long time. Perhaps never outside a movie.

"Good timing," he said, removing his coat and hanging it on a stand. "I just got back from lunch." He then removed his hat and placed it next to his coat, and I got the image of a man coming home from work in the fifties. I half expected a dog to scurry in and drop slippers at the man's feet.

"You're Clara," he said.

"I am."

He extended his hand. "I'm Dr. Miller. We spoke on the phone." His face was soft and smooth, his eyes more blue than gray, cool like stone.

"Hello, Dr. Miller. Clara Stowe."

I took his hand and felt fingers colder than my own, and I remember in the moment wondering when I'd last touched another person. His scent caught me, the aroma familiar but unplaceable. If a reliable source insisted this man was the ghost of someone I once knew, I wouldn't have argued.

"Please, just call me Landis," he said. Landis released my grip and gazed at me, smiling, as if I were a long-lost friend he'd just run into by chance. Before it got uncomfortable, he said, "I'm looking forward to helping you, Clara. Please, come in."

He escorted me to a small office, about as sparse as the reception area, containing only a metal filing cabinet, a mahogany desk-and-chair set, and a leather chair opposite the desk. The walls were bare save a framed diploma that was too far away for me to read clearly.

"Have a seat," he said, gesturing to the chair. He left the door open.

"Are you the only person here?" I asked.

"Yes. I am the entirety of Arete Memory Research," he said. "Of course, there are investors. But I'm the one doing all the work."

I sat, my posture rigid. "I...I have to say, coming here is outside my character. I'm not sure I'm right for your clinical trials. I just—"

He held up a hand. "Well, that's why you're here, right? To see if you fill the bill. But I think you do."

"Why's that?"

"Because something about the flyer piqued your interest, didn't it?" He took a seat behind the desk and rolled up the sleeves on his white button-down. "Did the image spark something in you? A feeling you didn't expect?"

"How...how did you know that?"

Landis opened the top drawer of his desk and took out something. It was a book, and not just any book. It was the book that led me on the path to where I am today.

The Responsibility of Death

He slid it over to me and I leaned forward, opening to the first page. There was the same image used in the flyer. I must have gasped, because Landis said, "It does resonate with you, doesn't it?"

"I don't understand," I said.

"I know. It's okay. You will." He gently pulled the book from my fingertips and closed it. "With your permission, I'm going to ask you some questions about your memory loss and just a few more about your medical history. Hopefully nothing too intrusive, but your answers will inform me as to your appropriateness for this trial. I can tell you we're only seeking a very limited number of participants, so maybe you'll be one of the lucky few."

"And what does the trial consist of?"

He nodded. "In due time, we'll get into the details, and lord knows there will be paperwork for you to sign if you're selected. But in short, the program is a regimen of visual stimulus complemented by advanced chemical compounds, all targeted to tap into the medial temporal lobe and unlock the memories you've forgotten. The research has shown tremendous results on rats, and we've just been granted approval for human trials." He tapped on the cover of the book. "But the trial isn't just about helping with your memory, Clara. The work we've been doing overlays with the part of the brain responsible for realizing one's full potential. In a nutshell, I believe we can help unlock both your past and your future."

There was a lot to absorb in his words, but the first question that came to me was unrelated to anything he had just said.

"May I see the book again?"

Landis flashed a smile of genuine enthusiasm. He slid the thin, hardcover book across the desk, which made a satisfying little *whoosh*.

"Yes, of course."

TWELVE
Jake

Thursday, October 11
Denver, Colorado

THE ADDRESS IS A quick walk from my hotel. Downtown
morning traffic hums and churns, and I pull my wool coat tighter
against my chest, shielding myself from the stiff winds that cut
through each alleyway I pass.

I've got work to do today, but I'm brain-fried from a shitty night's
sleep. The combination of too much whiskey and my bizarre plane
flight left me tossing around in the hotel bed all night.

God help me, I can't stop thinking about Clara. Thinking about
where she is now, or even if she's still alive. There were questions I
didn't ask her that I wish I had. Truths I didn't reveal to her. I'm
aching to see how much deeper our connection goes.

But she's gone.

Alexander Eaton's high-rise apartment building stabs into
the sky, cold metal and tinted glass. I walk into a modern lobby, all

angles and marble. The security desk houses an older man who looks comfortably bored. He barely looks at me as I approach.

"Who are you here to see?" he asks. A magazine is open on the desk in front of him.

"Alexander Eaton."

"He expecting you?"

"Yes. Jake Buchannan."

He studies me a moment, then reaches for a phone and dials.

"I have a Mr. Buchannan to see Mr. Eaton," he says. He listens for a moment, grumbles acceptance, hangs up.

"You know his apartment number?"

"Yes."

"Go right up." He returns his attention to the magazine, which has something to do with fishing.

I'm the only one in the elevator, which is paneled in brushed chrome and mirrors. There are so many reflections I can't help but look at myself. Funny how as I've gotten older, I have an increasing aversion to seeing myself in the mirror. I haven't gained weight since college, my short hair has so far avoided graying, and I'm in better shape now than I've ever been. But I don't like looking at myself; I fear the one moment I do and don't recognize the person at all. Not because I've changed, but because *I don't remember*.

Doors open, seventeenth floor. Down the corridor on the right. His is the last door, which probably means a nice corner unit. Lots of windows.

I'm looking forward to meeting the man so interested in my work he's willing to pay well above market value for my services. In my mind, Alexander is self-made and has amassed a small fortune along with a healthy ego. I picture him a bit shorter than average, with a perpetual golf tan and the paunch of a man who eats well and often, someone prone to wearing colorful sweaters over crisp, white oxford shirts. He wants his memoirs to serve as a testament to his brilliance in business, and he thinks, perhaps, this book could be a bestseller. He'll ask me which of the major publishers he should choose, as if they'll all be clamoring to buy his story.

That's okay. He's entitled to all his delusions. I'm here to write his life, and I'll give him my best work. And who knows? Maybe he has a hell of a tale to tell. Most likely he doesn't. Chances are, as I've discovered with many of my other clients, he'll have succeeded in business through a combination of basic intelligence, dogged tenacity, and an unwavering willingness to screw people over. I won't write that, of course. I'll use terms like *fiery competitiveness.* But his story will be similar to so many I've written, and Alexander Eaton will end up self-publishing his memoir, ordering a couple thousand copies, many of which he'll proudly distribute at board meetings and family gatherings. The remainder will forever occupy floor space in his office, pages fading as his skin wrinkles and hair grays.

I suppose it doesn't really matter. This is a guy who's helping me with Em's medical bills. In fact, he's my first significant writing gig since the accident, and I have a feeling more good things are on the way.

For the moment, I have a sense of regaining control. It feels good.

THIRTEEN

I EXTEND MY HAND.

Alexander Eaton is tall, but his thin frame sucks away any illusion of the strength I feel in his handshake. His head hangs a bit too far forward, as if too heavy for his body, a sunflower at sunset, drooping and resigned to the coming night. His shaggy hair is already gray, though he told me on the phone he wasn't yet forty. I would have guessed fifty, and that's being polite. He's dressed nicely: blue dress shirt, khaki pants, perfectly shined loafers. But if you put fancy clothes on a scarecrow, no one would remark *That's a nice-looking scarecrow.* They'd say *What the fuck is that thing?*

He is not the person I was expecting.

"Jacob Buchannan, how good of you to come."

I can't think of the last person to call me Jacob.

"Alex," I say. "Or do you go by Alexander?"

"Neither. Please call me Eaton."

He releases his grip first.

"Eaton, okay. And you can call me Jake."

"Come in." He takes a step back, giving me room to pass.

I step through the door, and there's a sudden and budding familiarity I can't define. My senses seem to be working overtime, and I wonder how much I can even trust them anymore. Still, there it is, as it was with Clara, yet markedly weaker. A sense I've met this person before.

Maybe it's because Alexander Eaton seems more a caricature, a cartoon figure I remember from a book or a show. Ichabod Crane, perhaps. Jack Skellington.

I walk inside, vaguely conscious of how far I am from the front door. It's a big apartment, but it's a palace of shadows. Closed shades against the morning sky and not enough overhead lights to compensate. Hallways lead three different directions, all to their own darkness. If he's trying to create an unsettling atmosphere, all he's missing is the sound of dragging chains or a distant, echoing drip of water.

Creepy as shit, in other words.

As if sensing my thoughts, he says, "Yes, I realize it's dark in here. Apologies. Sometimes I get these headaches, and dark rooms help. The Colorado sun is a thing of wonder, but it can also be a terrible weapon."

I turn. "Are you sure this is still a good time?"

"Nonsense. You came all this way. But we might have a bit of a shorter session today. I have good days and bad days."

Something sick people say.

"Yes, of course."

"Sit, please." He directs me to a taut leather couch.

I take a spot and set my messenger bag down next to me. Eaton slides into an overstuffed chair to my right and places both feet on the floor, his hands on knobbed knees.

"Jacob," he says. Not a question. Not a prelude before a statement. Just my name, and not the one I told him to call me. With that one word, I feel unsettled.

I don't say anything. He doesn't have the look of someone who would hear me anyway. Lost in thought. Or just lost.

Then he speaks again. "Jacob lived to be a hundred and forty-seven."

"What?"

"Jacob. From the Book of Genesis. I assume that's who you were named after. A powerful first name. I presume you're Jewish?"

"Um, no, actually."

Thin smile, no teeth. "Then, Jacob, what are you?"

In this moment, I'm happy I secured a large, nonrefundable retainer.

"I'm nothing."

He leans forward, a cat lured forward by a twitching string.

"Oh, no, you are most certainly not nothing, Jacob. None of us are. But I suspect you, more than most, are *something*."

I have to spend hours interviewing this man. If those hours are in the same bizarre vibe as the past minute, this job is going to be rough. I need to set the tone.

"First of all," I say, "as I already said, I go by Jake, not Jacob. Second, when I say I'm nothing, I mean religiously. Not that it matters, but I don't believe in god. Third, you and I have a lot of talking to do." I'm sitting fully upright now. "That's how memoirs work. I ask a lot of questions, and you give me a lot of answers. This is about *you*. If you start going into strange tangents and inquiries into my life, we're just wasting each other's time."

He laughs, lung-rattled.

"We do have a road ahead of us, *Jake*. But I will say you're wrong about God. Lord knows, I wish you weren't."

"Why do you want to write your memoirs, Eaton?"

It's a question I asked him on the phone but he didn't answer. It's the first question I ask all my clients, and I'm asking it here to gain control of the conversation.

He stops smiling and considers. "Because that's all we have in life, isn't it? Our memories. It's what makes the human experience. Best to get them onto paper before it's too late."

"It's a lot of money for memories," I say. "The fee, the first-class ticket, the room at the Four Seasons. You must have a lot to say."

"Indeed I do."

He leans back into the chair, which hardly seems to notice his presence. A small pool of light from a Tiffany stained-glass table lamp colors his face red and blue, highlighting a day's worth of stubble on sunken cheeks. "And yes, it's a lot of money. But it's money well spent, getting us together. This project is more meaningful than I've told you about so far. You see, the thing of it is, I'm sick." He pauses to cough into the crook of his elbow, perhaps for some kind of clichéd dramatic effect. "And I might not have that much time left."

This doesn't surprise me. How he looks, the sudden desire to write his memoirs at an early age. Still, I'm unnerved. It's the second time in two days a stranger has told me of their impending demise.

"I'm sorry to hear that. Can I ask…" I let the question trail, allowing him to fill in the rest.

"What I have? Of course you can, Jake. There won't be any secrets between us. You'll know everything about me once our time together is over."

"Yes, of course. I just thought you might not want to talk about it yet."

"Well, I'm sure we'll dive into more detail later, but I have a condition that is rather untreatable, at least by common Western standards. I'm hoping to find a more unorthodox convention to fight it, but haven't come upon it yet. Maybe I will, maybe I won't." Eaton shrugs his bony shoulders. "Hence the memoirs. I want to leave my story behind."

Condition. Not cancer. Not tumor. *Condition.*

"That's understandable. And you seem to have done well for yourself. I'm guessing you have the resources to seek alternative therapies?"

Eaton coughs again, a deep, echoing rattle inside paper-thin lungs. Maybe his condition has weakened his immune system. "I've learned money is a convenience but rarely a solution. Since I've become sick, I've put a lot of effort into finding an answer. And I think there's one out there, one particular way to make me whole again. But my instincts tell me it won't be money that gets me there. It will be something…serendipitous."

Goddamn interesting thing for a dying man to say.

"And so here I am, left with the one true currency all of us possess." Eaton lightly taps his index finger against his temple. "When we get to the point of death, whether we know it's coming or not, all we've ever accumulated in life that matters are memories. Things we've done. People we've loved. Lands we've explored. Memories are the truest measure of wealth, and yet they can't be passed down, not really. Stories can be told, but our memories, those things as unique as our fingerprints, all crumble along with our bones."

My body tenses at his comments, and not just because of the sheer morbidity of them. Within minutes of us meeting, he's talking about memories, my greatest vulnerability, as if he's toying with me.

This all makes me think of Clara. Again. I look at the window to my right, its shade drawn. That's west. Where the mountains are. She's out there, somewhere. Maybe at this very moment she's drawing her last breath.

The thought of it makes me feel helpless. *Damn it, I should have done something more.*

"What is it, Jake?"

"Excuse me?"

"You seem to be somewhere else."

I was somewhere else. I was up in the mountains, the Maroon Bells.

"Sorry, I was just…lost in thought a bit. Something you said."

He nods, accepting this, perhaps proud he triggered a suddenness of deep thought in me. Eaton gets up and disappears from the room, returning a minute later with two mugs. Hands one to me. Coffee with cream. I thank him and sip. No sugar.

It's not an imaginative leap to think a person might want a cup of coffee. But to know exactly how they take it?

He sits and holds eye contact as he sips his own.

"You and your wife are breaking up," he says.

The room feels suddenly darker. Smaller.

"How the hell did you know that?"

He cradles the mug in both hands, warming himself. "Jake, you're here to write my memoirs. That's a very personal thing.

Do you really think I'd hire you without doing some of my own research?"

"But how did you know about my marriage? I haven't told anyone."

"I only know because you just confirmed it," he says. "It's not like I'm having you followed. Or your phone tapped."

"So how did you—"

"All I know is an apartment was recently leased in your name in the same town as your home, an easy thing to find out. That, of course, doesn't really mean anything. But you're in your midthirties, married somewhat young, had a child soon after. Statistically speaking, assuming your marriage is now falling apart is the most logical conclusion."

"It's not falling apart," I say.

But isn't it?

"Okay, Jake."

"We're just trying to figure some things out. Not that it's your business."

Eaton nods. "Of course. I fully understand. Well, maybe not *fully*. I never married, you see."

I'm leaning forward. Body-language experts would call this a sign of attention, perhaps aggression. "What else do you know about me?"

"Relax, Jake. Nothing your car dealer didn't find out when you applied for the loan on your Toyota Highlander last year. Credit report kind of things."

"So you have my social security number?"

"Please don't be naive. It's not that difficult to get. Besides, I'm going to tell you my deepest, darkest secrets. It's only fair I know a few things about you."

"That's different. Your secrets are going into a book. You want them out there."

"How do you know what I'm doing with the memoir? Perhaps it's only for me."

"Dying men don't write memoirs for themselves. They want to be remembered."

A broader smile.

"Well, yes, I suppose you have done this kind of thing before. Though I admit I hate being categorized so easily."

This is going off the rails. I can't deny I'm curious to hear his life story—and I do need the money—but if he cat-and-mouses me the whole time, we'll never get anywhere.

"Eaton," I say. "We need to establish some boundaries here. Otherwise, this isn't going to work."

"Okay," he says, setting his mug down on a side table and sitting up in his seat. "Perhaps we're not getting off on the right foot, and that's my fault. I apologize. I won't try to use my illness as an excuse, but I will say I have been more…cautious as a result. Hopefully you can understand I don't want to waste any time, and please forgive me if I intruded. May we move forward?"

Eaton holds my gaze and I hold his, assessing him, struggling to read the energy on him as I now can with so many strangers. Yet he doesn't give me much to work with. It's like I'm trying to read the emotional energy of a hologram.

"I'm going to tell you right now," I say. "I don't like you investigating me. I know you're paying me a lot of money, but don't forget a good chunk is nonrefundable and I can just walk. You're the subject, not me. So from here on out, the questions are about you and you only. Can we agree on that?"

"Why, yes, Jake, of course. Now, tell me, how exactly does this all work?"

He stares at me almost too attentively as I speak, and more than once, I look away.

"I'm in town for three days," I say, "and over those days, we'll meet extensively. I'll be recording our conversations as I interview you about your past. That should be enough time to develop a base of material and, hopefully, find a thematic direction of the book, an element that informs the story of your life."

"Thematic direction?" A crooked smile.

"Everyone's life has a thematic direction," I answer. "But sometimes you have to do a lot of digging to figure out what that is."

He looks to have a thousand questions for me, but he manages to simply nod in acquiescence.

Eaton starts at the beginning, before he was born, and tells me about his parents. How they met, when they married, what his father did for a living. Then he tells me they both died when he was young, and for the first time since I arrived, I've found something in common with the man on the other end of the couch.

We were both orphaned at an early age.

And, along with impending death, being an orphan is another thing Eaton has in common with Clara. What are the odds that the only two people I've met in the last two days would have such very specific characteristics?

The universe continues to shrink.

I take notes, ask questions, try to lead him toward a narrative and steer him away from extraneous stories. Ghost-writing memoirs is much more than being able to transcribe a person's ramblings about their life. It's about knowing what's important and resonant in another person's history, what will connect with readers, and what's important to the subject themselves. But Eaton seems to sense this and has a surprising lack of ego as he speaks. He doesn't talk about his self-importance, or how things that happened in his youth became valuable lessons to his future success. He simply tells me the story of his family, just the facts, and lets me decide how those will ultimately take form on the pages.

And just as I'm thinking this will be easier than I expected, Eaton tells me he's tired and is done for the day. We've been talking just over an hour.

"Can we spend longer together next time?" I ask.

"Yes, of course. I know this requires more stamina from me. I simply don't have it right now, I'm afraid."

"Sure. I understand."

I say goodbye with a handshake, and as I do, I have another moment. Just a brief one, but it's there. A stronger sense of knowing this man than I felt earlier. Not quite déjà vu, but a close relative. A pang, almost nostalgic, softly painful.

"Are you all right?" He squeezes my hand a bit harder, as if thinking I might otherwise fall off a cliff. Maybe he's right.

"Yeah, I'm fine."

My chest wells with short but painful desperation, and I have a sudden desire to remember something. Anything.

I quiz myself. *What TV series have you been streaming lately?*

The answer comes quickly: *Better Call Saul,* season two.

A harder question. *What happened in the last episode?*

I think about this as I leave Eaton's apartment. I make it to the elevator, down to the lobby, out into the cool Denver air.

The answer never comes.

FOURTEEN

The Book of Clara
10/10/2018

The Responsibility of Death is a children's book.

There is no author name, copyright information, publisher, or ISBN. Nothing but the title.

The story centers on a young boy's long walk through a forest with his grandfather. During their walk, they encounter many creatures, all of which have advice for the two of them, but each time a creature speaks, the boy and the grandfather hear different things. A squirrel chitters, and the boy hears "Sleep heavily each night" while the grandfather hears "There's only darkness." It's nonsensical and disturbing, with the boy hearing only encouraging words and the old man hearing morbid advice, culminating with an old grizzly bear suggesting the grandfather might best be served by killing himself.

Accompanying the words are wondrous illustrations, all done in fine, black, hair-width pen strokes. Thousands upon thousands of inky wisps, collectively bringing to life the bizarre tale in the most depressing fashion. I think about how long those illustrations must have taken, how long this illustrator sat at a desk, hunched over paper, meticulously drawing one ink whisker at a time, trying to capture a scene of a snake telling the grandfather everyone is out to get him, while trees tower and loom, raining darkness. Each drawing is a piece of art, but one that somehow feels it shouldn't be seen by anyone. Mesmerizing and unnerving.

The story's simplicity is also why it's so disturbing. That, and the ending. On the penultimate page, the grandfather speaks for the first time. He looks down at his wide-eyed grandson and says, "I'll never come out of these woods, boy." The final page, formatted so it requires the reader to turn the book ninety degrees, shows the boy walking back on the path from whence they traveled, and the grandfather remaining behind. The old man sits stoop-shouldered on top of a tree stump, and in the background loom the eyes of animals, malevolent, glowing stars, watching. Watching and waiting.

I suppose the end is up for interpretation, but not much. Either the old man was dying and chose to let it happen in the woods, or he wanted to die and was sacrificing himself to the waiting teeth and claws of all that lived there.

I have read *The Responsibility of Death* enough times to recall many of the thousands of inked marks with precise clarity, but still have no idea what the book is about. What responsibility is the author talking about? The best I can come up with is the idea that once a person's time on earth is coming to an end, there's a responsibility to acknowledge that and, perhaps, do something to hasten the process. Making way for the younger generation, yielding land and resources to those who need them more.

I met with Landis twice after being accepted into the trial. The trial—which he called the *program*—consisted of a daily reading of the book and a weekly consumption of two tiny blue pills, which were so small, it was hard to imagine them having any potency. Landis and I discussed any changes I'd been feeling, any side effects. I expressed my concern that I hadn't retrieved any old memories—and in fact had been losing some of the recent ones—but he assured me this was all normal and, almost certainly, temporary.

I also informed him that, indeed, I had been feeling a shift in my life. In my mind, my emotions. This manifested itself in two distinct ways. One was positive, though it might not sound so. I became suddenly very certain teaching was not what I was meant to do. For years, I pursued teaching, thinking it was my calling. I believed myself to be good at it, and I loved the children. But then, soon after I started the program, my eyes just opened. I wasn't supposed to be a teacher. And the realization wasn't a moment of *I hate my job*. It was as if I realized I was filling my day with a respectable and fulfilling job, but I was meant to do something else. The *something else* remained hidden from me, but I was convinced I had to quit my job and let the answer come to me. That may seem like some kind of early-onset midlife crisis, but it was nothing of the sort. It was a stunning and soothing revelation that something most meaningful was right around the corner.

The other way the program was changing me was more jarring. I was suddenly feeling the emotions of others, as if I had turned into a Geiger counter of human energy. I could be on a bus with a stranger, and if they were having a bad day, I could sense it, and ultimately I'd end up soaking in their feelings, leaving me heavy. Alternatively, I'd catch the radiation of a joyful person, which would keep me smiling until counterbalanced by someone else's foul mood later that same day.

Landis explained that my empathy levels were elevating, which was expected. I told him I feared becoming exhausted by it all, and he said he'd look into changing my dosage levels if the issue continued to overwhelm.

During my last visit, Landis informed me the company was moving the office to a different state, but that he'd be following up with me by phone. The trial was to last a year, and he said there would be little need for contact unless I was experiencing significant adverse reactions.

Dear Reader, this is where you will be cursing at me. Telling me that I surely must have been mad to participate in any trial where I might develop *significant adverse reactions*. But how can I explain to you how the program made me feel? I had such a profound sense that discovering my true place in the world was imminent. It excited me. It drove my every waking thought.

Ironically, this enlightenment ultimately led to the idea of my own death. It crept onto me slowly at first, like a spider skulking along the backs of my fingers. Vapors of thoughts, here and there, flashes of how *light* death must feel. I kept sensing it as a hot-air-balloon ride, gently lifting, allowing me to float away and leave all earthly attachments behind. These weren't fully formed thoughts, but rather emotions, or even hazy memories. That I should be in the air, cold air, perhaps mountain air. That maybe I'd been dead before, and it was a wondrous astonishment, a dream to be first chased and then fulfilled. The ultimate pleasure.

Though these thoughts might be considered an adverse reaction, I didn't call Landis, and he didn't call me. I'm not ashamed to say I was addicted to the program. Very soon, nothing else mattered.

Two months after my last visit with Landis, I took to my life of seclusion. It all felt so right, so wonderfully predetermined. I don't expect you to understand. How could you? This doctor comes into my life, promises me a purpose, and I just do what he says.

I suppose it was a leap of faith.

Still, I leapt.

And have been falling ever since.

FIFTEEN
Jake

THE BAR AT THE Four Seasons has a steady stream of business. I'm sitting in a soft, oversize lounge chair, Dewar's on the rocks in a tumbler near my hand. I take a sip and let the alcohol slide over my tongue. It doesn't relax me, doesn't take off the anxious edge that I've been experiencing since the flight. I have this need to propel myself forward but don't know which direction to go. I keep telling myself to take control, but what does that even mean? Control of what, exactly?

Calm down, Jake, I tell myself. *Remind yourself of the why. Why you're doing what you're doing.*

To take care of Em, I answer. To pay the bills. To repair my marriage.

Aren't you doing that? Isn't the Eaton gig paying the most you've ever earned for ghostwriting?

Yes.

And, memory issues aside, haven't you been feeling good lately? More self-aware? More...actualized?

Yes. But my marriage is going to shit.

It's probably temporary. You're changing. That scares Abby.

What scares her—and me—is I'm forgetting things. I'm acting strange.

She's not scared of your memory loss; she's concerned. There's a difference. She wants to help you, but you won't let her in. The problem is, you haven't told her everything. She's smart. She senses it.

I know.

And you can't stop thinking about the woman from the plane. You might even be thinking about trying to find her, aren't you? Is she more important than your wife?

Clara is important. I know it. Our connection is important.

Okay, then let's cut to the chase with one last question. Do you like who you are as a person more than you did a year ago, or less?

I...I don't know.

Don't think about the events in your life. Don't think about the accident, or about your marriage. I'm asking about you. Who you are. What you feel. Are you happier with you *now than before?*

Yes.

There's your answer. Let that dictate what you do.

The last year.

I remove my laptop from my messenger bag, power it on. My fingers hover over the keyboard as I decide where to go first. I pause, take another sip of my drink, hoping for either inspiration or a completely numbed mind. The whiskey convinces me to do a Google search.

First, I try Clara Stowe. When the page loads, I click on image results.

Nothing immediately registers, and unsurprisingly, Google asks me if I meant Clara *Bow*, the silent-movie actress from the 1920s. I ignore Google and press on with my original search, loading pages of images. Scores of pictures resulting from the search *Clara Stowe*, some of people, others of documents and tombstones. A few nineteenth-century photos, and I half expect one to be of her. Maybe Clara is a ghost after all.

Back to the web-search results. I scan through the first three pages but find nothing remarkable. There's quite a bit about Clara Barton and Harriet Beecher Stowe. I think about that a bit, but struggle to find a connection. I dive into a few WikiTree results for Clara Stowes, but these are for other women. I hardly look at Facebook or Twitter profiles. If she's as truly disconnected from the world as she said, I won't find her on social media.

I need something, *anything*.

I search again, but this time not for Clara.

This time I search for a name known only to me.

Landis.

I wanted to tell Clara about Landis, but held back. I wanted to tell her he's the reason I started losing my recent memories, and that he's also the reason I like who I am now more than ever, despite all the shit going on. Hell, maybe Clara even *knows* Landis. But I said nothing about him.

He's been my secret for nearly a year.

He introduced himself as Dr. Landis Miller, but implored me just to call him Landis. In fact, I know almost nothing about him. When I Googled him after my first visit with him, I found nothing. But now, out of a hunch more than anything else, I try a new search.

Dr. Landis Miller "clara stowe"

The results are predictably unhelpful.

Then I try something new. The direct approach.

"jacob buchannan" "clara stowe"

As I press Enter, a bolt of nervous electricity shoots through my chest, as if I'm going to discover something insidious in the search result. That the internet somehow knows how Clara and I are connected, and the truth is something I don't want to know.

I'm both relieved and disappointed when Google yields nothing.

My mind wanders back to Landis. To the first time I met him, one memory still solidly lodged in my brain, fully intact.

Eleven months ago, I went to Landis's office in Boston, and that's when my world began to change.

SIXTEEN

Eleven months ago

THE FLYER ARRIVED AT Jake Buchannan's single-person office, which was housed in an aging four-story brick building in downtown Boston. Though Jake also worked from home, having an office was important to him. It gave him an identity, a place to meet clients, and five hundred square feet of total focus.

Mail was rare, usually consisting of take-out menus or trade magazines to former tenants. But the glossy-white flyer caught his eye, and it was specifically addressed to him.

MEMORY ISSUES?
Revolutionary Medical Breakthrough:
Volunteers Needed for Clinical Trial

The bold-font copy was enough to keep his attention—yes, in fact, he *did* have memory issues. But if those two words were enough to grab him, it was the image on the flyer that entranced him.

The hand-drawn image was of a king sitting on a throne. The picture was impossibly detailed, especially since it was a composite of seemingly thousands of tiny ink hashes, each little more than a millimeter in size. But the crown sitting atop the king's head was what made Jake stop, stare, and lose time altogether. The points on the crown were the heads of snakes, so realistic Jake could almost see them wriggling their way upward, like Medusa's hair.

Aside from the sheer oddness of it all, there was something about the image Jake couldn't quite shake. Though he threw the flyer away, that picture stayed with him, coming back in flashes throughout the day and evening. He might have even dreamed about it, but he wasn't exactly sure.

The next day, another identical flyer arrived with his office mail. That, too, he discarded, but not before staring a bit longer this time.

Jake worked from home the next two days. By Friday, when he returned to his office, the mail had brought with it three more flyers, each the same as the previous two.

A feeling gnawed at Jake. It wasn't so much that the image of the king had nothing to do with the text. Nor was it exclusively the stated purpose of the flyer, though the memory-issue subject did strike a nerve.

Rather, it was more that he couldn't stop thinking about the flyers as a collective message in a bottle. Something that required action and was not to be casually discarded.

A sign, Jake thought. Some kind of sign.

He had the growing sense that if he threw away these flyers, more would come. One a day, every day, until Jake did something about them.

He took the mail into his office, took a seat in his well-worn faded leather office chair, and dialed the number on the flyer from his landline.

The man's voice on the other end was soft, congenial.

"Arete Memory Research, may I help you?"

"Hi," Jake said. "I'm calling about the memory trial. I keep getting these—"

"Yes, of course. I'm so pleased you called. May I get your name, please?"

"It's Jake."

"And your last name?"

Jake paused. "Is that important right now?"

"No, it isn't, Jake. I want you to be comfortable with your experience with us. We can get that information later. My name is Dr. Miller, but you can just call me Landis."

"Okay," Jake said. "As I was saying, I keep getting these flyers. And I don't know what it is about them. I mean, this is going to sound crazy, but..."

"The picture triggered something in you, didn't it, Jake?"

Jake had a sensation of all his skin tightening at once. "How did you know that?"

"Because the flyer itself is designed in a very specific way," Landis said. "The image has seemingly nothing to with the clinical trial, and we don't state we're offering to compensate volunteers, so most people wouldn't bother calling us. But you aren't most people, are you, Jake?"

What the fuck? Jake thought.

"Is the picture some kind of...illusion?"

"Not at all. You see the same picture everyone else does. But your brain causes you to have an unusual reaction to the image, so you felt compelled to call this number. Exactly as we designed it. We're looking for people like you, Jake. There aren't too many of you out there."

Jake leaned forward in his chair. "What is going on here?"

He heard a soft chuckle on the other end. "A bit unsettling, yes?" Landis said. "*Apologies.* I'm so entrenched in the research, I sometime forget how this all appears to someone newly exposed to our work. Let me just ask you this, Jake: Do you have memory issues, either long- or short-term? It doesn't have to have been formally diagnosed, but it's more than just the occasional forgetfulness."

Jake took a breath, feeling more than ever as if he were at some kind of crossroads. "Yes," he said. "Long-term memory issues. My childhood."

"Excellent," Landis said, and Jake could hear a buzz of excitement in his voice. "Well, I don't mean excellent that you have these issues. But I think we can help you, Jake. Really help you."

"How…how exactly does it all work?"

"You come in and see us," Landis said. "You're located in downtown Boston, correct?"

"How did you know that?"

"That's currently where our flyers are targeted."

"Yes, I'm downtown."

"Good. So are we. Can you come over right now?"

"Now? You mean right now? I have work I need to—"

"It won't take long," Landis said. "And our trial is almost full of volunteers. I'd hate for you to miss out on something that could truly change your life."

Jake thought about it and realized he'd changed in the last week. A week ago, he would've been hesitant to engage in conversation with a stranger at Starbucks, let alone just leave his office to volunteer for some shady-sounding clinical trial. But the message-in-a-bottle metaphor wouldn't leave his mind, the feeling that maybe all this was happening for a reason. The universe slapping him in the face and telling him to pay attention. Even just seeing those flyers had… shifted something inside him.

"How long?" Jake asked.

"Thirty minutes, tops."

Jake shook his head and nearly smiled at doing something so uncharacteristic.

"What's your address?" he asked.

Seven blocks later, Jake walked into a nondescript office near the Public Garden. There was no sign on the door, but the logo on the interior wall read *Arete Memory Research*, the name Landis had used when answering the phone.

The reception area was clean, a tad dark, and empty. Seconds later, a man emerged from a back office, his gray suit and wool fedora packaging him neatly, vintage and clean, like a '57 Chevy rolling off the assembly line. Jake guessed him to be no older than himself, making the man's old-school styling all the more peculiar. And, anyway, who wore a fedora, especially while inside at work?

"Jake." The man beamed, extending his hand.

"You must be Landis."

"I am."

Landis's grip was strong. Borderline fierce.

In that moment, those few seconds of skin on skin, Jake had the same rush of emotion that he'd felt when he first looked at the picture on the flyer. A catch in his throat, a feeling of sudden vulnerability, a wave of undefined meaningfulness.

Landis didn't remove his hat. He wore it as he ushered Jake into a small office that contained little more than a desk and a diploma. He wore it as he explained to Jake about the clinical trial—the *program*, he called it—and how it was to help not only Jake's long-term memory issues, but in doing so, actually assist in creating a better future for him. Landis even kept wearing that hat when he opened his desk drawer and took out a book, which he slid across the top of the desk.

Jake studied the book. A slim but tall volume, hardcover, laminate finish. It had the shape of a children's book but the title—swoopy black font against a white canvas—suggested anything but. Jake read the title aloud.

"*The Responsibility of Death.*"

"Yes," Landis said.

"What is this?"

"It's part of the program. An integral part."

There was no image on the cover. Aside from the curious title, Jake couldn't imagine why anyone would bother to pick up the book.

"How…how does it work?"

"Open it," Landis said.

Jake did. Inside was a series of black-and-white drawings and almost no discernible story. But he realized immediately the style of the drawings was the same as the image from the flyer. Then, as Jake thumbed through the pages, he finally came upon the image of the king with his crown of snakes.

"Our flyer convinced you to contact us. Tell me, now that you have this book in your hands, does it seem familiar to you?"

Jake looked up. "Familiar how?"

"As if maybe it was something you once owned, a long time ago."

Jake shook his head. "No, nothing like that. Why would I own this book?"

Landis leaned forward over his desk, and as he did, he finally removed his fedora and placed it top down on the desk surface.

"Do *I* seem familiar, Jake?"

"What?"

"Even a little. Maybe you don't recognize me, but maybe you have a sense about me. A sense of the past."

"What the hell is going on here?" Jake asked.

Landis didn't answer, but he kept searching Jake's eyes. Finally, Landis leaned back and waved a dismissive hand.

"These are questions we ask any potential participant. I know they seem strange. Don't worry. You're doing just fine, Jake."

Jake closed the book and pushed it back toward the man on the other side of the desk.

"I'm not sure I want to be a part of this," he said. "I can't say I wasn't intrigued enough to get me this far, but you're kind of creeping me out now."

Landis gave Jake a full smile. Teeth perfectly straight with just a hint of yellow. His hand returned to the top desk drawer, and this time, Jake imagined him retrieving a gun. Or a long knife, serrated blade.

But what he pulled from the desk was a small, orange plastic vial with a white cap. The object was immediately recognizable to Jake;

every pill prescription he'd ever had filled came in one of these vials. But how different the ubiquitous container looked without a label.

Landis set the vial on Jake's desk.

"These go with the book."

"What are they?"

Landis kept his hands folded patiently in front of him as he looked at Jake. "The pills inside that container are part of the program, and the program is a means for you to become what you were always meant to be. A man of exceptional talent. And a man with memories. I'm sorry if I'm giving you any feelings of unease; that is certainly not my intention. But however you perceive me, Jake, I promise you that, if you follow the program in its prescribed regimen, you will transform in amazing ways. We've seen it happen."

Jake studied the vial but didn't pick it up.

Landis filled the silence. "You've already felt it with the image on the flyer, haven't you?" He opened the book and turned the first few pages. "I look at these images, and they do nothing for me. But you... you feel them. I know you do."

"Maybe I should just leave," Jake said.

Landis's smile disappeared, a cloud passing in front of the sun. "Of course, you can leave at any time. As I mentioned to you on the phone, our trial is quite nearly full. We don't *need* your participation, Jake. But I've been the project lead for some time now, and I know what it can do. If you've felt a reaction to these images, you are most likely a good candidate for the trial. If you want to stay a little while longer, I can vet you further and verify you're a good fit. Or you can leave." Landis leaned back in his chair and laced his fingers behind his head. "Life is nothing if not decisions.

It's up to you to determine when you're at a crossroads. I can't do that for you."

The word *crossroads* swirled around in Jake's head. He looked at the book, then shifted his gaze to the orange vial.

Maybe I'll stay a little longer, Jake thought. *Hear what he has to say. Maybe I'll even take the book home.*

He kept looking at the little plastic bottle.

But there's no fucking way I'm taking those pills.

SEVENTEEN
Jake

I REMAINED AT LANDIS'S office for another hour that day, and by the end of my visit, I'd been declared officially qualified for the trial, though I still wasn't sure I was actually going to participate. Landis had spoken in vague, sweeping terms, telling me that were the program successful, it would not only restore my forgotten past but embolden my future. Unlock talent I had never fully realized.

I told him maybe I didn't want to remember my childhood after all. What if something terrible had happened to me? Why would I want to remember that?

Yet he had this gentle way of assuring me I would be pleased with the results. And despite all the questions I had for which he had no concrete answers, Landis absolutely pinpointed many of my specific thoughts and feelings. Like how I've always had a nagging feeling I was meant to be something greater than I had become, and that maybe my inability to recall my childhood was part of my limitations. And finally, that I was more receptive than ever to recognize when I was at an important crossroads of my life. I felt like I was visiting a fortune-teller who, despite my skepticism, was telling me enough general truths to start making me a believer.

I asked how the program worked.

He told me it was simple: read the book every day, take the pills as prescribed.

I asked how often I needed to check back in with him.

He said it worked the other way around. He would reach out to me. The only formal check-in would be upwards of a year from then, when he would return to ask a very specific question.

What question?

He said I'd have to wait.

I asked what the hell kind of clinical trial worked this way?

He said *a life-changing one*.

I left his office that day with the book, the vial of pills, and no fucking idea what I was going to do.

I did look through *The Responsibility of Death* again that afternoon, and its hold on me was almost immediate. If I had been taken in by the image on the simple flyer, I was mesmerized by the book. It was the beginning of what Landis referred to as my transformation, when I first started having the sense of the universe contracting smaller around me, making me more certain of my place within it.

Self-actualization.

I didn't tell anyone about my visit to Landis, not even Abby. I can't explain that decision other than saying I wasn't sure what I was dealing with, and until I figured it out, I wanted to control the situation alone.

Apparently, I have control issues.

In the hotel bar, I finish my drink and slide the book from my messenger bag. I carry it around in the bag, which is with me most of the time. I wish I could rationalize my need to keep it near, as if it were some kind of talisman, shielding me from an unknown evil. For all I know, it's just the opposite, a source of harm, leaking radiation into my bones.

The book was the first thing to create a rift in my mind. I can't tell you if it had something to do with the hypnotic nature of the illustrations or the story itself, but it wouldn't be a gross exaggeration to say I have become somewhat obsessed with death. I now routinely scour the obituaries, reading of lives recently snuffed, and I've developed an uncanny ability to *feel* these people somehow, as if I lived a bit of their lives with them, and perhaps a little of their deaths.

A haunting, beautiful thing.

A part of me wishes I had never looked at the book, but, honestly, that part is pretty small.

"Jake."

I'm snapped away from my thoughts by the voice. It belongs to a woman, and it comes from behind my shoulder.

I'm thinking—*hoping*—the woman is Clara.

It can't be possible. Then again, I feel like I'm becoming fluent in the impossible.

I turn.

It's not Clara.

EIGHTEEN

The Book of Clara
10/11/2018

Last night, I booked myself into the Hotel Jerome in Aspen. The front-desk clerk seemed surprised I'd shown up at night without a reservation. He asked me how many nights I wanted to stay. Two nights, I told him. Perhaps I would change my mind, stay longer. He assured me that wouldn't be a problem, it being the off-season.

A light October morning rain spits outside my bedroom window. The Rocky Mountains, cloaked in gray, bruised and dull, the sun well away. Seems not the most favorable time of year to visit the Maroon Bells, but suicide isn't seasonal. Death cares little for blue skies and flowers in fierce bloom.

I have both the book and the pills with me. I don't really have a need for either anymore, but they go where I do, which is to the end.

I didn't start taking the pills immediately. Despite Landis telling me he was a doctor, the clinical trial was undeniably strange and Landis himself a bit unnerving. He knew more about my feelings than any stranger should, and that made me want to both trust him and run away screaming.

I did read the book, however, and it made me feel something. An understanding I couldn't explain, as if I was starting to finally see how I fit in the world. The book made me feel more...*me*, even if that new me became a shut-in a mere two months later. There I was, an orphan who couldn't remember her past, and suddenly I started thinking life maybe made a little sense. But it wasn't enough. I wanted to understand more. I wanted to *feel* more.

That was when I realized what the pills were for. Landis knew it all along, knew how the book would make me feel. Knew it would make me crave more of what I was feeling.

Maybe I was weak. Or perhaps I was enlightened.

I finally began taking the pills because I believed. Funny thing, that's how religions get started. Pure belief. A hope for something more. As a lifelong agnostic, I had finally found god.

The program was my deity.

The program has led me here, to the Maroon Bells. No, the program didn't drive me to depression-induced suicide. It made me realize death is where I belong, my rightful place. Death has a perfectly sized Clara-shaped hole, waiting to be plugged.

As for the book, I read it yet again, sitting on the thick

blanket of my hotel-room bed. This time, I stared even more deeply at the little boy in the woods. I've always wondered who that boy is supposed to be. He's not me. I'm the old man, the grandfather being coaxed into death by the talking creatures. That's never been clearer than now. But the boy?

Maybe Jake is the boy.

I don't know what to make of Jake. It's undeniable we somehow know each other. We both have a forgotten past. We both are orphans.

I would be mostly convinced he was an illusion were it not for the business card I have.

Jake Buchannan, Writer.

Either someone or the universe put us on that plane together. In either case, I think Jake represents some kind of test. Will I continue with my plan, or will I seek the answers he does?

I am unwavering. I will do what I've come here to accomplish.

I think of decades, *my* decades, specifically. My early thirties have been marked by loneliness, isolation, and, let's face it, probably some form of mental illness. I know my brain isn't right, at least not in a conventional sense. I try to look for clues on how I became what I eventually did. Those years weren't lonely, but neither were they full of happiness. I just...*was.*

Years of doing the same thing. Working as a teacher in the same school, teaching faces that never seemed to change. Same kids. Same subject. Same ticking minutes on the same wall clock, the second hand sweeping lives away.

I never married and dated rarely. I'm neither straight nor gay nor something else with a tidy definition attached. I'm an *undefinable*, a person with little need for human connection, despite an aching love of humanity. I'm capable of becoming obsessively attached to a character in a novel, for instance. Even feel real grief at the book's conclusion because that character is gone from my life. But I've met very few real-life individuals into whom I'd want to invest as much time as I would in reading a book.

I figured this out in my twenties, and by my thirties, I was quite content with the person I was. Not that my ambition was limited, but rather my definition of ambition was narrower than convention dictated. I was simple. I was existent, neither remarkable nor forgettable.

I'm back.

I stopped writing for a bit, because I had a moment. The same moment I've been having for the past few weeks. The first time it happened, it collapsed me. Now, I've built up a tolerance, but it still keeps me from functioning for a brief period.

I think it's some kind of breakthrough. A memory. A precious, rare, haunting memory.

This memory, when it came to me three weeks ago, hit me hard and fast, as if I were strolling on seemingly abandoned tracks when a freight train obliterated me from behind.

What a powerful thing, to remember something of such disturbing significance when I was so used to only forgetting! A repressed memory, I believe they call it. Whatever its name, when it first happened, it left me on my apartment floor, first with a ravaging headache, and then just an emotional heap, crying for hours, unable to do anything but loop the same scene in my head. When I finally came out of the cycle, I had more sense of purpose than ever.

Though I just recently recalled it, the memory is a singular one from my childhood. I don't know how old I was. Young, I think. At first, there was darkness. Memories rarely start without an image, but when this one first washed over me, it began with blackness. I saw nothing, but there was sound. There was screaming. A little child, uncontrollably shrieking.

I turned my head and saw glowing, orange numbers, floating waist-high.

1-2-3-4.

Just those four numbers. Like some kind of symbol. Maybe a puzzle. I focused on the numbers, adjusting my eyes. Then another form took shape, because the numbers were casting light. There was something beneath them. A surface, smooth and flat. My brain struggled to make sense of anything. Finally, even with the horrible din of the screaming child, something clicked. It was a clock. The numbers were part of a clock, and the clock was on a table. The numbers weren't a puzzle. They were telling the time.

12:34.

It was just after midnight, and I was in a room with a screaming child.

Then, there was light. Blinding, crushing light, assaulting me. My eyes took a moment to adjust, and finally, I saw him. The little boy on the floor, squatting on his feet, his arms wrapped around his knees. Little ball, in pajamas. Head raised to the ceiling. *Howling.*

I turned my head...forced my vision away from him. *I can't help you*, I thought. *I'm sorry, I can't help you.*

What I saw next plunged me into sheer horror.

I was at the foot of a large bed, and now I realized the boy was just off to the side by a bedroom wall. Next to the bed was a small table, on which stood the clock with its digital orange numbers. The light came from above. Somebody must have flipped on the switch, allowing me to see what was in the bed.

Blood.

Splattered on white sheets and blankets. Spray on the wall. Pools of red. Small rivers.

Two people. They were dead, flesh opened. Crumpled on the mattress, half-covered by blankets, ripped pillow stuffing mixed with their blood.

A man and a woman. Maybe. It was hard to tell.

Something bubbled blood. A wound on one of them, the heart ticking off its final beats. But neither of them moved. There was no saving them, even if I knew how.

I stared, paralyzed, wanting to turn my attention to

anything else, even back to the desperate child. My head wouldn't turn. But I did finally move. I took a step back, away from the bed.

Then, in my peripheral vision, I saw the others. They were like me.

Children.

The sight of them only lasted a moment. There were three or four other children, and collectively we all looked down upon the dead.

I reached out and grabbed a hand next to me, tethering myself.

"It's okay," the boy holding my hand says. His voice is shaking, and he's choking up. "It's going to be okay."

There, the memory ended. But the little boy on the floor kept screaming in my mind.

NINETEEN
Jake

"JAKE BUCHANNAN."

The way the woman says my name isn't posed as a question, the way an old friend might say it bumping into you on the street. It's a statement, the way a cop would say it when appearing at your doorstep.

The stranger doesn't ask permission before sliding in next to me at the Four Seasons bar. The corkscrew coils of her Afro brush the tops of her shoulders. Smooth, dark face. Lips drawn into a tight expression that falls short of a smile. Midtwenties, though I'm shit at guessing those kinds of things. What's most noticeable are her eyes. Though they dart from side to side, scanning the room, I connect enough to see sadness in her. A kind of longing, like the kid sitting alone at the cafeteria lunch table. I see all of this in seconds and wouldn't have noticed it at all a year ago. Finally, her gaze settles on me.

"Yes?" I say.

"I'm buying you a drink."

"I have a drink."

"I think you'll be needing another one."

"Why's that?"

She crosses her legs and signals to the waiter before turning her attention on me.

"Well," she says, "first off, I know how you like your whiskey."

"And how do you know that?"

Another scan of the room. "When a person is determined to find out as much as they can about someone else, it's a fairly easy task. Especially when that curious person is experienced, well equipped, and willing to break a few laws."

We hold our silence for a moment, as if daring the other to speak first. The waiter comes over, and she orders another Dewar's for me and a glass of pinot noir for herself. When the waiter leaves, she reaches across and lifts *The Responsibility of Death* from the table.

"This is a rare book," she says. "Very rare."

"You work with Landis? Are you part of the clinical trial?"

"I used to work *for* him. By talking to you, I'm effectively terminating my employment." This time when she scans the room, she actually turns her head.

I lean back. "Can you just tell me what the hell is happening here? And why do you keep looking around?"

"I'm not supposed to be here," she says. "They might be watching us."

"Who's 'they'? Landis?"

"Or other contractors of his I don't know about. Listen, Jake…" She's nervous; I can see it. The way her jaw twitches. Her fingers, constantly moving, as if trying to disperse the energy pent up inside her body. "I debated with myself a long time about whether to talk to you. Now that I'm doing it, there's no turning back. But it's a risk, for both of us."

"What do you…"

The drinks arrive. I don't finish my question.

She gulps her wine, and her lips leave a faint rouge impression on the glass. A part of me thinks I should take that glass with me, have it tested, and somehow find out who she is.

"I'll cut to the chase," she says. "Landis hired me to find you, which I now regret. He is not your friend. I no longer work for him. I don't know if I can help you, but I'm going to try." She nods down to the book. "You've read that, what, more than a hundred times?"

I nod, knowing she's way low on her estimate.

She leans toward me just an inch more, holds my gaze tight with hers.

"When you first looked through it, you were confused. Why would some strange doctor give you a children's book? You looked through it quickly, didn't quite get it, then dismissed it."

That's not exactly right. I felt something the very first time I read it. But I say nothing.

"But later, maybe after a few hours, you looked though it again. More carefully. Actually read all the words, looked at every picture. You became a little more intrigued." She flips to the first picture, one I've seen so many times, I could nearly draw it from memory had I the talent of the illustrator. "That night, you probably thought about it a little more, maybe even had a dream about it. In the morning, you had a third read, and something started to draw you in. Maybe the words. Maybe the direction of the simple story. Or maybe it was—"

"The pictures," I say, hardly aware I'm speaking.

"*Exactly.*"

"That's the key to whatever…" I don't want to say *power*.

"Whatever makes the book so intriguing. The illustrations. The way every pen stroke is just a tiny mark, yet thousands of them all build to make an image. It's like…it's like building a sandcastle out of dry sand. It seems impossible."

"Not illustrations, Jake. *Algorithms*." She leans back, flips another page. "I assume you've Googled the book. You've searched the title. Didn't find anything, did you?"

"Nothing," I say. "The book doesn't exist."

She holds it up. "And yet it does."

"How many copies are there?"

"Not many. But this one here? It's the only version like it. Of all the existing copies of the *Responsibility of Death*, each is different. No two stories are the same. All the drawings are unique to each edition."

I look down at the book in her hands, trying to picture other versions, other illustrations. My version is so ingrained in my mind that it's hard to imagine a wholly different edition.

"Have you been taking the pills?" she asks.

I don't want to admit it, but she reads my face and nods.

"The pills magnify the effects of the book," she says. "Stop reading the book, Jake. Ditch the pills. It's probably too late; the damage is done. But just get rid of everything."

"I wasn't going to take them," I say. "But my daughter, she was hurt in an accident…"

"Yes, the accident." Her face shows true concern, but I have no idea how much of an actress this woman is. "How's Em doing?"

"Christ, how much do you know about my family?" I ask.

"Enough to know you moved out recently."

"Whatever you're doing," I say, "it needs to stop. Leave me and my family alone."

"Take it easy, Jake. I *will* leave, if that's what you want. I'm no longer monitoring your family anyway. I'm here to help you. I'm not even sure I can, but I do know I'm the only one trying to right now."

I realize I'm sliding my ring up and down over my finger again, back and forth.

"What's your name?" I ask.

"You can call me Elle."

"As in Eleanor?"

"As in *L-M-N-O-P*." She takes another sip of wine, which just about finishes it off.

So I'm calling this woman an alphabet letter.

"And why do you think I need help?"

Elle leans in, forcing me to do to the same. "Because of Kate and Raymond."

"Who?"

"They're like you. Or, I should say, they *were* like you."

"And they are?"

"Dead." She leans back and takes another sip of her wine. "They're both dead."

I raise my hands in an attempt to actually grasp this situation. They're shaking. "Can you just tell me…in plain language…what the hell you're talking about?"

She gives me a furrowed brow, as if impatient I don't know all the things she apparently does. "I could have been helping all along, and I didn't. What Landis did with you, he did with Kate and Raymond, and they're both dead. That's what I'm talking about."

"The clinical trial."

"There *is no* clinical trial, Jake. Aren't you listening to me?"

Am I dreaming here? I actually take a moment to look around, take in my surroundings. Deep breath, inhale, smell. Listen to the clink of glasses at the bar. If this is a dream, it's the most goddamn realistic one I've ever had.

Elle leans toward me. "Look, if you've been taking the pills, then you've been changing. You've been feeling it, haven't you? Ever since you went to see Landis."

This woman even knows how I'm feeling?

"I have felt…changes," I admit.

"Good changes or bad changes?"

If I were to choose to answer, I'd say *both*. The bad change is the onset of more memory loss. The good changes? Well, how about the idea of seeing the entirety of my decade-long unfinished novel suddenly unfolding in minute detail in my mind? Or how I can connect emotionally with nearly everyone I meet, feel their essence, their undercurrent, with just a simple look in the eyes?

But I don't answer.

She leans in just a touch, locks in on my eyes. "I think, over time, everything Landis gave you becomes more and more suggestive. Starts giving you ideas. Are you having radical thoughts you hadn't had before?"

"Radical thoughts? Like divorce?"

"Divorce is a bit soft. I'm talking about something more significant. Like…thoughts of violence. Either to yourself or others. Have you had those kinds of thoughts?"

"No." But my answer comes only after a pause. I think about my growing obsession with death, my scouring of the obituaries.

"You say you want to help me," I say. "That's also what Landis said."

She pulls back and looks around the room, scanning. Then she leans into my ear. "He's not helping you. He's *experimenting* on you."

"What do you—"

"We need to find Clara."

Clara. The name sends a jolt through me.

"How do you know about her?"

"Do you remember her, Jake?"

Events are happening too fast for my brain to keep up.

"I met her yesterday. She was on the plane."

"No, Jake. Do you *remember* her? Not from yesterday, but from another time in your life?"

Coffee-brown eyes, flecks of cinnamon. The smell of citronella. Of nostalgia.

"Yes. I mean, I think I do. But I don't know how. Who is she?"

"She's like you," Elle says. "Another one of Landis's lab rats."

"You put us together on the plane."

"You were put together."

Not *I put you together*. But *you were put together*.

"I don't think anyone knows the complete story behind who you all are," she says. "Not even Landis, but he's trying. He hired me to track you all down so he could give you the books and pills. It's all part of *something…*"

"So Clara has a book as well?" I ask.

"She does. And the pills. Just like you."

Elle is tying my brain into tight little knots.

"I'm lost," I say.

"I don't think you have much time left. We need to find Clara."

"Why?"

She takes a sip of wine—more of a gulp—then sets the glass down and stands.

"Because you're the only two left, Jake. The last two names on the list. I know you don't trust me—I suppose there's no reason you should. But I'm trying to keep what happened to Raymond and Kate from happening to you."

I pound my fist on the table, which immediately seems ineffective. "*Save us from what?*"

Instead of answering, Elle looks around, as if assessing for the safest exit. "I have to go."

"Wait, you can't just leave."

"You'd be surprised how wrong you are." She turns and starts walking away.

"Wait. Just…just one more question."

She turns.

"What?"

So many questions swirl through my brain, but I only get to ask one. I straighten in the chair, lean forward. "How did Kate and Raymond die?"

She pivots so she's facing me fully, then pulls out a pen and writes a number on my cocktail napkin.

"If you want me to help, you can reach me at that number. As for your question?" She tucks the pen back into her purse and zips it. "Violently."

TWENTY

"HEY, SWEETIE."

"Hi, Dad."

My daughter's voice is the only thing I want to hear, yet it also breaks my heart. One of life's little jabs.

"Getting ready for school?"

"Yup."

"How are you feeling?" It was the new morning question. It used to be *How did you sleep?*

"Okay." Always the same answer.

"You have some OT today, right?"

"I dunno. I think so."

She does. Every Friday at 3:00 p.m., the occupational therapist works with Em for an hour. It's a form of play therapy, targeting anxiety and memory issues stemming from the accident.

I open the blinds of my hotel room, greeted by darkness. Five in the morning. Last night I made it until 3:00 a.m. before sleep decided it had had enough of me. I finally felt it pulling at me but forced myself up to call Em before she left for school.

"So, I'll be here a few more days."

"How's your trip?"

There are a lot of answers to that question.

"The guy I'm writing the memoirs for… He's a unique individual."

"What do you mean?"

"I mean I think he has an interesting story to tell. I'll tell you about him more when I get back."

"Okay," she says. "Mom says I need to go now."

"Oh…"

"Do you want to talk to her?"

God, yes. I miss her. I miss them both.

"Sure, if she's around."

Silence for a moment.

"She says she's getting ready and can't talk right now."

Can't or doesn't want to?

"Oh, okay, sweetie," I say. "In that case, I think I'm going back to bed. I love you."

"I love you."

We hang up, and I fall back on my mattress.

My copy of *The Responsibility of Death* lies on the right side of the king-size bed. I reach over and pick it up, its well-worn cover smooth and comforting in my hands.

There are several copies of the book, Jake, but each is different. No two stories are the same.

Did that really happen last night? Was that woman real?

If she was, that means the book in my hands is the only one telling the story of a king. He has no name and barely a face, but he and his kingdom are drawn from thousands of tiny pen marks. His face is shaded, almost blurred, as if he could be anyone, and his singular detailed feature is his crown. Here the illustrator abandons his whisker-style of art and strives for detail and realism. Though in black and white like the rest of the book, the crown is ornate in its detail, dozens of various-sized jewels layered on soft velvet, the gleam of gold wrapped around the base.

But most striking are the five points of the crown, each of which depicts a head of a snake, all with their eyes only the narrowest of slits, their jaws unhinged, mouths open to the sky, fangs bared and ready to pierce.

The same picture as in the flyer seeking volunteers for a memory-based clinical trial.

The story itself is simple and disturbing. I always wondered who thought it an appropriate children's book, but now I know the answer. It was never a book for children. It's only a book for me.

The man in the story wasn't born a king. He begins as an ordinary child, a poor one, the son of a cobbler. Yet he is happy and has many friends. On the second page are the first words of the book, in which one of the boy's friends says to him, "Let's play a game of war."

It took me several reads to understand the rhythm. The following pages—a total of forty-two—consist of the boy growing older alongside his friends, and on every page, a different friend makes a singular statement to the boy. Strange things, utterances that make no sense. Things like *Tickled alligators bare no teeth* and *Make me a sharpened stick from bone.*

The boy has no name. The boy never speaks.

He grows older.

The words in the book consist largely of these bizarre statements from the friends, and no one friend ever speaks twice. There is a lulling cadence to the language, which is almost poetic in nature but without any defined rhythm. No iambic pentameter, or any other metered types of verse I vaguely remember from school. But there's something congealing the collection of gibberish together in a satisfying way. On one of my many reads, it finally hit me.

Every statement from a friend contains exactly one of the same words as the previous one. It might be an almost invisible word, like *me* or *the*, or something more apparent, such as *castle*. I've checked every sentence, and no more or no less than one word is carried over from one to the next, and the same word is never carried over more than once.

Finally, in the last few pages, the boy has grown into a man, as have his friends. Suddenly, he is king, with no explanation or logic given. On the second-to-last page, the king sits on his throne in an impossibly large chamber, looking vastly bored and tired. His image is tiny—most of the page is blank space—making the detail of his crown all the more amazing. I've actually studied it through a magnifying glass, and I can't think of a pen with a fine-enough tip or a human with a steady-enough hand to create the detail of the snake heads as they are drawn on that page. Yet there they are.

A similarly tiny friend leans into the king's ear and says, "The life game commences, sire, and you decide who wins."

Turn the page.

In the very last scene, the king sits on this same throne, yet now he fills up nearly the entire page. And rather than bored, his eyes are wide with excitement. Another new friend leans in. His is the first face with a shadow of whiskers. He repeats the very first sentence from the book.

Let's play a game of war.

There is one remaining page after that, but it is blank. I used to give this extra page no thought; don't most books have blank pages at the beginning and end? Yet now I've come to consider this final, glossy piece of blank white paper as the king's oblivion. He played a game of war, and everything was wiped out.

Perhaps that's the key to the title. *The Responsibility of Death.* And whatever this book is, it's supposedly dangerous. The woman—Elle— said I need to stop reading it, though the damage might already be done.

She referred to the illustrations as algorithms.

I let the book slide from my fingers, and my head becomes impossibly heavy. I sink into the pillow and close my eyes, thinking, lost in the deepest of fogs. Five more minutes of sleep. Maybe ten. That's all I need.

Hours later, I awaken. Phone ringing. I recognize the number and try to sound as alert as possible.

"This is Jake."

"Did I wake you? Jake, it's nearly nine."

"No…no, Eaton. Well, actually, yes. I didn't get a lot of sleep last night."

"I thought we were meeting at eight."

"We were. I'm so sorry. This isn't like me. I can be right over."

A long pause. "Please come."

I apologize again, and we hang up.

In the bathroom, I splash water on my face. No time for a shower.

I get ready in ten minutes, grabbing a cup of coffee in the lobby on the way out.

Outside, an intense sun lights my face. Thick, gunmetal clouds lumber in from the mountains. As I look west, I let myself think of Clara for just a moment, long enough to wonder yet again if the girl from 2A is alive or dead.

Then I push her away in my mind. Not totally gone, but out of reach for the time being. I've got responsibilities here.

But later, I need to chase these ghosts.

TWENTY-ONE

I KNOCK. EATON DOESN'T answer the door, just barks at me to enter. I do. Again, the inside of the vast apartment is dark. Shades drawn, only a few lights on.

He's sitting on the couch, as if he hasn't moved since yesterday. I think his outfit is different, but it's hard to tell. His right hand grips his forehead, telling me the darkness hasn't quashed his headache.

"Come. Sit."

This is a different Eaton than yesterday. That Eaton seemed eager to leap into the work, despite his weakened state. This Eaton seems to want to pull his blankets over his head and turn the world away.

I sit. He doesn't look over at me.

"Sorry I'm late," I say. "Are you okay?"

He mumbles something. I don't ask him to repeat it.

The air is stale, stagnant, as if having been recycled by the same set of lungs, over and over. I try to picture Eaton outside of this apartment, in the world, conducting meetings, networking. Out to dinner. I don't know him, but I can't see it. The image of him here, on the couch, in a dark apartment on a sunny day, seems the only setting appropriate for this man. What does he do for a living? Where does his money come from?

When he finally speaks again, his voice is on edge, his words clipped. "I was there, you know."

"Where?"

"At the massacre."

The word *massacre* is about the last one I expected as a response. I gently reach into my messenger bag and retrieve my laptop and digital recorder. I power up my system and launch into the Word document I'd started for my notes on Eaton. I turn on the recorder, not asking him permission.

"What massacre?"

"The Water Tower Place mall shooting."

I try to process this. I was half expecting him to talk about some metaphorical massacre, but what he's referencing was very real.

"The shooting from last month?"

One of the worst mass shootings in U.S. history. Ray Higgins, dentist, walked first into a mall and then a hotel in Chicago with an assault rifle and just opened up. No apparent motive other than maximum body count.

"That's right," Eaton says.

"You were there?"

"In the hotel. Where it all ended."

Holy shit. This is hard to fathom.

"Were you hurt?"

"No. Not physically."

He goes quiet. Scratches his neck, then lightly squeezes his temples, as if coaxing his headache away. Part of writing memoirs is to act as a psychologist, knowing when to tease information from your subject, and when to remain silent and let the subject decide when to talk. This is a moment I remain silent. This lasts perhaps a full minute. Feels longer.

Finally, Eaton speaks.

"Raymond Higgins. A thirty-five-year-old dentist. Raymond Higgins started in the mall."

Raymond. All the news stories referred to him as Ray. You don't hear the name Raymond all that often, and I just heard this name off the lips of a woman who whooshed in and out of my life.

I know a coincidence when I see it, and this feels nothing like that.

"He walked in through Macy's carrying a large duffel bag," Eaton continues. "Headed straight for the changing rooms. Was in there for some time. When he came out, he was in full camouflage, Kevlar vest, and was carrying an AK-103. He also had pistols on each ankle."

I remember the grainy security footage. Images of Higgins walking out of the dressing room before the killing started.

"I was in the lobby of the Ritz," he continues. "I was there for the night on business and was just checking in. The hotel is connected to the mall, of course. I heard the shots, but it didn't sound like gunfire. It was just staccato popping in the distance, something unrecognizable. But the screams. The screams were unmistakable."

Eaton isn't looking at me as he speaks. His hand continues to massage his forehead, squeezing pressure on, then off. On, off.

"The first person he killed was a store clerk in Macy's. Three rapid gunfire bursts ripped open his chest. The victim was twenty-five, I believe. He killed indiscriminately. Seven more people died in that Macy's, and by the time Raymond reached the interior of the mall, everyone was running. Did you see any of the video footage?"

"A little. It's not something I felt compelled to watch. Reading about it was bad enough."

He doesn't even seem to hear me. "There's a young mother frantically racing with her stroller, trying to get away. It's all captured perfectly on mall security cameras. You see this woman running, but she's going too fast to control the stroller, and it topples, spilling her baby to the floor. Her instinct, her only option, of course, is to save the baby. Shield it. But she loses time in doing so, and as she bends to collect her child, Raymond walks up from behind and puts a bullet into the back of her skull, releasing her blood and brains on the tiled mall floor. She collapses next to her child, at whom Raymond then points the barrel of his rifle. The muzzle seems to actually touch the baby's forehead. Raymond pauses, seems to reconsider, and then he moves on. The baby was the only victim spared in the killing spree."

I had heard this story as well. Nearly as disturbing as hearing it recounted by Eaton is the fact he chooses to call the shooter repeatedly by his first name, and not even the shortened version of it. As if Eaton knew him.

"By the time he made his way into the hotel lobby, you could hear the sirens growing closer. Gunfire and screams louder. People in the lobby running for cover, and there I was at the front desk, not knowing what to do. He hadn't entered the lobby at this point, but I left the desk. Left and just pressed myself up against a wall. Seconds later, he entered the room and walked past me, sweeping his gun sights in front of him. He didn't see me as he walked past.

"In that moment, I could have done something. Rushed at him

from behind, knocked him over. Who knows? Maybe he would have turned around before I could get to him. But I had the distinct, immediate sense I could do something. Yet I didn't."

"Few people would have," I say.

Eaton now makes eye contact with me.

"Perhaps," he says. "Perhaps not. But it doesn't matter what other people would have done. I was the one there. Only my actions matter, and I did nothing. I had a *responsibility*, but I did nothing."

He draws out the word *responsibility*.

"Raymond shot the front-desk clerk in the head. She had just been checking me in, and now she was gone. I watched her die in a split second."

"I'm sorry, Eaton. I can't imagine."

"No, you certainly cannot."

"You shouldn't feel responsible."

"But I am responsible. I'm to blame, Jake." There is pain in his gaze, desperation. "People are dead because of me."

I want to assure Eaton he bears no burden of Ray Higgins's violence, but there is a confessional tone to his voice that keeps me silent.

"I remember hoping he would turn around and kill me," he continues. "I was ready for it. Ready for death. I think part of it was the shame of doing nothing. But part of it was...it just seemed like my time."

"Because of...your condition," I say.

"Yes." He closes his eyes, looking fatigued. "But he didn't shoot me, of course. Among the shouts and the screams, the sirens and the chaos, Raymond casually walked through the lobby, away from my view, and into the ballroom. I'm sure you know what happened in there."

"Yes."

The shooter had calmly walked into the ballroom, where a group of nearly one hundred real-estate agents were holding a luncheon. He didn't want to take hostages or make demands. He had come there to kill, and did so with devastating efficiency. It was only when he needed to change clips a second time that he was taken down by two men attending the conference, one of whom wrestled his rifle away. As Higgins tried to raise his pistol, the real-estate agent shot him through the left eye.

"All told," Eaton says, "Raymond killed twenty-three people and wounded eleven more. No suicide note, no manifesto posted on social media. He had a wife and three kids, a ranch home in Arlington Heights, and his own successful dental practice. No one even knew he owned a gun, much less an assault rifle."

I haven't typed a single note since he began speaking. I'll have to go through the recording later, but I'm thinking the memoirs have to start with this story. Eaton's thematic direction is nestled somewhere in these words.

"What did you do next?"

"I just left."

"Did you talk to the police?"

"No. I looked around the lobby. The front-desk clerk was dead; the shooting was just commencing in the ballroom. The screams were unimaginable. But there was nothing to do. No one I could help. I grabbed my suitcase and left through the front door. Hailed a cab. Went back to the airport. Took an early flight home."

"Just like that?"

Rather than answering, Eaton stands and walks slowly over to a small wet bar where he pours himself a glass of water. As he stands there, I appreciate how frail the man looks. It's not just that he's thin. It's the way he holds himself, as if each of his bones is barely connected, and only the right amount of balance keeps them all from tumbling into a heap on the floor. How is it he's just a few years older than me?

As he walks back to the couch, he finally answers.

"That's something you're going to learn about me, Jake. I'm exceptionally private. I've been able to do some great things because I keep my secrets closely guarded. Which, again, is why you'll appreciate what a huge departure this is for me, telling you such things. Putting them in a book. But there is a time in all our lives where our secrets must be told, and that time for me is now." A sip, a slight grimace as if the water is foul. "I wonder when that time will be for you, Jake. I imagine you have some pretty interesting secrets."

"Why do you say that?"

"Simple," Eaton answers. "Because we all do. Raymond Higgins had some secret, one we'll never know." He leans forward and locks in tight on me, so fiercely I want to look away but don't. "We are all capable of doing what Raymond did."

"I don't think that's true."

His head weaves ever so slightly, side to side, as if he's mulling my comment.

Then he says, "But *you* are, aren't you, Jake?"

"*What?*"

Eaton doesn't answer. Instead, he offers a grin, maybe a twisted *I'm just kidding* kind of smile. But I don't think Alexander Eaton is a man prone to jokes.

I'm about to say something, remind him as I did yesterday the subject of these discussions is him, not me. But there's a sudden depth in Eaton's stare that shakes me. I get a distinct sensation, a nudging in my brain. It's happened a few times over the eleven months, ever since I visited Landis.

I usually get this sensation when I'm trying to remember something but can't. This happened just the other day at Starbucks, the same one I go to all the time in Boston. I was making small talk with the barista, Sally, who was wiping down the counter near where I was sitting. I got this same sense I'm getting right now when Sally asked what grade my daughter was in. Just like that, I couldn't remember. I stammered for a few seconds before guessing one grade wrong, and then remembered with perfect clarity a few minutes later. But...*minutes*. It took me minutes to remember something I should have known immediately.

This feeling consumes me, and this time, it's significantly more powerful. What's normally a slight feeling of brain freeze suddenly erupts into the pain of smashing headfirst through a windshield. This time, it doesn't just cause me to shake my head, trying to jog my wiring back into place. This time, it collapses me. Actually collapses me, right to the fucking floor.

All I can think is I'm having a stroke. Blood must be filling my head.

Then, as I feel myself crumbling, something new happens.

I don't lose a memory.

I find one.

TWENTY-TWO

The Book of Clara
10/11/2018

When it first struck three weeks ago, the memory collapsed me, physically in the moment, mentally for days. How could it not? There I was, a child among other children, looking down upon mutilated bodies in a bed as a little boy shrieked and cried.

How had the people died? Who killed them?

The memory was real, but did the event actually happen? Or was it a trick of my fractured mind, a horrid effect of the book and the pills? If real, it goes a good way toward explaining my isolation as an adult. Imagine the impact of such a thing on a group of children!

Where were we, and what became of the others?

As horrible as it was to experience that recollection, something wondrous came from it. I believe having that memory was a breakthrough for me. Whatever the book and the pills are supposed to do, I think it culminated in that moment. Landis told me I had a chance to remember my past and, in doing so, expand my mind in the process. Shape my future.

It was after I had this memory that I knew there was no real clinical trial. No plan to study the human mind. Landis was not a doctor. He was an angel, sent to me to lead me to my final destination. My ultimate responsibility.

How does one reconcile the preciousness of life with a desperate hunger for death? I'm not depressed, in pain, afflicted with a terminal illness, nor, I think, mentally ill. What a waste, you say. To just throw your life away.

But that's the thing. I believe I'm more enlightened than you. I know things you don't, which means you can't comprehend wanting to kill yourself. But that's where you get it all wrong. I don't want to kill myself.

I need to.

It's a final piece to a puzzle I don't yet fully see. Perhaps I'm supposed to be in another world, another life, and I can't get there until I leave this one.

I won't know the answer until I get there.

Back to my twenties, to see if there are more memories left to recover. Once I've remembered back as far as I can, this book will be over, and so will I.

I have a sense of loneliness regarding the third decade of my life. I'd earned a liberal arts degree from Wyland

University in upstate New York, had been fortunate enough to receive a partial academic scholarship. Wyland was a prestigious yet bland school, though it had claimed some notoriety years before I attended due to a handful of students attempting to start a religion on campus.

There were some deaths.

I made some friends in college who quickly fell out of touch once we all scattered throughout the country. I returned to Maine, where I had lived before college, to my adoptive parents and an unknown future. They were happy to have me home, having always struggled with my decision to go away for college.

About my adoptive parents. They will be reading this, I'm guessing, so it's important for my words to truly reflect my feelings toward them.

First and foremost, I do not love them.

They are caring and supportive people who always provided for me. Never raised a hand to me, hardly ever scolded me. I've considered the possibility I do not love them because, perhaps, I am incapable of love for any real person. Certainly I will go to my grave having borne out that hypothesis, for if I've ever experienced the kind of soul-twisting love I've read about countless times in literature, it has only happened during a period of my life that I have forgotten. And, dear god, what a horrible shame that would be.

I do not love my adoptive parents, and that is little fault of theirs. Perhaps if I were to find points of blame,

I would say they were too passive in their approach to parenthood. I was their only child, and our conversations were dull. Tedious. Every day was a routine, and even our brief vacations seemed perfectly scripted from some travel brochure. A cruise to Acapulco was the most exotic of any trip we took, and even in that case, we never strayed from a detailed itinerary meant to shield us from anything out of the ordinary or unplanned.

Shield.

Yes, that's it. There was always a shield, and not just around the family, but specifically around me. There was always a concern I would stray too far from home, learn of the true nature of the world at large, and most likely get destroyed in the process. They always treated me as if I had been the victim of something horrible when I was young—something even beyond the loss of my birth parents—and it was their job to keep me locked away safely for the rest of my life.

I suspect I was a victim of something they know about and I don't remember. I've pressed them on this a number of times, but I was only answered with tight, uncomfortable smiles, pressed hands, and a simple, soft *No, dear.*

Maybe they knew about the bodies in the bed.

Still, I returned to them after college, not because I had to, but because it was a safe option. I knew how to take care of myself, and there were better career opportunities outside southern Maine, but I returned because of the grooves in my mind. I once read every time you do something, it gets literally etched into your brain, making it easier for that behavior to be repeated. The more times you repeat the same action, the deeper the groove, and like a record needle on vinyl, it becomes harder to leave that groove. Hence predictable patterns of behavior. Hence my return home.

I was miserable. They sheltered me as they always had, and I felt more like a pet than a daughter. Everything I needed was given to me, but what I wanted was to have some sense of the world. Some idea I fit somewhere, that there was a hole that could only be plugged by me. Even if that meant struggle, hardship, even danger, I wanted to be *out there*. How ironic that, ultimately, I would end up wanting nothing but being locked alone in my apartment.

I finally told my adoptive parents I was moving to Boston. What an upset, my father in particular. He insisted I stay, telling me there was no way I could make it on my own. That I didn't have what it took to *survive in the wild*.

I didn't understand. I had returned home of my own volition. I could easily have graduated from Wyland and struck out on my own, but after returning to Maine, it was as if they thought I'd made some pact never to leave again.

The day I left for Boston, my father said something to me. Strange, because I just remembered this only moments ago, and it's such a consequential statement.

He told me I would never make it on my own because I had been damaged all along. I never knew what that meant, but that was what he said.

You've always been damaged, Clara. And damaged people, left to their own devices, end up dead.

It seemed such a horrible thing to say at the time.

But looking back, I guess he was right.

TWENTY-THREE
Jake

I OPEN MY EYES. I'm on the floor, and there's an initial buzzing in my brain that quickly fades. The piercing headache doesn't.

Not a stroke. At least I don't think so. More of an entire mind shift.

I look up. Eaton hovers above me, leaning down.

"Jake, are you okay?"

No, I am absolutely not okay.

"I think so," I say instead.

"You grabbed your head and just fell. You blacked out for a few seconds."

"I did?"

"You did."

Eaton assesses me, not reaching down to help. Not offering me water. Just studies me as if I were an insect he'd never seen before.

"I'm not sure what happened," I say. This is partially true. I begin to stand, and Eaton backs out of the way.

As I rise, my balance is uncertain, and I make my way gingerly to the couch, where I sit.

"Can I get some water?" I ask.

"Yes," Eaton says. "Of course."

I massage my temples as he returns with a tall glass and hands it to me. I sip. It's warm.

"What happened to you?" he asks.

Then the memory plays all over again, and this time, rather than collapsing me, it squeezes my stomach. Squeezes with violence.

"I…I need to use the bathroom."

"Of course." He points me to one of the dark hallways past the living room.

I scramble to a guest bathroom, shutting the door and making it to the toilet just in time to unleash a torrent of puke. There's no way Eaton's not hearing this, but I don't care. My head pounds with each retch, and when I think I'm done, I reach up and feel through my hair for a bump. Maybe I knocked my head and have a concussion.

No bump. No blood.

Is this what happens when a repressed memory surfaces for the first time?

I flush. Twice.

Rise. Hold myself steady at the counter.

The soap in the tray is an ornate purple block, unused. As I splash water on my face and stare at my dripping reflection, I notice how pale and sickly I am.

I stare at myself and confront the pressing question:

What is real, and what isn't?

Focus, Jake. Go through what you remembered. Does it make sense?

I close my eyes and see it all again. A memory I've never recalled until now. The imagery and sounds are so clear, it *must* have happened.

In the memory, I'm a child. I can't see myself, but my certainty of age is absolute. A memory from my *childhood*, a time that's been nothing but a dark void my entire life. I should be thrilled with this breakthrough, but I'm not. It's just what I've always told Abby. People who can't remember their pasts probably had something horrible happen to them.

Turns out I was right.

I was in a house, a bedroom. It was nighttime, because the only light was from the moon through the windows and glowing orange numbers several feet away.

12:34.

I couldn't tell at first, but I later saw these numbers were glowing from the face of a clock radio next to a bed.

All of that wasn't so unusual or horrifying. What *was* horrifying were the screams filling the room.

The screams of another child. Hysterical, piercing.

Suddenly, the overhead lights come on, and everything became so much worse.

There was red, and it was everywhere.

On the sheets and walls. Blankets and pillows.

I stood at the foot of the bed and stared at two bodies, mangled in what surely must be death, blood still pumping from fresh wounds. They were adults. A man and a woman, I think, but I couldn't be sure.

And there, on the floor to the side of the bed, unblinking, a small boy, curled into a ball, fleece pajamas. He was the one screaming. There was no blood on him. Nothing seemed to be wrong with him at all aside from the shrieks coming from his mouth.

A hand touched mine, fingers grasping. I thought I was alone, but then realized there were other children in the room. I couldn't really see them; I only had a sense of them. I'm not sure how many we were, but the group of us just stared at these horribly mutilated bodies in the bed and listened to the shrieks of the little boy. I think the little boy was already in the room when we got there. I think… maybe this was the son of the dead people.

I squeezed back at the hand gripping mine.

"It's going to be okay," I said in my memory, staring straight ahead. I just said it reflexively, over and over, a chant. A mantra.

"It's going to be okay."

Nothing was okay.

TWENTY-FOUR

EATON'S BATHROOM IS NOW suffocating me, and I need all the effort I can muster to slow my breathing. I steady myself against the jolt of this memory, eyes still closed, almost afraid to open them back to reality.

I try so hard to remember *what happened next*, but I can't recall a single thing. The movie in my mind ends with a view of the bed, bloodstains inking white sheets, the child screaming. Nothing more.

Is this how repressed memories work? Is there truly no sense of what happened until it comes roaring back and tears through your head?

I splash water on my face, hoping it will help somehow. It doesn't.

There are two possibilities here, and only one of them can be true. One, what I remember is real, and I witnessed a horrific pair of murders when I was young. Perhaps...perhaps I even *participated* in it.

A rapping on the bathroom door.

"Can I help? You've been in there quite a while."

Collect yourself, Jake, because you can't stay in this bathroom forever.

You have to go back out there, and you have to decide what's real and what's not. No one else will do that for you.

Possibility number two: I've officially lost my fucking mind.

An image bursts into my mind. An image I've stared at a thousand times before, one I've struggled to understand. All those little scratches from a single pen that impossibly aggregate into an image. The image of a king, sitting on his throne, his crown adorned with the heads of snakes. The king's eyes are wide with excitement as a whiskered man leans into his ear.

Let's play a game of war.

There is a palpable shift in energy as I open the bathroom door. Sudden heat, a fresh pounding in my head. Sweat tickles my forehead, and when I try to ground myself and slow my breathing, I fail.

Eaton is standing just a few feet away from the bathroom, which feels intrusively close.

"Maybe it was something I ate," I manage.

I walk past him, avoiding direct eye contact. Back into the living room.

"I'll be okay," I say.

"You don't seem so."

I take my place back on the couch and wipe the sweat off my forehead.

Eaton sits, a bit closer to me this time, clearly unafraid I might spread some disease to him. In his weakened state, I would think this would be a concern, but it doesn't seem to be. Instead, he leans in closer, his eyes searching mine.

"What just happened, Jake?"

I take a deep breath. "I don't know. Like I said, maybe it was something I ate."

"No, I don't think so."

"What?"

He shifts closer. I drop my gaze because his stare is becoming uncomfortable. He almost seems to be excited about my current state.

"I don't think it was bad food," he says. "I think it was something else entirely."

"Are you a doctor?"

"No," he says. "But I am a bit of an amateur scientist."

"Look, I'm fine," I say. "We have a lot of work to do. Maybe we should just get on with it."

He doesn't listen to me.

"Look at me," Eaton says.

Having someone you hardly know say *Look at me* is an unsettling experience. But I look at him, and when I do, I see his eyes wide with…what, delight? He's barely suppressing a smile.

"Tell me what you saw."

The throbbing in my head is replaced with the feeling of ice being packed inside my chest cavity. I don't answer immediately, because I'm not fully certain what to say first. My instinct is to say I don't know what he's talking about. But whatever is happening here, I think we're past that point now.

"How do you know I saw something?"

"It's on your face. What was it?"

I'm not the only person good at reading others.

For a moment, I actually consider telling him. *I saw death. Horrible, mangled, gutting death.*

I don't say any of this. I sit here, head bowed. Eaton doesn't fill the silence, nor do I. Seconds pass. Maybe a full minute. It avoids being awkward only because I feel a shift inside me, as if the memory was the start of a metamorphosis.

I can't get the word *death* out of my head. It flashes over and over, pulsing, the letters growing larger, darker. Thicker.

"Jake, tell me what you saw."

Then, an urge both incomprehensible and overwhelming floods me.

Kill him.

Right now.

Kill Eaton.

He's weak, frail. Get on top of him, wrap my hands around his throat. Squeeze his windpipe until he's dead. It would be easy. Over in minutes.

I squeeze my eyes shut against this irrational thought, pushing it away as much as I can. This is crazy. This is crazy.

I am crazy.

I can smell him. Smell his fear, his excitement. Smell the blood coursing through his thin veins, and for a moment, I can taste it. Warm and salty, thick like milk.

Sweat seeps from my forehead. Bile starts creeping back up my throat. My sudden rage is as indecipherable as my recalled memory, as if I've transported into someone else's body and mind. My body craves control, my mind craves direction, and everything suddenly is telling me the only way to attain those things is through violence.

Kill him, Jake.

"I…I have to go." I jump from the couch and stuff everything back into my bag as fast as I can. "I'm sorry. I don't know what's wrong with me."

Eaton stands in an effort to block me.

"Tell me. You can tell me."

I've never been in a fight, never had a tendency toward violence. But this unthinkable urge to tear this man apart is now beyond an irrational desire. It's a primal hunger.

He reaches over, places a hand on my shoulder.

"I can help you, you know."

I'll attack him if I don't leave right now. I can *see it* happening. The blow to his jaw with my right hand, dropping him. My body on top of his, legs straddled firmly over his bony torso. Fists flying, knuckles smashing against cheekbones, over and over, each punch filling me with more rage, finding no satisfaction as long as he continues to breathe. Blood spurting, splattering the floor, my shirt. Finally, his face caves in, a rotten pumpkin, moist and meaty, fresh only in death.

I push his arm out of my way and nearly run to the front door, not bothering to look back or say anything else.

Into the hallway, an interminable wait for the elevator. Down, into the lobby. I pass the security guard, who offers me a quizzical look. He surely sees the sweat on my face, hears my labored breathing.

I pass through the lobby doors and into a cold and rapidly clouding Colorado morning.

I hear her voice in my head. Elle.

Are you having radical thoughts you hadn't had before? I'm talking something significant. Like…thoughts of violence.

Yes. Yes, I am.

TWENTY-FIVE

JAKE LOVED PICKING EM up from school. Wright Elementary was out of district from their home, but the highly rated charter school made the easy six-mile drive more than worthwhile. The trip was only ten or so minutes, but it was alone time with his daughter that Jake cherished. The smile on her face when she spotted his car in the school pickup area, that instant flash of love, was enough to make his day.

Em picked up her pace as she approached Jake's Subaru and, rather than entering the back seat, she opened the front passenger door.

"Can I sit in front today?"

She'd started asking this every time Jake picked her up, which was usually two or three times a week. Abby never let her. Jake usually didn't, though he was guilty of letting Em get her way a few times here and there.

"No, sweetie."

"Please? It's the last day of school. It's special."

She had perfected the art of puppy eyes, which she used with particular flair right now. Jake looked at her as light snow started to fall. It was the Friday before the school's winter break, and Christmas was just a week away.

He was in a good mood; the week leading up to Christmas was one of his favorite weeks of the year. So he caved.

"Okay, only because it's the last day of school. Not because you're cute. Though that helps."

She gave a little squeal, threw her backpack to the floor, and climbed in the front. Jake eyed the rearview, scanning for the scolding glances of other parents in the car line. Em buckled and he drove away, feeling a little guilty about his decision and hoping Abby wouldn't see them when they arrived in the driveway. He wouldn't tell Em to keep it a secret—he'd never ask his daughter to keep anything from his wife. But that didn't mean he wanted Abby to find out.

They talked about school, and Em pulled Jake's iPad from his messenger bag, then launched a game. Jake glanced over as he turned onto a four-lane thoroughfare that ate up four of the six miles on their path home.

"Let's not play a game right now," he said.

"Aww."

"Come on, Em. You have enough screen time as it is."

"Can I take a picture of the snow?"

He noticed it was coming down heavier now, though not sticking.

"Sure."

Em launched the camera on the iPad and held it in front of her face, arms extended, aiming out the front window.

"Pretty," she said. Then, "Music?"

"Music what?" Jake asked.

"Can we listen to music, please?"

Jake sped up to merge with traffic, which seemed heavy for this time of day. Almost as soon as he reached the speed limit, the cars in front of him slowed down, causing Jake to do the same.

A little snow and everyone forgets how to drive, he thought. *Every single year, it's the same thing.*

"Sure," he told her. He quickly looked down at his phone and launched a Spotify playlist that he and Em had built together. It only had about thirty songs at this point—and Jake was sick of nearly all of them—but Em never tired of their little music collection.

Three Dog Night started belting out "Joy to the World" when Jake remembered something.

"Oh," he told her. "There's a new song that I meant to add to the list."

Traffic sped up again, and Jake inched the car just past fifty. Maybe a little fast given the weather, but still within the speed limit. Seconds later, traffic slowed again, forcing Jake to brake, though not too hard. He looked ahead and couldn't see any reason for the slowdown other than the car in front of him being overly cautious. Jake moved to the right lane.

"What song?"

"Have you heard the new Imagine Dragons?"

"I don't think so. What's it called?"

He couldn't remember. "Powerful"? No, that wasn't it.

"I'll find it. It's definitely an Em song."

He'd love to take Em to an Imagine Dragons show. She'd never been to a concert, and that would be an amazing first one. He reminded himself to Google when they were next coming to Boston.

Jake passed the car that had been braking in front of him, seeing an older woman hunched over the wheel, both hands death-gripping the steering wheel. He wasn't technically supposed to be passing her on the right, but others were doing it. She was going at least ten under the limit.

He looked down at his phone in two-second bursts, navigating to the search feature in Spotify. He knew he wasn't setting a good example here, but he was good most of the time about using his phone while driving. He never texted or replied to emails (though he was occasionally guilty of checking them). Navigating music and podcasts were his sins, though he'd mastered how to do those things while barely taking his eyes off the road.

Em kept taking pictures of the snow with the iPad. Jake knew none of them would be much more than a blur, but kids didn't care about those kinds of things.

He looked down and thumbed in the letters *I-M-A*. Sure enough, Imagine Dragons was the first result to return. He clicked on the link to the group as he flicked his gaze back to the road.

The snow wasn't falling any faster, but the flakes were definitely getting larger. Jake hoped for a white Christmas. It had been years since they'd had one, and Em had even added that request in her list to Santa.

Up ahead, the traffic light turned red. Jake took his foot off the gas but didn't yet brake, nor did the car in front of him. There was time.

He glanced down at the list of popular songs suggested for Imagine Dragons. The title "Beautiful" stuck in his head, but that wasn't quite right either.

He scrolled through, looking.

Damn it, he thought. *Where is it? I'll know it when I see it.*

Then.

There.

"Natural." Yes, that's it. It's called "Natural."

"Here it is—"

Em screamed. "Daddy!"

The sound pierced him as he looked up. The car in front of him had braked, and it was close. Too close. Jake knew immediately in each and every one of his bones that there was no way to stop in time before hitting it. The inevitable and horrible was happening, and Em was in the front seat. Jake braked as hard as he could. The tires on the aging Subaru still had tread, but no amount could keep the car's grip on the wet road. Hurtling. Metal facing metal. The glowing red eyes of the brake lights in front of him, looming larger as time slowed.

Em screamed. Not his name. Not any word. Just screamed.

In the final moment before impact, Jake pulled the wheel to the right. They'd been in the right lane, so there was just the shoulder next to him. He didn't have time to see what he was pulling the car toward, but he knew a one-car accident was better than a two-car accident.

The Subaru missed the car in front by inches.

Over the shoulder. Into the scrub. There was no controlling the car. There was no control of anything. Jake was always so good at being in control, and now he helplessly floated in time and space toward whatever life had planned next, which maybe was death.

In the distance, a copse of trees. But they were far away.

The ditch, however, wasn't.

The Subaru flew over the edge of the ditch, which was less than five feet deep. The nose slammed into the other side, bringing the car to a shattering stop.

The sound of airbags, exploding like cannons. Glass shattering somewhere. Sickening crunch of plastic and metal. Jake's airbag delivered a punch like a heavyweight, pummeling his torso and head.

No sound from Em.

Em. Oh my god, Jake thought.

Em.

He wrestled out of his deflating airbag and clawed over to his little girl. Her airbag had deployed as well.

"*Em!*"

She didn't make a sound.

Honking in the distance, behind him, another world.

Then Jake saw the blood on her airbag. He ripped it away from her and found the source.

The iPad. She'd been taking pictures when they hit. The airbag had smashed it against her face, lodging a long slice of broken screen glass above her temple. Blood streamed from her wounds at an impossible rate. Her eyes were closed, and Jake told himself she wasn't dead.

She isn't dead. She can't be dead.

He reached over and desperately clutched her body, holding her against him while thinking he shouldn't be moving her. Her blood spilled onto his face, his neck, his shirt. God, how could he stop the blood?

Jake held his daughter and told her the same thing over and over, the thing he always said when things were rough. But they'd never been as rough as this.

"It's okay. It's gonna be okay. You're okay. Everything going's to be okay."

In the distance, sirens.

TWENTY-SIX
Jake

NIGHTTIME.

I'm back in the hotel bar after having slept most of the day. I haven't day-slept like that since... Well, I can't remember. Probably years ago when I had the flu. Makes me think what happened at Eaton's apartment was some kind of illness, but I don't think so.

There was so much to process that I think my body just overloaded and shut down. Now, as I sit at the bar counter and wolf down a twenty-dollar burger and beer, I allow myself to think about all that's happened, taking it a little bit at a time.

I meet a woman on a plane whom I'm convinced I know, and she tells me she's going to kill herself.

Another mysterious woman approaches me and says there's a group of us—myself and the woman on the plane included—being targeted for some kind of... What did she say? *Experiment.* That Landis is not who he claims to be, and this bogus clinical trial could end in violence. That, in fact, two other participants in Landis's program are already dead.

At a work meeting, my client tells me of his presence at one of the worst mass shootings in history. Immediately after telling me this, I black out and have a sudden memory from my childhood. A repressed memory. One of a brutal set of murders.

Finally, all this culminates in a sudden and inexplicable rage toward my client, one so powerful, I had to force myself from his apartment to keep from hurting him.

I shove the final bit of burger in my mouth and barely chew it before swallowing.

A name pops into my head.

Raymond.

Raymond.

The mysterious woman, Elle, mentioned the names of the two others in Landis's program who died. Kate and Raymond.

Eaton told me this morning about being at the shooting. In the media, the shooter was referred to as Ray Higgins. But Eaton didn't say that.

Eaton called him Raymond.

I don't know how all this relates, but I feel an urge to continue. Continue with my Eaton project, because as bizarre as the man is, the work is necessary. And continue with figuring out what's happening to me, to understand exactly what Landis's intentions are.

I dial Eaton and get his voicemail, telling him I'm okay and apologizing for leaving abruptly. I end the message saying I'll be ready to resume work in the morning.

Then I fish the cocktail napkin from last night out of my messenger bag and dial the number Elle scribbled down.

There's an automated greeting, followed by a beep.

"This is Jake. I'm at the same place we met last night. I want to talk some more."

So I wait.

Elle said we have to find Clara, but I'm not certain how we do that. Just drive to the Maroon Bells and look for a woman wandering around carrying a noose? Besides, I can't just go up there now and forfeit my work with Eaton.

Besides...

Clara is probably dead.

I have no idea if Elle will even hear my voicemail, so I nurse a couple of drinks as I wait. It's a slow stream of business tonight. A young couple at the bar. An exec on a laptop, the serious expression on his face washed in screen glow. An old man sits twenty feet away in an overstuffed lounge chair, a hardcover of a Lee Child book held firmly in his wrinkled hands. A glass of red wine rests on the table next to him, but he rarely reaches for it. Nor does he read much. Rather, he peers up from the pages and scans the room, and once in a while, his gaze simply rests on the window next to him. Maybe his wife has passed away, and they used to come here together, so now he continues the tradition and wonders how much longer he will have to endure a life of loneliness.

It's not that I want to attach such a sad story to this man. For all I really know, he's waiting for his wife to meet him here, and his life is full and complete.

But I don't think so. I think he's a desperate man wondering what's left for him.

We lock eyes for a brief moment, and he offers a polite nod. I do the same, and then he looks away.

"Hey."

I don't know how she did it, but the woman appears so suddenly, it's as if I'd lost time for a moment. But here she is.

She looks to the old man, and I follow suit. The man is giving her the faintest trace of a grin.

"We have to assume there are eyes on us," she says. "Be better if we got out of here."

"And go where?"

"My car. You okay with that?"

I don't answer, and she starts walking away, forcing me to follow if I want answers.

We exit through the bar and out a side door of the hotel. When we reach the parking garage across the street, it hits me I didn't even pay my bar bill. Third level of the garage. Gleaming black Lexus sedan.

"Never rent a boring car," she says, chirping the car unlocked with the key fob. "That's one of my rules for the job."

"What job is that?"

She ignores this. "Also, never wear more than one-inch heels. Just in case you have to do some running."

She eases into the driver's seat, and I just stand on the other side of the car. She rolls down the passenger window and leans toward me.

"Are you going to get in or stand there like a lost child at a county fair?"

"Where are you taking me?"

"Does it matter?"

"It does if it's a place I don't want to go."

"I'm not the one you need to be afraid of, Jake."

"Yeah? How do I know that?"

She lets out an impatient sigh and lowers her head. "We can just sit in the car and talk, if that makes you feel better. I'd rather drive around a bit to make sure no one's nearby, but if you want to sit here, we can."

A vibration in my front pocket. Rather than getting in the car, I reach for my phone. A text from Abby's phone, but the message is from Em.

New haircut!

The image loads, and I see my beautiful eight-year-old daughter staring at me. Her thick, chestnut hair is just a bit shorter than before, and her beaming smile pushes her dimples nearly to her eyes. Her scar is several shades lighter than the surrounding skin, seeming to glow on her face. She's in the kitchen, the kitchen of the house I used to occupy. Behind Em, the framed photo of the three of us in Barbados hangs on the wall. That vacation was only three years ago, but that memory feels like it belongs to someone else entirely.

"Jake, get in the car."

"No," I say. "Not yet."

I call my girl.

"Hi," she answers, a beautiful enthusiasm in that single word.

"I like your hair." My voice sounds too loud in the concrete parking structure.

"I know, me too. It's not that much shorter, but feels good."

I hear a little slurring in the word *shorter*, but I'm still amazed at her progress. Her speech therapy sessions have really helped.

"What are you doing up so late on a school night?"

"I dunno. Mom didn't tell me to go to bed yet. When are you coming home?"

Home feels so distant.

"A couple more days."

I look down at Elle, who gives me a frustrated wrap-it-up motion with her hands.

Em asks me the one question I usually ask of her. "What's the most interesting thing that happened to you today?"

Christ, where to even begin? The naked truth would probably not be a good bet in this instance.

"I saw snow on the mountains," I manage. "I have a good view from the hotel. They're far away, but pretty cool."

"Sounds like a boring day."

"I suppose, Em. It's late. Time for you to get to sleep."

"I will."

"I miss you," I say.

She sighs with a heaviness no kid her age should have to carry. "I miss you too, Daddy. I just want things back the way they were."

I don't tell her there's no going back in life, only forward. Instead, I tell her the one thing I always do whenever she has a worry or fear.

"Everything's going to be okay."

"I hope so. Good night."

"Good night, Em."

I hang up and feel myself smiling, because no matter what happens, my daughter exists.

I look up from my phone.

Elle is staring at me, and for a second, I float out of my body and look down at this scene, almost smiling at how little sense any of it makes.

Almost.

I get in the car. I'm not totally convinced Elle is here solely to help me, but I can't deny I want to know more—*need* to know more—about what she said earlier. About Raymond and Kate, and how I am part of some select group, apparently destined for death.

She starts the car, and we pull out of the garage and onto Fifteenth Street, each of us remaining silent. I catch the scent of her perfume for the first time. I can't pinpoint what the smell is, but it makes me think of the ocean. Elle checks the rearview mirror every few seconds.

"Do you think we're being followed?" I ask.

"Can never be too careful," she says.

"Here, get on the interstate." I point to the sign for I-25 North. She eases the car onto the highway, where traffic is still heavy despite the later hour. A few minutes later, I suggest taking the exit for I-70 West, toward the mountains.

"Why?" she asks.

"I don't really know." Which is the truth, though I feel a pull toward the west, toward the Rockies. Maybe I'm being lured toward Clara.

On I-70, traffic is lighter, and we head west as night descends. I don't know how far we'll drive, but I suppose far enough for me to get some answers.

"My first question," I say. "If you were me, would you trust a stranger swooping into your life and telling you she wanted to help you?"

"Fair point," she says. "My answer is I'd trust that person more than a fake doctor promising me memories."

"That's not really an answer."

Elle looks over. "You really think I'm trying to fuck up your life more than it already is? Because that'd be hard to do."

"Jesus, can you just... I don't know. Give me *something*, Elle. I don't know anything about you, and you're telling me I'm in danger. *Why do you want to help?*"

Her jaw muscle twitches. Teeth clench, and the tightness seems to spread down, tensing her whole body. Finally, her shoulders slump a half inch, and then she leans back into the seat.

"I'm a glorified PI. I'm thirty-seven years old," she says. "I'm strong, independent. I'm good at my job, and that means a lot to me. I take pride in my work. But, shit, who cares? What am I actually doing besides taking orders for lots of money? Tell me, can you picture me going to the movies on a Saturday night with friends, drinking and bitching about life?"

"No," I reply honestly. "I've known you for maybe a collective thirty minutes, and I can't picture that at all. I also would've pegged you to be ten years younger."

A small laugh comes out, the short, barking kind that's usually followed by tears. "I don't go out with friends because I *have* no friends. I travel all the time. I don't get close to anyone. I live what I've convinced myself is some sexy life of intrigue, but it's *shit*, Jake. It's complete shit. You know what my last gig was before Landis came into my life? I had to follow the wife of some tech company guru because he was convinced she was cheating on him."

"Was she?"

"Damn right she was. And there I was, setting up surveillance. Getting pictures. Recording audio. All so I could give it to him."

"Well, maybe you helped them. Got them out of a bad marriage."

"Or maybe he was an abusive husband and she found someone she really loved, but then the husband used my handiwork to leave her without any claim to their assets. Divorced her and didn't have to pay a dime."

I'm tempted to tell her the husband would have found someone else to do the surveillance work if Elle hadn't, but she already knows this.

"Few people ever find great satisfaction in their work," I say. "I mean, I write other people's memoirs. Not even interesting people. How sad is that?"

"Sad," she says. "But not harmful." She exhales, and I get the feeling this is the most she's shared with another person in a long time. "Last year, I adopted a dog just to have some kind of companionship. You know how that went? I had him a month and then had to take him back to the Humane Society because I think the thing was dying from boredom. You ever hear of a dog that actually doesn't care when you get home at night? Like, he just lay there. I thought he was sick, so I took him back to the clinic at the Humane Society, and as soon as this animal was back in dog prison, he perked right up. He just didn't want to be around me."

"All right, I'm sure it wasn't because—"

"So when you ask why I want to help you," she interrupts, "the only answer is I have to do *something* different. You need to understand, Landis hired me to find all of you. You, Clara, Kate, Raymond. Two are now dead, and I didn't expect that. I certainly didn't want that. I can't just sit back and do nothing, because I know the pattern. The pattern ends in violence."

"Okay," I say, trying not to focus all my fear on the word *violence*. "What happened to Kate and Raymond? Who are they?"

She edges up the speed a bit more, as if we have somewhere to go.

"We'll get to them," she says. "But let me start from the beginning."

TWENTY-SEVEN

The Book of Clara
10/11/2018

I've traveled all this way with a singular purpose, yet I don't know how I'm going to kill myself. Seems odd, doesn't it? But while the idea of death is inescapably luring, the thought of *dying* is horrifying. So that would lend itself to something simple and painless. An overdose of prescription pills, perhaps. Clean. Or a gunshot to the head or chest. Grisly, but fast. But I have neither a gun nor pills, so I will have to be more resourceful.

I need to keep reminding myself none of this is romantic. That what I'm doing is, by conventional standards, an awful thing. Someone will have to deal with my body, which may be badly decomposed by the time I'm found. Perhaps even ravaged by wild animals. So I apologize to whomever is the unlucky soul making the ghoulish discovery, and I hope I didn't ruin more than your day. But you are also likely the one to find this journal, and perhaps that discovery will make everything at the very least intriguing.

I'm getting toward the end, which means I'm going back to the beginning. Or, at least, as far back as a beginning exists for me.

In my twenties, my adoptive father told me I was damaged. In my teens, my adoptive parents never dared say anything so directly, but their every action supported his eventual declaration. They handled me with kid gloves, ensuring I was always protected, always shielded from any situation that could be adventurous. The thing of it is, I never rebelled. Not really. Never threw a tantrum. Never snuck out at night. Never yelled back or insisted they were ruining my life. I can't even tell you they were wrong, because I think they knew me better than I knew myself. Back then, I *liked* being protected. I wanted to grow up inside a cocoon. I think I knew I had been damaged, but didn't know the extent of it.

Since recently having the flashback of the two people horribly murdered in that bedroom, I now believe my adoptive parents must have known I'd witnessed such a thing, and also knew my brain was suppressing the memory. So they handled me like ancient, sweaty dynamite: gingerly. They didn't want me to explode. Turns out, three decades later, what I'm actually doing is imploding.

Forgive me if I skip what, for me, were uneventful and

dull teen years, time spent reading escapist fiction and being unrelentingly committed to achieving good grades. I don't remember most of it. Most years are a blur, or even a blank, as if I've suffered so many concussions, I've simply lost time. I have memories of *having* memories, meaning I have a distant sense I used to remember my past, but even that has eased away from my consciousness. All I'm left with from my teen years are snippets, flashes, and general impressions, and all of those tell a story of a very boring and sheltered girl who was less *raised* than *kept*.

But there is one memory that stands out. I was about ten, and this is the clearest remembrance I have of my second decade. It was October in Maine, the trees still on fire with brilliant-colored leaves before shedding them to wind and winter. A beautiful day to be spent outside, unseasonably warm that close to Halloween, yet I was home from school, sick. I have vague memories of being sick often in those years. Strep throat, nagging colds, ear infections.

This time, it was strep, and every time I swallowed, razor blades sliced new grooves inside my tender throat. We had just returned from the doctor with antibiotics. My mother told me to go upstairs and make myself a bath. *Soak your bones*, she told me, making me feel like I was some kind of stew ingredient to be tenderized.

I went to my bathroom and drew a bath, adding in an excessive amount of bubbles, which grew into a city of clouds rising atop the water. I slid in, the cool of the bubbles quickly replaced by the nearly unbearable heat of the water. I loved to make the baths as hot as I could, to test my limits, force myself to bear extremes. Inch by inch, I disappeared beneath the cloud city, thousands of tiny bubbles popping faintly in my ears, my skin flushing with the heat. Finally, I was fully submerged with the exception of my face, which poked through a pocket of foam that tickled and teased my cheeks.

Eyes closed. Deep breaths. I avoided swallowing as much as I could, not wanting to spoil the moment with pain. I imagined the bubbles would soak in and somehow cure me. Not just my throat, but *me*. Because even at that age, or maybe especially at that age, I felt I wasn't right. That I was broken.

I imagined these magical, healing bubbles making me normal. As I did, the water temperature and my body temperature began to converge until everything was the same. I became part of the water, and the water became part of me. Then I had this thought. No, not a thought. An impulse.

Go under, Clara. Everything is safe beneath the surface. In the beneath, you are protected.

Hidden.

Slowly, I lowered myself, the edge of the water creeping up my chin, over my lips, into my nostrils, until finally my entire face was beneath. I didn't even take a deep breath as I went under. I didn't have to. I would be fine.

In the beneath, an ease at first, followed by the familiar pangs for air. I counted. Ten seconds. Twenty. My lungs tightened, legs twitched. Thirty seconds, and my body became seemingly hotter than the water. All I needed was to breach the surface two inches away and I could breathe, but something, somewhere deep in my mind and perhaps my past, told me to stay.

One minute.

I almost came up when the panic began to overwhelm me, that desperate need to breathe, but I pushed a little bit harder. In fact, I pushed all the way through to the other side.

At a hundred and seven seconds, a calm like I've never experienced settled over me. My whole body stopped moving, and I *became* the water, and if the drain had opened, I'm certain I would have been sucked right down. There was no part of me warning I could die in that moment, no automatic reflexes lifting me to the surface.

I stopped counting, because seconds no longer mattered. I would do whatever the water wanted me to do, and if it was my purpose to forever exist beneath the bubbles, so be it.

There was...something.

Now, as I write and recall this, sitting here in this Aspen hotel, I expected to tell the story of feeling an overwhelming, irrational sense of peace under the water. But I didn't remember until this moment the reason I returned to the surface.

There was another memory.

One that my ten-year-old self had in the beneath, and I'm suddenly having again right now. It's as clear as watching a movie, and this is perhaps the most vivid memory I've had since...well, since the poor people stabbed to death in their bed.

As with that one, I am a younger child in this memory. My parents are dead, but I am not yet with my adoptive parents. It is the *in-between time*, the lost time. I've been told I was in an orphanage of sorts, but only for a short while. Math dictates it had to have been over a year, and somehow I eventually became fine with the fact my memory of that entire period has ceased to exist.

I am in a room. A classroom. There are a handful of other children there, but I can't make out their faces. I look up and see a man. The teacher. On his desk, a name painted in sparkled gold on a clunky wooden block. Black outlines.

Mr. Müller.

He walks among us carrying a stack of books, each of them wide, white, thin. Laminate hardcover. He begins handing them out to each student.

Now he is here, standing over me. Peering down.

Here is yours, Clara. But before you read it, take your vitamin.

On my desk, a plastic cup of water and a smaller container with a single, tiny blue pill in it. I don't want to take the vitamin, but I do want my book. So I gulp it down, its aftertaste familiar, as if I've taken many before.

Mr. Müller nods and smiles. *Good girl.* Then he hands me my book, and I see it for the first time.

The Responsibility of Death.

Mr. Müller continues on, and I crack open my copy to

the middle, to a page of overwhelming artwork, a thousand pen scratches forming the image of a little boy and an old man walking through the woods. An owl hoots out from the top right of the page, and the figures hear different interpretations.

The boy hears *Follow the path to your dreams.*

The old man, in a much bleaker vein, hears *Yield your space for others.*

"I think they're all different."

The voice comes from behind. I turn, and the boy leans forward and whispers again.

"What's yours about?"

"I don't know," I say. "I've only just opened it. There's a boy and an old man."

I stare at the boy seated behind me, searching for familiarity, his blue-gray eyes the color of river rock. Sandy hair, tight little nose, Tic-Tac teeth crooked and white. He's younger than me, I think.

"What about yours?" I ask.

His face scrunches, brows narrow. Leans back into his plastic chair and looks down again at his book, which is open, like mine, somewhere in the middle.

"It's weird," he says. "I think it's about a painter." His head tilts in confusion. "But all his paintings seem to be about dead people."

Mr. Müller's voice materializes as if over a loudspeaker, deep and resonant, making me jump.

"You're right, Landis. The books are all different. Each

one is perfect for its owner, and they are yours to keep and study. To absorb. They might not make sense to you now, but someday they will." Mr. Müller strolls back to the front of the classroom. "Someday, each of you will do great things. Memorable things, I'm certain. And these books and your vitamins are an important part of that. So, for now, no talking. Everyone read your book all the way through. Just once, and from the beginning. Appreciate how special this is. The first step along quite a lengthy road."

The memory-within-a-memory ends there, quickly dissolving. No more schoolroom. No more mysterious books. No more familiar vitamins.

The next thing I recall, I was above the bathwater, gasping for air. Panting, panicking, unsteady, and uncertain what I had seen. Uncertain how close to death I had been.

Was any of this real?

My hand shakes as I write this.

I look over at the book next to me, the book I've been carrying for over a year now, and for the first time, I realize it's been part of me for much longer.

Not just me, but others.

There were other kids, and we were all in that class-room. Not many, maybe three or four more. Just as there were in the bedroom the night of the murders. I think this was the same group of children. The same time period.

And the boy. The one with the tight little nose and the book about paintings of dead people.

Mr. Müller called him Landis.

TWENTY-EIGHT
Jake

"I GET PAID A lot of money," Elle says as night whooshes by outside the car. "I earn every penny, because I'm good…no, *great*, at what I do. What I do is find people, then surveil them. You have an ex who's skipped town? Call me. You have a whistle-blower who went off the grid? I'll find him. I've done some dirty work for dirty people, and I take their money with a smile. My services aren't hard to find with a search engine."

"I don't doubt any of those things."

"This quirky guy named Landis gives me a call," she continues. "Says he hears I know how to locate people. I say, sure, yeah. That's what I do. Who do you need me to find? And then he says there's more than one. There are four. That he needs these people found and monitored. So I listen to this, take it in, decide the guy has no idea what he's doing, and I don't want to waste my time with amateurs, so I quote him this crazy fee. Like, *crazy* fee. And you know what he says? He says, 'Money is no object.' Who says that? It's not a real thing, right? Only in movies. So I start laughing, and he just sits there in silence. When I'm done laughing, he calmly asks for my retainer amount and wiring instructions. I tell him, and we hang up. Two hours later, I get a wire notice from the bank. The next day, the money is in my account."

The same method Eaton used to engage my services, I think. A willingness to pay an outrageous fee.

Elle continues. "Like most clients, Landis isn't real forthcoming to me about the *why* of what he's doing. But he's got to give me as much information as he can in order to help with my search, and it quickly becomes clear this isn't some run-of-the-mill search for people who owe him money."

"How so?"

"I'll tell you how so. I'll tell you exactly what he told me, right after he made me sign a confidentiality agreement. I've already broken the agreement by talking to you, so I may as well tell you everything." She stares straight out the window for a moment, seemingly collecting her memories. A few moments pass, then she says, "Landis said he had an old journal that belonged to his father, and this journal documented some kind of psychological experiments being carried out on a group of children. The names of four children—the subjects of whatever experiment it was—were in the book. These are the people he wants found. Landis say the names were written down in the early nineties, and that most of the people now should be in their midthirties. Last names likely changed, as well. Your name was on the list. And Clara's."

"Early nineties," I say. "I was in an orphanage then. I don't remember any of it."

She shakes her head.

"Not an orphanage, Jake. A *school*."

A chill worms through my guts.

"A school?" I ask. "What kind of school?"

Elle shakes her head. "A school consisting mostly of orphans… That's all he said. I figured if the journal belongs to Landis's father, then his father must have somehow been a part of it all. I think Landis himself was even there."

"Did you ask him?"

Elle nods. "Oh, I asked him *lots* of things. Because I'm thinking maybe this guy is actually out of his mind, and that's obviously something I would want to know if I'm getting into business with him. I asked him where the school was. What did it look like? How were the students chosen? Etc., etc." She's getting more animated, speaking with one hand off the wheel at a time. "But here's the thing. He doesn't know anything, Jake. He says he doesn't *remember*. All the information he has is from this journal."

Landis doesn't remember. Just like me.

"So why the hell does he want to find us?" I ask. "I mean, what's the point?"

"The most he said was that the program was incomplete. The *program*. That's what he called whatever experiments were being done on the children. He said if he could find the children from that school, he could continue his father's program. That his father was working on a medical breakthrough that could… How did he say it? *Create exceptional people.* He said even as adults, the program could still work, but it had to be done only with these four specific people."

"Wait," I say. "You said you think he was at the school too. Which would mean Landis would've been a little kid at the time, just like me. You even said he doesn't remember, which is the theme here, right? I don't remember. Clara doesn't remember. Landis doesn't remember. So why isn't Landis going through this program himself? What does he need us for?"

"I have no idea, Jake. Maybe he is." Then she looks over with tightly drawn lips and narrowed eyes. "Or, think about it this way," she says. "What do researchers do when they're developing a new drug? Before they try it out on people?"

It clicks in place. "They test it on animals," I say. "Fuck. That's what you meant when you said he was experimenting on us."

"Right. Maybe all of his promises are rooted in truth," she says. "Maybe the program *can* work. But what if he doesn't know for sure? I sure as hell wouldn't want to take a chance with my own life, and maybe neither would he. Not when he can find some lab rats."

"Have you seen this journal?"

"No."

"What happened to his father?" I ask.

"Dead," she replies. "Not sure how."

"Okay, so Landis hires you to find us. What then?"

"Then it only gets stranger," she says. We are now well past Denver, which glimmers in the distance in my side-view mirror. We're climbing into the mountains with no destination that I'm aware of. "I'm able to locate all of you—which was no easy feat—and then he pays me to keep tabs on you all. Very light surveillance, just making sure I'm aware when you're traveling, that kind of thing. He even pays me to help lure you into his clinic."

The clinic in Boston, I think. A few plants, barely anything on the walls besides the lab name and logo, and no other employee besides Landis.

"How did you help?"

"Those flyers you received every day? That was me."

"Did you understand the…the meaning of the flyers? The picture?"

"I asked Landis. He revealed a little more to me after I'd been successful in locating all of you. He said the program was a mix of different types of stimulus. Visual stimulus…the books. Chemical stimulus…the pills."

"He told me he was a doctor," I say.

"Which I'm sure you were happy to believe. Predisposed to believe, even. But no. He said probably none of you would remember the school or your time there, but you'd all respond to the images on the flyers. That was why it had to be you four specifically. Those images were somehow meaningful to you, even if you couldn't remember them. You each had your own picture book, which was integral to the program. A book that would create a positive response in you."

"You said the pictures were algorithms," I say.

"That's what Landis told me. Each book was apparently tailored to just one individual."

Hearing her fill in these pieces stirs even more angst in me, because I still can't put the whole picture together.

"So you just helped him pretend to be a doctor and sell some bullshit story to us?"

"Yes, Jake, I did. I won't deny it. But you did walk into his clinic. All four of you. Willingly. It was bizarre to watch. And you all agreed to be in the program."

"I didn't…not really." My defensiveness comes off as weak.

"You did. Eventually, you all did. Which brings me to Kate and Raymond."

I want to know about them just as much as I don't want to know. "*Okay.*"

"Kate was the first one I found," Elle says. "Followed by Raymond. Landis approached them first. Or, I should say, got them to approach *him*. And things worked just like Landis expected. They each went to visit him in a makeshift office he put up, and he put them in his 'clinical trial.'" She air-quotes those two words with one hand. "He had me keep loose tabs on them while I worked to find you and Clara."

"And what then?"

"Then, nothing," she says. "At least for a while. I thought the whole thing was pretty ridiculous, but it was a very well-paying kind of ridiculous, so I was happy to keep doing the work. After I located each of you, none of the rest of what I had to do was all that difficult. But then there was an incident about a year after all this started."

"What incident?"

She takes a moment before answering, and when she does, her tone is flat.

"Kate blew her fucking head off."

TWENTY-NINE

"SUICIDE," I SAY. "JUST like Clara." God, how awful. Maybe *The Responsibility of Death* isn't a book teaching self-actualization. Maybe it's an instruction manual.

"Clara's going to kill herself?" Elle asks.

"She told me on the plane to Denver," I answer. "We had a connection. A sense of knowing each other. We tried to figure out where we knew each other from, but couldn't. All we really found we had in common was we were both orphaned at a young age, and neither of us have memories from back then."

I don't like the progression here. Each of the other three people Landis inducted into his program has either died or is planning to. I'm the fourth on the list.

"Did she say where she was headed?"

"The Maroon Bells," I say. "Near Aspen."

"Good, that's a start. That might be enough to find her."

"If she's even alive."

Elle says nothing to this.

"So Kate killed herself because of the program?" I ask. "She didn't have depression or anything?"

"As much a happy soccer mom as you can imagine, up until the moment she sucked on that gun. My money says it was related to the program."

"Did you confront Landis?"

"Of course I did."

"And?"

"He's the one who told me she'd been making good progress, as far as he could tell," Elle says. "He said he'd anticipated behavioral changes with all four of you, but the program was designed to effect positive changes. Increase your emotional intelligence, unlock potential, and restore your long-term memories." She looks over. "Did you have any of that?"

I think about that. "I didn't start taking the pills right away. And once I did, I didn't have any memories of my past."

Except for that horrifying one in Eaton's apartment, I don't add.

"In fact, I even started losing some of my short-term memory," I say. "As for emotional intelligence? That's true."

"How so?"

"I could read the sadness on you even before you told me a single thing," I say. "The moment I met you, I saw it. All that stuff you said about being lonely? I had an immediate sense of it. Before I met Landis, I don't think I would have noticed at all. But I can read people's… I don't know. Energy is probably the best thing to call it. Is it a positive change? Yeah, I think it is. It's caused upheaval, but I also feel more certain about who I am."

"That's pretty vague."

"Maybe. But in terms of unlocking potential, I can give you a concrete example. For the first time in my life, I *know* I'm supposed to a writer. I mean, I've always had a knack for it, and I certainly have improved with years of practice. But ever since I've been part of whatever all this is, I know writing is what I was meant to do. There's even a novel that I've been thinking about for years and have barely written any of it. Just a few months ago, the entire plot came to me. I mean, *entire* plot. All the details. I haven't even written it down yet, but it's clear in my mind every day." I lean back against the leather and think about all the things I've felt since Landis came into my life. A desire to kill myself hasn't been one of them. "I suppose Kate never had that kind of epiphany."

Elle shakes her head, her curls jiggling in the light of the dashboard. "Landis called it 'an unfortunate and unexpected side effect.'"

"Jesus. And what about Raymond?"

I can sense her tense immediately. Can almost hear her gripping the steering wheel tighter.

"What Raymond did was worse," Elle says.

"Worse than killing yourself? How bad?"

She gives a sharp exhale, the kind reserved as a precursor to giving really unpleasant news.

"Water Tower Place mall bad."

The words hit me immediately. "Wait, Raymond *Higgins*? Are you saying Raymond is *Ray Higgins*?"

"I told you it was worse."

"He killed *twenty-three* people. And you're saying he's one of the four of us?"

No, I think. *It can't be.*

"Yes," she says. "That's exactly what I'm saying."

Confusion dizzies me. I knew there was something strange about the name Raymond popping up in different places, but it never consciously occurred to me that Raymond Higgins was one of the four of us.

And Eaton. I think of Eaton.

Eaton arranged my flight to Denver. The flight for which Landis knew my seat assignment.

Eaton, in whose apartment I had a sudden, violent memory of my past.

Eaton, who I suddenly felt unspeakable rage against.

Eaton.

What the fuck?

Elle interrupts my thoughts.

"I didn't go to the police," she says. "I was too freaked out. I mean…shit…I had helped deliver flyers to Raymond's dentist office. I had surveilled him and his family. I didn't see any signs at all. He just…snapped. I'm ashamed to admit it, but I didn't even confront Landis. But it was the moment I knew I had to get out. I knew I had to warn you and Clara." She turns to me, and for a second, her eyes catch just enough ambient light for me to see her fear. "The last thing I did for Landis was help arrange for you and Clara to sit next to each other on the flight. I had her upgraded. Then I followed you both out here. I'm trying to help, Jake. I swear. The thing is, I just don't really know how to do it."

I stare out the windshield as we wind up Interstate 70 and deeper into the mountains. I'm trying to process the things Elle is telling me and reconcile them with my own experiences, but it's pretty damn hard to move on from the idea I could be some kind of time bomb.

"Does the name Alexander Eaton mean anything to you?" I ask.

"No. Should it?"

"He's the reason I'm out here, the memoir guy. Just this morning, he told me he was at the scene of the Water Tower Place shootings."

"Seriously?"

"Yeah. Seems like a hell of a coincidence," I say.

"Or not a coincidence at all. You think he's somehow involved in everything?"

"It's a possibility," I say. "All three of the others on the list seem to have snapped at some point. Something must have gone off in their minds. I'm wondering if that happened to me this morning."

After I say this, Elle signals and takes an exit for some town called Idaho Springs. She pulls into a dark and empty parking lot next to a diner that looks permanently closed. With the car off, she turns her full attention to me.

"What did you do, Jake? What happened this morning?"

"I didn't really *do* anything," I say. "It's more of what I felt. I... After this Eaton guy tells me this story about being at the Water Tower Place shootings, I kind of blacked out." *Well, that's not exactly true, is it?* "Actually, I had a memory."

"What kind of memory?"

"One from the time I can't ever remember. When I was young."

"What was it?" she asks.

For all I've been sharing with Elle, I don't think I'm ready to talk about what I remembered. About the glowing orange numbers, the screaming boy, the bed soaked in blood.

"It was…violent. That's all I'm going to say."

She nods, giving me my space. "And you think this memory was…I don't know…the same trigger experienced by the others?"

"No. Afterward…after the memory hit me, I threw up. Almost as if I was concussed or something. And Eaton was asking me if I was okay. Then suddenly…" I can feel my chest tightening just recalling the anger.

"Suddenly what?" she asks.

"I wanted to kill him," I say. It feels so foreign hearing my voice mutter those words. I turn to Elle. "Really, actually, no bullshit *kill him*. I had this rage come over me that I've never felt in my life. He didn't do anything wrong. I was just struck with an urge…no, *a lust*… to beat him to death."

"Holy shit."

"I had to leave his apartment just to restrain myself. The feeling went away slowly, but it did go away. But for all I know, it's going to come back. And with what you told me about Raymond Higgins, what if it comes back again, and next time, it's directed at many people? Or even my family?" *Or even myself*, I think. Like Clara and Kate. Suicide.

"I don't know," Elle says.

"I don't want to become another Raymond."

There's no turning back. I feel it deep in my bones.

Eight months ago, I finally started taking the pills after vowing not to. All I wanted to do was fix my daughter by fixing myself, and now I fear there's no gluing either of us back together.

THIRTY

Eight months ago

JAKE BUCHANNAN SAT ON the carpeted living room floor
with Em, playing checkers.

"You're turn, hon," he said.

"Oh, okay."

He seemed to startle her out of a mini-fugue, and she immediately moved a piece one position rather than capturing the obvious
piece Jake had left vulnerable to her. A few months ago, Jake had to
put in real effort if he wanted to beat his daughter in checkers. Now…

He slid his piece one space along the board, rather than capturing
two of hers. If she noticed this tiny act of mercy, she didn't indicate it.
Her head was lowered as she stared at the board. A minute passed,
maybe longer.

"It's okay, sweetie, take your time." He wondered if she was lost
back in her fugue.

Then Jake saw the tear fall on the checkers board, landing smack
in the middle of one of his pieces.

Em looked up, her left eye welled with tears, her right eye pulled narrow by the bandage they replaced every day.

"I'm scared, Daddy."

Jake scooted over and held her. "I know. It's going to be okay."

"It's not," she said.

It was the first time he'd heard her say this since the accident a month ago.

"Why do you say that?" he asked.

"Because I don't think right any more. I can't… My brain just doesn't go where it's supposed to when I try."

"We just have to train it again, like the doctor said. Then you'll be good as new, maybe even better."

"No," Em said. Jake heard anger in that one word, not sorrow. Then she took her hand and swept all the checkers pieces off the board and onto the carpet, a gesture of finality. "I won't be better. I'm different, and I don't like it. I looked at pictures from kindergarten, and I didn't even remember being there."

The idea of her not remembering the past was an especially exquisite torture to Jake.

"It'll come back, sweetie. It just takes time." His words sounded hollow, for they were things he'd told himself for years.

"And I hear you and Mom arguing, saying how you're worried about money."

"Oh…oh, Em. I'm sorry. That's not okay for us to—"

"I feel broken." There was such a distance in her gaze, as if she suddenly saw the raw truths behind all the false comforts children are told. "And nobody can fix me."

It was the last sentence that did it. He would think of it often in the upcoming months, certainly once a week. Every time he put a little blue pill in his mouth.

Nobody can fix me.

He heard her voice later that night as he sat alone in that same living room. Em was in bed, hopefully not having the same dreams he often had, the dreams of exploding airbags, crunching metal. The blood. The long shard of glass impaled in his daughter's face.

Jake heard her voice that night as a fourth pour of whiskey numbed his mind to the point he didn't care Abby had gone to bed without him. The routine was becoming too common. The arguments, the fear. The guilt.

I feel broken.

And I broke you, Jake thought. *I fucking broke you because I wanted you to hear a song. And it's not just you. I broke our family.*

Jake knew he was going down a treacherous path of self-destruction, self-pity, and blame. None of it was helpful. In fact, the only thing that seemed to soothe him these days was a children's book, one he read in moments of solitude.

He rose, stumbled over to his study, and pulled the slim volume off the shelf. Abby had never seen it, and Jake had never told her about it. But keeping it on the bookshelf among hundreds of the other books wasn't really hiding it, was it?

Standing there, Jake read it again, flipping the pages, soaking in the illustrations, and as he did, it even seemed to clear the fog of whiskey in his mind (if only a little). The book had a hold on him. He couldn't explain it, and he didn't really want to. He just liked how he felt after reading it. As if he understood things a bit more.

Like the universe was contracting tighter around him, making more sense.

In all the chaos and hurt and struggle, the strange book from the strange doctor was a rare source of comfort. Hope, even.

Now, the voice in his head was no longer his daughter's. He heard Landis.

More than anything, you want to grow. To provide the best for your family.

Yes.

Jake didn't even remember if Landis had said these words, but that was what Jake heard. Landis had promised memories of a past, but moreover, a vision of the future. An ability for Jake to become a better version of himself, a chance to unlock abilities dormant inside him and, by doing so, help him become a better provider.

Help him fix broken things. Like Em.

Still, the only thing Jake had ever done was read that book. Over and over and over again. And goddamn if it didn't make him feel a little exceptional, a little more aware of his place in the world, at least in brief moments.

Without thinking about it, Jake reached his hand over the tops of the books on the same shelf and felt around in the empty space until his fingers found the plastic bottle. The little pills gave a soft rattle as he brought the bottle in front of his face.

Jake unscrewed the cap and took out the piece of paper.

One pill, once a week. Same time. Don't take on an empty stomach.

That was all it said.

Jake tipped the container into his palm, and a few of dozens of tablets poured out, each half the size of a Tic Tac. He tilted his palm back toward the open top until only one pill remained in his hand.

I'm broken. Em's voice was back. *And no one can fix me.*

Maybe not yet, Jake thought. But what if I could fix myself? It's like what they tell you about oxygen masks dropping in an airplane. You have to put on your own mask before helping others.

He took another sip of his whiskey, large enough to finish what was in the glass. He held it in his mouth, which was already numb enough that the alcohol barely tingled, much less burned.

He was out of ideas except one.

Take the pill. Just one time. It's so tiny… How much of an effect could just one have? See what happens.

The book made him feel good. Jake had a sense the pills would too. Maybe even better.

What he had vowed never to do was now what he saw as his only option.

But that was before the accident, Jake thought. *Things change. Life has twists and turns.*

He started to think about it a little more. Think about what if the pills were actually poison. Or if mixing them with alcohol made them deadly.

But Landis was a doctor. Doctors prescribe medication all the time.

Then Jake stopped all these opposing thoughts and forced his mind blank.

Deep breath through the nose.

I just need a little more help, he thought. A leap of faith.

Just this once.

Jake pushed the pill between his lips until it swam into the whiskey in his mouth. With no more thought, he swallowed.

It didn't taste like anything at all.

THIRTY-ONE
Jake

ELLE AND I SOAK in the silence of her car. She doesn't know how to help; I don't know what to say.

Then a thought hits me. "Did you ever see Raymond's book?"

She nods.

"What was it about?" Maybe there was something in Raymond's book that gave clues to the horrible act he committed. If so, that could help me figure out if I'm headed down the same path.

Elle takes her time to gather her thoughts.

"It was pretty messed up," she begins. "It was about a mouse."

"A mouse? That doesn't sound so bad."

"A mouse that lived in a graveyard. It had dug a massive system of underground tunnels that connected each casket and had chewed through each of them. I only read the book once, because it actually made me nauseated. Dizzy, even. I'm telling you, there's something about those drawings."

"Believe me, I know. So what did this mouse do?"

Elle gives her head a single shake. "This goddamn rodent would spend night after night going to any fresh casket and worming itself through the corpses' ears and into their brains."

"Do mice do that?"

"This one did. In their ear, straight into their brains."

"That's disgusting."

"It gets worse. It would reach their brain and then start eating it. *Eating it.*"

"Jesus, why?"

"Because each time the mouse ate a bit of brain, it would live a part of that person's life. As if the person's memories were transferred to it. Somehow that made the mouse smarter. Made it something more than just the nasty little creature it was. I think the mouse just wanted to be human, but it never happened."

I can't imagine why anyone would conceive of these books, much less take the painstaking hours to construct the elaborate, apparently hypnotic illustrations.

"How did the book end?" I ask.

"The mouse ate too much one night. Got himself fat and stuck in one of his own tunnels. He died. Last page was a worm coming along and eating the mouse's brain."

I try to find meaning in this, knowing what Raymond Higgins eventually did.

"Circle of life," I say. "Maybe the book convinced Raymond he could become something greater than he was by taking away from other people."

She turns her head to me. "Or the drugs he took drove him insane and homicidal. Maybe that's not the intention of the program, but what ends up happening anyway. Which is why Landis wants to test it on others before himself."

I'm about to respond, to ask her if she ever talked to any of the others, and if so, if they ever reported any of the feelings I'm having. The good feelings. The sense of place, and of being.

But I don't ask, because our attention is commanded by the sudden swirls of red and blue light flooding our car.

THIRTY-TWO

The Book of Clara
10/12/2018

I'm here.

The Maroon Bells.

Morning. It's cold. A crisp wind swirls, chilling me. A thin dusting of windblown snow stripes the two peaks, making them look like massive bar codes. I had no intention of buying any clothes during this trip, but I realized I needed something warmer than what I'd arrived with, so I found myself in an Aspen boutique. If I was concerned about my bank account, I would never spend seven hundred dollars on a leather jacket. But living expenses are for the living and won't long be a concern of mine.

I'm sitting on a rock, writing next to a lake, the sky menacing above me. I am not alone. A few families walk the trail nearby; a little boy tries to skip a rock and fails.

A man holds his little girl on his shoulders, gloved hands wrapped snugly around her ankles. They pay me no attention, nor should they. Just a woman on a rock in one of the most beautiful locations anywhere. Journaling. Meditating. At peace, likely.

I've decided to drown myself. To be precise, I'm going to slit my wrists and throw myself into this lake.

So, Dear Reader, I suppose this is the end of the Book of Clara. I have remembered all that I can, and looking back through it, I can't say for sure what the sum of my life totaled. More than others, less than most, I suppose. Yet most people's life goal is not death, so in that, I still have one major accomplishment ahead of me.

One more day, I've decided. Tomorrow morning. I will come back here, to this place I've never been but that feels so familiar. Look up at the mountains, those peaks I've seen countless times in photos. The aspen trees on fire with the colors of October. And the lake. The cold water, black under the cloudy skies, a keeper of secrets. The kind of water in which nothing floats, and all sinks.

Goodbye.

THIRTY-THREE
Jake

"THIS ISN'T GOOD," ELLE says.

We're still parked in the empty lot in Idaho Springs. I didn't even see the police cruiser snake in behind us until the flashers lit up the night.

"They're probably just wondering what we're doing here," I say.

"Maybe," Elle says. "Maybe not."

The dashboard clock reads just after ten. If there's a moon out there somewhere, it's swallowed by the mountains. Or eclipsed by the cruiser lights.

Now, a new light. Flashlight beam. A rap on the driver's window. Elle lowers it, and a rush of cold mountain air invades the car.

"Evening." The disembodied voice is somewhere behind the beam, which fixes on Elle's face.

"Hello, Officer." Elle's voice is smooth, calm.

The beam sweeps and lands on my face, blinding. I squint against the glare, and the harshness of it starts to piss me off. I remain silent.

"I need IDs from both of you," he says.

"We were having a bit of an argument," Elle says. "We pulled over so I wouldn't be driving distracted."

"Understood. Need to see your ID, ma'am." His voice is graveled. An older cop, still driving patrol. Is that weird? I don't know. "Sir, you hand your ID to the officer outside your door."

I turn my head and see him right outside my window, a figure silhouetted by pulsing red light, hands on hips. Boogeyman.

I reach into my back pocket and grab my wallet, then thumb for my license. Elle reaches for her purse, and for a split second, I imagine her pulling a gun. Or Mace. I can see it so clearly, this all ending badly in this mountain parking lot deep in the night. But it's just a wallet she grabs.

The cop on Elle's side of the car looks at her license, and I suddenly wonder what name appears on it. Surely not *L*.

He doesn't ask for her registration. Instead, he calls out over the top of the car to his partner. "Whatcha got?"

Three knuckled raps on my window. I lower it. I see the gun on his hip. Handcuffs. No nightstick. He reaches a hand inside.

I give him my license.

He clicks on a flashlight for the first time and studies my ID. Then, in a deep voice, he calls back over to his partner.

"This is him."

This is him.

Elle turns to me and whispers, "What did you do, Jake?"

"Do? I didn't do anything."

Elle's cop leans in, and the first thing I notice is he doesn't have a badge. No badge, no stitched name on his shirt. He's maybe in his fifties, salt-and-pepper beard.

"Stay in the car," he says. "I'll be right back."

He disappears, but not the guy on my side. My guy stays right where he was. It's too dark for me to make him out, to see if he's wearing a real uniform or not.

The chill intensifies. I start to raise my window.

"Keep it lowered."

I turn to Elle and speak as softly as I can.

"They're not police."

"Yeah, I'm getting that vibe," she says.

"So, who are they?"

"Find out soon enough."

Elle's right hand rests on top of the gearshift, and she drums her fingers, left to right. She reaches out and presses the button for the hazard lights. Lights flash. Clicking, like a metronome.

Ticktock, ticktock.

This lasts just shy of forever.

Then.

"Get out of the car."

Not *Step out of the car, please.*

It's the man on my side. He's talking to me.

"Get out of the car. Sir. *Now.*"

Elle looks at me, and in her expression, I can see she's just as confused as I am.

I'm not seeing a lot of choices right now.

I open my door. He backs up. I get out. There's just enough ambient light to make out some distinct features. He's younger than his partner. Shaggy hair. Beard.

Not a cop. I know this as clearly as I know the number of stitches needed to sew up my daughter's face.

Without pause, I take a swing. Just like that, no logic, no hesitation, barely even consideration for the gun on his hip. I took boxing classes years ago, and though much of the training has long since left me, my balance is solid and my knuckles connect with the side of his head, a few precious inches above his jawline. He falters but doesn't collapse, grabbing his face as he stumbles backward under the red hue of the swirling cruiser lights.

This is not the me of a year ago. Then, I would have run through every scenario in my mind before taking such dramatic action, and then still probably wouldn't have.

But, fuck, it's apparently who I am now, and I'm going with it.

I move in for a second strike, knowing I need to get the gun before he pulls it. I lunge, allowing my torso to be exposed while I twist toward the holster. But he doesn't reach for his gun. Instead, he twists toward me, slamming his fist directly into my stomach.

I've had the wind knocked out of me playing sports as a kid, but I've never experienced the sudden and shocking pain of a grown man's fist pounded into my abdomen. The blow upsets my balance, and I fall hard on the lot's cracked asphalt.

Another fist in my side, just under my ribs. More jarring than painful.

He yanks my hands behind my back, then I feel the bite of plastic on my wrists. The unmistakable *zooop* of zip ties cinching into place, cutting into my skin.

I twist my head back to the car. "*Elle!*" My scream is hardly more than a wheeze.

I'm yanked to my feet, as easily as strings lifting a marionette. The older man has joined in, and each has one of my arms, their fingers pythoned around my biceps. The passenger door is still open, and all three of us are facing the inside of the car. The dome light casts a noirish glow on Elle, who watches the scene unfold.

"You can go," the older man tells Elle.

She doesn't move. Frozen. Watching. Deciding.

"*Go*," he says, louder this time.

I lurch forward, managing to break from one of them for a moment, but the younger man holds firm. Seconds later, all four hands secure me even tighter than before.

"*Leave*," the older man barks at her. Then he kicks the car door closed, and any chance of further communication with Elle is gone.

Instead of being shoved into a caged back seat of a police cruiser, they drag me to the back of an unmarked sedan and pop the trunk. I catch one glimpse of Elle's car as I scream some of the worst profanities I can muster at the men cramming me into the tight, black space.

Trunk closed. My breaths are heavy, which I can't afford in the suffocating space. Are there air holes in trunks?

I feel the car rumble awake, and my body pitches hard as the car jolts to the left.

Despite my disorientation, after two turns, I have an idea which direction we're headed.

Back toward Denver.

THIRTY-FOUR

Saturday, October 13

I'M NO LONGER IN the trunk, but still captive.

How long have I been in here?

Eight hours? Ten?

Can't say for sure. They took my phone. My watch, my wallet.

But it seems at least that long. And no one has come in through that door. No offer of water. Food. Not even a bucket to relieve myself in.

Motherfuckers.

Some undeterminable time ago, I pissed in the corner of the room like an animal. Afterward, I pounded on the door. Shouted a few choice words.

But nothing.

Silence.

I've paced the room and counted. Eight feet by ten feet. Bare white walls. Gray linoleum floor. Fluorescents raining harsh light from above, so bright that closing my eyes is barely a relief. Two aluminum chairs, facing each other. Nothing else.

I tried to use the chairs to reach the ceiling, hoping for a way out. Couldn't reach.

One door, no windows.

One vent, pumping unnecessary AC constantly. Has to be sixty degrees in here. I think the shivering is the worst part of all this. The constant shivering.

When they put me in this room and locked the door behind them, I sucked in a deep breath and assured myself someone would come in soon. After all, there are two chairs here. Someone wants to have a conversation.

But no one's coming.

This isn't jail or a federal detention center. This is someone's shoe box, and I'm a memory to be stored and tucked in a closet. A flower petal, pressed between pages, crisping in death.

I check in with my brain, giving myself a memory test.

What's your room number at the Four Seasons?

The answer comes faster than I expect. Maybe five seconds.

201.

A small victory, followed by a strained yawn.

Fatigue pulls at me. They took me late at night, and I would normally have been asleep even before then. Now I sit against a wall, knees up to my chest, wrapped in my own arms, head down. I tried this earlier and fell asleep for a brief moment, but I soon fell over and jolted awake. I was tempted to stay there, fetal position, a ball on the floor. But somehow that's the surest sign of defeat, so I'm back to the wall again.

Good thing I slept most of the day yesterday.

I can't get sucked into a whirlpool of panic. So I repeat a mantra, over and over, believing it with all my soul and despite all evidence to the contrary.

I'm in control.

Everything will be okay.

I'm in control.

Everything will be okay.

I'm—

THIRTY-FIVE

THE DOOR OPENS, AS if they've sensed my final breaking point.

One person enters.

Landis.

Landis and his stupid, fucking fedora.

Tight smile, smug almost. Gray suit, sleek like sharkskin. Jacket buttoned. Black shoes, polished to an obsidian glaze. He's carrying a plastic bottle of water.

He walks in, shuts the door behind him. Someone on the other side locks us in.

Landis says nothing as he hands me the water. This is where I'm supposed to refuse it, not playing the role of the pawn. But no. I need it, so I take the bottle and down the contents in seconds, discarding the empty container to the floor.

Landis unbuttons his jacket, takes a seat in one of the chairs. Looks left to right, as if there's anything else to see in this room, then removes his hat and holds it in his lap.

He says nothing, but I don't fill in the silence.

I stand, not wanting him to be above me. I have no idea if he has a gun inside that jacket. I'm not even sure if I could take him one-on-one. I'm bigger than him and in good shape, but he has the look of someone who can take care of himself. Carries himself loosely, like a boxer. But it doesn't really matter. He wouldn't have walked in here without a plan, were I to suddenly lunge at him.

He clears his throat, says, "Sorry to keep you waiting."

I don't give him the outburst he likely wants. I'm counting that as a victory. The water already starts rumbling in my stomach, churning.

"No problem," I say. "I was appreciating the minimalist decor in here."

He looks to the corner of the room, to where I urinated.

"Looks like you added a splash of color."

I shrug.

"I asked to use the bathroom; no one answered."

"Again, apologies."

He wants me to ask what he wants, and I want to know the answer. But I keep silent. If I'm trying to get control, I have to start with this conversation.

"I suppose you're wondering if we intend to let you out of here."

We.

"Well, Landis, seems you know everything about me. You shouldn't have to suppose at all."

"Have a seat."

"I prefer to stand."

He sits up a hair more, squares his shoulders.

"Jake, the way this works is you do as I say. Now, I know you're a man of intelligence. A man who has studied communication, probably knows how to use body and verbal language to gain power over situations. You might even think you can somehow talk your way out of here. But you're also a man of emotion, of tremendous sensitivity. And, it seems, based on recent actions, a man prone to rash bursts of violence."

"It wasn't rash. I was trying to protect myself from being exactly where I am now."

"Yes, I suppose so. My men tried to take it easy on you. How are your ribs?"

"Just fine. I can handle a little pain."

"You may not fear a little pain, but I do know you fear something happening to your family."

The word *family* stabs me, but only for a second. There's an energy to Landis I can read, maybe because of the program. His threats resonate as hollow. There's a mask on him, a forced edge to his tone, as if he's an actor playing a role he's not fully prepared for. Still, I need to tread carefully here.

"Please, Jake. Have a seat."

I think about what choices I have, and I count only one. I take a seat in the remaining metal chair. Back straight, hands on knees. The fatigue has left me, replaced by adrenaline.

A wave of familiarity from Landis washes over me, just as it did the first time we met. Faint.

I focus on him, saying nothing. Just focusing.

There. As stone-faced as he is, I detect the faintest wave of desperation. Of some kind of longing.

This could be a vulnerability.

"You came to me nearly a year ago," he finally says. "And I gave you a book. You've read it hundreds of times by now. Maybe thousands."

"Yeah," I say. "You told me you were a doctor. What do you really do? How do you have the time and money to fly around the country luring people into your weird psych experiments?"

"I have outside funding for this," he says. "As to what I do? Actually, I sell insurance. I'm on leave," he says.

"Most people go on vacation. Beach, Disney World, you know." I jab an index finger in his direction. "Though I gotta say you don't strike me as the Disney type. Nah, can't picture that at all."

He doesn't get pulled in by anything I say.

"I gave you a book, and I gave you pills," he continues. "You probably thought about throwing the pills away, but you kept them, didn't you? Surely you didn't plan on taking them… What sane person would just ingest some little blue tablets given to them by a stranger? But the book made you start thinking things. Feeling things."

He leans forward a few degrees. His face isn't menacing. If anything, it's full of boyish wonder, as if he's looking down at the first flower he himself ever grew.

"You knew then, right?" he continues. "After feeling what the book was doing to you, you took a pill. Because at that point, you believed in me. Not trusted me, but *believed* in me."

"Let me out of here," I say.

"No. Not yet. I will, but not yet. I just want to chat, Jake. That's all."

"Fuck you."

"You have confidence. You can thank me for that. Thank the program."

"Fuck the program."

"Oh, is that how you feel?" An eyebrow delicately arched. "So you haven't been taking the pills?"

"I have," I admit. "But it wasn't because I believed in you."

"What then?"

I swallow, suddenly craving more water. "It was desperation."

His eyes narrow for a second before widening in understanding. "Your daughter. The car accident."

"Yeah. The accident."

"Interesting. The accident drove you to taking the pills."

"And if I didn't remember so clearly how it was completely my fault, I'd think maybe you caused the accident just to get me where I am."

Landis shakes his head. "No, Jake. I'm not a monster. So you took the pills, kept reading the book, felt the changes. The program is working for you."

"Yeah? And this is part of the program? Throwing me in here for hours? How exactly is that supposed to help me?"

"It might not help at all," he answers. "But I believe shocks to the system may help at your point in the program. But I don't have all the answers. I actually don't know much more than you."

"Look," I say, staring directly into his unblinking eyes. "When you first gave me that bullshit about a clinical study, I bought into it because some things you said rang true. So, yeah, I looked at the book, and it was a head trip. Literally. Started to think maybe you were actually onto something. I had no intention of taking the pills until I hit rock bottom after the accident, and even then, I was probably driven more by whiskey than reason. But your doctor act was convincing enough to get me to take them, I suppose. Did I start to feel more of a change in my emotions? My perception of my *potential*?

Yeah, I suppose I did. But I also started losing my short-term memory. Maybe that's just what happens when you take psychotropic drugs."

"They aren't just psychotropic drugs," he says. "They—"

"But *now*," I say, cutting him off. "Now you've had me abducted. Beaten by your thugs, thrown into a car, and kept here against my will. So when I get out of here—and I *will* get out of here—I'm going to the police and making sure they find and arrest your ass."

"The program *is* working, Jake." He doesn't seem to have heard a word I said. "And it only works because of *who* you are. You're one of only a few. People without pasts. People who always had a twitch in their soul, who knew they weren't quite normal. Always expected they were destined for something more than how they ended up, because once upon a time, you started the program but never finished it. It's been slowly burning inside you for years, and I'm here to stoke those flames."

"What…*the fuck*…are you talking about?"

His eyes grow a smidge wider. "I told you last year I'd come back to ask you a question, so I'm going to do that now. Is that okay with you?"

Of all the things giving me fear in this room, his asking me permission for something is probably the greatest.

My silence is apparently good enough for him.

Landis stands, takes a step toward me, and lowers his hand onto my shoulder. No rings, no watch. His bare hand, bony knuckles. A light squeeze, as if he's consoling me.

He looks down, and it's all I can do to hold his gaze. I don't want to look away, because that feels like some kind of defeat.

"Was it you, Jake?"

What?

He pauses a few seconds, leans down, searching my eyes, as if there's some secret just beneath my surface and he might just be able to catch it in the right light.

"*Was it you?*"

"I don't understand."

His hand squeezes harder. Leans in more, eyes wider. He suddenly seems more familiar than ever.

"Was…it…*you?*"

"Was *what* me?"

I'm waiting for him to ask me the question again, but he doesn't. He's locked in tight, focused intently on my eyes, looking for a tell, a giveaway, some proof I'm lying. But I can't be lying when I don't even understand what he's talking about.

His right hand balls into a fist, then uncurls. Balls, uncurls.

"We went to school together," he says. "Do you remember that?"

"Yes," I lie. "Yes, I remember."

"Do you really?"

"Yes." Take another chance, put the pieces together based on what Elle told me. Might be my only way out of this. "Clara was there too. Raymond. Kate. We were all in school together."

Now his eyes widen further. "Yes. Yes, that's right."

I remember none of this, and he's so desperate to believe me. Landis's edge is softening.

"You don't remember, do you?" I say. "You don't remember any of the school, and that's what you want more than anything, isn't it? I think your father was one sick bastard who had some theories, and now you're taking over his work. I think you believe whatever this fucking program is, it will restore our memories and maybe…I don't know…

maybe mess with our minds enough so we feel enlightened. But you're too chickenshit to take the damn drugs yourself, so you're trying them out on us first. Tell me I'm right, you coward. *Tell me I'm right.*"

His lower lip trembles. Almost imperceptible, but I see it.

"Was…it…you?"

Evade, Jake.

"The program doesn't help us, does it?" I say. "It makes us do horrible things. Is that intentional, or just an *unfortunate side effect?*"

Landis returns to his chair, crosses his legs, considers my question. He never answers. Instead, he asks me something that is terrifying mostly because I don't know the answer.

"Did you kill my parents, Jake?"

PART II

Final page from Clara's copy of The Responsibility of Death

THIRTY-SIX
Clara

Saturday, October 13

IT'S A BEAUTIFUL MORNING. I am minutes from death.

Earlier, I checked out. Hardly said a word to the clerk. Didn't even look at the total on the bill.

My next stop was a nearby supermarket, where I found the aisle with the household goods. Light bulbs. Tape. Screwdrivers. Then, there. Box cutter.

I paid and left.

After that, an Italian café. Expensive, as you would expect in Aspen. It was quiet, and I told the hostess I wanted to have some breakfast.

I wasn't hungry, but it seemed at least ceremonial to treat myself. I ordered an omelet, which ended up just cooling in front of me as I picked around the edges. The waiter was very concerned I didn't enjoy my food, but I assured him the problem wasn't the food. He must have read something on my face, because he asked if I was okay.

I told him that was an impossible question to answer and then ordered champagne. He asked if I meant a mimosa, but I said no. Just champagne.

And there I sipped and considered my life, such as I could remember. The culmination of all I'd become, the hours learning, experiencing, and forgetting. The moments of laughter and pleasure, which were too few. The relationships, the people, even the pets I'd once had. All the living things that had floated around in my world, all for different lengths of time, plunging to various depths within me. Some leaving marks, others not. Everything I experienced that added up to what became Clara Stowe, the thirty-four-year-old woman who sat in an Italian restaurant alone, not even eating her last meal.

I'm back in the car, making the short drive to the Maroon Bells, my final stop. My journal rests on the passenger seat. I had this romantic image of leaving it on the rock where I will slit my wrists, but it has a better chance of being read if I leave it in the car. I don't know why the book being read is important to me. I think I'm ready to be dead, but not yet forgotten.

It's almost Halloween, a holiday I haven't celebrated in years. Halloween, promptly followed by the Day of the Dead.

The mountain trees are a blaze of yellow, with evergreens spotted throughout, unchanging. I open the moon roof. Crisp air swirls around me, sun beats down. I navigate the hairpin turns cautiously, because plunging off the road is not the plan.

Finally, I arrive, and the Maroon Bells don't even look real. They are a Disney photo, airbrushed perfection, streaks of snow and rock against the bluest of skies. I pull into a gravel lot, which is occupied by three other cars.

I get out and survey the scene. The lake is calm, not a hint of a breeze. Small ripples erupt here and there, little creatures coming up from beneath. Or insects landing for a drink.

Though I can barely make him out, on the far side of the lake, a man is fishing.

I had hoped to be alone.

I locate my rock, the one where I'll be standing when I do it. I have it perfectly planned. Slice my right wrist, lengthwise, not across, then quickly switch hands and do the other. Shouldn't take longer than ten seconds, if I do it right. Then all I have to do is fall forward, into the lake, and breathe in the depth of it all.

Then I will be at the next stage. The stage of existence I haven't been able to stop thinking about. I'll have accomplished my greatest achievement.

The responsibility of my death.

Suddenly, two children scurry from the hidden side of the rock, up and over. Siblings, perhaps. Blond and joyous, girls. One of them, the larger of the two, stands on the top, the place where *I'm* supposed to stand. The other scampers, tries to get to the top, but is denied by her sister's stomping feet. Squeals of laughter. Shouts of life.

King of the mountain.

I turn my head and locate the parents standing nearby, hand in hand, facing the Bells. *Look at this*, I imagine them saying. *Look at where we are. Isn't this beautiful?*

Now, I have to wait.

Strange that this fills me with a flush of impatience. *What's the rush, Clara? What do you really think will be on the other side?*

The father turns his head and sees me, offers the slightest nod.

I smile and nod back. He doesn't notice the box cutter in my hand, because I'm palming it out of view. Don't want to alarm him. His children are closer to me than they are to him, after all.

So I walk, taking a nearby path that extends from a trailhead and winds to the south. A half hour should do it, most likely. I'll check back then, see if I have the rock to myself.

It only takes minutes before I'm deep in the trees, and the shade brings on a sharp chill. But the cold feels good, making my senses more acute. Leaves crunch beneath me. Bare branches rustle in a sudden light wind above.

Deeper into these woods.

The smell of soil. The musk of moist, decomposing vegetation.

And then something else. A new scent, so deeply familiar.

Citronella.

My pulse quickens, and I push deeper still, yanking aside branches and stepping over the bodies of trees fallen long ago. I don't know what I'm looking for, or if I'm even looking at all. I'm following this smell, and it's almost as if it exists as a single line of direction, a trail of bread crumbs left for me to follow.

The woods draw tighter around me, closing in.

I'm no longer on the path. No sense of how much time has passed. Maybe ten minutes. Perhaps much longer.

Darker now. Colder.

I stop and listen. Something moves near me, little paws springing along the ground. Not a squirrel. Bigger.

Flashes of my book. Not my journal, but the *other* book. The one sitting along with my journal in the front seat of my rental car. The children's book first given to me a long time ago.

A little boy and his grandfather, taking a walk in the woods, with forest creatures portending death for the old man. At the end of the story, the grandfather speaks for the first time, looking down at his wide-eyed grandson and saying, "I'll never come out of these woods, boy." On the final page, the old man sits stoop-shouldered on top of a tree stump, alone, the background peppered with the eyes of animals. Watching and waiting.

There.

A tree stump.

Not unusual, certainly. But there it is. Just like in the book.

I'm drawn to this stump. Compelled to sit on top of it, its rough surface scraping against my jeans. My feet just touch the ground. I wrap my arms around me as I scan the surrounding trees, waiting for a creature to reveal itself. Maybe this is how it's supposed to be. Maybe I'm not supposed to be in the water, but in these woods. Just as in the book.

I'll never come out of these woods.

More rustling somewhere out of view. I picture a wolf. Though unlikely, it sticks in my mind. An animal with impressive teeth and a hunger to use them.

The box cutter feels reassuring, and I thumb the blade from its casing. A small triangle of perfect steel, the razor polished and smooth. So sharp I might not even feel it as I pierce my skin, slice upward, and ribbon my arteries.

The scent of citronella hits me again, bringing with it a wave of familiarity. A déjà vu that overwhelms, that feeling of *I've been here before*. Right here.

I push it away, just as I pushed Jake away.

Then I place the tip of the razor against my left wrist, deciding.

Until this visceral moment, the idea of suicide has been nothing but a desire, an overwhelming sense of purpose. But here, blade against skin, it's very real and humbling. All my years, over in seconds. An affront to life. A spit in the face of whatever it was that created us. Is this really what I'm supposed to do?

An image. From a movie, I think. Years ago. A girl in a hotel room on LSD. She walks barefoot to the balcony, a dozen stories up. Climbs the railing and stands on the edge, arms out, wearing nothing but a loose T-shirt that ripples in the city breeze. The hum of traffic down below. She is smiling because she is happy. And she is happy because she thinks she can fly, that if she just launches herself off the balcony, she will soar like Peter Pan, swooping over London. She doesn't want to die. She just wants to fly, and the LSD tells her she can. And so she plummets, arms still spread, until her flight of fancy is brought to an end by a concrete sidewalk.

A voice asks me a question from deep within my own mind.

Is that you, Clara?

No. I'm not her.

But you've actually taken mind-altering drugs, containing who-knows-what.

It's different. It's not a drug. It's a substance my body needed. A vital element. Just like the book.

You're delusional.

I've never had such clarity in my life.

My stomach knots as I apply the faintest pressure against my wrist, and seconds later, a single drop of blood snakes down. Maybe this will change my mind, seeing the blood. The reality of it all.

But it doesn't.

I want to do this.

No.

I need to do this.

I don't know why, but that part is losing its importance. I'm not depressed. I don't hate my life, meager and isolated as it is. And this world...I do love it. Life is a gift, a cosmically improbable fortune, and it *should* be cherished.

But death.

Death is a reward. My death is meaningful. In some way, I'm helping the world by dying.

My entire core becomes a rock as I draw the blade a quarter inch along the inside of my wrist. I haven't hit the artery...yet. Blood trickles but doesn't spray.

Tears form, filling my eyes, blurring my vision. They are a mix of happy and sad. Beauty and loss.

A single breath, held in my lungs.

Go, Clara. An inch more, then you'll hit it. Then the other wrist.

Then just lie down. Let the forest take you. Do your duty.

Then, a rustle.

I look over to my right.

There's a creature in the woods after all.

THIRTY-SEVEN

TEN FEET AWAY, A crow stares at me from the ground. Black, glimmering feathers. Graphite eyes.

He jumps in place, and something is clearly wrong. One wing is neatly tucked behind him, and the other juts out at an unnatural angle. Broken.

More hopping. Then a feeble *caw*.

He is old. Old and wounded.

Ready to die, but fighting against it.

I try to ignore him but can't. He hops around more, this time inching toward me. Then a screech. An awful screech.

I stand from the stump, lightly bleeding.

I walk in his direction, wondering what I would do if he let me reach him. Put him out of his misery? What an improbable scene. A murder-suicide with a crow.

The old crow turns and scrambles away from me, but he cannot fly. All he can do is hop, three or four bursts at a time before having to rest. But maybe he's not resting. Maybe he's waiting for me to catch up.

I get closer, my steps small and cautious. Trying to make myself as nonthreatening as I can, because I want to help. But really, what can I do? Fixing broken creatures is not something I do.

The box cutter warms as my hand starts to sweat. I imagine the razor glowing with heat. I *can* help this poor, old bird.

Another caw. Harsh, urgent. Three more hops.

Up a path, a narrow and uneven dirt trail partially obstructed by overgrown trees. If I didn't really focus on it, I could hardly say it was a path at all. But it is. A path not taken in some time.

The crow shuffles under branches and directly along the trail, which itself is no more than a few feet wide. To follow him any more would take effort. And will I really kill this creature? Even if I caught up to him, could I really take him in my hands and slice through his throat, or twist his neck until it cracks?

The idea of his suffering is suddenly unbearable.

I crouch, the only way through the branches. Sharp wooden fingers scratch my neck and back, grasping at me like greedy witches. The crow keeps moving forward, squawking at me, a few feet away but forever out of reach.

This is beyond reason, but of course, beyond reason is by now an old and familiar place.

Closer, until the crow makes a last-gasp effort and hops frantically forward without stopping. Going and going, up the path, calling out as if summoning every creature of the woods to its aid.

I don't want to hurt you, crow. I only want to kill you.

Blood from my small nick drips over my jeans. Drops fall to the ground.

I move faster, trying to keep up, pushing branch after branch out of my way. Some are dead, snapping like brittle bones. Others bend unwillingly. I scramble over a stump teeming with ants.

Finally, after what seems an eternity lost in the bramble, I see it. A small clearing. Fifteen more feet, maybe twenty. The crow stands under a shaft of light that has found its way through the towering trees. The bird turns to me, good wing flapping. Caws at me yet again, raspy enough to sound like a hiss. Jumps in place, up and down, five or six times. Then, like a drunk realizing the night has finally caught up to him, stumbles on its feet before falling onto its side.

I push a branch out of my face and stare at it. So disconcerting, the sight of a bird on its side.

I push past into the clearing, and one final broken branch catches my cheek, tearing at me. Pain sears my skin, and I reach up and feel the blood seeping from the fresh wound. It's not deep; at least I don't think so. I suppose it doesn't really matter anyway.

I reach the crow and sit next to it.

It's alive. Puffed chest heaving in rapid bursts. One eye fixed on me. Maybe it's scared; maybe it's past that point. A drop of my blood falls from my cheek into the dirt next to the bird.

The animal is dying. He doesn't need my help.

As I look down and as he looks up, I consider that we will likely be each other's last creature.

I reach. He doesn't resist as I use one finger to stroke the top of his head. So smooth. Silky and perfect.

And then the bird seizes, a death rattle. Not a sound in its final seconds. The old crow stops moving entirely, now and for all time, and in its death, I see myself, lifeless on the forest floor, another piece of carbon returned to the land, no more or less significant than the thousands of those before and after, just a collection of bones from a transient passenger.

I look up, as if perhaps I can catch a glimpse of the crow's ghost as it slips away. Yet I see something else entirely. Something quite real.

Windowless with rusted-steel siding. A storage facility, or a maintenance shed.

There is a single door, secured with a padlock.

I know this place.

As much as I've ever remembered anything with my unreliable mind, *I know this place.*

My fingers graze the side of the shed, feeling the cool of the metal. Motes of rusted dust flake off, float to the ground. I walk around to the back, seeing nothing remarkable, but sensing something extraordinary. The scent of citronella is so powerful, it threatens to make me gag.

I feel both scared and excited, and for a second, I wonder if I'm dead after all. I look down at my wrist. The wound is small, the bleeding stopped.

No. I'm alive. This is real.

I complete my loop of the shed, passing around the one side I haven't yet seen, and this is where everything changes.

This side of the shed is identical to the other, with one exception. There's lettering painted on it, still visible through the rust.

Industrial lettering, like army stencils.

Two lines, the first reading *Grounds and Maintenance Storage.*

But it's the second line that reaches into my stomach and squeezes. Words that should be meaningless to me, but I know they are anything but. Because now, right now, I remember.

Arete Academy.

My god.

I remember.

THIRTY-EIGHT
Jake

"WHAT?"

Landis holds his gaze tight and fixed.

"Did you kill my family, Jake? My mother and father?"

I don't know how to answer his question.

Because…what if I *did* kill his family?

The one memory I've had, the one that buckled my knees and roiled my stomach back at Eaton's apartment. The memory of the bloody bed, the screaming child.

The child.

Now I understand.

Landis was that child.

Those were *his* parents.

Ripped apart. Blood on the walls. Ceiling.

The screaming. The little boy who'd seen it all.

I was there, but there were others too. Other children, one of whom clasped my hand in fear. We all stared at the bodies together.

"What do you remember?" he asks.

My head spins as I struggle to make sense of this. All I know is the memory is real. Has to be.

I was there during the killing of Landis's parents.

"I was a child," I say.

Landis pushes out of his chair and leans over me.

"Yes," he says. "We were all children."

"You were on the floor. You were screaming. You were so little."

"Where were we?" he asks.

"A bedroom. It was night. Someone turned the light on, and that's when I saw them."

"Where?"

"In the bed. There was…"

"What? What did you see, Jake?"

"There was blood."

He turns and belts a guttural cough, as if just sucker punched. When he turns back to me, he wipes his lips with the back of his hand.

"Were they alive?" His voice is straining, starting to crack.

"I don't think so," I say. I remember blood still oozing. Maybe a moan. "At least I don't think they could have been saved."

"So you did it? You killed them?"

"No, I… There were others in the room. Other children."

"Aside from you and me?"

"Yes. Someone else turned the light on."

"Who else was there? *Tell me.*"

"I don't know. This memory just came back to me. I didn't really see them as much as I sensed them. Vague shapes. Maybe two, three others. They were children, but I'm not sure how I'm certain of that. I just know."

"That's it?"

"Someone grabbed my hand. One of the others. I think…maybe for protection."

"Think, Jake. Think of the other children. Were any of them holding a knife?"

A knife. I try to remember more, but it's starting to wisp away in my mind. I know someone grabbed my left hand, which means the hand in which I'd hold a knife was empty.

"It's not that clear. This memory, the whole thing was a few seconds."

"Did you hear anything?"

"Just you. You were screaming. Maybe you were hurt too. I don't know."

He shakes his head. "I don't have any scars. You must remember something more."

I lean forward in my chair, put my palms on my forehead, my view now only of Landis's shoes.

"Listen to me," I say. I decide to try a different tack. Reason with him instead of threaten. "I'm in town for important work. I *need* this work, and I have a client who's expecting me." Though I know this is all likely bullshit. My doubts about Eaton's real motives have soared since my time with him yesterday. "Just let me do my work. We can meet again and discuss this, but it doesn't have to be this way. You don't need to hold me like this."

"What's happening to you is happening to me," Landis says. "And that's the important thing at the moment. Your memoir can wait."

I look up. "I never mentioned I was working on a memoir."

He immediately averts his gaze and looks to the side, as if there's something to see besides a blank white wall.

I'm now certain Landis and Eaton are working together. Everything is an elaborate hoax, which means the memoir—and my fee—are as real as Landis's medical license.

"I know about the nasty side effects of your programs," I say. "Side effects like suicide. Mass murder. I know all about Raymond Higgins."

"I assumed as much," he says. "Elle wasn't supposed to make contact with you."

"*She's* the only one trying to help me."

"No," Landis says. "Maybe she thinks she's helping, but all she's doing is interfering. Not only is that a breach of contract, but it taints the program."

I lose it. "Enough about the fucking program—*I just want my life back.*" I jump out of my chair and pick it up, holding it over my head. It's cast in light aluminum but still could do some damage.

"Easy, Jake," he says.

"Why?" I'm sweating in this freezing room. "Why am I not allowed to lose my mind? The others did. Maybe my psychotic break starts with you."

"They are not psychotic breaks," he says. "They are break*throughs*, and I think you had one earlier. But these breakthroughs aren't what we anticipated. They weren't supposed to be violent. We've been tweaking the program, trying to get the desired results. I thought for a moment you might be the first one we succeeded with, but it doesn't appear so." He remains seated, seemingly unconcerned about the raised chair. "Jake, if we can get the program to work, then we all benefit. We all get to remember. Which means I can know who killed my parents. Moreover, it means I get to remember who they were. What they were like."

Of everything he just said, one word stands out most. I set down the chair.

"When you say *we*, who else is involved? Is it Eaton?"

His face softens a touch, and in the ensuing silence, his mind is churning. Considering. I think he might tell me. I think he *wants* to tell me.

Then, the sound of the lock opening on the other side of the door.

The door opens.

THIRTY-NINE
Clara

IMAGINE A DÉJÀ VU so real, it swallows you, threatens to pull you into its own reality, yanking you permanently from your current one. It's more than a nagging sense of familiarity. It's a universe created just for you, one of sights, sounds, smells, all of which you know to your core.

Arete Academy.

I have been here.

A breeze ripples through the aspens, bringing a littering of freshly deceased leaves raining around me. Even this is unnaturally familiar.

The smell is powerful, the smell of Jake, of my past, of lost time.

Citronella.

I walk back to the front of the shed, the door secured with a padlock.

My whole body is tingling, as if warming by a fire after rolling in snow.

I scan the area. There. A rock. Might be big enough.

I hold it with two hands and smash at the lock. A chunk of the rock is the first thing to break, but I keep hammering. More bits crumble to the ground, and the repeated impacts send shock waves up my arms.

Then, as I fear the rock with simply disintegrate, the lock breaks.

I let the granite remnants fall to the ground as I stare at the door.

In the distance, the laughter of children. It must be a trick of my mind. But still, there it is.

I open the door.

FORTY
Jake

LANDIS TURNS HIS HEAD to the door. As do I.

It's the younger man with the shaggy hair and beard who threw me in a trunk. He's got a reddish welt just outside his left eye from where I punched him. It looks wonderfully painful. He's holding up a cell phone, and I recognize the case. My phone.

"What is it?" Landis asks, an impatient edge to his voice.

"He's got a voicemail. You're going to want to hear this."

"Fine." Landis turns from me as the man enters the room. He's still in the same outfit as before, black button-down, not a trace of wrinkles, tucked into black slacks. Polished black shoes, though not as gleaming at Landis's. He could be a waiter in a nice restaurant, but the giveaway of his menacing true profession is the utility belt around his waist. Pistol, cuffs. Folded knife.

Landis takes the phone and listens to the message. The younger man glowers at me for a moment, then shifts his focus to his boss. In the brief eye contact, I could read the anger on his face for me getting a punch in. He's pissed because he truly doesn't see me as a threat, which is obvious in his casual stance and averted gaze. He thinks I got lucky, and besides, he ended up winning the fight after all, didn't he?

He underestimates me, which I see as an opportunity. This asshole doesn't understand my newly discovered capacity for violence. My *desire* of it. Landis understands, but he's distracted with my phone.

I might die in here if I don't make a move. Maybe I'm failing at whatever the program is, and they're just going to kill me instead of releasing me back into the wild. Prevent me from becoming another Raymond Higgins.

I have just these few seconds to act. Might be my only window.

I'm just a few feet away. The man's gun sits snugly in its holster on his belt, but the strap that should be securing it in place is unsnapped. Dangling open.

Trust your instincts.

Now.

I lunge and, in a perfect motion, reach for the gun. The man reacts quickly, begins to turn to me, but it doesn't matter. There's nothing he can do, because my timing, my movements, my senses...all perfect. It's like I'm watching another person.

I snatch the gun and bound backward to the edge of the room.

The man is furious, probably more at himself than at me. He starts walking toward me. There's caution in his small steps, but confidence. I can read it all over him. He knows I'm capable of throwing a punch, but doesn't think I'm a killer.

Are you? I wonder. *Are you a killer?*

"Cason," Landis says. "Stay back."

Cason. He doesn't look like a Cason.

Cason doesn't listen to him. He doesn't even tell me to put the gun down. No *Take it easy, buddy.* He just keeps walking toward me, and there's even a hint of a swagger in his walk. I think he's excited he has a reason to come over and properly beat the shit out of me after he takes his gun back.

I take another step back. My heel hits the wall. Nowhere else to go.

I raise the gun, which shakes in my unsteady hand.

I don't know if the safety is on.

I don't know if it's loaded.

"*Cason*," Landis barks.

Cason reaches for the folded knife in his utility belt, and in that second, I see the scar on my daughter's face. Em, who needs me almost as much as I need her.

I fire.

The report is deafening in the small room, but I don't even blink against it.

Cason's head snaps back with an unimaginable jolt, as if his puppet master yanked the string attached to it.

Brilliant red spray. A violent wet burst.

He collapses into a heap on the floor, blood pumping and spurting from his head.

And there, because it's so distinct against the otherwise whiteness of the room, a piece of his skull with a clump of his long hair still attached.

Yes, I tell myself. *You're a killer after all.*

My heart's pumping so hard, I imagine my arteries bursting, bleeding me out from the inside. But as I train the gun on Landis, my hand is remarkably steady.

Landis's voice is calm. Almost remorseful.

"You showed promise, Jake. As far as we know, you were the first one to remember anything at all. But…now this. Everything ends in blood. Again."

I could argue his point. Tell him this is self-defense, and that I'm not turning into Raymond Higgins. But I don't even know what the truth is.

"I'm leaving now," I say.

"And where are you going to go?"

"Give me my phone."

"Jake, I can help you."

"*Give me my fucking phone.*"

His thumb hovers over the screen, and in an instant, I realize he's considering deleting the voicemail. Whatever it says, he's already listened and can delete it.

"Don't," I say. "Put it on the floor. Kick it over to me."

Landis hesitates, then finally does what I say.

"And now what, Jake?"

I reach down and pick up my phone, slide it into my pocket.

"Where's the other one?" I ask.

"The other what?"

"The other rent-a-cop you have. The older guy."

Landis remains silent.

I shout. Not because I have to, but because it feels good. "Is there anyone outside that goddamned door or not?"

All he does is shrug. "I guess you'll be finding out one way or another."

I sidestep toward the door, and as I do, my foot catches the edge of the blood pool, and I nearly lose my balance.

"We can still work together, Jake. I'm not your enemy."

I ignore him. I don't want Landis to convince me of anything. I just want to get the hell out of here.

I reach the door, which is still open.

The last thing Landis says is, "You still have potential, Jake."

Once I'm through the doorway, I turn and lock Landis inside. I half expect him to start pounding on the door, but he's quiet as I scan the space I've just entered.

It's an unremarkable, vacated office space. No furniture, just well-worn industrial carpet, eighties-era wooden cabinets and counters, and rectangular markings on the wall where art once hung. Could be a former medical office, I think.

My messenger bag and wallet are on top of a counter. There's overwhelming reassurance in getting them back.

If there's anyone else here, they're concealing themselves. I don't want to go looking for them.

My best option is to run. Just run until I find a door that gets me out of here. If I see anyone along the way, I'll shoot.

I take off through the office, hurrying down a hallway lined with doors, then enter a vacant reception area. Empty banker boxes and network cables litter the floor.

Tinted windows line the front wall, framing a single glass door. Outside, an empty parking lot. It's too normal. Too easy. I resist the urge to sprint for the door and instead pivot around, sweeping the gun with a two-handed grip at eye level. Years ago, I took a gun class with a friend who was more interested than I was. But I can still hear the instructor's voice as if he were right behind me in this moment. *Don't lock your elbow. Align your sights. Keep light pressure on the trigger.*

It's quiet. No movement. I wait a few more seconds, straining my ears, listening for the faintest creak, or distant, deep breath. Anything.

Nothing.

I sprint to the door. It's unlocked. I push it open and burst outside, where nothing more than a stiff, chilling October breeze greets me.

This is just an empty office building in some suburb. The parking-lot asphalt is old and faded, with snakes of tar covering dozens of cracks. The brick-and-stucco building is starkly ordinary, and judging by the unruly juniper bushes, the area hasn't been maintained in some time. I take a few tentative steps into the daylight, feeling very much as if I'm stepping into a sniper's sight.

The car that brought me here is parked maybe fifty yards down to the right, the only car in the lot. Tinted windows. If there's someone inside, I can't make them out. But they could certainly see me.

I run my ass off in the opposite direction. I realize I'm still holding the gun, so I stop and put it in the messenger bag, sliding the safety on before I do. At least I think it's the safety.

When I get up an embankment and reach a street humming with traffic, I look back. The car is still there, motionless. No one's coming after me. The world seems abruptly normal. Even as the sweat glazes my face and my heartbeat is double what it should be, cars whiz by as if nothing is out of place. As if there's not a dead man in the building behind me.

After I make my way to an intersection, I slide the phone from my pocket and swipe the screen open. It seems not having a pass code was a good thing, because otherwise, my phone would have been useless to them. But it wasn't. Someone left me a message, setting forth a sequence of events that freed me.

Battery at 80 percent. They must have charged it.

I notice the time on my phone.

10:34 a.m. Saturday, October 13.

I was in that room for more than ten hours.

I swipe to my missed calls, the most recent one about thirty minutes ago. The caller ID lists a 970 number assigned to a Conoco gas station. That area code is Colorado, I think.

Who would be calling me from a gas station?

The answer lies in the twenty-seven-second voicemail listed at the top of my received messages. The voicemail that saved my life and ended another.

"Jake, it's Clara. I found it, Jake. Not only did I find it, but I remember. Not everything, but some things. But I know how we know each other, and I don't want to die anymore. You need to come here too. Maybe…maybe you'll remember. It's amazing. I can't tell you how it feels. You have to come here."

She leaves the name of a hotel in Aspen, the Hotel Jerome. Gives me her room number, and says that she'll be waiting.

Clara.

What do you remember?

FORTY-ONE

"HI."

"Hi."

In a single syllable, I hear the distance in my wife's voice.

"Do you want to talk to Em?" Abby asks. "She's upstairs."

"I wanted to talk to you."

A long pause, the kind that would never have been noticeable between us. Now, it's deafening.

I dive into the silence.

"Things aren't okay," I say.

I'm sitting in the corner of a nearly empty Starbucks somewhere in central Denver, out of earshot from the two other customers. A large, black coffee warms my hands. Gray, muted sunlight filters in through the ceiling-high windows, highlighting two perfect infant-size handprints on the glass. I picture a mom sitting here earlier, wriggling child in lap, juggling coffee and phone, as the child leans over, places her little palms on the window, and stares at the outside world.

"I know, Jake. I know things aren't okay."

"I don't just mean with us. I mean with me. I'm in a situation here, and I'm not sure how it's going to end."

Hesitation on her end of the line. "What does that mean?"

"This last year has been…" What's the word I'm looking for? "Inevitable." Yes, that's it. Because it has been, hasn't it? "And it's all culminating here, in Denver."

"I don't know what you're talking about."

I stand, needing to pace.

"There are things you don't know, because I don't even know. My past, my forgotten memories. The time when I was a kid that I don't really remember. I'm getting answers now, but there's a price with that. Maybe a steep one."

"Okay, you're scaring me. Please tell me what's going on."

"I'm not trying to scare you. I just want you to finally know the truth, at least as much as I understand it."

"Okay, what's the truth?"

"The truth is all I want is to be with you and Em."

She's crying now. Stifled sniffles on the other end of the line. The sound of her crying is as unique as her fingerprints. So distinct and heartbreaking every time I hear it.

"Then why are we going through this?" Her voice cracks.

Here is what I've never told her. "Because nearly a year ago, I went to visit a man."

"What man?"

"I think we knew each other a long time ago. From the time I don't remember. He doesn't remember either. But he wants to. Desperately."

"Why haven't you told me this?"

"Because I'm scared." *No, Jake. That's not the entire truth. Tell the truth.* "It's…it's more than being scared. After the accident, I hit bottom. I've never wanted to change the past more than after Em got hurt."

"But you can't, Jake."

"I know I can't. All I can control is where I'm headed, but I felt like I was even losing my grasp on that. I felt like I could no longer take care of my family."

An exasperated sigh. "We don't exist just to have you take care of us. We all take care of each other. That's how it works."

"You're right, I know," I say. "But you might feel differently if you'd been the one driving that day."

Silence. Then, "Okay, I get that. But what does this have to do with this man?"

"He…asked me to participate in a kind of therapy."

"What kind of therapy?"

Oh, just some unlabeled drugs and a hypnotic children's book about death.

"He calls it 'the program.' It turns out to be something I was part of when I was a kid, and he's continuing the research. He thinks it will restore our memories. And…well, there's a deeper element to it. This program is also supposed to make you realize things about yourself. Become more… I don't even know how to say it. *You.* Unlock your potential, he said. I was only following part of it at first, and I did start to change. You noticed the changes. I had more of a sense of people around me. Deeper feelings. More…intuition. And then the accident happened. After Em was hurt, I don't know. I got desperate. I felt like the only way I could take care of her was by becoming a better version of myself. So I started following the rest of the program."

"Which means what?"

I just say it before I change my mind. "It involved taking some drugs. Drugs the man gave me."

"What do you mean? What kind of drugs?"

"I'm not sure." Which is the truth.

"Is he a doctor?"

"That's how he presented himself. As a doctor in a medical office in Boston, running a kind of clinical trial. But I found out later he's not that at all."

"*Jake.*" She's trying to control her voice; I can hear it. "Are you telling me your mood swings, your recent memory issues…*our separation*…are all because you're on drugs?"

"Not *on* drugs," I answer. "I'm not taking meth or anything. These are… Fuck, this is so hard to explain. These are drugs meant to help me, and they're not the reason for our separation." As long as I'm telling her the things I've been holding back, might as well fire off this one. "We're separated because you blame me for what happened to Em, and you don't know how to move past that."

"That's not true. I—"

"It is true, and it's okay. I understand. I can't say I wouldn't feel the same way in your position. All I can do is try to grow, and that's what's happening."

"Tell me how you're growing," she says. "Because I'm really struggling here. I've only seen things fall apart in the last year, so tell me one thing that Jake Buchannan has done to grow. Because, shit, maybe at least something good is coming of this."

I press on with the truth. "My book," I say.

"What book?"

"My novel, the one I've been working on for nearly a decade and still don't know what to do with it."

"What about it?"

"The whole thing. It's written. In my head."

"That's great." Her voice is flat.

"You don't understand," I say. "I have it all outlined in my head. Start to finish. Every chapter. I *see* it. I don't even need to write down notes, I see it so clearly. I've never had anything like that happen before. I was going to start writing it, and then I got the call for the memoir job."

"So, this is another thing you never told me."

"Abby, I—"

"And your novel isn't more important than your family."

"I know it's not. That's not what I'm saying. I want to be with you and Em."

"Then *be* with us, Jake. It's not hard. We've done it for years. Come home."

"I can't. Not yet. Things have happened here."

So, do you tell her about Eaton? That he might be a part of everything, which probably means no more money other than the retainer he already gave you?

She's crying harder now. "What does that mean?"

"The man who runs this program. He's here. In Denver."

Abby's frustration spills over, and I understand every ounce of it. But I don't have all the answers, and those I have will probably only frustrate her more.

"Come home," she says. "We'll get you more counseling. We'll get *us* more counseling."

"I will, soon. But I need to keep moving forward right now. I need to *remember*. I think… I think if I can do that, I'll be okay."

"Tell me where you are. Let me come get you."

"I need to do this on my own."

"Do *what?*" She's shouting through her tears, and I don't blame her. I know this is a selfish call, meant to somehow make me feel better despite how much confusion and pain I cause in the process.

"I'm sorry," I say. "I didn't mean to upset you. I just wanted to tell you I'm sorry for everything. I love you."

"I love you," she answers, but her tone sounds far removed from love.

I end the call, regretting I placed it at all. I've only created more chaos and confusion around me.

She texts.

Come home.

I will, I reply. I promise.

I desperately want that to be true.

I put the phone in my lap and close my eyes for a minute, trying to shut out the hurt. I don't get there, but I manage to clear my head enough to do what I need to do next.

Eaton.

I pick the phone back up and dial him. He answers on the second ring.

"Jake, I was getting concerned about you. I feared that after your… your incident, you might have decided to abandon our project."

"I can see how that would concern you," I say. "With the nonrefundable retainer and all."

"No, that's not the issue. I just want to make sure you're okay."

It's hard to discern what the truth is behind his words, but I can tell the words themselves are empty. "Actually, Eaton, I'm not okay. Not at all."

"I'm sorry to hear that. What happened?"

Time to call his bluff. "You know exactly what's happening."

There's a silence, one long enough to tell me Eaton is carefully considering what to say next. Finally, he says, "I don't know what you're talking about."

"I'm sure you don't."

"Tell me where you are. You don't sound well. Perhaps you shouldn't be alone."

"How do you know I'm alone?" I ask. "Maybe I'm at the police station."

"If you are, I hope they are helping you. You sound rather unsettled."

A swell of the rage I felt earlier at him rises in me. "I took the pills and read the book," I say. "That's on me. I *chose* to do that, because maybe I thought there was something to the program after all. But what happened last night and this morning? That's on all of you, and now there's one less of you."

"Jake, you need to calm—"

"You're part of this," I say. "Deny it all you want, but I'm certain of it. And the program… People have died. You held me captive. Landis even threatened my family. I'm not going to be your guinea pig anymore."

I can hear his shallow breaths over the phone. "Like I said, I don't know what you're talking about."

I squeeze the phone in my hand. "I'm coming for you."

Then I disconnect, fighting the urge to smash the phone into a thousand pieces.

Now what the hell do I do? I consider calling Abby back, telling her to take Em and stay in a hotel for a couple of days. But Abby probably wouldn't do it anyway, and all I'd be doing is freaking her out more.

I play Clara's voicemail a second time, and then a third. I get chills with each listen, as if hearing the last recording of a dead person. Then I dial the Hotel Jerome and ask for her room number. The hotel operator transfers me, but no one answers.

I'm suddenly frantic to talk to her, find out what she remembers, if only to provide me with forward momentum and to keep me from being swallowed by the thought that's been creeping up on me for the last few minutes. The thought that now has its mouth around my feet and inches up along my legs, digesting as it crushes me.

I fucking killed someone.

My hand hits my coffee cup, which was sitting on the armrest of my chair. The cup hits the floor and the plastic lid bursts off, gushing my drink along the slate-gray tiles. I immediately kneel down to…to what? To scoop it all back in my cup? There's nothing to be done, but here I am, on my knees, bowing before a Starbucks river.

Then my chest tightens, like hands squeezing my heart until it has no choice but to burst. Accompanying this is a sudden inability to breathe.

I suck in a breath, and it just stays there. Suck in more. Makes it worse. I can't exhale. I'm vaguely aware I'm grabbing my chest. Panic consumes me.

"You okay?"

Well-worn Vans attached to the feet of a kid wearing a green apron. I look up. I nod. Of course I'm okay.

I'm only dying.

"Don't worry about that. I can get it. Happens all the time."

Finally, the air escapes my lungs, and I let out a desperate moan. My hearts pounds with the relief I'm not going to take my last breath on the floor of a coffee shop. I breathe in slowly. Breathe out.

"Thank you," I wheeze.

"You sure you're okay?"

I lift a hand and wave, as if it's some kind of universal indicator that all is just fine in the world. It seems to work.

"I'll go grab a mop," he says.

I'm still on my knees, collecting myself, steeling my mind against the reality of all that I cannot change, when two more feet appear next to me. They belong to a woman. Flats, not heels, in case she needs to run.

"God, you look like hell."

"Hello, Elle."

FORTY-TWO

ELLE EXTENDS A HAND, and though I can get up on my own, I take it. I take it as a lifeline I desperately need.

She leans over and picks up my phone from the small table next to me.

"Your signal registered a little while ago—I had nothing to go on until then. Figured they turned your phone off or took you somewhere with no reception."

"You were tracking my phone?"

"I installed a hidden app months ago when you left your phone in your office and went to lunch. I figured I was the only one using the app, but they found us last night, didn't they?" She looks around, apparently seeing nothing that alarms her. "I'm shutting this off."

She powers the phone down and hands it back to me.

"They took me to a room—"

"Not here," she says. "Come."

Elle walks out of Starbucks, and I follow her to her car.

"Let's drive a few blocks. Enough to see if anyone's following."

She pulls out and cruises down the nearest boulevard, changes lanes several times, then turns into a strip mall parking lot. "I was naive to think I was the only person working for Landis. I guess I was just reconnaissance, and those guys were security." She parks, scans the lot for anything suspicious, then looks at me. "Are you okay?"

I search her face, asking myself again how much I should trust her.

"You were pretty quick to leave me last night," I say.

"What choice did I have? I wasn't armed. I followed the signal as long as I could, then it dropped." She nods to the back seat. "That's where I slept, waiting to get a ping from your phone. I was about an hour away from going to the police."

"You slept? Lucky you."

"What did they do to you?" Her gaze tracks from my face to my neck. She squints, looks closer. "Is that blood?"

I reach up, feel nothing. Look at my fingers. Slight tinge of pink.

"Oh. Hell. It's…it's not mine. It's—"

We remain parked in the lot while I tell her everything that happened. The ride in the truck, the white room where they abandoned me for hours. Landis asking me if I killed his parents. I detail Clara's voicemail.

Elle absorbs everything with an ease that amazes me. "Okay," she says. "But you still haven't told me whose blood that is."

I tell her about the man I killed, who, for a brief period of time, I came to be aware had a name. Cason.

"Is he dead?" she asks.

"Oh…oh, yes."

"Shit. Where's the gun?"

"In my bag."

"Let me see."

I grab my messenger bag, open it up. She peers in.

"We'll need to figure out what to do with that. And you locked Landis in the room?"

"Yes."

"How far away was that place?"

I point down the road.

"I don't imagine he's still in there. And the body…I don't know. My guess is it'll be cleaned up without leaving any trace of what happened. The logical thing is to go to the police, but if we do that, one of two things will happen. One, you'll tell the whole story, and they won't believe you. Then you'll take them to the room and it will be spotless, and then they really won't believe you."

"Or two," I say. "We go to the room, and there's a body in there with my DNA all over the place. And I have the murder weapon on me. There'll be no way to prove self-defense."

I look out the window. A teenage girl in PINK sweats rushes from the Starbucks gripping a venti something-or-other.

"I just want to go back to who I was," I mumble, knowing that's not exactly true. I want to go back in time, but not back in person.

"Well, you can't, Jake," she says. She makes me think of Abby, telling me I can't change the past. "You can only move forward. Your choices are to go to the police or go find Clara. If you choose the former, you're on your own. But I can help you find Clara."

Find Clara. That would make the most sense, I think. But it's not my instinct. I want to make another stop before going to the mountains. A stop not too far from here.

"We need to see Alexander Eaton," I say.

"Alexander...oh, the memoir guy."

Memoir. The irony of that word truly hits me for the first time.

"Yeah," I say.

"You still think he's involved?"

"He has to be." I think about all the connections as I check them off on my fingers. "He calls me out of the blue and offers me a shit-ton of money to write his memoir. He's the one who booked my flight out here, and somehow, Landis knew my seat assignment. He tells me he was *at the scene* when Raymond Higgins went on his killing spree, the same Higgins who Landis put on the program. And it was in Eaton's apartment where I had my first-ever childhood memory, triggering some fucked-up rage inside me. Yeah, I think he's involved."

She nods. "Hard to argue those points. So we go see him, and then what? How does that help us? How does that help *you*?"

"I don't know yet, but I'll figure it out."

Which is only partially true. When I called Eaton, I heard the vulnerability in his voice. The tinge of fear. I even told him *I'm coming for you*, as if I'm some kind of vigilante.

Maybe I am. Maybe this is the true *me* that's been building my whole life. The program enhanced my emotional awareness, but right now, there's only one emotion that's spreading up through my chest, into my throat, infecting my brain. It's the rage I felt earlier with Eaton.

All I want to do right now is confront him. Stand right in front of him, stare into his eyes, ask him what he knows. He won't want to tell me, I think.

Good.

Then I get to make him.

FORTY-THREE
Clara

IMAGINE A PAIN SO throbbing, so pervasive, consuming your entire being. It won't go away. After a while, perhaps you become numb to it, grow the smallest bit accustomed to the misery. But not really. And then someone gives you a shot of morphine, and like that, it's gone. You don't just feel a return to normal. You feel superhuman.

Now imagine that instead of pain, what you feel is a compulsion to kill yourself. And the morphine is a sudden memory. A real memory. And just by remembering, that compulsion you've felt for a long time is wiped away in an instant.

You don't want to die anymore. You want to live. *Really* live. Perhaps for the first time. I don't feel just superhuman. I feel like a god.

I'm sitting on my bed at the Hotel Jerome, and it's early in the afternoon on a day when I never expected to live past morning. I'm in a different room, of course, because when I checked out this morning, I couldn't imagine I'd be returning. The front-desk clerk was surprised to see me return.

"Change of plans," I told him, smiling. It felt so different, so odd. I was *smiling*. I went up to the room, giddy. Opened the shades, let the sky fall all over me. What a day. What a beautiful, eternal day.

Then I flipped through my journal, toward the back, the place where I stuck the one thing that now was more important than anything. Jake's business card. *Jake. You made me take your card. You knew it would matter somehow, didn't you?*

The call went to voicemail, and I'm sure my message was borderline incoherent. But the point was simple.

I remember. Come to me. I want you to remember too.

Because if I can feel like this, maybe he can as well. I hope so. I want this for him. I want this feeling for everyone in the world.

It all happened the moment I opened the door of that maintenance shed. I'm clutching my new memories, though now bits are fuzzy. It doesn't matter. I'm going to live. I *want* to live. A gift I didn't even know was a gift.

I'm ashamed I ever wanted otherwise.

The inside of the shed was dark, the only light coming from the door as I slowly opened it. Fear rippled through me at first, as if a collection of dry, dusty bones was bound to spill around my feet. But it was an ordinary shed. Tools on walls, an old snow-removal machine. Tarps and hammers, everything layered in a dirty film of time and neglect. The smell of citronella, overpowering. I thought that must be my imagination, but there it was. An entire metal shelf of bottles filled with citronella oil, and next to them a dozen or so tiki torches, the kind you'd see at a luau. So out of place in the mountains, but there they were.

Seeing the tiki torches brought everything back.

A little boy, his face streaked with the red glow of a late-summer sun. Eyes vibrant and wide, a touch of mischief.

He's so clear. His name was Jacob.

And me, just a little girl, no more than seven. I remember Jacob was a year older than me, and every day, we had chores at the school, and for this particular chore, Jacob and I were always paired together. The headmaster called us the mosquito patrol, for it was our job to refill the citronella torches each evening at dusk.

In the summer, we ate our dinners outside. Picnic tables just outside the small school building, surrounded by mountains. A circle of torches surrounding the tables.

We weren't allowed to light them. Usually that was a job for a grown-up. And, when lit, how the torches would glow, flames dancing, black smoke rising, the acrid fumes keeping the biting bugs away.

Jacob and I sometimes spilled the oil, and it was a smell that seemed impossible to wash off our skin.

It's…

It's fading.

I didn't stay at the school; I had to come back and contact Jake. Navigating to my car was a bit difficult—I was deep in the woods and got turned around more than once. But finally, I made it, making note of the way so we can return together. I've been back at the hotel for a few hours, and ever since, I keep trying to picture myself back at the shed. Try to pull myself back to the things I remembered, but some of it is already beginning to wash away.

There were only a few students. The school was our home. Two teachers, maybe three.

Müller.

Yes, that's right. Headmaster and Headmistress Müller.

They are a vague notion to me. I can hear his voice but not picture his face.

This book is yours, Clara. Make sure you take your vitamin before you read it.

The vitamins. They made me start feeling strange. And the pool. The swimming pool where we had to hold our breath underwater. Hold until we very nearly blacked out.

It was all for our potential.

And then I see them again. The Müllers. That's who they were.

The bodies in the bed.

Was it—

There's a knock on my hotel door.

Jake.

FORTY-FOUR

THE SECOND I OPEN the door, I curse myself for not checking the peephole. Such a basic reflex, but in my excitement, I just assumed this was Jake at my door.

The man standing in front of me doesn't appear to be hotel staff. No uniform. Maybe management? But…I don't think so.

He's tall. Rail-thin. Older than me, but hard to tell by how much. Graying hair, sunken cheeks, stubble like a fungus. Nicely dressed, but not in a thoughtful way. He's holding a slim leather briefcase in his right hand.

I sense an immediate malevolent energy to him. Not on a high level, but subtle, nearly undetectable. Like radiation that settles in your bones, biding its time to eat you from the inside out.

"Miss Stowe?" he says. His voice is higher pitched than his looks would suggest.

My grip on the door handle is firm.

"Yes."

"My name is Eaton. I'm sorry to bother you, but I have some pressing business to discuss with you."

"I don't think so," I say. "You must have the wrong person."
Though he just said my name.

"I promise you I don't."

I take a deep breath. The last time I had an interaction with an
odd man, he gave me a book about death and a vial of unlabeled pills.

"I just want to be left alone."

"I want to give you what you want, Clara. I just need to ask you
some questions first."

"Are you the police?"

"No."

"Then who are you?"

"I'll explain everything in short order."

And there it is. That vague and untouchable sense of familiarity.
I think I've met this man before, which, unlike with Jake, instills fear
rather than intrigue. I have a sudden feeling there's something very
dangerous in that briefcase of his. Perhaps a knife, long and serrated.
Or hypodermic needles, filled with an array of poisons.

"I just want to be left alone."

He stiffens his posture and seems to grow six inches in the
process. A monster animating.

"I'm afraid I must insist."

With that, a rush. But not him. Someone else, suddenly in front
of me, then behind, spilled into my room like midnight fog. I turn
and look.

Landis.

He's holding a gun.

I should have checked the peephole.

FORTY-FIVE
Jake

MY PLAN WAS TO confront Eaton in his apartment, shove him against the wall, threaten to snap each and every one of his brittle bones until he tells me how he's involved and exactly what, the *fuck*, is happening to me. Then maybe still break his bones.

Elle quickly pointed out how bad a strategy that was. Not just criminal, but absurd. If he's truly part of everything, she argued, surely he'd protect himself, especially after being told *I'm coming for you.*

We compromised. We agreed to go to his apartment, ring him from the lobby, and if he isn't home, we'll try to break in and see if we can find anything. If he is home, we'll see how receptive he is to a visit.

I promised Elle I wouldn't attack him unless threatened myself. But I was sure as hell taking the gun we have with me.

As we enter Alexander Eaton's apartment-building lobby, I admit to myself I don't have any real proof he's part of everything. Maybe he really was surprised by my accusations during the phone call. Perhaps he's indeed just a lonely man with a lot of money and a need for a memoir.

But I don't think so.

Sometimes you just have to go with your instincts, though at the moment, mine might be dangerously uncalibrated.

The security guard is here. He recognizes me, nods. Reaches for the phone.

"Here to see Mr. Eaton?" he asks.

"I, uh…yes. We are."

"Your name again?"

"Jake Buchannan."

The man dials.

"He's not answering."

"He just called us five minutes ago," Elle says. "He's expecting us."

I look at her, wondering what she's doing, then realize she's trying to get us access without Eaton being home.

"You're welcome to take a seat, and I can try again in a couple of minutes."

I look to Elle. She nods.

We wait on a stiff, backless couch. A few minutes pass, and I'm aware I'm sliding my wedding ring up and down my finger again.

"Can you try again?" I ask.

He tries. No answer. "Like I said, I don't think he's home."

"Can we just go up and knock?" Elle asks. "I'm sure he's there."

I look over at her, unsure what she's thinking.

"Well, that's the point of phoning, isn't it?" the guard says.

"Maybe his phone is off."

"I thought you just talked to him."

"Look, I'm certain he's home."

"I'm not supposed—"

If not for the sudden presence of a FedEx worker hauling a dolly's worth of boxes into the lobby, I could have pictured an ineffectual back-and-forth for another minute until we were asked to leave. But the guard looked over at the FedEx guy, and there was a look of mild disdain on his face, as if the two men were professional enemies who engaged in some extremely low-stakes battle every day.

The guard waved us off. "Fine, you can try."

"Thank you," I say, moving quickly to the elevator before he can change his mind. Elle is right behind me.

We stop on Eaton's floor, then walk at a slower pace as we approach his unit.

"This is it," I say.

I stand there, thinking, but taking no action.

"Are you going to ring the bell, or do we just stand here?"

We're whispering. It all seems so ridiculous. What am I going to say if he answers?

I ring the bell. My stomach knots. I have my messenger bag with me, gun inside. I'm wondering if I should take it out.

Wait thirty seconds. A minute. No answer.

"Okay, I think we're good," Elle says. She digs into her purse and pulls out a small tool.

"Did you notice a security system when you were in his apartment last time?"

"No. I mean, I don't think so. You think you can get us in?"

"Fifty-fifty chance. If not, we leave. Or we might get in and an alarm goes off. Then we leave."

I scan the hallway, looking for cameras. I see none, so I take a step back from the door.

"Okay, let's do it."

She steps up to the door, huddles over the knob. I don't even watch. Instead, I turn my back and keep scanning the hallway, left to right. Right to left. The first minute feels like an hour. The second minute a full day. I'm waiting for a neighbor to come out, ask us what we're doing.

"It's an older lock," Elle says, her voice barely audible. "Which is good. But it's not cooperating."

"Maybe we should just go."

The ding of the elevator, the soft *whoosh* of the doors opening. I turn back to Elle, because facing away from her appears too suspicious. But I chance a half tilt of my head down the corridor.

The security guard. He must be second-guessing his decision to let us up. He walks toward us, not fast, but with purpose.

"We gotta go," I whisper.

"Hang on."

He's getting closer, and my pulse races as I wonder what he's going to do when he reaches us. He's not a cop. Doesn't have a weapon. I can't imagine how he could detain us. But I think about the man I killed. The body in that small, white room. My DNA swimming in the piss in the corner, my fingerprints on the doorknobs. Not to mention that the murder weapon is on me, in my bag. I don't want any possibility of being questioned by the police.

"Elle, come *on.*" I give a light tug on her arm, which she shrugs off.

I'm just about to turn to the guard, tell him he was right and that Eaton's not answering, when the door flies open.

Elle looks up into the apartment and says in a loud voice, "Alex, we were worried about you." She then lifts her arms as if to hug the imaginary man and steps inside. I turn to the guard, who is now less than twenty feet away but too far to actually see into the apartment. I do the first thing that comes to mind, which is to lamely give him a thumbs-up.

He narrows his brows but says nothing. I step inside the apartment and shut the door behind me.

"I don't hear an alarm timer," she says, scanning the walls. "No keypad. I think we're okay, unless he has a silent system. Guess we'll find out if the police come kick the door in." Elle steps in and swivels around. "So, now what?"

"I don't know. But let's be fast." I twist and turn, looking at everything and nothing at the same time.

She walks into the living room. "It's like a morgue in here."

The apartment is characteristically dark, though the idea of turning on a light makes me nervous. But not Elle. She immediately snaps on the overhead can lights, which hit me like prison-yard spotlights.

"What are we looking for?"

"I don't know." My instinct is to check his bedroom. Isn't that where secrets are kept?

"Ten minutes," she says. "Then we leave. Let's split up and search."

"Should we be worried about fingerprints?"

"Yes, we should be. Be aware of what you touch, and we can wipe down when we leave."

"I'll look in the bedroom."

"Fine," she says, then heads down a short hallway and disappears into the first room on the right.

I continue down the corridor. Three more doors, all closed. I check the first one. Small bathroom. Second door. Linen closet, almost completely devoid of any linen. I reach the last door. I assume this is a bedroom. Who lives alone and closes the bedroom door when they're away?

The thought of opening the door fills me with the memory I had when I was last in this apartment.

The bedroom.

Orange, glowing numbers from the bedside clock.

12:34.

Blood. So much blood. On the sheets and walls.

The bodies, mangled and ribboned.

A little boy curled on the floor, crying in horror.

I put my hand on the knob. The brass feels warm to me, warmer than it should be, as if recently gripped by a hand.

Or maybe it's all in my mind.

I begin turning the knob as slowly as I can, exhaling along with the motion.

Just as I'm about to open the door, Elle calls to me from down the hallway.

"Jake."

I turn. She's poking her head out of the office doorway.

"Come see this."

I feel a tinge of relief that I don't have to open the bedroom door, at least not yet. I release the handle and head back down the hallway, then into the office. As in the rest of the apartment, the shades are drawn. Here, the only light comes from a brass desk lamp, heavy and ornate, the kind I'd expect to see in an old public library.

There's a large wooden desk, maybe teak, the top of it covered with the wounds of carelessness and time. Pushed a few feet back from the desk, a chair. Simple and black, modern. Aside from the desk, chair, and lamp, there's no other furniture in the room.

The walls are bare. Not even nail holes where pictures once hung.

No computer, no cables.

A stack of papers in a manila folder on top of the desk.

"What'd you find?" I ask.

"Look at the top sheet."

A photocopy of a drawing. I know the artist. Ink scratches, thousands of them. Taken all together, impossibly, they form the image of an exotic bird in a tree.

This has to be a page from *The Responsibility of Death*. But not from my version.

I shuffle through the pages, seeing more copies. I don't take the time to read any of them, but I do find a photocopied sheet from my version. Page twenty-six. The boy is now an adult but not yet king, and one of his friends whispers in the man's ear. *A simple rock makes a formidable weapon.*

I try the top drawer, the thin, wide one directly beneath the desk's surface. It slides open easily.

Another folder.

More photocopies, several pages. These aren't from the varied editions of the bizarre children's book. These are handwritten notes. A journal. Tight, mesmerizing script, sharp and piercing. Too much to absorb at once, but I scan a few sentences from one of the pages.

DECREASING THE DOSAGE FOR CLARA, GIVEN HER WEIGHT.
ONSET OF FATIGUE NOTED IN RAYMOND. POSSIBLY RELATED
TO ALTITUDE.

JACOB HAS A STUNNING IMAGINATION. I SUSPECT HE HAS A FUTURE IN THE ARTS.

There are a couple of formulas toward the bottom of the page, along with a vector drawing. There are also two small sketches, one of which is a simple mountain range. The other drawing is strange and chilling: a disembodied face, appearing to be just above the surface of water.

"What is it?" Elle asks.

"Notes. Lots of notes. A few sketches."

"Notes from what?"

I thumb through a few sheets, all of which are in the same script.

"I'm not sure," I say. "Journal entries, looks like." There are dates at the top of each page. "From 1991."

I keep flipping through, sheet after sheet.

The final two copies in the stack are in entirely different handwriting. Feminine, flowing.

It's a letter, dated just two years ago.

It starts:

Dear Landis.

That's all I read before I hear a sound somewhere in the apartment. Someone is here.

FORTY-SIX

THE FAINTEST CREAK, BETRAYAL of a hinge.

I can't tell if it's the front door or maybe the bedroom door I just left. Elle's wide eyes tell me she's heard it too.

She points, jabbing fingers. It takes me a moment to figure out what she's telling me. *Hide.*

Three steps later, I'm there, pressed up behind a hollow-core door that won't conceal me for long if someone takes more than a casual look in the office. I reach into my bag and take out the gun. I assume it's loaded, though I know one bullet is missing.

There's a thumping in my ears, and it takes me a second to realize it's my heartbeat. Adrenaline brings tingles to my fingertips and shortens my breath. I squeeze the handle on the gun, feeling its heft.

Another creak. Someone's weight on the floorboards. Picturing Eaton's skeletal frame, I'm surprised the floor would give even the slightest beneath his weight.

There's no chance we're not getting discovered, so I suddenly wonder why I'm bothering to hide. I came here seeking answers, and I'm going to get them.

I step out from behind the door, and the first thing I see is Elle. She's flat against the wall adjacent to the open door. She's taken the desk lamp, unplugged it, and holds it high above her head, ready to use it as a club.

She looks at me and mouths, *What are you doing?*

I stand a few feet inside the office, directly facing the open door, and wait. Arms by my side, ready to face Eaton. The gun is in my right hand, pointed at the floor. No reason to raise it now—I'm sure I look threatening enough.

A leg is the first thing to appear in view. It's coming from the direction of the living room, which means it was the front door I heard, not the bedroom door.

Eaton must have returned from wherever he was.

The figure appears in the doorway, turns to me.

It's not Eaton.

It's Cason's partner. The other, older fake cop who threw me in the trunk of a car.

There's a gun in his right hand, which he brings up to eye level and aims at me.

"Drop it," he commands.

My stomach drops, as if I've swum too far out to sea and just realized the riptide is washing me away.

Logically, I know I should drop my weapon. But all logic evaporates in the moment. In this instant, I see what I did in the white room. A man who is a threat, coming for me. He underestimates me; I'm certain of it. Doesn't think I'm capable.

I start to raise my gun when he shoots me.

FORTY-SEVEN
Clara

THEY'VE TAKEN ME TO a different room, two floors above mine. We took the stairs, at one point passing a housekeeper, who greeted us warmly in accented English. I wonder if she read anything on my face, saw a look of concern.

I'm in a large hotel suite, seated at a living-room table, flanked by each of them. When we arrived, Eaton put his briefcase on a nearby sofa, and I've yet to see the contents. There is the faint wave of familiarity about both men.

I'm surrounded by my past and unclear of my future.

"Can I get you anything?" Eaton asks. "Tea? Coffee?"

"Coffee." I almost add *thank you*.

"Of course." He walks away to a bar area, and Landis sits quietly next to me. These few seconds of silence reveal the hierarchy between the two men. Eaton, whoever he is, is very much in charge.

He returns a moment later with two porcelain cups of coffee and offers one to me.

"I'm assuming you take it black."

"I doubt you're assuming anything," I say. "I think you already know everything about me."

I take the coffee, wondering for a moment if he's put anything in it. I set it on the table.

"That's actually not true," he says. "I don't know *everything* about you, and that's why we're all here in this room. Because there's more I want to know."

So I have information he needs, which means I have some control here. A morsel of power.

"How does it feel?" he asks. "Being out in the world after being a recluse?" He spreads his arms out. "Out here in the vastness of the mountains. Is it unnerving?"

I decide to be honest, answer his questions until there's a clear reason not to. "It's wonderful," I say. "Nature doesn't unnerve me. It's the people in the world I find best to avoid."

"Why the Maroon Bells?" He leans in just a tad, angles his head in interest as he studies my face. I instinctively lean away, but then realize I'm that much closer to Landis, who sits in silence on the other side of me. Two men, studying me like an insect in a jar.

"Why not the Maroon Bells?" I reply. "They're wondrous."

"They are, Clara. Are you going to drink your coffee?" His cup and mine sit untouched on the table. I reach forward and switch them, then sip from his.

Eaton laughs, and it rattles his lungs.

"You're worried I'm going to drug you?"

"It doesn't hurt to be cautious."

"No, I suppose it doesn't. But it's far too late for that kind of caution."

"Meaning?"

He shrugs.

"You've been taking our drugs for some time. It's a bit reactive to be concerned now."

Our drugs.

The coffee sits on my tongue, dark and bold, but the savory taste turns instantly acrid. "Yes, I did take them. I don't regret it."

Landis speaks for the first time. "Nor should you, Clara. You have to understand we're trying to help you. The book. The pills. They're for your betterment."

I don't argue his point, because even in retrospect, I'm in awe at how I feel. I was so convinced suicide was the answer, but now consider perhaps I was supposed to inch as close to death as I did, so that the taste of ensuing life would be so much sweeter. Still, I wonder what's in it for him.

"And why are you so concerned with my betterment?" I ask.

He looks down and smiles, as if my question were steeped in naivete. "Because your progress gives hope for others." When he raises his gaze to me, I'm taken aback by the menace in his face. "Namely, me."

Landis changes the subject. "We know you left Jake a message. That's why we're here."

This shouldn't surprise me, but their ability to burrow so deeply into my life is nonetheless unnerving.

"In your message, you said you remembered everything," he continues. "We're very interested in what exactly it is you remember, Clara."

I think back to my sudden childhood memories. Some have faded enough that I only have a feeling about them, while others remain vivid. Arete Academy. Tiki torches. The headmaster handing out copies of *The Responsibility of Death*. The little boy turning to me at his desk, asking what my copy was about.

Landis. That little boy was Landis.

"A painter," I say, remembering. I look at Landis.

"What?"

"Your book was about a painter, but all he ever painted were pictures of dead people."

"You remember my book?" Landis asks.

I shake my head. "I never saw it. What I remember was you telling me about it."

His gaze fixes on mine, and for a moment, his eyes glisten.

"Excellent, Clara," Eaton says. His voice is a bit higher pitched, more excited. "What else do you remember?"

As I turn back to him, things are snapping into place. I know Landis was at Arete Academy with me. But...

"You were both there," I say. "We were all there, weren't we? Us. Jacob, who must be Jake."

"Yes, very good, Clara. Tell us."

I swivel my head back and forth between them, then push my chair back from the table far enough that I can look at them both at the same time. They're both leaning toward me with rapt attention.

"You don't remember," I say. "You were there, but you don't remember anything, do you?"

Landis leans in further, now hovering only inches from my face.

"My parents were murdered there," he says. "Can you tell me anything at all about that?"

I'm immediately transported to the memory, the one that germinated my suicidal impulses. A screaming child, two bloodied bodies in a bed. A group of children. I'm holding someone's hand, staring at the carnage, but it's just…chaos.

I shake my head, as if I can just fling the image away. This is one memory burned into my brain.

"I don't know," I say. "Maybe."

Landis starts to say something, but Eaton cuts him off immediately.

"We'll get to that," Eaton says. "I want to know more about the school itself. The lesson plans. Anything you can recall about dosages or specific instructions. We need to know more about the program. You're the closest we've been to getting it to work."

"And I'd like to know if she remembers my parents." Landis pushes out of his chair and stands. He looks down at Eaton, who doesn't bother looking back. "Jake remembered their murder, said there were kids at the crime scene. It was a bedroom. I want to know if Clara remembers this as well."

Yes, I do. But I say nothing.

"*Enough about your parents.*" Eaton's voice has a hard edge, and he still doesn't look at Landis as he speaks. "That's secondary to the information we need right now. In fact, I need you to go back to Clara's guest room. Jake will likely be arriving soon, and that's where he'll be headed. When he arrives, bring him here."

Landis looks back and forth between Eaton and me, seeming to decide what to do.

Eaton takes a breath and speaks in a calmer tone. "I promise we'll find out everything we can about your parents' death," he tells Landis. "We have time. But if Jake goes to her room and no one answers that door, then we'll lose him. So, please, do as I ask."

Landis considers, then turns to me and says, "Let me have your room key."

I do as he asks, and after taking it, Landis takes the gun from his ankle holster and offers it to Eaton.

"I think you'll need that more than me," Eaton says. "Jake might need some convincing."

"What about her?"

"Oh, I don't think she'll be a problem." He cracks a thin smile as he stares me down. "Will you, Clara?"

His arrogance forces me from silence. "I'm stronger than you think," I say. "You look like you'd snap in a stiff breeze."

At this, Eaton laughs, which descends into a minor coughing fit. "Quite so," he says once he's controlled his lungs. "But I think you want to stay. We each have answers for the other. Besides, you want to see Jake, don't you? If you stay here with me, I'll make sure Landis brings Jake to us in good health. Can we agree on this?"

A thinly veiled threat. An easy trick, but effective.

"Yes," I say.

"Good."

Eaton offers a simple nod to Landis, who takes his gun back and leaves the suite.

It's now just the two of us.

This man named Eaton. I don't recall his name in any of my newly found memories.

I expect him to flash me an evil smile, say something sinister.

Instead, he says, "Clara, please help me."

His eyes are filled not with evil, but sadness. Resigned and a little desperate.

"I don't know how I can help you," I say.

"I want what you have, even for a moment. You have to show me how. It's the only thing that can save me."

"Save you from what?"

"I'm dying."

I can't tell whether he's lying, but there's a very dark energy about this man, and perhaps that is indeed a terrible illness. Death inside him, waiting to eat its way up through the skin.

"Perhaps it's what you're meant to do," I say.

FORTY-EIGHT
Jake

ELLE SAVED MY LIFE.

Just before the gunshot, I saw her arm swing down, smashing the man's outstretched forearm with the table lamp as he fired.

If she waited a split second longer, I'm sure I'd have a bullet in my chest. Instead, I have one in my leg.

The impact collapses me, like a high-voltage current to my muscles. As I hit the floor, my gun releases from my grip and slides toward the wall. I can't reach it, and now I'm waiting for the second bullet, the one that ends everything.

Elle pounces, her fierceness efficient. She smashes the lamp against his head with a crack. Neither lamp nor skull seems to break, a surprise.

She's knocked him out. Elle slides the gun from his grip.

"Jake, talk to me."

I groan, grabbing my leg. "What do you want me to say?"

"Are you hurt?"

Blood breaches the dam of my locked fingers.

"Yeah."

She takes another glance at the man who shot me and seems to decide he's no longer a problem, then rushes over to me.

"Where?"

"My leg."

A hole in my jeans, just above the knee, over to the side. I *think* it hurts, but it's hard to tell. Either shock or adrenaline is compensating, and I'm hoping it's the latter.

"Can you stand?"

"I have no idea." It's as if three-quarters of all the muscle in my right leg suddenly vanished.

I struggle to get up. I'm not quite standing. I'm *listing*. Good enough.

"Okay," she says. She races over and picks up the gun I dropped. "Let's get out of here."

My impulse is to agree, but I look at the man on the floor, and rage suddenly burns through me. That same feeling as with Eaton. So white-hot and consuming, it makes my whole body itch.

"Kill him," I say.

"What?"

I answer without pause. "I'll do it."

God, I want to. I don't even want to use the gun. I want to club him to death, watch him break into pieces. Sharp pieces at first, then I'd keep pounding until they're reduced to pulp.

"Jesus, Jake, no. What's wrong with you? He's not a threat anymore. Let's just go. We need to get you help."

I can't reconcile my sudden violent cravings with who I am as a person, but I suppose who I am is changing. Maybe I've reached some next level in the program, just as Raymond Higgins did. My enlightenment seems to end in deep pits of darkness.

I force myself away from my compulsion. Focus my energy on leaving, which, given my wound, is a damn good distraction.

Elle supports me, and we make it to the living room before she says, "Hang on." She lowers me to the floor, where I bleed on Eaton's hardwood.

She disappears for a year, or maybe a minute. When she comes back, she has a belt, which she tightens around my leg.

"Good idea," I say.

"You have two holes in your jeans," she says. "The bullet went through."

"That's good, right?"

"The hell do I know?" Elle says, tightening the notch. "My trauma knowledge comes from TV."

"I thought you…knew stuff."

"It's all I can do not to puke right now."

The pain starts now in earnest. A dull, aching throb, as if my lower thigh is trapped in the jaws of a mountain lion.

"Get up."

I do. It's harder this time.

The man on the floor emits a groan. He's coming to, but not yet moving.

"Okay, we have to get out of here," Elle says.

We make our way to the door.

"Wait," I say, just as we reach it.

"What?"

"The papers." I point back to the office. "Get the papers."

She has that look on her face where two perfectly logical and opposing thoughts are battling for dominance in her brain. Finally, "Fine."

I lean against the wall as she rushes back to the office. I experience a spike of concern, wondering if maybe the man is getting up off the floor. But Elle comes back only seconds later, a fistful of papers in her hand. She stuffs them into my messenger bag, which still hangs across my chest.

"Let's go."

We leave the apartment, make it to the elevator. Inside, Elle pushes the button for the lobby level, and I take my first few seconds to acknowledge I've actually been shot. It's not terrible. Maybe I'm tougher than I thought. Maybe the wound is minimal. Or maybe the adrenaline is masking the real misery.

Elevator doors open, lobby level. I hobble out, supported by Elle. There's blood in my shoe, slickening my foot. For some reason, this is the most unnerving of my current sensations.

We shuffle past the security guard, and there's no hiding my condition.

"Jesus," he says. "What the hell happened up there?"

I guess no one reported a gunshot, at least not yet. I try to think of something to say. My career is hinged on finding the right words, but now I come up empty.

Elle, likewise, remains silent.

We pass the guard, push out the front door. The chill of the air feels like a morphine injection.

Elle and I make it to her car, where I collapse in the passenger seat.

"Hospital?" she asks.

I shake my head. "Walgreens."

Then I take out my phone and power it on.

"Jake, what are you doing?"

"What?" I reply. "They already found us." I thumb to my call history, then dial the Hotel Jerome again. The same hotel operator from before answers in an exceedingly chipper voice, and once again, I ask for Clara's room number.

It rings. Once, twice.

I expect it to go to a message or bounce back to the front desk.

Then, an answer.

My heart skips a beat. Clara.

"Yes?"

Not Clara. A man's voice. But not just any man.

A man I know.

"Landis?"

FORTY-NINE

"YOU GOT OUT," I say. My last image of Landis was his calm face as I locked him inside the white room with Cason's corpse.

"Of course I did."

"Where's Clara?" I ask.

"She's fine, Jake."

"*Where is she?*"

"She's with Eaton. They're having a discussion."

"Don't hurt her," I say.

"Why would we do that?"

Blood from my wound drips onto the smooth leather car seat.

"Because your hired gun just shot me."

"What?"

"Eaton's apartment. We were there. So was your thug. He shot me in the leg."

"How hurt are you?"

Elle jolts the car out into traffic, sending a fresh wave of pain through me.

"I'll live."

"He wasn't authorized to do that. He was just supposed to bring you in. But you killed his nephew, so that might be the reason he acted as he did."

I almost say *I didn't know that was his nephew.* But what does it matter? I still would have pulled the trigger.

"Where's Markus?" he asks.

"Who?"

"The man who shot you. Where is he now?"

"I have no fucking idea. We clubbed him and ran away."

This quiets Landis for a beat.

"Is he alive?"

"Yeah. I think so."

"I'll contact him and tell him to back off," Landis says. "Are you going to the hospital?"

There are two holes in my leg. Blood oozes, but doesn't spurt.

"I'm guessing you're going to tell me not to."

He sighs, then pauses. When he speaks again, Landis's tone is different. It's not the steely monotone from before. "Jake, I think you should get up here as soon as you can. Eaton is more unsettled than I realized."

"Unsettled?"

"Just get up here, Jake. Hotel Jerome, Aspen. We're in suite 317. We'll all talk, and things will make more sense. But come as soon as you can. We'll make sure you get medical attention."

"What's Eaton doing with Clara right now?" I ask.

"He's interrogating her, Jake. She *remembers.*"

Clara's voice from her message echoes in my mind.

I remember, Jake.

The last thing Landis says before disconnecting the call is, "We all still have a chance, Jake."

I have no idea what he means.

FIFTY

I FILL ELLE IN on my conversation as we drive to the nearest drugstore. Once there, Elle stops and runs in. As I wait in the car, the pain blossoms. I've never even had stitches, and now there are two holes in my leg. *Holes*. I'm afraid to look, but I have to deal with this.

She comes out a few minutes later, a stuffed plastic bag in her hand. She gets in, hands me the bag, and we drive around to an empty part of the lot before she pulls into a space and turns off the car.

"How do we do this?" I ask.

"You know as much as I do. I bought a ton of bandages, gauze, rubbing alcohol."

I look in the bag and see everything. I'm thinking about where to even begin, and then I realize it starts with needing my pants out of the way.

I unbutton my jeans. "This is by far the least pleasant reason I've ever taken off my pants in a car."

She manages a laugh. I bleed.

Shoes off, pants off, and it's awful. Bloodstains streak past my knee, down my calf and ankle. My once-gray sock is black and soggy. I take that off as well. I see the hole in the front of my leg, off to the side, a few inches above the knee. Blood continues to bubble from it, a volcano showing the first signs of activity. It's small, maybe a half inch, but I nearly vomit thinking I could just stick my index finger right into it, probably down to the second knuckle.

This is not good.

"Can you run in and get me some socks and paper towels?"

"Sure." She bolts out, probably very happy to be out of the car.

I look down at my wound and think, *I can do this*. The momentum builds in me, the welling belief I can take care of my problems, no matter how great. I ride this wave of confidence long enough to open my car door and stick my bare and bloodied right leg out into the parking lot. Without pausing to reconsider, I open the bottle of rubbing alcohol and pour half of it directly onto my wound.

Blinding pain ravages me. My leg is on fire, and it's all I can do to keep from screaming. The pain is quickly paired with instant nausea, and my sheer fear of puking onto the wound keeps everything down, at least for the moment.

Breathe through it.

Elle's back. She comes up to my side of the car and suppresses a gag. "Can…can I help?"

"Give me a towel."

She unwraps, unrolls. Hands me a clump of paper-towel sheets.

I wipe off my leg the best I can. The paper clump turns a fierce red.

"How does it feel?"

"Like being speared with a white-hot iron," I say. Rising out of the car just a few inches, I put a little weight on my leg, testing it. It throbs, but I can bear the weight. "I think the wound is far enough to one side that it didn't do too much damage. Didn't hit bone. Maybe not even much muscle."

"You need a doctor."

"I can just wrap it up for now."

I go back through the bag, find the gauze and tape. With a swift motion, I wipe the oozing blood a last time and then press a wad of gauze over both holes in my skin.

"Here," I say, pressing down hard. A fresh wave of pain roils me. "Wrap tape around this while I hold."

Elle takes the tape, then inhales deeply. I don't think she even exhales as she quickly wraps it around me. Five loops, tight enough to threaten my circulation. At first I think it needs to be relaxed, but then figure it's also serving as a tourniquet, which is probably what I need.

"Think that will keep the blood inside you?" she asks.

"I don't know. I guess we'll find out."

I look up and see a woman a couple hundred feet away walking to her car in the lot. She glances over and holds her gaze for a few seconds. I can't make out the expression on her face, but I can imagine.

"We need to get moving," I say, eyeing the woman. What would I do if I saw this scene? Would I call the police, or just go about my day? When I look at the wad of bloody paper towels on the ground, I decide I might just call the police.

I grab the wet clumps of paper, lean back into my seat, and shut the door. Elle circles back around and gets in the driver's seat, then starts the car. As we leave the lot, I wiggle back into my pants, which are now unpleasantly cold with my blood. But at least fresh socks warm my feet.

"So, Aspen?" she asks. "Are you sure you don't want to go to the hospital? That could get infected fast. I'm here to help you, not—"

"Aspen."

She sighs. "Going to be at least a couple of hours. Maybe you should get some rest."

I look through the bag and see Elle thought to buy some Advil and water. I immediately wash four pills down, then look at the dashboard clock. Just after one in the afternoon. I do the math. Landis must have gotten out of that room very quickly if he called me from Aspen. Most likely Cason's body is still in that vacant office building, unless Landis has another minion he was able to summon to clean everything up.

I lean back in my seat, hoping the Advil kicks in soon.

"I need to figure out where we're going," she says. Elle swipes the screen of her iPhone. "What's the name of the hotel again?"

"Jerome," I say. "Hotel Jerome."

She navigates through city streets and finally reaches the on-ramp for Interstate 70, heading west. The sky is darker over the distant mountains, building with dense, gray clouds. We merge into the freeway traffic, silence between us, each of us lost in likely similar thoughts. Wondering what happens when we get where we're going.

After a few miles, we begin a slow incline, which gradually becomes steeper as we start making our way into the mountains. Exhaustion pulls at me, but I'm not yet ready to sleep, so I grab the pile of papers we stole from Eaton's apartment. There was something in particular I wanted to read.

I thumb through the pages until I find it.

There. The letter.

It begins *Dear Landis.*

FIFTY-ONE

December 6, 2016

Dear Landis,

You don't know me now, but you once did. You were a child, and I was your teacher.

My terminal illness has given me the courage to locate you and send this. I'm ashamed it has taken me so long. I owe you more.

I took away your mind when you were six, Landis. I didn't feel I had a choice. We had a protocol to follow in the event of an emergency, and I erred on the side of caution. I drugged you. All of you. That drug was experimental back then, still is now. Its purpose was to block the memories of traumatic events so the subject can have a normal life. But you weren't supposed to have a normal life. You were supposed to be extraordinary. Each and every one of you. I am sorry if that is not the case.

As I said, I was your teacher in a school you once attended. A teacher, researcher, lab technician. The only adults were myself and the headmasters, William and Catherine Müller. They were your parents, Landis. I wonder what, if anything, you've been told of them. Did you know your parents worked for a time in the Department of Defense? That's where I met them. Did you know your father was a chemist by training and your mother a psychologist? I suspect not.

I loved your father. Silently, never sharing my feelings, never wanting to be the "other woman." He died never knowing how I felt. That's its own special kind of death, I suppose. That's a story for another life.

I have much to say, but even more not to. My goal isn't to cause pain; rather it is, as it always has been, to teach. I want to teach you to remember, Landis, because every child deserves to know their parents. I want you to see your father's beautiful smile. Feel your mother's warm embrace. I want you to remember, because I took those memories away, and for that, I am weighed down with regret.

Your parents created an experimental school, a school known to almost no one outside the small government department responsible for its funding. The school's enrollment was small and specific. Only orphans, and then only those with little to no other family. The school was year-round, and we all lived together in an isolated pocket of nature, as it was important we didn't have outsiders interrupting or questioning our work.

I felt privileged to be a part of the work, to be a part of the lives of you six children. To see what you could become. You were *just ordinary kids when you came to the program, unremarkable. Lumps of clay waiting to become art.*

Your parents learned things in their time at the Department of Defense, and what they learned they thought could be modified to teach children to become exceptional. Everyone has limitless potential, Landis, yet few ever tap into even a fraction of their own. Your parents created a system to expand young minds. That system became a school. Your parents named it Arete Academy for good reason. Arête means a sharp mountain ridge, well fitting for the school's location. But it's also an ancient Greek word meaning "living up to one's full potential." A perfect term.

The teaching was highly unconventional, and your ability to learn was influenced by a drug your father developed. This drug was based on scopolamine, a centuries-old chemical extracted from the flower of the South American borrachero tree. In very small doses, scopolamine is used to treat motion sickness and nausea. But in concentrated form, the drug is known for its ability to completely remove free will from those who take it, making them dangerously susceptible to suggestion. A side effect is memory loss.

Your father's work was a byproduct of some of the darker government programs from the Cold War. All you need to do is research MK-Ultra to see its origins. William was interested in the benefits of the research. It was his theory that the same brain centers that controlled aggression also represented emotion, potential, and aptitude, and thus the compounds developed for the Department of Defense could be modified for a better purpose. Rather than creating super soldiers, William was intent on activating natural talent and potential. He hoped his research would lead to the formation of a private company, which he and your mother would lead. I think he deeply regretted his complicity in some of his earlier government work, and this research would be his ability to help move society in a powerful and positive direction.

William believed he found the answer in scopolamine, or at least a modified version he created that boosted the positive properties while suppressing the negative ones. The drug he created enhanced all your receptors, opening you to expanded thinking while heightening your emotions. For most of you, memory loss was not a problem, and in fact you showed deeper levels of intelligence, more ability to process and retain information, and an increase in recall.

Another integral part of the teaching program was the use of suggestive imagery. Your mother's specific field of study was the functional impact of mental imagery on conscious perception. In short, one's "mind's eye," or how you perceived your own reality, could be greatly influenced by external visual stimulus. The impact of mental imagery could greatly influence a number of high-level cognitive functions, including one's ability to store and retrieve memories, emotional intelligence, and empathy.

She designed a series of textbooks, each titled <u>The Responsibility of Death</u>. After each of you had taken a series of personality tests, she crafted a book specific to each student. She referred to the drawings in the books as algorithms, saying they were designed to trigger emotional responses in the targeted child. The one common thread in all the stories was death. While the most critical part of the books themselves was the visual and spatial representation of the imagery, the concepts of aging, death, and dying were somehow necessary elements meant to complement the drug. Your mother told me that, in tandem, these elements would help unlock natural ambition and drive in you, all stemming from a place of deep emotion and empathy.

And then there was the pool, the third part of the program. I admit not understanding or enjoying the work with the children in the pool. But your parents insisted it was an integral part of the process. Once a week, each student was taken to the pool and had to stay submerged, eventually working up to two full minutes. You had to learn to overcome fear, push past the idea of death. Welcome it, even. You all struggled at first, but eventually grew to master it. Combined with the books and the drugs, your time in the pool resulted in breakthroughs, reaching another plane. Self-actualization. I could see it in you, at least most of you students. Your ability to learn expanded exponentially. Your communication as a community, your levels of profound group awareness. If someone got hurt, it seemed you all felt the pain. It was working.

Then something terrible happened. I'm sorry to tell you this, Landis, but one of the students killed your parents. Killed them, then set fire to their house, a fire that quickly spread to other buildings on the small campus. It's my belief the student who did this had an adverse reaction to the learning methods. Perhaps a reaction to the chemicals. Something snapped. I won't tell you who did it, because I don't think, truly, they should be blamed.

The drug I used to wipe your memories was another

derivative of scopolamine, but much closer to its original chemical composition than the special version crafted by your father. In fact, the two drugs were closely related but have very different effects. The version I gave you created complete suggestibility while also erasing memories, and this drug was to be used in only two circumstances. One, in the event any student was determined unreceptive to our teaching methods, and only as a last resort in the case they were removed from the program. And two, in the case of an emergency. The murder of your parents created an emergency situation. The school had to be abandoned, both physically and in memory, and none of you were allowed to remember your time there. It was considered too much of a risk.

I hate myself for what I did, and seek only the slightest comfort knowing I didn't kill anyone.

After I administered the drug, a man from the government came in and took over, placing you very quietly back into homes with new parents who were all told well-crafted lies about your pasts. The school was abandoned and, for all I know, forgotten about. I've never returned.

You simply grew up, Landis. Unaware, and likely unexceptional.

Perhaps that can be changed. I've enclosed in this package what I've salvaged of your parents' work. A journal of your father's, the only one undamaged by the fire. Five copies of _The Responsibility of Death_ (none of them your personal copy, I'm afraid). Some vials of the pills we used in our teaching. We called them vitamins, which made it easier to get you to take them. I have no idea if their efficacy remains or if they have lost all their properties over time, but it's my hope they can undo the damage caused by the drug I gave you. An antidote.

Your parents truly discovered something powerful. Were it not for their deaths, I'm convinced you and the other children would be household names now, in whatever industry or art you chose. Maybe it's not too late. Perhaps you can learn from your father's writings and resurrect the program. Become what you were meant to be. In the process, I believe there's a chance you can undo what I did to you. Recapture your memories. Remember your true parents.

I hope so, Landis. I should have allowed you to remember all along.

I'm sorry.

Forgive me if I choose to remain anonymous. Even as I die, I cannot push past my shame.

FIFTY-TWO
Clara

TIME PASSES SLOWLY AS we wait for Jake to arrive.

Landis rejoined us in our room some time ago, announcing Jake is coming to the hotel. Though Landis holds the gun, Eaton carries the more menacing presence. I remember only flashes of their childhood faces. In this room, however, I have a strong read on the energy radiating from each man.

Landis isn't as harsh as his demeanor suggests. There's an underlying softness, perhaps even a kindness, he isn't allowing through. It's as if he's playing some role that is necessary for this program. Maybe the success of this grand experiment, whatever it really is, depends on him playing this character. He doesn't seem to want the same thing as Eaton. Landis just seems to want to remember his parents.

Eaton is different. There's seething desperation just beneath his surface. He's tight and coiled, and I picture a wholly separate and brutal creature bursting though his skin at any moment, fangs flashing, lunging for my neck. He's a man of darkness. I don't know his intentions, but it's clear he's in charge.

I don't doubt Eaton would harm to get what he wants, but I also know I'm valuable to him. He might hurt me, but I doubt he'd kill me.

I'm desperately curious to piece together my childhood. My memories were of Arete Academy, clearly some kind of school. Other children. Books and vitamins. But, in all, I don't remember enough to explain my lost time. It's as if I watched a few short scenes from an epic movie, just enough to get a flavor of the story. I suspect there is much Landis and Eaton can tell me to fill in the blanks, but I don't ask. I wait.

We all wait.

Landis has brought *The Book of Clara* from my hotel room. At the table, the two men read the pages together in silence.

After several minutes, Eaton looks over to me.

"You've documented much of what I was going to ask you. It's fascinating to see how the program drove you to seclusion. That didn't happen with the others. Your dosage was a bit higher, so perhaps that's the reason. It's a difficult task, you can imagine, figuring out dosages for a drug for which we have so little information. But with you, Clara, we decided to give the highest concentration of the drug. It's all guesswork, but I think it paid off."

Landis takes the book into his hands and continues reading on his own, his eyes widening with interest.

"When Jake gets here, we'll have a talk," Eaton tells me. "We need to understand all of what you remembered. You just might be the key to the program's success."

Landis lets out a small gasp.

I switch my gaze to him. He's clutching my journal.

"What is it?" Eaton asks him.

"It's…"

"What?"

"My parents," Landis says. He hands the book to Eaton and points to an entry I remember well.

"Look," Landis says. "It was her triggering moment. A memory of my parents."

"Really?" Eaton starts reading, but there isn't excitement in his face. There's hesitation.

"I see," he says, then snaps the journal closed.

Landis looks as frantic as someone like Landis can look.

"You were there," he says to me. "You witnessed the murders."

I shake my head. "I don't think I saw them happen. Maybe I did. I just saw the…the aftermath."

"Do you know who did it?" he asks.

I look back and forth between them, and they both cling to my gaze, trying to read my mind. The truth is, I don't know the answer to his question. There's a seed of fear that's been growing in me ever since I first remembered the killings. It's a fear *I* was the one who killed Landis's parents. Maybe that's why I longed for death ever since that memory first returned to me. I was a killer and therefore deserved to die. There were only a handful of children in the room, it seemed. One of us likely committed the act. There's no reason to think it wasn't me.

I don't feel like I could have done such a horrible thing, but neither would I have imagined wanting to kill myself.

Now I'm uncertain who the real Clara even is.

FIFTY-THREE
Jake

ON THE DRIVE UP to Aspen, we pulled the car over to a quiet trailhead, and I disposed of my gun in a deep creek. We kept the one Elle took off the thug in Eaton's apartment, and since we had that one, I wanted to get rid of the weapon directly tied to a killing. Never in my life had I imagined myself needing to ditch a murder weapon, but I suppose there are a lot of things about my current life I never could have predicted.

The Hotel Jerome is a quaint, three-story brick building that stands with quiet permanence, likely little changed since whenever in the long-ago mining days it was built.

We pull into the parking lot, and I leave my messenger bag with the papers in the car. Elle walks in first. I follow. My leg stiffened during the car ride, and every step feels like knives repeatedly stabbing into my knee.

Inside the hotel, the tight lobby is stuffed with elegant furniture—hard leathers and darkened woods—giving the feel of a luxury train car from an Agatha Christie novel.

We know what room we're going to, but it turns out we'll be accompanied.

Markus.

The fucker who shot me is waiting in the lobby, occupying a chair next to the fireplace. Landis must have summoned him, and Markus probably sped past us while I was in the drugstore parking lot, bandaging the wound he caused. I'm not happy to see him.

Though, even from thirty feet away, I can see the welt on his forehead where Elle smashed him with the lamp. That makes me smile.

Elle stops and turns her head back to me. "See him?"

"Yup."

He sees us too. He stands the moment we make eye contact.

"Ideas?" she asks me.

"I've gone this far. I'm going to keep going. But seriously, Elle, you don't need to do this. I can do the rest from here."

"The rest of what, exactly?" she asks.

"I have no idea."

She smiles. "Oh, Jake. Are you trying to be brave?"

I know she's playing with me, but I think about her question. Being brave in a situation implies fear. Honestly, I'm not scared. This is likely delusion, but it fuels me enough to limp past Elle and directly up to Markus, who folds his arms across his chest.

"You look like hell," I say.

"They're waiting for you."

"Aren't you going to apologize?" I nod down to my leg. As I do, I'm suddenly aware how conspicuous a heavily bloodied pair of jeans is in the lobby of a small luxury hotel.

"No."

Markus wears a blue blazer that he opens just enough to show me he has a gun.

"I always carry two," he says. "And I'd like my other one back."

I'm starting to regret getting rid of our other gun.

Elle has come over and joined the group. "No way."

The gun is in her purse, where she seems content to leave it for now.

The two stare at each other. "Fine." He sighs. "I'll get it back later."

"No," she replies.

I step between them. "Let's go."

He nods, then sweeps his arm to make it clear I'm to lead the way. "Third floor," he says.

"I know."

I go first, and when I look back, I see Elle and Markus awkwardly walking shoulder to shoulder, neither willing to offer their back to the other. We head into the elevator, which we share with a fur-draped woman wearing sunglasses and clutching a pocket-size dog. The dog sniffs the air, gives out a little whine, then goes back to shivering. I wonder if it's sensed my blood.

The woman gets out on the second floor with a brief look back before the doors close. After she does, I say one thing to Markus.

"I'm sorry about your nephew."

He says nothing at first, but it's almost as if I can hear his entire body tense.

As the elevator heads up one more floor, he finally says, "He wasn't going to hurt you."

"You locked me in a room for hours. After you both threw me in a trunk. You had already hurt me."

"It was what I was hired to do," he says. "But no one was supposed to actually hurt you."

"You *shot* me."

"I acted on impulse. I'm not going to apologize."

The doors open. Third floor.

"Yeah, well, neither am I." I step out, and Elle and Markus follow. I'm hardly aware of them following me as I limp to the hotel room.

In front of the door, and for a moment, only a moment, I close my eyes. In the darkness, I see the universe, and it continues to shrink around me. It collapses in on itself, into a singularity, which is this place. Right here, now, this very point in time.

I let out a long breath, open my eyes, and knock.

FIFTY-FOUR
Clara

I JUMP IN MY chair at the knock on the door, and Eaton reaches over and places his hand on my arm. He's not calming me as much as telling me to stay put.

Landis gets up and heads to the door. The second he opens it, I stop breathing.

Jake.

He's not alone. There's a woman and another man. I have no idea who they are.

Tears well in my eyes for a man I barely know, but for whom I desperately yearn. When I left him at the airport, I felt connected to and curious about Jake, but was singularly focused on my mission of death. But now that the mission has shifted to life, all I want to do is share my experience with Jake. I want him to feel what I've felt. I want him to remember.

This is how he must have felt in the airport terminal that night, this intense pull. And yet I just walked away.

I hear his voice first.

"I'm here."

FIFTY-FIVE
Jake

"I'M HERE."

I hear the anger in my voice.

"Jake, welcome." Eaton smiles. His yellowed teeth strike me as rotten. How is it he seems to have aged even more since I last saw him?

He stands aside, and I walk into the room. I'm vaguely aware of Landis, but my immediate focus is Clara.

Clara.

Very-much-alive Clara.

She's sitting at a mahogany table in the middle of the suite, her kinked hair flowing over her shoulders and a look of sheer hope on her face.

I limp over as she rises, and a second later, we're hugging.

This woman I've only known on a flight from Boston to Denver sinks into me, and I'm immediately dizzied by her presence. Her essence of time. Nostalgia. It radiates from her with such power, it nearly overwhelms me, and I feel myself immediately choking up. Whenever this life ends, I'm certain I'll discover Clara and I were intertwined in a previous one.

"Jake," she says. Her voice is a sob. She squeezes me harder for a second, then releases, pulls back, and directs my gaze right into her eyes.

I see a fresh cut on her right check, about an inch long. I reach up and touch just beneath it.

"Did they hurt you?"

"No, that was a tree branch. But listen, *I remember*. We were children together at a school."

"I know," I say, thinking of the *Dear Landis* letter.

"I don't have the urges anymore. They just...evaporated."

"That's wonderful," I say.

"I was close, but..."

Eaton steps up. "But what?"

Clara gives him a hard stare and shuts down. He's fishing for information, but she's not biting.

"Who are they?" Clara asks.

Elle and Markus walk into the room. Elle concedes and walks in first, giving her back to Markus. He behaves. No gun drawn yet.

"This is Elle," I say. "She used to work for Landis. But she's trying to help us. She's on our side."

That last sentence sounds like I'm trying to convince myself. But I can't doubt Elle at this point. She's followed me into this lion's den.

"There are no sides," Eaton says. "We're here for the same thing."

I ignore him. "And that guy is Markus. He also works for Landis, but he's not on our side. That motherfucker shot me."

Clara looks down at my leg, which she must have noticed when I limped in the room.

"Oh my god. You need a doctor."

"Soon," I say.

"She has a gun," Markus says, pointing to Elle. "In her purse."

"Oh?" Eaton turns to Elle. "Please hand your weapon to Markus, dear."

Elle looks Eaton up and down with just a flash of her eyes. "Your apartment is creepy as hell," she says. "Way too dark, hardly any personal effects. You can tell a lot about a person by how they live."

"I know you don't know my involvement here, Elle. You only know Landis. But Landis and I are a team, so you need to also consider me your employer. How do you think you got paid, after all?"

"I know enough. And by the way, I already quit."

"Very well," Eaton says. "Markus still works for me, and he is both loyal and capable. Isn't that right, Markus?"

Markus hesitates for just a moment. "Absolutely."

Elle remains frozen just inside the doorway. Markus finally closes the door, the lock clicking into place with finality. This luxury-hotel suite suddenly feels like a tomb.

"We're here to see this to the end," I say, my attention on Eaton. "You're not going to hurt us because you need answers. Elle's not going to shoot unless we're threatened. She keeps the gun."

Eaton considers this. "Fine. Landis has another one anyway." He looks around the table and adds, "Such a violent little group we are." Then he takes a seat at the table, sitting down with enough slouch to show fatigue. He's a weak man, I think. Physically. Emotionally. But not mentally. I need to remember this. Eaton is smart, and whatever his endgame is, I can't underestimate him.

"Sit," he commands. "Let's talk."

Markus walks over and stands at one end of the table. Elle follows suit, standing at the other end. Opposing pieces on a chessboard.

There's no way I'm standing; my leg is throbbing. I nearly collapse into the chair across from Eaton. Clara joins my side, and Landis sits opposite her.

Here we are.

The last of the orphans.

Reunited.

FIFTY-SIX
Clara

JAKE SITS NEXT TO me, and I feel myself listing in his direction. He's hurt, and I can feel the pain coming off him. He's poker-faced, but his anguish seems to flow into me.

Eaton begins.

"Clara, you've had a breakthrough. Please walk us through exactly what you remember, and where you were when the memories came back."

"No," Jake says. He reaches over and puts his hand on top of mine. "Whatever they're doing, they need our information. Once we give it out, we're expendable to them. There were two others like us, and they're both dead."

"What?" This is the first I've heard of two others like us. "Who were they?"

"Kate and Raymond," Jake says. "Kate killed herself."

"Oh," I say, unable to find more words. It sounds so tragic, though it was exactly my own path until just hours ago.

"And Raymond was Ray Higgins," Jake says. He looks at me as if I'm supposed to know that name.

"That's right, you've been in seclusion. Ray Higgins killed twenty-three people in Chicago recently. Shooting spree."

If hearing about Kate felt tragic, this news is soul-shattering. Tears immediately well into my eyes, and I can't tell if fear or sadness weighs heavier on me in the moment.

"You're making us into monsters." My voice cracks as I speak. "Is that it?"

Eaton shakes his head. "You don't understand. This is what we're trying *to prevent*. That's exactly why we need your information."

"Don't, Clara," Jake says. Then he jabs a finger at Eaton. "I know all about the school."

Markus, beefy arms folded across his chest, jumps in. "They took some papers from your office," he tells Eaton. "From the desk."

"I see." Eaton is locked on Jake, directly across from him. "And what is it you think you've found?"

"I found the letter written to Landis by the other teacher. And some pages from a journal. Handwritten notes, which refer to us all when we were kids. They detailed our daily activities in the school, what we learned, our *weights*. There were also notes about dosages and our reactions to copies of books given to us."

"Do you understand these notes?" Eaton asks.

"I understand enough. Between what we found and what Landis and Elle already told me, I have a good idea what's going on."

Eaton clasps his fingers together on top of the table and hunches forward toward Jake.

"In that case, you clearly know we don't have all the answers either. But we *do* know from Müller's journal that every action we take in the program, every piece of information we choose to reveal, can affect the outcome. You and Clara are both subjects, each given slightly different dosage instructions. Clara has had a breakthrough in her memory, which means she might be the key to making the program work for all of us."

"Don't tell him anything," Jake tells me. "The letter written to Landis… It outlines everything that happened." Then to Eaton, he says, "I already know enough from the letter to taint whatever this program is, and I can just tell Clara all about it. Hell, the letter's in our car. We can bring it in, and she can read it. What I want to know is if what happened to the others is going to happen to us." Jake squints and drills his gaze deeper into Eaton. "Because if *I'm* going on a killing spree, you can damn well be assured I'm going to start with *you*."

"Jake, if you—"

I interrupt. "If we're all truly in this together—*really* together— let's sit here and share our information. Right now."

In this moment, I realize the extent of my power. Jake's right: I hold information they need. I remember things they don't. Knowledge is power, and memory is currency.

"Tell us everything we want to know," I say, "or I'll stay silent."

"Maybe I'll have Jake shot right here," Eaton says.

Elle visibly stiffens.

"No, you won't," Jake says. "I'm valuable to you."

"But not as valuable as she is."

"Enough," I say. "You have my word. Answer our questions, and we'll answer yours."

Eaton glances around the table, stopping on the face of each orphan for a moment. Landis offers him a single nod.

"Fine," Eaton says.

"Good," Jake says. "Now tell us what you know. And start from the beginning."

"In that case," Eaton says, "there's something I need to read to you."

FIFTY-SEVEN
Jake

MY LEG THROBS, AND I squeeze my fists into tight balls, trying to distract myself from the pain.

Eaton stands and walks over to the couch in the living-room area of the suite. I hadn't noticed it earlier, but there's a very thin leather briefcase propped against the back cushion. He brings it to the table and *thunks* open the brass latches. I can clearly see there's only one thing inside, which Eaton lifts in front of his face.

It's a worn leather journal, its cover no different in tone than a saddle with hundreds of miles of wear, in addition to what appears to be some smoke damage. The full-size sheets number enough to make the sheaf nearly an inch thick, by my best guess. I know immediately what this is.

"This is the only known journal of Dr. William Landis Müller," Eaton says. "Landis's father. William and Catherine Müller—Landis's mother—started a small, very private school nearly thirty years ago. The four of us at this table were all students."

He sits back down at the table.

"The school was somewhere in the mountains," he continues. "Where exactly, I don't know. It's not documented in any public records, on any maps, or anywhere in the vastness of the internet. It wasn't meant to be discovered." He looks at Clara. "I'm hoping you remember the location, Clara, because we might be able to find more journals, additional research."

"What was the name of the school?" I ask.

"Arete Academy," he says. "But you already knew that."

Clara whispers the name of the school.

Eaton says, "Does that name sound familiar to you, Clara?"

She remains silent.

"Fine." Eaton continues. "There were only six students at this school and three teachers. The students were all orphans with the exception of Landis, whose parents ran the school. They selected orphans with no deep family roots. No family members who would be wanting to check on these children. This was a year-round school, and I suspect visitors weren't openly welcome."

"It sounds more like prison," I say.

"No." Landis speaks for the first time since we've sat at the table. "My parents were running a special school, but their intentions were good."

"An *experimental* school," I say. "Good intentions or not, we were lab rats."

"What was the purpose of the school?" Clara asks.

"The *program*," Eaton answers. "We only have this one journal from William Müller, so we don't know all the nuances of the program, which is the root of the problem. I suspect there were many more journals. Dozens, perhaps. I'm sure there were computer files as well, so we're likely going on a fraction of the information that once existed. But to answer your question, the purpose of the school was the program. We all started the program as children, but we never completed it." He opens the journal to the first page. "Here, I want to read this to you," he says. "This journal is numbered *seven*, and on the first page, there's an oath written by William Müller. I suspect he wrote this at the beginning of each of his journals."

He holds the journal outstretched with both hands, like a parishioner holding a Bible at service.

"'Do something positive with your life, because life is fleeting,'" he starts. "'This was always my promise, but one I broke. I have helped my government hurt unsuspecting people. I have created things that have ended lives and promoted suffering, and this I fully and freely confess, because it is the truth. Since I cannot hide that from God, I won't pretend to hide it from anyone else.'"

"Some dad you had there," I say, throwing a hard gaze at Landis.

Landis remains poker-faced.

Eaton continues. "'This is my new promise, one I shall repeat every day. From here on out, my commitment is to science and its ability to benefit, not damage, society. Arete Academy will help children in need and position them for the greatest possible success in life. The program administered on this campus may be unconventional by societal standards, but its unwavering goal will be to use science to unlock the inherent potential and talent that exists in each of its participants.'"

Eaton looks up and closes the journal. "He goes on to write about how we all have natural abilities, which very few of us live up to. Think of all the brilliant would-be artists in the world working in Starbucks. Or world-changing statesmen who only have a sense of their ability and end up in middle-management office roles. The Müllers' work intended to tap into that talent…chemically. Psychologically. Tap into it, unearth it."

"So they wanted to create superior human beings?" Clara asks.

"No," Landis answers. "They wanted to unleash all the superior qualities that human beings already possess."

"It's fucking science fiction," I say.

"I think you know it isn't." Eaton tilts his head toward me. "If the program had no effect, you wouldn't have continued with it. But you did continue, Jake. You felt yourself changing. I'm certain of it."

"Yeah, drugs can do that to you," I say. I don't want to give him an inch, as much as I have to admit there's truth in his words. Within a couple of months of taking the pills, I had visualized the entire story line for my manuscript, something I hadn't been able to do in the nearly ten years I've been working on it.

"And none of you remember any of this?" Clara asks. "This school, these people?"

Eaton and Landis shake their heads. "Just you, it seems," Eaton says. "You're the first to remember anything substantial, which is why we want to talk to you. You're remembering for all of us."

I say, "I don't remember the school, but I did have a memory a couple days ago." I've already told Landis about this, back when he was holding me in that cold, white room. "I saw his parents. They were dead. And I think…I think we were all in the room. We were just kids."

Clara sucks in a breath. "I saw the same thing. We were at the foot of the bed. It was awful."

"Amazing," Eaton says. "I'm guessing it was your triggering event. The same memory."

"What?"

Eaton turns to me. "Müller documented it. It's a sort of mental breakthrough. A shift."

"It's after that memory when I started to feel the desire to die," Clara says. "It wasn't a sad feeling. It felt like a noble purpose. A destiny."

My breakthrough was the moment I started feeling rage. In Eaton's apartment, after the initial rush of the memory and the ensuing wave of nausea, I was left with a stunning desire to hurt—kill, even—Alexander Eaton, a pull so strong, I had to leave his apartment. The urge for violence has been simmering just below the surface ever since.

All the breakthroughs lead to violence. Sure doesn't sound like what William Müller was trying to accomplish.

"What is it you want?" I ask Eaton. "Is there…some treasure buried somewhere you're hoping one of us remembers?"

"Jake, you're not understanding."

"Of course I'm not understanding, because you're not telling us anything."

Eaton takes his index finger and points it around the table. "We're the treasure, Jake. The program can let us tap into our real potential, but it only works if we can find the right way to administer it. And Clara is the closest one we've had to success in that she finally had extensive memories of her childhood. If we can replicate her success, we can all reach the next level. Maybe she remembers more details of the program itself, like if the dosages were supposed to change over time. Any information can help us refine what we're doing. Refine it and avoid…"

Eaton just confirmed what Elle and I had pieced together. "Avoid what Raymond and Kate did, right? Because you want to subject yourselves to this program as well, but you don't want to lose your mind and turn violent, is that it?"

Eaton hesitates in answering, and Landis fills in the silence.

"Not quite," he says. "We did try it ourselves, but not for long. The results were proving to be…inadequate."

I explain to Clara. "We're just expendable test subjects, as were Raymond and Kate."

"No," Landis says. "Not expendable."

"Yet," adds Eaton.

With all my will, I resist snatching the gun from Elle and shooting Eaton, Landis, and Markus all cleanly through their heads.

I can almost taste how satisfying it would be, like a perfectly cooked piece of meat.

04-18-1991, 6:27

Temperature reached 44 today. Clear skies after brief thunderstorm late last evening. Hydro-Patientia sessions for Raymond + Jacob. Raymond's time was 1:44, a decrease of seven seconds from previous session. No breakthrough; though he reported a series of colors immediately before surfacing. I suspect he said that out of fear of disappointing us. Onset of fatigue noted in Raymond, possibly related to altitude. Jacob's time was 2:03, his first past two minutes. He reported a "scary stillness," which is promising. When asked to describe if he saw anything in the stillness, he told me he visualized a waterfall in reverse direction, throwing fish high into the air. Jacob has a stunning imagination. I suspect he has a future in the arts. We must, as always, be careful not to bias his direction. At weigh in, Clara dropped 1.2 pounds, down to 46.3 pounds. I will be decreasing the dosage for Clara, given her weight. Considering .25 (45.17 vs. 31.47, P=.04; adjusted odds ratio=1.9; 99% confidence interval, 1.03-3.5).

R	1:44 ↓⁰⁷, .6, ±V	
J	2:03 , .6, +V9	
C	↓1.2W, .3→.25	
L	n/t, +S	
A	n/t, -2/10.9	

Diet to be reexamined, more protein. Lucius had a good day with his studies, and his writing is showing promise. Margaret and I continue to debate including our son in the program, with her voice the dissenting one. Keeping watch on Alex, as he's been more withdrawn.

$C_{17}H_{20}NO_4$ [21]

View out the front

FIFTY-EIGHT
Clara

JAKE IS OPENING AND closing his hands, making fists, then releasing them. Perhaps he is doing this subconsciously, but he has the look of a man intent on fighting. Someone ready to brawl because it's all he knows.

"After hearing your father's words in his oath," Clara says, looking at Landis, "it does seem your parents' intentions were good. But clearly this…this outcome wasn't what they envisioned. How did they even come about the idea of this program?"

Jake answers.

"His parents used to work for the government." Jake doesn't look at me as he speaks. He's drilled directly into Eaton. "They worked for the Department of Defense. William and Catherine Müller. His father was a chemist and his mother a psychologist. Correct?"

Landis nods. "As far as I know. We've both read the letter, and that's the only information I have. I don't actually remember anything about them."

Jake continues. "This is all back in the eighties, I'm guessing.

Whatever they did at their job, I think it involved manipulation of the mind. I mean, you have a chemist and psychologist. They were apparently continuing a branch of work shut down after the Cold War."

"Psychological warfare programs," Eaton says. "MK-Ultra, among others. Those were all programs meant for defense. The creation of hypereffective soldiers, advanced interrogation techniques, even psychological torture."

"Good god," I say.

"Exactly," Jake responds. "Crazy dark shit. I mean, we all heard it in his oath, right? Müller said he did bad stuff for the government."

Landis is shaking his head. "Their intent was to repurpose some of the work from the shuttered programs and use it for a greater benefit. That was the point of his oath. That's the point of the *program*."

"Some benefit," Jake says. "Experimenting on children. Like Mengele. We were basically in a fucking concentration camp."

"You have a flair for the dramatic," Eaton says.

Jake looks ready to pounce, bad leg notwithstanding. Both Elle and Markus stiffen their posture, ready for anything.

"My father synthesized a drug rooted in scopolamine," Landis says. "It's been around for a long time, and it's used to manipulate the mind and cause memory loss. He modified it to enhance its beneficial properties and minimize the damaging ones. The effects of the drug were supposed to be enhanced through suggestive visual stimulation—"

"The books," Jake says.

"Yes. And some kind of water therapy."

Jake looks at me. "Get this. *Water therapy*. Basically nearly drowning the kids in order to...I don't even know, reach another plane of existence."

Drowning. I think back to my other memory, the one of the classroom. That memory came to me as a teenager when I was holding my breath underwater in the bathtub.

"How was any of this even allowed?"

"No one knew about it," Jake says. "It was a small school. Probably not formally approved by anyone. Like a shadow program," he adds.

Landis reaches over and picks up the leather journal. He doesn't open it, just holds it, as if absorbing some stored energy from his father. "There's enough detail in here to understand what they expected to happen as a result of the program," he says. "Each student was anticipated to develop extremely high emotional intelligence, particularly empathy. They believed supercharging those areas of the brain would unlock a person's natural talents."

"Meaning?"

"Meaning if you had a natural tendency to be artistic, this program would allow that talent to develop and become your life's focus. If you had a mind for science, you'd have a greater chance at becoming the next Stephen Hawking."

Jake takes over. "But in reality, their theories were only that. Theories, right?"

Landis stiffens in his chair. "You've felt the effects. You said so yourself."

"Doesn't matter," Jake says. "*Trying* to do good and *doing* good are different things. Besides, even if it did work, you're trying to cobble it all together based on one goddamn journal. It's like you've been given all the ingredients for a five-course dinner and only one sentence from the recipe. So here you are, taking your best guess and ending up with a shit sandwich."

"Exactly," Elle says. Heads turn to look at the woman who has remained very quiet this whole time. "*Your* program doesn't work at all. Raymond Higgins slaughtered dozens of people. Kate left her children without a mother. Jake is literally bleeding *right now*."

"What happened to the school?" I ask. "Did it get closed?"

Landis's voice turns icy. "One of the students killed my parents."

My stomach tightens. "You read this in a letter?"

Jake nods. "There was another teacher in addition to the Müllers. This teacher sent a letter to Landis explaining what happened... She wrote it as a deathbed confession. She said the night of the killings, someone started a fire and burned down parts of the school. The teacher followed some kind of emergency protocol. No one was supposed to know this school existed, so she couldn't just summon help. So she drugged us, Clara. She fucking drugged all of us."

"Drugged us with what?"

Eaton says, "Scopolamine, in its purer form. There were two drugs, each based on scopolamine. One was modified and used as part of the program. The other, related to the first, had very different properties. Extreme suggestibility in whomever takes it, along with pronounced memory loss. In high enough doses, it can kill, and it's surprising none of us died. Apparently the bad version of this drug was to be administered to any student removed from the school, or in the case of an emergency."

Jake's voice is a notch louder. "Which means they would just wipe the memory of any kid who didn't fit in and put them back up for adoption."

"Yes," Landis says. "So in the instance of my parents' murder, it was given to all of us."

Jake barrels over him. "And whoever was ultimately in charge of this deranged experiment created new histories for us, got us placed in new homes. That's why none of us remember. They just wiped our slates clean."

Elle speaks again. "This is some messed-up shit."

Eaton squeezes his temples and looks down at the table. "This teacher salvaged most copies of *The Responsibility of Death* and the drugs from the program. She also kept one of Müller's journals. She tracked down Landis and sent everything to him two years ago, telling him she regretted what she did to us."

Then Jake stands, and the sudden movement is startling. He lists toward his good leg and points a finger at Eaton.

"You're just guessing how this all works. And you failed. You didn't create exceptional people. Kate killed herself. Clara wanted to kill herself. Raymond Higgins murdered."

Eaton stands in a direct face-off. "And you, Jake? What do you feel?"

"I feel hate. Right now, right here, nothing but hate."

"So, you're more like Raymond, I suppose."

"No, there's only one person I want to kill," Jakes says. "You turned Higgins into a monster, and you could have stopped him. Assuming you were even really there for the shooting."

"Oh, I was," Eaton says. "We went to see him, just as I had you come out to see me. Landis and I wanted to see how Raymond was progressing on the program. Our meeting was...not fruitful. He didn't know how to handle what we were telling him. He had an episode similar to what you experienced in my apartment. The next day, we followed him to the mall, but we were too late to stop him."

Jake looks at Landis. "You were there too?"

Landis nods. "It was terrible."

Jake spins to Elle.

"You knew about this?" he asks.

"No," she answers. "I swear. I had found Higgins originally, but by then, I was only loosely keeping tabs on him. I had no idea they both went to see him."

Eaton scratches his cheek. "I think telling you about the shooting was the trigger for what happened in my apartment," he says to Jake. "I didn't realize that would occur, but still, it was a breakthrough for you. An episodic event. We learned from Raymond. If we had locked Raymond in a room as we did with you, he wouldn't have killed all those people. We attempted to be vaguer with you in the hope of more favorable results. There are always casualties with chemical trials."

I feel the hate radiating from Jake. It's so pure, so undiluted. His rage will consume him, as did my desire for death. I need to take him to the school site. I need to cleanse him, just as I was.

Eaton's voice isn't the same as Jake's. Eaton's is calm. Hauntingly so. "No one forced you to follow the program," he says. He then glances at me. "You both did it because you knew there was something to it. You wanted to change. And you wanted to remember."

Jake offers him the cold, fixed stare of a predator moments before an attack. "Yet I don't remember anything, and I'm losing even more memories. Plus, if I thought I had the slightest chance of becoming violent, I never would have taken anything."

Eaton opens his hands, and the immediate, dissonant image coming to me is of Jesus breaking bread. "Everything we've done has been measured as carefully as we could, given the confines of what we know. After the unfortunate outcomes with Raymond and Kate, we tried a different tactic with you. We thought we could trigger something by getting the two of you together. That maybe if you connected, it would yield different results.

"We put you on the plane next to Clara after she booked her trip in order to see if that jogged anything in you, and it seems it did, at least based on her own notes. I created the ruse of hiring you for the memoir to try to trigger something in you, and it *did*. You were taking the drugs and reading the book because you knew—deep inside, you *knew*—you had potential that vastly exceeded your current accomplishments. You *wanted* to change, Jake. To be more than who you were, because when you were a child, you had started on that path and never finished it." Eaton takes a moment to look at each of us. "The program *can* work. Clara is proof of that." His eyes bore into me. "We all started it as children but never finished. Now is the time to complete the work."

Jake seems barely able to control himself. "No matter what happens, you have blood on your hands," he says. "Everything Kate and Raymond did, that's on you."

Eaton nods. "Yes, Jake, I do have blood on my hands. More than you'll ever know. I want to change, perhaps more than all of you."

"Oh, yeah? You're dying anyway, you told me so, so what's the point? You're sick, or was that a lie too?"

Eaton shakes his head at Jake. "I'm certain I will die if I cannot change who I am. The program can help me."

"So fucking experiment on yourself," Jake says. "Leave us out of it."

"Oh, I have." Eaton nods at Landis. "As Landis said, our results were unfavorable."

"How?" I ask.

Eaton pauses for a moment. "For Landis, it had little effect overall. For me? Let's just say I have an addiction, and the program merely increased my cravings. My uncontrollable desires."

"Addiction to what?"

Eaton doesn't answer. He just sits there, still as rock.

Jake's hands are shaking. "So the pills are, what, twenty-five years old? You had no idea if they'd lost their chemical properties. Or became harmful. Not to mention we're all adults now, not children. How could any of this possibly work?"

"And yet it's working. We're close."

"Fuck you," Jake says. "I want to go back to who I was. I don't care about remembering my childhood. I just want to be who I was a year ago."

Eaton gives Jake a thin smile. "I don't think that's true at all."

"I could have hurt my *family*," he says.

Eaton's smile grows wider. "It seems to me you've been effective at hurting them without any of our influence."

Jake takes this comment in unusual stride, even laughing faintly at Eaton's horrid reference to Jake's daughter.

"Yeah," he says, looking down at the table in surprising and calm contemplation. "I suppose you're right about that."

Jake's coolness is revealed to be a mask he sheds with stunning abruptness. With the speed of a disappearing memory, he lunges from his chair and throws himself at the man across the table.

FIFTY-NINE
Jake

THE SECOND MY HANDS are squeezing his throat, it's like a pure heroin rush.

He falls to the floor, and I collapse with him, but my hands never leave his neck. The red haze fills my eyes, and for a moment, I think it's blood. No. Not blood. Lust.

Shouting.

I don't look over. Just at him. I start drilling my thumbs into the soft tissue beneath his Adam's apple, convinced I can push all the way through. God, how satisfying it would feel to have my thumbs pop right through his flesh!

Eaton looks up at me, his eyes wide, more with surprise than fear. He doesn't fight back. Maybe part of him wants to die, or perhaps he just thinks I won't have time to finish the job before Markus puts a round in the back of my head.

An arm hooks around my neck. I twist my neck and see Landis as he tries to pull me off.

He's strong, but I just need a few more seconds.

There's noise behind me, another scuffle. Someone knocks a chair over, and then I hear Elle shout.

"*Goddamn it.*"

Landis continues to pull, but I remain focused on my prey. Spittle flies off Eaton's lips as his face grows a deeper red.

"Jake!" Elle yells. "He took my gun."

Then, cold metal against the back of my head.

Markus's voice is hauntingly calm. "Drop him, or I'll kill you right now. Then I'll kill Elle, just because I can."

I need more time to finish this, but that time just expired. I give one last squeeze with my fingers before finally releasing. As I do, Landis repositions his arms around my waist and finally manages to heave me sideways. I fly off and hit the wall a few feet away, my fingers bent as if still clutching Eaton's throat.

I try to get up, but Markus rushes over and stomps my chest with his right foot. Pain sears through my core, almost masking the fresh throbs from my leg. I look up, expecting another blow, but it doesn't come. Markus is pointing his gun directly at Elle, who is sitting on the floor next to an overturned chair. When I attacked Eaton, Markus must have rushed over and overpowered Elle before she could react.

Now we have no weapon.

Elle and I make eye contact.

"I'm sorry," she says.

"Me too."

I shift my gaze to Eaton, whose sweat I smell. I have a visceral urge to attack again, to rip into him. This is what a shark must feel in a feeding frenzy. The unbridled ecstasy of violence.

He rubs his neck. Bruises begin blossoming on his pale skin. He holds out his right hand to Markus.

"Give me the gun," Eaton says.

Markus hesitates, then slowly lowers the gun from Elle's direction and hands it to his employer.

Eaton takes a step closer and aims the barrel directly at my face.

"You can't control yourself, can you, Jake? I suppose that's somewhat my fault."

"Come closer," I say. I don't even think he's listening.

"I don't need you anymore, Jake. As far as all this goes, you only have one more purpose to serve."

Landis, now a step away, says, "This isn't necessary, Eaton. We don't need more death."

"Quiet," Eaton tells him.

"A gunshot is going to be loud," Landis says. "If you pull the trigger, we'll have to leave immediately. And our prints are all over this room."

Eaton either isn't listening or doesn't care. His entire focus is on me. The image of the king in my book flashes in my mind. The king so easily coaxed into violence.

Let's play a game of war.

"I will shoot you, Jake. It's not the way I usually do it, but the result is the same."

The way I usually do it? What does that mean?

"Clara," Eaton says. "Jake is depending on you to answer my questions. So please tell me exactly what you remember, and how you came to remember it."

"Clara," I wheeze. I think Markus broke a rib or two. "Once he has what he needs, he'll kill us. You, me, Elle. He won't need any of us."

I believe this to be true, because the energy coming off Eaton now is the purest evil I have ever felt. It's as if he's been wearing a second skin that's finally shed, and now I'm exposed to the utter essence of Alexander Eaton. It's not just that I believe this man will kill. I think he wants to. Actually would take pleasure in it.

"Clara." Eaton's voice is louder now, more commanding. "I can stand here and try to convince you how I'm trying to help us all, which is the truth. But I've lost my patience. Tell me what happened to you, or I will kill Jake. Right here."

He's close enough I could try kicking the legs out from under him, but it's a long shot. In any event, Markus will just subdue me immediately.

I rest my head back on the floor and look at the ceiling for a moment, then close my eyes.

Deep breath, slow exhale. I feel my body, the pain rising and falling with my breaths.

The room is silent. I consider telling Clara once again not to say anything, but I no longer know what's the right answer.

Goddamn it all.

I'm tired.

I'm so fucking tired.

SIXTY
Clara

I HAVE NO CHOICE. My vow of silence is immediately invalidated once Eaton points the gun at Jake. I can't lose him. I'm unsure why I have such a connection to this man other than we were once friends at a school, long ago. As he lies on the floor and closes his eyes, I feel a deep pull toward him. His pain is mine, his life is mine. Whatever happens next, it must happen to us together.

"I was going to kill myself," I say.

Eaton cocks his head to me, but the gun doesn't waver from Jake's direction. "Good, Clara. Yes, the Maroon Bells. I read what you wrote about it. Where were you?"

"On the lakeshore. There was a rock. I was going to climb the rock and slit my wrists, then fall into the water."

Jake opens his eyes, stares directly at the ceiling. I turn my head briefly to the woman, Elle, who looks at me with a mix of confusion and pity.

"Why there?" Landis asks. "Why that specific location?"

There isn't an easy answer to this question. How does one describe an indefinable magnetism?

"I wanted to die in the water. When I first remembered the school, I was underwater. It seemed like the completion of a cycle."

"All right," Eaton says. "You're on the rock. Then what happened?"

"I never got on the rock. There was a family there, so I had to wait. I went for a walk on a trail as I waited for them to leave."

"That family saved your life." Jake's voice is calm, resigned.

"Yes, I believe they did."

"Okay, then what?" There's a sharper edge of impatience to Eaton's voice.

"I walked deeper into the woods. Off path. I started to change my mind."

"About killing yourself?"

"No, about the location. As I got deeper into the woods, I realized everything was mirroring the story in my book. The old man who dies in the woods. There was a tree stump, just like in the story. I thought…maybe I should just sit on the stump and do it there."

"But something stopped you. You had second thoughts?"

"There was a crow."

"A crow?"

"It wasn't the family who saved me. It was the crow. I was sitting on the tree stump, and it just appeared. It was wounded. A broken wing."

"And?"

"And I started thinking I should help it."

"How were you going to do that?"

"I was going to kill it. In a way, it was going to be an act of mercy for us both. And the way it looked at me and called out… I had to do something. It started hopping away, and I followed it."

"Had you remembered anything else at this point?" Eaton asks.

"No."

"And you still planned to kill yourself? After killing the bird?"

"Yes."

"Okay, so then what?"

"Then I followed the crow. It couldn't fly. Only hop. But it started to go through an area of overgrown thicket and fallen branches. An old path that had been covered over. I had to crawl to get to it. Finally, it reached a clearing, and I managed to get close, at which point it collapsed and died on its own."

This story sounds crazy, and perhaps it is. For a moment, I wonder if any of this actually happened. And if the crow wasn't real, what about everything else I discovered there?

Landis and Eaton offer quizzical looks and furrowed brows. Jake continues to stare at the ceiling, taking it all in. Or perhaps he's in some other world altogether, one where he doesn't have a gun pointed at his skull.

"Okay," Eaton says, his tone growing more impatient. "The bird is dead. Then what?"

"Then the smell of citronella grew stronger."

"Citronella?"

"Yes. It's a smell from my past, and it was there. It grew stronger as I followed the crow."

"You weren't imagining this?"

"How would I know?" I ask. "How does one know what's real and what's not? When you're by yourself, the entire world could just be a trick of the mind."

Landis speaks. "In my father's journal, there was a note about the program enhancing olfactory memory in some of the subjects. The sense of smell is the strongest trigger of memory, and if yours was enhanced, it could explain sudden smells."

Jake turns his head and catches my eye.

Eaton presses harder, growing more impatient. "What happened next?"

"I realized where I was."

He gives a rapid, scooping *come on* gesture with his free hand.

"Where were you?"

"I was at the school."

Landis stiffens at this comment, and Eaton lowers his gun and turns fully toward me.

"You were *where?*"

I feel myself smiling, not because I'm giving them information they desire. I'm smiling because I'm remembering how it felt in that moment. It was like feeling sunlight for the very first time.

"Arete Academy. I found it. I found our school."

PART III

December 6, 2016

Dear Landis,

You don't know me now, but you once did. You were a child, and I was your teacher.

My terminal illness has given me the courage to locate you and send this. I am ashamed it has taken me so long. I owe you more.

I took away your mind when you were six, Landis. I didn't feel I had a choice. We had a protocol to follow in the event of an emergency, and I erred on the side of caution. I drugged you. All of you. That drug was experimental back then, still is now. Its purpose was to block the memories of traumatic events so the subject can have a normal life. But you weren't supposed to have a normal life. You were supposed to be extraordinary. Each and every one of you. I am sorry if that is not the case.

As I said, I was your teacher in a school you once attended. A teacher, researcher, lab technician. The only adults were myself and the headmasters, William and Catherine

Page from "Dear Landis" Letter, Author Unknown

SIXTY-ONE
Jake

THE BANDAGE AROUND MY knee is dark with blood, but not dripping. Knives pierce my torso with each breath. At least I'm still breathing.

Our two-car caravan heads deeper into the mountains. Landis is driving Markus, Clara, and me. Eaton and Elle follow behind.

It's a thirty-minute drive. The afternoon light grows heavy, adding an extra layer of saturation to the blazing trees outside. This time of year, it won't be long before dark.

Markus sits in the front passenger seat, half-turned, the gun pointed directly at us. Clara and I share the back seat.

"That's really not necessary," I tell Markus.

"Not necessary? You tried to choke out my employer."

"But he's not in the car," I say. "I don't feel the same hatred toward either of you."

I think about explaining to him how my aggression had nothing to do with trying to escape. I wasn't trying to wrestle a gun away from Eaton—he didn't even have one at the time of my attack. I knew as I attacked there was no logical reason for my decision, and I would be jeopardizing my life even more. It was pure lust for violence.

"Yeah, well, forgive me if I don't believe you."

I look at Markus a little longer, taking in the faint crow's-feet around his eyes and the faded acne scars from his youth. But what I notice most are his eyes. There's nothing remarkable about them except the wells of emotion he probably doesn't know are emanating from them.

"You're an incredibly desolate man," I say.

"What?"

"Just fucking *sad*. I can tell." I examine Markus. "I'm guessing you're an ex-cop, maybe retired early, maybe got fired. Probably never advanced too much, maybe you always had someone or something to blame, but at some point, you hit a ceiling and couldn't push past it. That's obvious to anyone looking at you."

"Oh yeah?" Markus smiles, but it's twisted, uncomfortable. "All that is obvious about me?" The smile is followed by a tough-guy laugh. Hollow. Something to fill silence.

"Yeah," I reply. "But what's not as obvious, but I can see, is the weight on you, pushing you into the ground. A desperate, crushing sadness, the kind you can't ever get rid of." This sense wasn't as strong about him before, and maybe that's because my focus was never fully on him as it is now. "The kind of sadness where you wake up each morning and have to make an active decision not to put that gun in your mouth." As I say it, it becomes more pronounced, to the point where some of his pain seems to transfer to me, and I have little capacity to bear more.

"Maybe you should shut your mouth," he says. The smile is gone, but the teeth are still bared.

Then it hits me, but Clara says it before I do.

"You've lost someone," she says.

"Yes," I add. "And not just your nephew. Someone much closer, I'm guessing."

Markus says nothing. He doesn't have to; his face says it all. I've sensed this on a few other strangers, that these people all carried incredible burdens they could not unload. Until I started having this ability to feel other people the way I do now, I'd never appreciated the massive pull some people have to fight against every day. The slog of living through some incredible loss. Where once life was a field of grass, it's now an endless stretch of waist-deep mud. Every step an unthinkable burden, every inch a fight, and with no end in sight, no destination in view, a question of whether the journey is even worth taking.

"I'm sorry," I tell him, meaning it. I'm thinking he lost a child, which makes me think of Em. It was stupid and selfish of me to attack Eaton back in the hotel room—I could have gotten myself killed. She and Abby have to remain my focus. Whatever happens this afternoon, I have to think of them.

Clara fills the silence with a question directed at the back of Landis's head.

"You're different from Eaton," she says. "You don't want the same thing from all this, do you?"

Landis keeps his gaze straight ahead, both hands on the wheel, jaw tight. A few seconds pass.

"I just want to know my parents," he says.

"You mean you want to know who killed them," I say.

"That's just part of it. I want to *know* them."

We hit a hairpin curve that he navigates with caution. The

barrier on the road's edge, the thin ribbon of metal separating life and death, has a substantial dent along one section but is otherwise intact. Someone must have had a hell of a scare.

"You think if you can experience what I did, you can remember them," Clara says.

"Every child should know their parents. I want to know who they were, what their faces looked like. I want memories of them, and not just…from the night they died."

"And then what?" she asks him. "What happens in your life after you remember them?"

He looks in the rearview mirror, and we catch each other for a half second. In that instant, it's clear to me he hasn't thought much about this answer before. He's driven only to remember his parents, remember their killer. Those are the only important things to him.

"I still don't remember my birth parents," Clara says.

"Nothing?" There's a crack in Landis's voice.

"No. Or maybe I did, but it's gone now. Maybe this time." Her eyes glisten. "Or maybe that was it. What if it never happens again? What if I was allowed one moment of memories, and nothing more?"

"We'll find out soon," I say.

A few minutes pass as we wind toward our destination, then Clara points and says, "We're close. Jake, look."

I look out the window on her side.

"The Maroon Bells," she says.

She told me about the twin mountains on the plane, and her description didn't do them justice. It's not just that the snow-peppered peaks rise so dramatically out of a low-scooped valley, adding to their majesty. It's not just the freckling of yellow and red trees at their base, splashing color against the stark granite. It's something else, and only the orphans from Arete Academy would be able to pinpoint what it is.

I know. I see it immediately.

The way the gray of the rock and the wind-whipped snow intertwine. It looks like a very fine pen drawing, as if someone spent endless hours and thousands of tiny ink strokes to create the two peaks I'm looking at now.

"Landis," I ask. "Do you know who drew the books? Was that in any of the notes you have?"

He nods. "My mother. There was a reference to that in my father's journal."

"Up here," Clara says, and directs Landis to turn down a road ending at a trailhead next to a small lake.

We pull over, and Eaton's car soon joins us. I wonder what he and Elle spoke about for the last thirty minutes. Unlikely to have been small talk.

At first, we don't get out. We just look through the windshield at the Maroon Bells, which reflect imperfectly in the rippled water of the lake.

"Do you see it?" I ask the others.

"See what?" Markus says.

He won't see it. The others might.

"The Maroon Bells look like they were drawn."

Perhaps Landis and Clara notice it as well. The Bells look like ink drawings fashioned in the same style as the images in *The Responsibility of Death*. They were an inspiration for the artist, and I feel that same pull toward them, that same hypnotic gravity, as when I first read my book.

Patterns. Everything's a pattern.

I get out of the car, struggling against fresh waves of pain, and hobble a few feet closer to the lake's edge. I'm aware of car doors opening and closing, but I don't even see Clara until she's standing right next to me. The wind that ripples the water buffets against me, cold but not fierce. As I keep staring at the peaks, mountain air flows through me, deep and familiar, and despite my wounds, this is the most alive I've felt since I can remember.

I ask Clara, "You felt this place all along, didn't you?"

"Somehow, yes. I don't know how I knew to come here. A little bit of magic."

I shake my head. "It's not magic. You must have seen a picture at some point, and it looked just like this."

"That's true. I have seen pictures."

I turn to her and see the outline of her face as she looks forward. She evokes a single word in me, which loops a few times in my brain before dissolving.

Home.

"You saw the pictures, and it evoked something in you. You probably weren't even consciously aware of it, but it was enough to compel you. The shapes of the rocks, and how the snow is blown against the black and gray of the granite. It looks like the images in the books. It's a pattern, Clara. Landis's mother used these rocks as a basis for her illustrations, I'm guessing specifically to make a connection. However their program works—if it works at all—must have connected everything with this *place*. Maybe at some point we were supposed to come back here all along." I turn my attention back to the peaks and see the first of a wave of clouds beginning to crown over the tops.

"Maybe." The voice comes from Landis, who is now standing behind me. "There are references to peaks in the journal. I knew the school was somewhere in the mountains, but never considered the location itself may be part of the program."

"*Arête*," I say. "A sharp mountain ridge."

Eaton's voice calls out from behind us.

"Where is it?"

I turn to him. He's standing next to Elle, who carries more concern on her face than when I last saw her getting into Eaton's car. Markus has moved to their rear, the gun in his hand. The sheepdog, making sure he has full view and command of the herd.

"*Where is the school, Clara?*"

Eaton's head is tilted to the side, as if he's losing the muscle to hold it upright. His shaggy hair is even more unruly, and there's a quiver in his stance, a tremor in his body, and I don't think it's from the growing chill in the air.

I think Alexander Eaton is coming apart. Right here.

He staggers a few feet forward. "Take me there, now."

Even Landis eyes him with wariness.

"Do you feel it?" I whisper to Landis. "Do you feel this place?"

He nods, almost imperceptibly, his gaze on Eaton. "I do. Just a little. But it's there."

I lower my head closer to Landis and keep my voice soft enough so Eaton can't make out my words. "He's erratic," I say. "We can come back here another time. I need medical help. We all need sleep. We can do this together, but it doesn't have to be right now."

"Stop talking!" Eaton shouts.

Landis turns his face to me. The gray-blue of his eyes turns nearly white in the afternoon light.

"I'm sorry, Jake," Landis says. "It needs to be now."

"Why?"

He sighs. "Because I don't know how to stop it anymore."

"What does that mean?"

"Today is either a beginning or an end. It's only one of those two things. It's not a pause. Ever since I received that letter, I've been consumed with thoughts of who my parents were. The second I stepped out of that car and looked up there"—he points to the peaks, where more clouds gather by the second—"I knew there was no turning back. There are a lot of things I'm capable of, Jake. But turning away now is not one of them."

"We have to go now," Eaton barks at Clara. "*Show us.*"

Silence for a moment. No talking, no breeze. No distant birds. Pure, heavy silence.

Then I feel what Eaton and Landis must feel, a sudden urgency to unveil all the mysteries. The treasure we seek is buried deep within all our minds, memories waiting to be released, and the key is somewhere nearby, a place where Clara can lead us. Of course we can't wait any longer. It's as if we found an ancient sunken vessel full of gold bars and I suggested coming back another day to explore.

In this moment, I release all my questions, all my doubts, all my concerns about what's happening and just allow everything to *be*. At the edge of this lake, I choose to release it all, and as I do, I turn east and whisper something, thinking maybe my soft words will carry fifteen hundred miles to my daughter's ears.

"Everything's going to be okay."

Then I turn to Clara.

"Let's do this."

"This way," Clara says.

We follow.

SIXTY-TWO
Clara

THICK, MENACING CLOUDS PASS in front of the sun, pulling a shade down across the landscape, muting colors and bringing an increased chill to the October air. The clouds could bring rain, hail, snow, or nothing at all. Such is the power of places like this, ruled only by nature. I wonder if these clouds scared me as a little girl.

It doesn't take long for the trail to snake away from the lake, up along a dusty ridge, and eventually into a deeper section of trees and scrub. I know exactly where I'm going, and even if I didn't, I could lead by sense. It's pulling me, this thing, this place, my past. No, that's not quite right. Pulling implies I might be resisting. I want to go back to this place. It's not pulling me. It's luring me.

I reach a fork in the path and know which way to turn, but I stand a moment, considering, stealing some time. I want to go to the school, but I don't know what will happen when we get there. There is beauty ahead, yet there is violence here in this group. Those two things are often found in nature together, one sometimes begetting the other, beauty and violence, the end becoming the beginning. Raymond and Kate were seeking a kind of beauty, I think, as was I.

Eaton is the problem. As I lead the way, he follows directly behind, his feet nearly entangled in mine, his breath coming in huffs not from exertion but from anxiety. It's hard to tell if he's anxious for something he's seeking ahead or leaving behind. But he's become even more erratic since the hotel, a man losing more of his mind the closer he gets to the thing he wants most. I fear if it's not what he expects, reality will eat him alive, perhaps taking us along with him.

We form a single line, though the path is wide enough to accommodate at least two. Behind Eaton is Elle, this poor woman ensnared in something far stranger than she likely imagined. She came to help, but is herself helpless. What she doesn't know is by being here, she *is* helping, because despite her uncertainty, she is strong, and I draw from that. I know nothing of this woman other than she is good, and that energy might somehow prove a tipping point as we move deeper into these woods.

Jake is behind Elle, limping and wheezing. He has no business being upright, much less hiking, and when we stop, we do so for him, as if a momentary pause will help him regain strength. In one of these moments, I take his face in my hands. Soft, silent. I feel him diminishing, and I want to fuel him, but I don't know how. Of all of us, I'm here for him. I want him to experience what I did, to remember it all, if even for a moment. That will heal him faster than any doctor.

We continue.

Jake leads Landis, who is dressed in a suit with his fedora snug on his head. He couldn't look further out of place and time on this mountain trail, and I suppose there's meaning in that. Of all of us, he holds the quietest desperation. There's no anger with him, no fury or threatening anxiety. He just wants to find his parents, and I don't know if he ever will.

Markus brings up the rear, and every time I look back, his gun remains firm in his right hand, pointed to the ground, his gaze sweeping over us, back and forth. This man belongs to Eaton; that much is clear. I wonder how much a person needs to be paid in order to do whatever another will tell them. Twenty thousand? Fifty? Whatever the number, I have no doubt Markus will do as commanded, just as I have no doubt Eaton is increasingly unfit to command.

It takes less than a half hour to reach the small clearing with the tree stump. I stop as the others gather around.

Eaton asks, "Is it here?"

"Close." I glance to Jake. "Do you smell it?"

Jake nods. "Yes."

"Smell what?" Eaton lifts his nose and snorts.

"Citronella," Jake says. "The scent has been getting stronger for the past few minutes."

Landis gives a slight nod but says nothing. Eaton sniffs the air a few more times and, by the look on his face, smells nothing other than the decay of leaves.

"This is crazy," Elle mutters, and I can tell by Markus's expression he agrees with her.

Rather than letting Jake rest his leg, Eaton sits on the tree stump and places his hands on his knees. Landis walks over and whispers something in his ear. Eaton nods and then stares straight ahead, looking deep into the woods, far beyond us.

"It's my book," Jake whispers. He's close, and I'm the only one who can hear him.

"What?"

"Right here. This scene. This is the end of my book. A king sitting on his throne, someone whispering in his ear."

"It's the end of my book too," I say.

"Really?"

"In the end of mine, an old man waits on a tree stump in the forest."

"Waits for what?" Jake asks.

I look at Eaton in this moment, seeing him as nothing but old and brittle bones.

"Death," I reply.

Jake takes in the sight of Eaton a moment longer, then turns his head, as if not wanting to accept the parallels of the book and reality. The magic of it all. Though if there's any magic in this spot, it seems of the dark sort. That tree stump was where I was going to slit my wrists. But for the wounded crow, my blood-drained body would be among the fallen leaves and pine needles, mulching the earth.

"We need to keep moving," Eaton says, rising from the stump.

"It's not much farther," I say. "But Jake needs to rest."

"No."

I start to protest, but Jake waves me off. "I'm okay."

"Let me help you," Elle tells him. Jake resists for only a moment, a knee-jerk reaction, and then puts his arm around her for support.

I spy the patch of ground where I first saw the crow and lead the others off path and through a maze of trees. As before, my feet sink into fallen leaves and pine needles, and the deeper we go, the less of the tree-filtered afternoon light reaches us. For a moment, I think I've lost my way, but just as I'm about to try a different direction, I see the remnants of the old path.

Here it was that the crow stopped and squawked at me.

"This part is harder to navigate," I tell the others.

I go first, crouching beneath living low tree limbs and climbing over dead ones. I push some out of my way, while others claw at me, leaving white scratches that soon turn a dull pink.

There seems no other way to stay on this path but to push through, and this growth doesn't appear to be a natural occurrence. This path was covered. A collection of branches and limbs meant to obfuscate, though whoever did this didn't take too much care or attention in the effort. A sloppy and hasty job, though perhaps it was enough to keep the remains of Arete Academy hidden from most explorers.

Surely there have been others who have found the small campus throughout the years. Though I didn't explore farther in my earlier journey here, a sweeping glance at the school revealed much had been burned down. Any hiker stumbling onto the old school would have found it a curiosity, and likely little else.

Or maybe the school knows how to hide itself. A lost world, available for discovery only to those attuned to its specific frequency.

Like us.

For those following me, what lies ahead could change their lives forever.

"How much farther?" Eaton's voice is on that edge between anxious and frantic, and I turn to see a spindly, dead branch scrape against his face. He winces and snaps the offending arm in two.

"Not much," I answer, then call to the back of the pack. "Jake, are you doing okay?"

"I'm managing," he replies, adding, "The smell is stronger."

"I know."

Eaton sniffs the air again. "Faint," he says. "But it's there."

"I think I remember you as a child," I tell Eaton.

He peers at me through the branches.

"Hopefully soon I'll be able to say the same about you."

"I only remember snippets. But you were the oldest. And you were never happy."

Eaton pushes through the limbs separating us and walks up to me. Sweat trickles down his forehead, which on him looks more like a by-product of sickness than physical exertion.

"*Happy* is an emotion I've never known," he says.

"That's such a sad thing."

"It's neither here nor there. It's just who I am."

"How have you made it this far in life without happiness?" I ask.

"I haven't found it to be a necessary ingredient for success," he replies. "My adoptive parents came from old money, mostly from banking. I've never had to work in my life. Money hasn't bought me happiness, but it did purchase everything I've ever needed. And without my money, I doubt we'd all be here right now."

The others are catching up, but I take a moment. Here, with this man at the root of everything, I take him in. His smell, his energy. There is the familiar scent he carries, as I noticed when I first opened my hotel-room door. A rot. A core of putrescence, deep below his surface.

"And you think if you can experience what I did, it will change you?"

"I don't know. All I know is I cannot continue living as I am."

As I am. Such a lost man.

"Keep moving," he says. "We only have so much daylight left."

I turn and continue to push myself through.

The metaphor hits me as I get closer to the end.

This is a birth.

We are being born today, the orphans. Reborn, perhaps. Reborn in the mysterious world that's always been a part of us but hidden out of view.

I fall silent as I focus on my task. Whatever time I wanted to kill is gone; there is no more contemplating what will happen when we arrive. There is just fate.

At last, I reach the small clearing where I watched the crow seize up and die. I push into the open with Eaton on my heels, and the first thing I notice is the maintenance shed. There's an audible gasp from Eaton as he looks upon it, as if finally seeing a ghost he'd only ever heard about in stories.

My focus, however, is on the ground.

There is no dead crow. No trace of the bird I watched convulse and perish just a few hours ago.

I suppose it wouldn't be unusual that another animal came along and took it in its jaws.

And yet.

I can't help myself from wondering if it ever existed at all.

SIXTY-THREE
Jake

SOMETHING IS HAPPENING.

I fucking *feel* it.

A shiver runs through my entire body, the kind you get after a long run, when the sweat runs cold on your skin and your body has nothing left to give. I'm suddenly raw and vulnerable, and though I'm sure some of it has to do with blood loss and fatigue, there's something more.

My god, this place.

I've just made it past the fallen trees with their bony branches, earning scratches on my face and arms. My leg hurts, but the real pain comes from my upper body. I've never had a broken rib, but I'm certain there's at least one inside me. Every breath is a struggle, and bending over and under the tree trunks has become an advanced course in pain management.

Worse than the pain from the hike was watching Eaton ahead of me, scrambling behind Clara, so close to her heels, he kept threatening to trip her up. As I struggled along the path, the rage continued to well in me, and I kept thinking about how I could take him out, resisting only because I knew I had no chance of hurting him in my condition.

Then, the clearing.

I tripped on the final fallen tree, and when I tumbled into the clearing, a fresh wave of pain shot through my midsection. I managed to get onto my knees when Clara turned and rushed over to me, asking if I was okay.

Elle came from behind, and when she and Clara helped me to my feet, a shiver of ice shot through me, and I wondered if I was going into shock.

Now, as I stand here looking at an old metal shed, the shiver fades, leaving a tingle on my skin, as if I momentarily grabbed a low-voltage electrical wire.

The smell nearly overwhelms.

"This is it," I say. "Right?"

"Yes," says Clara.

I begin walking forward and nearly lose my balance, but Clara and Elle seize me, holding me upright.

"Walk me to the shed."

Eaton has already disappeared inside the small, metal structure, followed by Landis. Markus is behind us, keeping guard.

The door is half-open, a broken and rusted chain on the ground.

"I can walk the rest," I say. Clara and Elle release me, and I hobble inside.

It's an ordinary shed. Tools on the walls, an old snow-removal machine in the corner. No one has been here in here for years, I think. This place is stuck in time.

And the smell of citronella, stronger than ever. Now I see the source. An entire metal shelf of bottles filled with citronella oil, and next to them a dozen or so tiki torches.

I reach up and touch one of them, and this is when it happens. A found memory, something I last experienced in Eaton's apartment. That was a memory of horror. Not this one.

As in the last memory, in this one, I'm a child.

Standing here. In this shed. I reach for the bottle of citronella oil, but it's a stretch for my little arms. The bottle nearly topples but I seize it, then lower it to my chest. I turn and see her.

Clara.

She can't be more than seven or eight, but it's her. Kinked red-brown hair, which falls well past her shoulders. Pale and thin, almost scrawny. A little gap between her front teeth, which I see because she's smiling at me. She holds a tiki torch to me.

"Fill her up," she says.

I unscrew the bottle as she removes the top of the torch. I tip the bottle over the torch, but the liquid weight shifts faster than I'm expecting, and the oil sloshes over the side, splashing on my skin.

"You spilled!" she shrieks, laughing.

"I didn't mean to," I say, resting the bottle on the floor. "It's all over me."

"It stinks!"

I reach over and wipe my bare arm on hers, ensuring I'm not the only one slicked in oil.

"Yuck. What'd you do that for?"

"Now we both stink," I say.

Her smile is eaten by a frown, which itself doesn't take long to disappear.

"We're never going to get that smell off."

"Look at the bright side," I tell her. "You're also never going to get a mosquito bite."

Like that, the memory is gone and I'm back in the shed, dizzy.

Her voice. Clara's voice as a child fills me with such longing, I don't know if my ribs or my emotions are causing the pain in my chest. I think it reminds me of my daughter, only with deep sorrow, as if my daughter had died and I'm hearing her voice on an old recording.

"Jake." It's Clara, coming up behind me.

She doesn't even need to ask the question.

"Yes," I say, turning to her.

She smiles. That smile—no longer gap-toothed—but still the same. Same kinked, red-brown hair. Same bit of scrawniness to her.

"Yes, *what?*" Eaton leans in and studies me, his eyes darting back and forth, as if trying to read in mine a language he doesn't know. Sweat glistens his forehead. "Are you feeling something, Jake? What is it? Tell me."

I have to steady myself against one of the walls.

"I remembered something."

Landis walks in, and Eaton immediately interrogates him.

"You? What about you? Do you remember anything?"

Landis barely acknowledges his presence. He steps inside the shed—which now barely contains us—removes his hat, and squints.

"No," he at last proclaims. "I don't feel…really anything. Maybe a light current of electricity. But very light. I don't remember this place."

Eaton snatches a bottle of citronella oil off the shelf, holds it against his nose, breathes it in. He closes his eyes for a few seconds, and then twists his face in frustration. He throws the plastic bottle against the wall, where it doesn't even give him the satisfaction of breaking open.

"Me either," he says.

"It's okay," Landis assures him. "We have time."

As if to prove otherwise, a rumble of thunder fills the shed, and seconds later, rain assaults the metal roof, sounding less like water and more like thousands of insects trying to break in and consume us.

"So, what now?" Elle asks.

I turn to Clara. "What else is here, besides this shed?"

"I don't know, some burned-out buildings. I haven't explored anywhere else yet. I wanted to bring you here first."

I reach out and hold her hand, which feels so natural, as if we did this as little kids. Maybe we were each other's crush at this school.

"I only saw… It was brief," I tell her. "We were here, in this shed. I spilled some of the oil, and you laughed. Somehow the smell of the oil became a memory, I suppose."

"I remembered more than you," Clara says. "I remembered the school grounds. Faces of the others. The recollection hit me for several minutes, then started to get fuzzy." She looks over at Eaton and Landis.

Eaton wears a feral snarl as he turns around in the shed, as if looking for an elusive clue.

Eaton.

It just hits me as I watch him. He hasn't changed in the last few minutes, but I have.

I take a step closer to him.

"Don't get any ideas," he says. "Markus is just outside."

We lock onto each other. In the moment, I feel a shallow kind of sorry for him, like I would seeing a mean stray dog stranded in a downpour.

But there's one thing I don't feel.

The rage is gone. I even try to summon it, to hate this man, to will myself the desire to hurt him. Yet I'm completely unable to bring myself beyond anything but pity and, perhaps, compassion.

That's the pattern.

Clara and I had the same memory of Landis's dead parents, and immediately thereafter, we became consumed with violent urges. For Clara, it was a desire to kill herself. For me, it was an urge to kill Eaton. The same thing must have happened to Kate and Raymond, who carried their own urges to completion.

But here, in this shed, on these old school grounds, the urges dissolved. If Kate and Raymond had come here, I'm certain they never would have done what they did.

This place is some kind of closed loop. A circuit completed. Whether this is a beginning or an end, all I know is I feel good. Damn good. Despite the physical pain and a heartache I cannot explain, I feel *alive*. Purely, viscerally alive, in the way someone who has just fallen in love, or maybe found their version of god, or has simply walked outside into the fresh air after a lifetime locked indoors might feel.

Christ, I want to go home. I want to tell Abby everything is okay now, that whatever was happening to me has reached the place I was hoping for. A plane of existence that will make us better as a couple, as a family. I want to touch Em's face, because I feel as if I could simply wipe her scars away, erase all the pain, restore to her all she's lost.

Maybe this feeling will be fleeting, but right now, wounded and hobbled, I feel whole. I am in control.

It's fucking elating.

This is how Clara felt when she was here. Why she rushed back to the hotel to call me. She wanted me to experience this, and now I have.

"Thank you," I tell Clara, who doesn't need to be told what I'm talking about. I can see it on her face, and she gives me a smile and a nod. My chest wells with emotion, and I push away tears.

My emotions seem to enrage Eaton further, as if I've stolen something precious from him and smashed it on the ground.

"We need to keep going," he says.

"This is crazy," Elle counters. "It's raining. It's getting late. Jake needs help." She steps up to Eaton. "I don't know what you're expecting to happen to you, but it's clearly not happening. You're a lunatic, and standing in a magical shed isn't going to change that."

Eaton pushes past her and reaches the door of the shed. Markus has moved just inside, though he's already wet from the rain. He's holstered his gun away, perhaps worried about it getting wet.

"We keep going," Eaton commands him. "And if any of them try to get away, kill them."

With that, Eaton walks out into the rain, a lone figure trying to find direction. He trudges along a mud path until the rain blurs his image, dissolving him, breaking him into pieces, until finally he is gone.

"Out," Markus orders.

We all hesitate for a moment, perhaps testing him, seeing how willing he is to do what his boss has asked. The answer becomes clear when he removes his gun and points it directly at Clara's head.

"I said *out*."

Landis sidesteps and places himself between the gun and Clara. "It's okay, Markus. They understand."

Then, turning to us, Landis says, "Let's see this thing through, shall we?"

He slips on his fedora and is next to leave the shed and step into the downpour.

The rest of us file out, and the rain is an instant chill on my skin.

I look up to the heavy clouds as I hobble through the fresh mud.

Darkness creeps.

SIXTY-FOUR
Clara

WE FAN OUT, LIKE soldiers on patrol. Only Markus hangs back, shepherding us through the grounds of the old school. The rain shifts from pelting to spitting, and despite the bitter cold, it's invigorating. Cleansing.

None of this is familiar, yet all of it is.

The small campus consists of a cleared piece of land, perhaps five acres at most, with the maintenance shed the only structure set apart by a path. Four buildings occupy the clearing, three of them fire-damaged and partially collapsed. Each building blends into the mountain environment, no more than two stories high, and each consisting of log-and-stone construction. Ahead to my left, a house. This is the most damaged structure of all. A sand-filled playground occupies a swath of land next to the house, with rusted swing sets and slides that haven't held the weight of a child in decades.

A larger building lies straight ahead, half its roof collapsed under the weight of time and neglect. I'm guessing this is the main school building. I try to remember it, but I have only a sense of familiarity rather than direct memory. Three wooden picnic tables sit in front of the building, and these seem the most recognizable things to me.

Tucked behind this building is a simple boxy structure. The word that comes to mind is *barracks*. Maybe that's where we lived. I start walking toward that structure, but Eaton has something else in mind.

"Over there," he says, jabbing to the smallest structure of them all. It's the only one appearing undamaged, at least on the outside. A small, one-story log cabin with, curiously, no windows.

He pivots toward the cabin as we cross a large, overgrown field. Two soccer goalposts decay on each side of the field. I imagine myself running along the field as a little girl, kicking the ball, squealing. I imagine it, but don't remember it.

Eaton beelines to the cabin, and the rest of us follow. He's losing it; I can tell. He's desperate for even a hint of his past, and I'm worried what will happen if he doesn't find it. A treasure seeker finding an empty chest.

As I get closer to the building, the tingling in my skin begins, as if the structure itself is alive, pulsing its energy outward. Just like what happened outside the shed.

Eaton reaches it first. He stares at a sign on the outside wall, the letters artfully carved in wood. I can't make it out until I'm standing next to him.

Hydro-Retinentia Room.

The name is meaningless to me, but apparently not to Eaton.

"Yes," he says. "Of course. *Yes.*"

The others soon join us. I look to Jake, who appears no more enlightened than I am.

"What is this place?" Elle asks.

"Perhaps exactly what we need," Eaton says, quietly enough that I suspect I'm the only one who heard him.

Markus's voice grumbles from behind. "Whatever it is, let's get out of this goddamn rain."

We file in, Eaton again leading.

The outside door is unlocked and opens into a small room, cedar-plank floor and walls, wooden pegs on the wall. It reminds me of a sauna, minus the heat. Two of the pegs hold simple white towels left behind years ago.

A second, solid-wood door is the only option for going farther inside this building. This time, I go first.

The door pushes open easily, and I'm immediately struck by an intense smell. A faint scent of chemicals, but it's overpowered by a musk of decay.

There's only one thing in this room.

A small, square pool.

SIXTY-FIVE
Jake

HYDRO-RETINENTIA.

I don't recognize the name, but I think I know what this is.

The smell is terrible. Death kind of terrible.

"Shit," Markus complains. "I liked it better out in the rain."

"No," Eaton says. "This is exactly where we want to be."

There is nothing more to the room except the pool—a square measuring maybe a hundred square feet—and a narrow surrounding deck. The side closest to us contains a set of metal bars angling down toward the water, and I'm assuming there are steps descending into the pool. I limp up to the edge and peer in. After all these years, there's still water in here, though it's not the kind of water anyone would want to swim in. It's the water of a bayou pond, dark green, a thick film of slime on top.

Fucking disgusting.

"That's the worst swimming pool I've even seen," Elle says.

"It's not for swimming," I say.

Landis takes a few steps forward and stands next to me, looking down. "It's a therapy pool. In fact, it's one of the most important parts of my parents' work, and the one part of the program we didn't repli-cate. *Couldn't* replicate."

"We intended to," Eaton says. "But the complexities of getting you to agree to it presented a problem." He goes up to the edge, squats, and breathes in the stench.

"Therapy for what?" Clara asks.

I recall the words from the *Dear Landis* letter. The author wrote about this pool. The unconventional teaching methods that focused on an intimate understanding of death.

"Two minutes," I say. "We had to hold our breath underwater for two minutes here. It was a part of the program. The books, the pills, the pool."

Clara looks down into the brackish water and then looks at me.

"So that's why," she says.

"Why what?" Landis asks.

"I used to hold my breath underwater when I was taking baths as a teenager," Clara says. "Sometimes…sometimes I would remem-ber things."

"What things?"

She shakes her head but doesn't answer.

Elle speaks before Landis can continue questioning Clara.

"Two minutes? That's a long time. And they made you do that as kids?"

"You wouldn't understand," Eaton snaps. "You're not like us." He walks along the edge of the small pool and breathes it in as if smelling the sweetest nectar and not murky rot. "Yes, this is important."

Elle takes a few steps and stands next to me. She leans in closely. "We need to do something about Eaton."

"I know," I reply.

"It's a balance," Eaton continues, seemingly talking to himself. "A balance of the chemical stimulus, the visual stimulus, and the water therapy. The program never succeeded for us as children because the Müllers died. Our memories were wiped so no one could ever know what was being done to us. But the *roots* remained." He turns to me. "We all feel it. We've always felt it. It's just a matter of finding that balance. Now, we have the final piece. It has to be here. This pool. This water."

"What the hell are you talking about?" I say.

"It's the one thing we never incorporated into what we've been trying to achieve over the past year." He points to the murky water. "We need to re-create a therapy session. We need to get into the pool. All of us."

Elle points at my leg. "Are you crazy? He can't get in that water… He's got a gunshot wound. That pool has more bacteria than water. He'll get an infection in seconds."

Landis takes off his hat, tosses it to the deck. Then he removes his coat and lets it drop. When he starts unbuttoning his shirt, Clara says, "Wait, you're not really doing this, are you?"

"Eaton's right," Landis replies. "It's the one variable we didn't replicate. This place…this campus. The whole area is a trigger. Just because Eaton and I aren't remembering anything right now, I agree something could happen by replicating a hydro-retinentia session. Particularly here, in the original pool."

"Look at the water," Clara says. "It's filthy. And probably freezing cold."

His shirt is now off, and his torso is lean and toned, like a welterweight. He begins unbuckling his belt.

"Clara, I know this is difficult. But think of what you've already experienced here. You've *remembered* things. You had a profound shift in your thoughts, and your suicidal impulses instantly disappeared the moment you found the school." He slides his pants off, revealing boxers, which he then casually takes off, along with his socks.

Landis is now completely naked.

"*Shit*, man," Elle says. "Seriously?"

Landis clearly doesn't care about modesty in this moment. He's in his own world.

I realize there's no gun along with Landis's pile of clothes. He carried one in the hotel, so he either left it there or in the car. Markus still has two guns, but at least Landis isn't armed.

"When I got that letter," Landis continues, locked on Clara, "our teacher thought there was a chance to get our memories back. Now we know it's possible. *You're* the evidence of that. If there's still a chance it could happen for me, I need to try."

"And then what?" I ask. "If you find out who killed your parents, so what? What's your plan then?"

He glances over at me, and his eyes are the color of glacier water. "I just want to see them, Jake."

Without answering, Landis walks to the metal support rails and takes the first step down into the pool. He descends slowly but with a steady, smooth motion. No reaction to the temperature or the filth of the water. Once in, he turns and faces us, and the water level comes up to his navel.

Eaton starts taking off his shirt.

"This is fucked up," Elle says.

Shirt off, Eaton barks at her. "You don't have to approve, and fortunately for you, you don't even need to join us. You're not one of us."

The man is a scarecrow. Pale skin, lanky arms, desperately underweight. Ribs protrude.

"Clara, Jake, you too," he says. Eaton strips to boxer briefs, the elastic of which struggles to hold on to his bony hips. Thankfully, he leaves them on.

"Why?" I ask. "What does it matter if we join you?"

"We need to see if it works for any of us," Landis replies.

"Yes, exactly," Eaton says.

"I'm not getting in there," I tell him. "Elle is right. My leg will get infected in that muck."

Eaton squeezes his temples with his right hand, then looks up with an exasperated expression. Rather than arguing my point, he walks over to Markus and demands one of his guns. Markus—after a moment of hesitation—acquiesces.

Eaton holds the gun with the barrel pointed down, as if the gun itself is too heavy to raise.

"In the pool," he says.

Clara shifts her weight and looks over to me.

What do we do?

"Fuck you," I tell Eaton.

"I'm not asking, Jake."

"We're not getting in there."

Eaton sighs, shrugs, then lifts the gun and points it at Elle.

I yell to him to stop, but my voice is drowned by a deafening gunshot, which echoes endlessly in this tiny room.

Elle falls to the deck.

As I stare in disbelief, blood pools around her writhing body.

SIXTY-SIX
Clara

MY INSTINCT IS TO rush to Elle's side, but Eaton turns the gun on Jake and me, keeping us back. He's proven he'll kill to get what he wants.

Eaton squeezes his eyes shut for just a moment as he shakes his head, as if trying to rid his brain of controlling thoughts. He appears calmer when he opens them again.

"I didn't want to do that," he says. "In fact, this is exactly the kind of behavior I'm trying to change. I'm hoping you'll listen to me now."

Jake's face is a mixture of horror and rage, but he remains in his place. Elle twists on the deck, grabbing her side and moaning.

Landis says nothing.

Eaton hands the gun back to Markus and turns to us.

"She can be saved. The faster you do what I say, the sooner she gets help. Now get in the pool."

Elle's fear and pain stab at me with every moan, and in between her labored breaths and curses, she lifts her bloodied hands from her side and says, "It's bad."

I start to undress. Eaton wins. I will not let this woman die.

"Clara," Jake says. "We have to."

I would be lying if I didn't admit I want to know what will happen in the pool. Despite my sheer disgust with the idea of entering that water, I'm ready to remember more. I *want* Landis and Eaton to be right.

I strip down to my bra and underwear, feeling no shame about my vulnerability. In fact, I don't feel vulnerable at all. Despite the roiling storm of violence and suffering in this room, I have a strange sense of peace.

Jake finally gives in. "I think my ribs are broken," he says. "I can't lift my arms to take my shirt off, and I'm keeping my bandage on my leg."

He turns and hobbles to the edge of the pool, then starts a slow and obviously painful descent into the water. Once it reaches his wound, he gasps.

"Christ, it's cold."

Eaton follows and stands in the small pool near Landis.

I'm the last to join, and before I do, I walk over to Elle and place a hand on her shoulder. A wave of cold washes over me, and I hope that means I'm absorbing some of her suffering, if even for a moment.

"We'll get you help," I tell her.

She doesn't reply. She's still conscious, but every bit of her energy seems focused on staying alive, and nothing else. I'm not even certain she's aware of me.

Then I stand, feeling every gaze in the room on me. Landis, Eaton, Jake, all in the dirty water before me. Markus stands behind us, gun in hand.

I walk to the pool's edge and descend the steps. Jake was right; it is bitterly cold. As the water reaches my thighs, my muscles involuntarily contract, threatening to buckle my legs. My body adapts after a few more seconds and I keep going, the stench growing stronger. I finally reach bottom. The water's surface is nearly to my chest, and the water is so dark, I cannot see past my navel.

I glide to Jake, and when I reach him, I walk to within an inch of his body. He leans his head down and our foreheads touch, and as they do, I close my eyes. For a second, the smell of citronella is back, and in the darkness inside my eyelids, I see Jake as a boy.

He is smiling.

SIXTY-SEVEN
Jake

I BEND MY NECK, and Clara and I touch foreheads. It feels so natural, as if she's an extension of me. For a moment, I close my eyes and breathe her in, which is perfume compared to the foul smell of the water.

"Everything's going to be okay." I'm not sure if I'm saying this more to her or myself. Clara reaches up and puts her hand around the back of my head, pushing our foreheads harder together.

"I know," she says.

There's another world beneath the surface of this water, and we don't know what it contains. Wonders, horrors, or maybe nothing at all. Maybe just an endless nothing.

"We go under at the same time and stay under for two minutes," Eaton says. Then he turns to Markus. "Time us and yell out when it's been two minutes." He points at Clara and me. "If either of them come up before then, shoot them."

Markus looks more scared than confident. He holds the gun loosely in his right hand, shifting his weight back and forth between his feet.

"Do you understand?" Eaton asks him.

"This is fucked up," Markus replies.

"That statement tells me you don't fully understand. You do what I ask, and I will add 10 percent to your fee. Does that help?"

Markus's eyes narrow. "Fifteen."

"Fine."

The grip on the gun tightens. Whatever his fee is, he's clearly motivated by the idea of more of it. Markus shifts the gun to his left hand and looks at the watch secured around his right wrist.

"Let me know when you're ready."

Clara has separated from me, and we've all naturally drifted to the four corners of the small pool. Clara to my right, Landis to my left, Eaton at the opposite corner.

The absurdity of this isn't lost on me, the four of us in varying degrees of undress standing waist-deep in decades-old freezing pond scum. Not only are we here, but under the threat of death, we're going to submerge ourselves to the point of drowning in the hope something, *anything* will happen to our minds as we do. Hell, two minutes? How am I going to hold my breath that long?

Yet maybe this really is the moment I've been waiting for. Ever since the fedora-wearing stranger gave me a book about a king, I've been undergoing a metamorphosis. Maybe this is the day I emerge from the chrysalis.

There are only a few outcomes here. One: I'll come up early for air and be shot. Two: I'll stay under too long and drown. Three: I'll come up after two minutes, and nothing will be different. Or four...

Four is the completion of the program.

The remembering.

The fulfillment of something wondrous. Or terrible.

As I have been so many times in the past months, I'm hit with a wave of emotion that threatens to take my breath away before the water does. I close my eyes and see my daughter's face. I would die to see her right now.

Maybe that's what it'll take.

Deep breath in, slow exhale.

Steady yourself, Jake.

"On my order," Eaton says.

Eyes open. Clara and I instinctively turn to face each other.

Deep, deep breath, as much as my lungs can handle.

"Now."

We lower. Clara's face is expressionless as she descends. Before her chin reaches the surface, she closes her eyes. I do the same.

The smell is overwhelming as I go under.

Water over my head.

SIXTY-EIGHT
Clara

THE STENCH IS OVERPOWERING as I lower myself, and the moment I'm under, I fight against bursting immediately back to the surface. I steady myself, ease my mind for a count to ten. That's enough to bring a granule of calm against all that is happening, all that surrounds me, all that clings to my skin. The filth of the water, the threat of death. Elle, bleeding and helpless on the surface above.

I count higher, just as I did as a teenage girl in the tub. I remember that now, the counting, chunks of ten, manageable pieces. If I can count to ten underwater, surely I can make it to twenty. And if to twenty, then certainly thirty.

Two minutes.

That's a count to 120.

No, Clara, don't think of it that way.

Ten at a time.

Only ten.

I'm up to thirty, and my lungs begin to seize. Heat rising through me, and the fingers of panic beginning to pinch. Soft at first, then harder, warning me to listen.

You're running out of air, panic says.

Forty, then fifty.

I can do this.

You will do it until you don't. And then you die.

I try not to listen to the panic, or the other voices insisting on things to say. It's almost impossible to do.

Sixty, then seventy.

I'm aware of my arms moving, and I stop them to conserve energy. All my focus must concentrate on remaining under.

Eighty, then ninety.

Thirty seconds left, and nothing matters except my need to breathe. My head is exploding, and if I still wanted to die, it would be easy to give in, to let this black water take me. But now all I want is to live. I want it even more than I craved the death I came seeking here in the first place.

Small chunks, ten at a time. Three chunks left.

Suddenly, the heat vanishes from my body. I am heavier, a piece of granite, and would surely sink were I in deeper water. My desire for air is replaced with a need to sleep.

One hundred, I think.

I warned you.

It would be so easy. There's nothing I need to do but let it happen.

Death lures you.

An incredible peace rushes through me, a morphine injection. Everything is fine. There is no life. There is no death. There's just the moment, and nothing existed before or after, and it's all perfect.

I've stopped counting. Numbers don't even exist anymore.

I'm going to sleep now.

My body stills. Soon, I will open my mouth and the water will fill me, and I will become the same as it.

Then.

Light explodes in my brain.

A surge.

Overload.

This must be it, the end, and I no longer want to come up for air.

Images. So many of them. Flashing through my mind in millisecond bursts, but I'm able to study them all, as if doing nothing more than leisurely looking through the pages of an old photo album. Some images are frozen snapshots, while others have motion. Home movies.

Everything is here, at this school.

I'm a little girl.

The classroom. Chalk on the board. This pool. I'm scared, cold, shivering in a bathing suit. Running on the soccer field, the grass lush and forest-green. Climbing a tree, worried about falling. Studying the strange children's book, not understanding it. Sharing a room with Kate, crooked teeth and freckles on her nose. We tell stories at night after the lights are out.

Then Jake, standing next to me. We're securing tiki torches to the holes in the ground outside the dining hall. He lights them and gripes about smelling like citronella.

The way he looks at me, it's different from the others. I chase him at sunset through the grass, tackle him though he's bigger and older. Climb on top of him, both of us laughing. We are close. He protects me, I think. And I protect him.

Then, a final series of images.

Near total darkness. Sneaking through a house. The others are here. We're looking for something but can't find it. We've broken into groups, and I can't see who's with me. Whispering.

It's not here.

What do we do?

I don't know.

I'm scared.

Me too.

Then, a scream.

A terrible, night-piercing scream.

SIXTY-NINE
Jake

IN THE WATER, IN the deep, I'm taken to an impossible blackness.

I don't think I can do it. Two minutes is too long.

Jesus, what is happening? I'm going to die in this pool.

Em. I'll never see her again.

Don't think that way. Think of every challenge you've ever had. The moment you wanted to give up, then pushed harder. You need to do that now.

It's not possible.

It is. Hell, you did it as a kid. Just a few more seconds. Push harder, Jake.

I can't.

Markus will shout, then you can get your air. Until then, push harder, goddamn it.

I'm trying. I'm trying so hard.

Seconds pass. Maybe years.

Keep going. Just a little more.

Suddenly, a blinding light.

Then,

I'm back.

I'm a child.

I'm lighting tiki torches with Clara. She tells me I stink. I tell her she's ugly. She's right and I'm wrong, and we both laugh. Raymond comes over and asks if we want to throw the football. I don't want to, but I say yes because I feel bad for him. No one likes Raymond, which must be hard, I think. There are so few of us.

He seems angrier lately. I think since we've gotten our books. We throw the football, but he wants to play tackle. One on one. I ask him how it works, and he just says whoever has the ball gets tackled. Without me agreeing, he just comes over and knocks me to the ground. The air rushes from my lungs, and I struggle to replace it. As I lie wheezing, Raymond rips the ball from my hands.

There. That's how you play.

I'm still aware I'm underwater, but that's a distant thought. Hardly a concern, though I must be near death now. Somehow, that doesn't matter. All that matters are the images flooding my brain. The memories.

I have *memories*.

I'm willing to die just to have more.

Maybe that's what death is. A permanent state of remembrance.

The scene changes, like an abrupt movie cut.

It's dark. I'm in a house with the others. It's the home of the headmasters, and we're looking for something.

The vitamins. We're searching for the vitamins.

Another child is in charge. The Leader. It's the Leader who convinced us all to break into the headmasters' home at night.

The Leader told us we have to find and destroy the vitamins. The vitamins are hurting us. The headmasters are experimenting on us.

I think…

Eaton is the Leader. But he's not Eaton. He's just Alex.

I don't know what to believe, but we're all here. Except Landis, who's six but seems even younger. We didn't warn Landis. He might tell his parents.

We've split into groups. I'm with a girl in the study. It's either Kate or Clara, but I can't tell, even when I hear her voice.

Maybe they're in here, she whispers.

I'm looking at a large wall safe, my flashlight beam sweeping along the numbered keypad.

How do we open it?

We don't, stupid. That's why they call it a safe.

We could guess some numbers.

And we do, but nothing works.

The image dissolves, replaced by darkness. I'm still in the house, I think, but I can't see anything.

There is no more sight. There is only sound.

Someone is screaming.

We race upstairs, toward the sound, the horror.

There, at the end of the hallway.

Into the bedroom.

Dark. Mostly.

The screams are in here. They pierce through me.

I think they come from a child.

Orange numbers glow near the bed, perfectly sequential.

12:34.

SEVENTY
Landis

I SEE THEM. MY god, I see them. First, only snippets. They flash by so quickly, I cannot keep up, but enough shape and color stick to my brain to understand what they looked like. Mother, her hair a chestnut brown, pulled back so tight, it gives a severe look to her face. But when she smiles, it radiates, and she smiles often, especially when she looks at me. Father, so busy, pen to paper, or at his computer, never ceasing with his note-taking, studying, experimenting. He is stern yet caring, his face as pale as mine, his eyes more blue than gray. He believes in what they are doing, believes it so much, he's willing to put his own child through the program. But that's the thing. We are all his children in his eyes. The six of us, all orphans but me. The others, are they jealous? That I have parents and they don't?

The images slow and my brain fills with memories, and it's dizzying and painful to contain them. I'm a starving man suddenly feasting, unable to stop the consumption. A small corner of my brain reminds me I'm submerged in the foulest of water, that my brain is nearly depleted of oxygen, and I will die if I don't surface soon. But the rest doesn't care. It wants me to stay right here, absorbing my childhood memories until I implode under their crushing weight.

Then they stop. No more colors, no more light. Blackness. Then a door opening. Another memory comes, but this one is slow to build.

My little hand is on the doorknob, and I enter more darkness. The only light comes from glowing orange numbers. My parents' clock, garish and utilitarian.

I'm in their bedroom, and I shuffle up onto their bed, squeezing between them.

My father mumbles.

What are you doing?

I was scared. I wanna sleep with you.

You're six, Landis. We've already had this discussion.

Just for a few minutes. Please? I promise.

My mother's voice, groggy with sleep.

Let him stay, William.

Okay, but just for a few minutes.

They fall back asleep quickly. I do not. I fixate on the glowing numbers, watching them change.

12:17

12:18

12:19

At 12:20, I get out of bed, knowing I'll never sleep if I keep watching the clock, but unable to look away. I'm still scared, so I don't want to return to my room. I choose to sleep on the floor, between the bed and the wall. Somehow, there is safety here on the floor, but not in my room.

My eyes are closed, and things begin to feel heavy, and I sense myself drifting away.

Then, wet, punching sounds, and a terrible thrashing coming from the bed. My mother—I think it's my mother—makes noises I've never heard come from her, somewhere between a scream and a gurgling plea for help. She's drowning, I think. It doesn't make sense.

12:32, the clock glows.

My father shouts, not from anger, but from pain. The light from the clock shows me nothing more than shapes twisting and convulsing on the bed, and all my mind can conjure is *animal attack*. A bear has broken into our house and is killing my parents. I am helpless to stop it. In fact, there's nothing I can do but add my own screams to theirs, which I do with every fiber of my six-year-old being.

It doesn't do any good.

12:34

Lights flood the room.

My parents are just meat and blood. The attacker isn't a bear at all. It's a boy.

I know him.

SEVENTY-ONE
Eaton

BIRTH OR DEATH.

That's what this is.

I hold my breath and count the seconds in my head.

Thoughts about God.

It's too late to ask for forgiveness. Any god who created me will discard me as the waste I am.

I want to change. I always have. No one will believe me.

Not even God.

But You made me like this. The irony of it all.

The program is my only hope. It all starts or ends here, in this water.

Seconds pass, a full minute. Another count to thirty, and I'm reaching that space between will to survive and a nudge toward endless sleep. The sleep begins to win. I think how comforting death would be.

Then a sudden, blinding light, followed by a kaleidoscope of imagery. Images twist and turn, dissolve and reappear, but somehow I can focus on them, tune into each frame, put them in a logical order.

Memories.

Actual memories.

From childhood. The first I've ever had.

A policeman holds me, telling me my parents are dead.

Somewhere in the distance, another officer utters, "Murder-suicide."

I want to push away from the arms of the man who holds me. They think my parents killed each other. They don't know the truth.

About who really put the poison in their coffee.

I didn't hate them. I didn't love them. I didn't feel anything.

I just wanted to see what they looked like dead.

Then, a flash to the school. This school. They're trying to help, make us better versions of ourselves. They say.

Don't fear the methods here.

Don't fear death. It's natural.

Do take your vitamins. Every week.

The headmasters make promises. I want to believe them.

Whatever natural talents you have, our methods will make you use them to your fullest potential.

I want to raise my hand.

I want to ask them the question that's been festering inside me since I arrived here.

Surely they've thought of everything, so I want to ask:

What if my natural talent is killing?

Because I think the headmasters did not account for that.

Maybe they do in their final moments, as I stab them in an uncontrolled frenzy in their bed.

In my frenzy, I briefly spy the orange numbers on the bedside clock.

12:33

Maybe in these final seconds, they realize they made me into an extraordinary version of the monster I've always been.

I wanted to stop them by destroying the vitamins, hoping that would be enough.

But the moment I entered the house with the others, I could not help myself. The others searched for the pills. I went to the kitchen and grabbed the knife.

Landis is screaming nearby, but he does nothing to save his parents. He's too young to help. All he can do is suffer.

12:34

Someone turns on the light. I've left the bed and steadied myself against a wall in the back of the bedroom. The others don't yet see me. Maybe they hear me wheezing from exhaustion. I'm still holding the knife. Blood paints my body.

Little Landis, on the floor, hugging his knees, his face bright red and contorted in horror, mouth wide open in a permanent shriek.

He's the only one staring directly at me.

SEVENTY-TWO
Clara

A GUNSHOT, UNMISTAKABLE AND deafening, even underwater. It jolts me instantly from my past, severing the thin and fragile cord connecting this world to the other. It also saves me from drowning, because it forces me from the water.

Markus is shooting. That animal has shot someone, just as Eaton instructed. It has to be…

Jake.

I push up through the muck and burst through the water's surface, becoming an easy target for the next bullet. I expect it to come, yet I don't cower from the thought. Air floods my lungs, nearly toppling me with relief, and as I open my mouth, I take in a mouthful of this putrid, slime-filled water.

I gag as I lunge to where I think Markus is standing, but even as I storm through the pool, I know this is a suicide mission. He's already shot Jake, maybe killed him. I can't save Jake, and now Markus will kill me.

Still, I advance.

I'm at the edge of the pool by the time I fully open my eyes. I wipe algae from my face as my stomach lurches, and without any ability to stop myself, I heave water and my last meal onto the concrete pool deck.

"Don't shoot him!" I can finally make out the watery image of Markus, gun held high in his right hand.

Nearly the same words are shouted from behind me.

"Don't shoot her!"

I spin and see Jake, gasping for air as he rushes over to me. What I don't see is fresh blood. I don't think he's been shot.

"Relax," Markus says. "I shot into the ceiling. You couldn't hear me when I yelled that two minutes had passed."

Another *whoosh* of water, and Landis spears through the surface, gasping nearly as much as Jake. Three of us are now above the surface. Eaton is nowhere to be seen. Elle is still writhing on her side, in obvious pain. At least she's still moving.

Harsh rain assaults the roof, and water dribbles through a leak in the ceiling. The bullet hole.

"Eaton?" Landis says.

"Still under," Markus replies.

The three of us in the pool share a collective gaze and, likely, the same thought. Eaton has either drowned or is close. Do we make any attempt to pull him from the water? Or will Markus?

No one moves. Five seconds, then ten.

Finally, movement.

Eaton surfaces, and not with a rush and a gasp, but calmly, still breathing just through his nose, as if he could have remained under another five minutes.

Markus speaks first. "Everyone was under for two minutes. Unbelievable. You all made it for two whole minutes."

Eaton says nothing. The only sound is the rain pelting the roof and a muffled groan from Elle.

Jake fills the silence.

"Okay, we did what you wanted. Now we need to get Elle help."

Eaton says nothing. He even has the trace of a smile on his face.

"For fuck's sake," Jake yells. "*We have to save her. So, now what?*"

Eaton slowly lifts his hands, slicks back his hair, then wipes a thin layer of green slime from his face.

"Now it ends."

SEVENTY-THREE
Jake

EATON MUST HAVE FINALLY lost his fucking mind underwater. That means I need to act, and now.

I take small steps until my lower back touches the edge of the pool.

The only real threat here is Markus, who's standing directly behind me on the deck of the pool. I don't turn around, but I should be within an arm's reach of his legs.

Deep breath.

I have memories now. Not complete, but they're there. Colors and smells, smiles and tears. I saw my parents—my birth parents—for a thousandth of a second, but that was long enough for me to capture them. And I saw Clara. She grabbed my hand in the bedroom that night as the Müllers' blood poured from them.

I know it was her because I turned and saw Clara's face, and in it, I saw the face of my own daughter. That's when everything clicked.

In that moment, all the responsibilities I carry became fully realized. A responsibility to raise Em, to be a true partner to Abby. A responsibility to life, to complete whatever journey this is with more joy and less resignation. To be better today than what I was yesterday, and be better still tomorrow.

I don't know Eaton's intentions, but I'm done waiting.

You're in control, I tell myself. *You've always been in control.*

Markus begins to speak, and I don't even know what he's saying.

Now, Jake.

I push off the floor of the pool as hard as I can, spin, and lunge for Markus's legs. As my body turns, I see he's as close as I hoped, but my bad leg fails me. I hoped to clear the top of the pool. Instead, my chest slams on the concrete pool edge, rearranging my ribs once again in a fresh torrent of pain. I've managed to catch one of Markus's ankles and, just by virtue of falling uncontrollably back into the pool, I yank his legs out from under him, sending him crashing to the deck.

But it's no use. I've fallen back in the water, and it's all I can do to keep my head above the surface. Markus can just stand up and start shooting.

As I finally find footing, shouts erupt all around me. I think Markus is cursing at me, but then Clara's voice rings in my ears.

"Stay there. Right there."

I finally stand, my ribs like snapped matchsticks. Clara is out of the pool and holding a gun on Markus, who is flat on his back. She's leapt from the pool and taken his gun.

"Take it easy," he says. He starts to get up.

"Don't move," she says.

He does. He very carefully gets to his knees, and as he starts to stand, he takes his other gun from his ankle holster.

Clara doesn't shoot. Her hands shake.

"Shoot him," I tell Clara.

She doesn't. She can't.

By the time he's fully upright, they're standing five feet from each other, gun barrels pointed at each other's faces.

Clara is panting. Elle, close by, has stopped moving.

"I won't if you won't," Markus says. His face is rigid as stone, but now I see the slightest shake in his outstretched hand.

I don't feel the rage I did earlier, but goddamned if I'm going to die in this filthy muck.

"Shoot him," I say again. "If you don't, we'll all die."

Each of them stiffens, their arms stretching out an inch more, their guns seeming to lean in for a kiss.

The next spoken word is "no." It comes from Eaton.

I turn.

"Both of you, put your guns down," he says, his tone less bitter than resigned. I turn back, and neither Clara nor Markus has obeyed, but Clara has pulled her arm back a few inches.

"Him first," I say.

"Markus," Eaton says. "Put your gun down and take Elle for help."

This is the last thing I was expecting him to say. He remembered something under the water. Something changed him.

"Are you sure?" Markus says.

"Yes, just go. Save her, if you can."

Markus still hesitates, and then I yell, "Go!"

This works, and Markus holsters his gun back to his ankle, then walks to Elle and lifts her with ease. Elle is limp in his arms, and blood trails along the pool deck as he leaves the room. I can't imagine how he's going to make it through the fallen trees and branches along the path and back to the car while carrying Elle. In the rain. And near darkness. But at least she's being moved. Here, she'd die.

I know with immediate clarity that, as quickly as Elle entered my life, this is the last time I will ever see her.

Now we are alone, the orphans. Landis, Eaton, and myself, still in this cold, black-green water. Clara, nearly naked and shivering, standing on the pool deck, gun still in her hand.

Landis's gaze is fixed on Eaton.

"It was you," he says. "You killed my parents."

Eaton nods. "Does that surprise you?"

"No. In fact, I had always suspected it. But I had to know for certain."

Through chattering teeth, Clara tells Eaton, "It was your idea. You were the oldest. You called yourself the Leader. You told us the vitamins were making us crazy. That's why we were in the house that night, to destroy the vitamins. But then you snuck away by yourself and went up to their room."

I wade over to the edge of the pool, pushing away a pain-induced desire to vomit. "Give me the gun," I tell her. "Get dressed. You're freezing."

She hesitates. "No more death, Jake."

"I know. I don't want anyone else to get hurt. But we have to protect ourselves." Eaton and Landis can hear us, but I don't care. Nor does it seem to matter, for after Clara bends down and hands me the gun, I turn and see the two men locked deeply into each other's stare. They don't even seem to be aware of anyone else in the room.

"What did you remember under there?" Landis asks him.

"I remember enough," Eaton says. He takes a few slow and deliberate steps in the water toward Landis, who is so motionless, he could be carved from stone. "I remembered my boyhood tendencies, well before coming to the school. How I used to play with fire all the time. What I did to animals: first bugs, then lizards, and then finally a stray cat." Eaton takes a long, slow breath and briefly looks to the ceiling. "I remember what I did to my own parents, which is how I ended up at this school. But your parents, they had no idea what I was. Not really. No one knew."

He takes a step closer, and now the two men are within two feet of each other. I hold the gun tightly but don't point it at either of them. They remain a threat, but only to each other in this moment.

Eaton's voice is soft, a stark contrast to earlier. "I wanted to change, I *did*. I thought I had a chance when you came to me, and I'd hoped the program was a way to finally become someone different from who I am." A half step closer. "But that was the problem all along, Landis. Your parents developed a program meant to augment our natural talents." He gives a shake of his head. "They didn't know my natural talent all along was death."

I inch away as Eaton confesses this. The pieces lock into place with what he said earlier about the things he's done, and the clouds of confusion start to dissipate. Who knows how many lives he's taken, or if it was indeed made worse by the Müllers' work. But where Landis's motivation to reestablish the program was to remember his parents and find their killer, Eaton just wanted to change, to be something different from what he was. I suppose the program was never meant to domesticate a feral animal.

Eaton reaches out and places a slime-covered hand on Landis's bare shoulder. For a second, I expect some kind of attack from either man, but it doesn't come.

"I would say I'm sorry, Landis, but I'm not. I'm incapable of feeling sorry. I just am who I am."

Landis barely moves his mouth as he speaks. "I forgive you," he says.

I think Landis has been waiting his whole life to speak those words. He just didn't know who to say them to.

He gently takes Eaton's hand off his shoulder and, with a preternatural calm, raises his own arms and places his hands on top of Eaton's head. Eaton nods in some kind of agreement only the two men share, and then Eaton begins to lower into the water, an inch at a time, first chest, then neck, then jawline. Landis keeps his hands on Eaton's head but does not appear to be forcing him down. He's just a part of this ceremony.

Before Eaton is fully submerged, Landis tells him, "May your last memory be a good one."

Then Eaton is gone into the beneath. One minute passes. Landis's hands remain softly placed on top of Eaton's head.

"No," Clara says.

I look over and she's now dressed, with her soaked bra and underwear discarded on the deck. "No more death."

"It's his decision," Landis replies, looking down into the pool. "His responsibility."

The seconds tick by. Two minutes surely have passed by now, and Eaton's mind must be flooding with imagery. I wonder what he sees as his final seconds transpire. Is there one good thing buried in that brain of his, something soft and sweet to take him from this world?

Or maybe his mind contains nothing but death.

Eaton. We were all supposed to be great through an innate understanding of death. You understood it better than us all, and look where you are.

Then, a small thrashing in the water, and for the first time, Landis applies force to keep Eaton underneath. This is the moment suicide and murder intertwine, and it doesn't last long, only seconds, a final splash, and then stillness and calm. Landis keep his hands in place a while longer and finally lets go. Eaton's body rises, facedown, floats gently in the algae, as if just a natural extension of all the decay and bacteria already here.

Landis doesn't even acknowledge what's transpired as he gets out of the pool and puts on his clothes. He fully dresses, including tucking in his shirt, securing his belt, and placing his fedora back on at an angle. His clothes spot from the water still on his skin, but he doesn't seem to care.

"I'm going home," he says.

Then Landis walks away, leaving me wondering to what home he's even referring.

SEVENTY-FOUR
Clara

TOGETHER WE WALK, JAKE and I.

The rain has moved on, leaving behind a chill that burrows into my skin, threatening my bones. Jake is colder yet, having gone into the pool fully clothed, and his wet clothes hang heavy on him like freshly applied papier-mâché. We each shiver as we walk the grounds of this place where we once knew each other.

One of the places, I should say.

The sky turns a fierce, rusted orange for a brief moment, then bruises over and continues to darken.

We walk into the remains of the Müller house, a two-story structure consumed by fire and time. We don't stay long. The house is the kind of dark and cold place that just begs to be left alone. The stairs are still intact, though I can't say for sure what remains of the bedroom where the child Eaton murdered the husband-and-wife headmasters of this ghost of a school.

I shudder, thinking their bones may still be up in that bed.

Most likely some anonymous workers from an anonymous

agency disposed of the corpses. If not, the bodies have surely been picked over by animals.

I know Landis has come to the house because a set of car keys is on the kitchen counter. He may even be upstairs right now, eyes closed, in the room where he watched his parents die, filling himself with memories until he's drunk with them.

We don't go up to investigate, but we do take the keys.

Next stop, the fire-eaten ruins of a nearby building, the one I thought looked like barracks. I think this is where we slept as children. Four rooms, and we explore each. Children's clothes are littered in the remains. Sweatpants, T-shirts, winter gloves. I kick through the ash and rubble, looking at the things that used to be ours, memories forming and fading almost simultaneously, zeroing each other out, leaving me dizzy.

Something sparkles, catches my eye. In all these remains, something shines, catching the embers of the dying sun. I reach down and pick it up.

A watch. Gold edging around the glass.

Child's size.

A smiling Mickey Mouse splashes across the face of the watch.

"What is that?" Jake asks.

I hand it to him. He studies it a moment before his eyes widen.

"Oh my god," he says.

"What?"

"It's the watch from my father. My biological father. I don't remember it, but I have a picture of me wearing it on my sixth birthday." He looks up at me. "On the plane, you asked me if I'd ever lost something and then found it in a place I was sure I'd already looked.

That made me think of this watch. I don't know why, since I'd never found it. But this is what I thought of." He smiles, seems to fight back tears, then slides the watch into his front pocket.

"A little bit of magic," I say.

"I suppose so."

Back in the main building, Jake and I decide what to do. Night closes in, we're cold, wet, and hungry, our fatigue pronounced, and his injuries aren't going to get better on their own. But I don't see how we can navigate the tree-covered path back to the car in the dark, and if we somehow manage it and drive away, Landis will be stranded here in the mountains. Maybe he prefers it that way, and perhaps he plans to simply give himself fully to this place. But wherever he is in this moment, we agree we're not ready to abandon him.

There's no power in the building. We find flashlights with dead batteries, but we also find several boxes of matches. There is food, most of it rummaged or rotten, along with cans of soup and vegetables that expired decades ago.

Jake is unable to move without pain, but I use the remaining light to race around the small campus and gather some supplies, returning each time with arms full. Bathrobes and blankets from the Müller's house, which I found in a downstairs closet. A first-aid kit. Two tiki torches and a bottle of citronella oil from the maintenance shed. And, miraculously, a bottle of red wine. Jake unearths a corkscrew from the kitchen.

We fill and light the torches, which give off an acrid smoke that smells of my newly discovered childhood. Outside, on an old picnic bench by the firelight, Jake strips and cleans his wound the best he can, which mainly consists of pouring rubbing alcohol on it until he nearly passes out from the pain. He then wraps it in fresh gauze.

I slip on the robe, monogrammed WLM, and its softness reminds me just how exhausted I am. Likewise, Jake slips into his robe and we open the wine. We have no glasses but are comfortable taking swigs back and forth. It's cheap red wine, the kind that doesn't get better with age, but it's the best thing I've ever tasted.

I look up and see the stars, which are packed so densely together, it looks like a phosphorescent fog. Not too often a girl from Boston gets to look to the sky and see the Milky Way, but I vaguely recall doing this very thing, night after night, long ago.

More and more memories return, some of them finally staying put, letting me rebuild my past. It's not the feeling I imagined. I always thought if I could suddenly remember, it would be overwhelming. A sensory and emotional overload. But it's not that at all. It's just a feeling of needed comfort, like sitting by a campfire on a brisk night.

Maybe the overwhelming part comes later as I really start to process all the images in my mind. The school, the other children. The Müllers. The vitamins and the books.

And even before that. My birth parents, looking back and smiling at me as we eat ice cream in our car.

That is one memory standing out above all others, and perhaps it will overwhelm me, but right now, it just feels perfect. So unexpected, but now it makes sense.

It's a memory of Jake from when we were children.

But this memory is from before the school.

That image of eating ice cream in the car. My parents look back and smile at me, but they smile at Jake too. He is sitting next to me in the back seat. Mussed hair, scrunched nose, and a tiny brown spot of chocolate ice cream on his chin, which he doesn't even know about.

I take a swig of wine and pass the bottle to Jake.

"Do you remember?" I ask him.

SEVENTY-FIVE
Jake

WHAT A HUGE, OPEN question.

Do you remember?

A few days ago, the answer would simply have been *no*. There were no memories of anything a few days ago. Now there are thousands of them.

But Clara isn't asking if I remember things in general. She's asking about one thing.

One specific memory from my past.

It came to me as I was underwater, when I thought I was on the losing side of the life-death balance. A memory of Clara from the lost time. The time before the school.

"I do," I say.

She stares straight ahead at the torch flame and reaches her hand out to me, which I take. I know now I have a history of holding her hand. I did it when we witnessed the murders in the house behind us. I did it when we were told our own parents were dead. As a child, I would always grasp Clara's hand when she was scared, telling her *Everything's going to be okay.*

That's just what a big brother does.

SEVENTY-SIX

One month later

JAKE BUCHANNAN STARED DOWN at the checkerboard and waited for his daughter to make a move. As he did, he gave himself a quick test.

What did I have for dinner last night?

The answer came after a few, long moments.

Chicken piccata. Asparagus.

He'd quizzed himself frequently since coming home. The answers to his short-term memory questions weren't coming much faster than before, but they came. He rarely searched his mind only to find blank space, certainly not as frequently as before.

And the past.

The *way* past. The lost time.

Jake had found it.

His childhood, his early years. Even as far back as age four. It was all there. Mostly.

Jake wanted to think he was becoming normal, but that wasn't quite it. There was nothing normal about the sudden wells of creativity and inspiration he'd experienced since his time in the Colorado mountains. It certainly wasn't normal for him to take these bursts and contain them, absorb them, and use them with such high degrees of productivity.

Jake had finished his novel.

The one about nostalgia, the novel that was nearly as old as Em and had still been sitting half-written on his laptop's hard drive. He'd had it all visualized in his mind but had not yet written anything down, maybe a little out of fear of his ideas turning rotten once they were actually written down.

In the past month, he'd restructured and rewritten all of what he'd had, about forty thousand words, and then added an extra fifty thousand to complete it. He was on his second draft now, excited at all the ways he'd been finding to make it better.

The entirety of it simply unfolded before him soon after he started the program, and all he had to do was type the words. Even though he'd since discarded all remaining pills and hadn't taken another look at the book, all his ideas about the novel remained firmly rooted in his mind.

The novel wasn't quite about nostalgia anymore. When he thought about it, he realized it was about finding things long since lost. Time. Love. Money. Memories.

Magic.

Em made her move. With ruthless efficiency, she jumped three of Jake's black checker pieces and landed on the edge of the board.

"King me," she said.

Jake topped her piece with one of hers he'd captured earlier. As he did, the word *king* stirred the faintest quiver of panic inside him.

Let's play a game of war.

"Tell you what," he said. "I'll *queen* you."

"What does that do?"

"Gives you the same power as a king, but also makes you nicer and smarter."

Em shrugged. "Fine. I'm still going to win."

"So much for being nicer," he said.

Em burst out giggling, which always ended in a snort of delight.

Jake decided then and there he could listen to that sound for the rest of his life.

At the game's end (she won, with only the slightest lack of effort on Jake's part), Jake cleaned dishes in the sink and told Em to get ready for bed. Abby was entrenched in a show on the couch, and Jake planned to join her after getting the mail. He didn't even like the show, but wanted just to sit next to her and not think about anything.

He fetched the mail in the dark, which grew ever earlier this time of year. He tried to rifle though the pieces under the streetlight but gave up.

In the house, he looked again, finding an assortment of the usual crap. He felt the slight twinge at a bright-pink flyer, remembering the flyer that had started everything. But this wasn't an ad for a revolutionary clinical trial. It was the announcement of a new car wash.

Tucked inside the small bundle was the last piece of mail he inspected.

A postcard, with a picture he knew well. A photo of the Maroon Bells.

He almost didn't turn it over to read the back. He almost didn't want to know who had sent this and why. It could be good; it could be decidedly not good. But in the end, he flipped it over and was glad he did.

Should have ducked was the extent of the message. That, and a signature, which was nothing but a letter of the alphabet.

L

EPILOGUE

The Book of Clara
1/7/2019

Final Entry

I've just come from a visit with Em, and upon my arrival home, I saw this journal where I left it at the far end of the kitchen counter, tucked next to the coffee maker. It's been sitting there for over two months, collecting dust, as I have a daily wrestle with myself over what to do with it. It is, after all, a suicide note. A collection of scattered memories of a fractured and incomplete life, peppered with deathly overtones and moments of wonder. I can't bring myself to throw it away, because, after all, it is *me*. But it saddens me to look at it, as if reminding me of something from my past that has long slipped away. So this is nostalgia, I suppose.

After visiting my niece—a niece I never knew I had until recently—I am reminded again of how beautiful life is and have decided this book should have one final chapter, one filled with hope, such as I define it. In my daydreams, I imagine taking this book and having Jake add to it, telling what he remembers since the day he went to visit Landis in his little Boston office. We'll add in the photocopies of the Müllers' journal, and perhaps the letter Landis received from the anonymous teacher. An illustration from *The Responsibility of Death*. We'll bundle it all together and maybe have it published as a curiosity, or even a warning. I have even thought of the title. *The Dead Girl in 2A*.

Truth is, I'm not allowed to say anything to anyone. I will likely just bury everything in the back of a closet somewhere and let it sit untouched, until either it disappears for good or someone finds it after my bones have finally settled into silence.

I have a brother.

I knew Jake and I were connected at a deeper level than merely orphans thrown together at a school, but it all came together beneath that rotten water. In the slideshows that flashed as my air ran out, I saw us all together. Jake, myself, our parents. I remembered Jake holding me when we were told our parents had been killed in a car accident, knowing what death meant but not understanding the foreverness of it all. He squeezed me tightly and told me everything would be okay, but he was also just a child, scared, confused, full of tears, and suddenly lost in the world.

Washburn.

That's our real last name. Jake and Clara Washburn. Brother and sister orphans, and one-third of the enrollment of Arete Academy, a school that technically never existed. We were drugged after the death of the Müllers, then separated and given new names, new stories. Just like that, the only family ties we each had left were conveniently severed by those for whom the truth only sears and burns.

It makes sense to me now the Müllers used orphans in their program. It wasn't just the convenience of having little family left. The program hinged on an innate understanding and acceptance of death. The orphans in the school were already tragically qualified.

After Eaton took his final breath underwater, Jake and I spent the night at the school, cold and uncomfortable, with him in considerable pain. Yet it was also wonderful, being there with him, talking of our past lives, each of us filling in gaps for the other. We slept some, and when we woke at dawn, we went back into the Müllers' house and called for Landis. He did not answer, nor did we find him anywhere else on the school grounds. The man in the gray fedora disappeared from our lives as quickly as he'd entered, like a specter from a Dickens story. Whether he's now alive or dead, I like to think he's where he wants to be.

On the way to the hospital, Jake called his wife, Abby, and could hardly talk through his tears. He wept and wept, not out of sadness, but I think out of love. He explained little but promised Abby he was fine and would be coming home soon. For her part, I think she was rightly concerned about his state of mind, but they hung up with her telling him she loved and missed him. It was what he needed to hear.

Jake's injuries were treated back in Denver. We knew the police would become involved once the gunshot wound was revealed, and indeed they were. Jake and I had discussed this, deciding there was no way around the truth, so the first person to whom we began telling our truthful story was a young patrol officer. She did a poor job hiding the disbelief on her face and quickly summoned a detective. The detective seemed more curious, especially with Jake's revelation about the man he killed in a Denver office park and of Eaton's body, which could be found floating in a small indoor therapy pool in the mountains. We even inquired if there was any interhospital information about a woman named Elle—last name unknown—treated for a gunshot wound. The hospital staff replied they couldn't reveal such information, were they even to have any.

Neither of us was charged with a crime or held for psychiatric observation, which surprised me. We were simply told to remain in Denver for a few more days in case there were follow-up questions.

We went back to the Four Seasons, with Jake bandaged for the gunshot wound and wrapped up with three bruised ribs, and both of us shot full of antibiotics. Eaton's credit card was still on file, so we used it to secure an extra room. A small favor the dead man could do for me.

That first night away from the school, I slept a long,

dreamless sleep, and when I woke, I was disoriented and unsure of my surroundings, needing a full minute to remember where I was. I had a moment of panic that the solid sleep had erased my old memories, shaking me like an Etch A Sketch, wiping me clean. But no, I could still remember whole swaths of my distant past. Disney World with Jake and our parents. First grade at an elementary school, before Arete Academy. Later, dinners in the mountains, citronella-filled tiki torches blazing the mosquitoes away.

The memories were still there, and moreover, new ones kept coming, as if a tiny fissure in my mind was opening wider by the moment, allowing my old life to spill into my current one.

I was no longer bothered by the outside world, no longer afraid to be around people. If anything, I gained more a sense of wanderlust than anything else, wanting to soak in the world as much as I could. I had a sudden, innate understanding that life was short, precious, and not to be wasted tucked inside a shoe box like a keepsake.

On the second day at the Four Seasons, a man came to visit Jake and me. An avuncular man, short gray hair, compact, round glasses, and a gray suit a bit too large for his body, as if his advanced age had caused him to start withering away.

He introduced himself as Charles Manheim and claimed he knew the Müllers quite well when they worked first with the Department of Defense, and then with Arete

Academy. Mr. Manheim said he still worked with the government in an advisory capacity, but didn't provide any specifics.

He said we were free to return to Boston and that there would be no continued criminal investigation against Jake for what was clearly a self-defense killing. But he made it very clear that the condition for our freedom was to keep what happened to us a secret, telling no one other than those closest to us. If the story of the school and what happened there began appearing in the media, they might have to reassess Jake's criminal culpability.

Manheim stressed the school site would be appropriately sanitized—something poor government communication had prevented from happening long ago—and that were Jake to make claims, proving them would be an impossible task. The only residual evidence amounted to no more than bizarre children's books, some unlabeled medication, and photocopies of a journal and a letter. He was confident our story wouldn't register with more than the fringiest of conspiracy theorists.

Jake and I agreed to his demands. Jake did, however, tell Abby everything. She reacted appropriately: disbelief and anger at first, as if he was concocting an impossible story for no discernible reason. Then gradual acceptance, coupled with a fresh volley of anger for keeping it a secret so long. Then the anger shot outward—to Landis and Eaton, to the Müllers, to the government as a whole, for creating and fostering such a program to begin with.

Jake didn't tell Abby that Raymond Higgins was one of the orphans, fearing if he did, she might not remain silent.

Yet her anger was ultimately overpowered by concern and her love for her husband and, perhaps, relief there actually was a reason for his changes.

They are working things out. Abby has gone back to work in marketing, and Jake has contracted for two more ghostwriting projects, so they seem to be keeping up with Em's medical bills. He's also landed an agent for his novel, and she's starting to shop the manuscript out to publishers. I asked to read it, and as I did, I had a constant catch in my throat, a heaviness in my chest, and a tear always falling (or threatening to). It's about all the things we lose in life, and having lost so much myself, I was caught in the ineluctable current of his narrative and swept away. It's beautiful, haunting, and sometimes desperately sad. A perfect parallel to life.

The best news is Jake's moved back into the house. He and Abby are going to make it, he assures me. Actually, what he said was "Everything's going to be okay."

Abby and Em also had to accept a new woman in their life: me. The sister-in-law and aunt no one ever knew existed. I've visited a handful of times, awkward at first, and then smoother with each subsequent meeting. And Em. Oh, what a wondrous girl. She and I have developed a bond, and she has told me quite a bit about her accident and recovery. Her occupational and physical therapy have helped immensely, and she tells me the doctors believe there will be no long-lasting effects from the accident. *Good as new*, she tells me. She even says she's growing to like the scar on her face. That it makes her feel special, like Harry Potter.

I see much of Jake in her, though truth be told, I still hardly know my own brother. I have finally found my family, and I'm going to make sure I continue to build memories with them.

As for my adoptive parents, I haven't told them anything. I will someday, when I'm ready to reconnect. To them, I'm sure, I'm as damaged as ever.

Eaton is gone, his body *sanitized* by those responsible for such things. Jake received a postcard we're certain was from Elle, and finding out she was alive filled me with immeasurable joy. Though I only knew the woman a few hours, I'd felt a responsibility for her, wanting to save her as much as she was trying to save us.

As for Landis, I like to picture him very much alive and holed up somewhere, experimenting with the program, with himself the sole test subject. Perhaps he's becoming the great person his parents envisioned for all of us, blossoming from his natural talents. Maybe in the process he's adopted the same philosophy as Jake and me, which is to appreciate what we've become and to seek no further. We have new memories. We remember the good things along with the bad, and through life, however long it lasts, I'm not sure how any person can ask for more than that.

I remember.

How I've wanted to say that for so long.

I remember.

So no more book and no more pills for either Jake or myself.

Now I begin a journey, this one physical instead of mental. I'm going to take the funds I have left and visit all those places I've only explored within the stacks of books in my tiny apartment. Venice, Istanbul, and Paris...just for starters. I'll run out of money, and then I'll figure things out from there. I'm sure I'll eventually come back, but for now, I have the deepest, insatiable desire to wander. Perhaps wandering has always been my natural talent, and now I will become exceptional at it.

I never used to believe the cliché *Life's too short*. Life always felt painfully slow to me, a job that had to be done, clocking in and out every day with little understanding of purpose. But then a strange man with a fedora appeared in my life, and now I get it. I'm awake. I'm alive. I can *breathe*, and that's a gift not to be wasted, because some day, those breaths will stop and I will be gone, as lifeless as that old crow on the leaf-strewn grounds of the woods.

So here's my promise to myself: Whatever time I have left I will fill with joy, love, compassion, and—above all else—grand adventures.

So goodbye, Dear Reader.

I'm walking out of these woods.

It's my responsibility to do so.

Clara Stowe
Boston, Massachusetts. For now.

Author's Note

The chemical compounds fictionalized in this book are rooted in the quite-real drug scopolamine, which is derived from the borrachero ("drunk") tree found throughout regions of South America and most prevalently in Colombia. The drug has been used recreationally for inducing hallucinations, used by the CIA as a truth serum during the Cold War, and employed by the Nazis during WWII in experimentation on prisoners. Side effects consist of pronounced memory loss and a relinquishing of free will, which is why the compound has become a horrifyingly effective weapon for street crime around the world. It can be transmitted by simple touch, rendering the victim susceptible to any suggestion the assailant chooses.

In this novel, William Müller created two derivatives of scopolamine, one of which was meant to magnify the suggestibility effects of the drug and pair its administration with other psychological methods, with the intention of creating high-achieving children. The other derivative intensified the memory-loss aspects and was only to be used to wipe the memories of the children in the case of an emergency or abject failure of the program. Müller was, at best, only guessing to the best of his scientific abilities as to the efficacy of the compounds, not actually knowing how each child would ultimately react.

For a more detailed look at the powerful effects of scopolamine (also known as Devil's Breath), I highly recommend the VICE documentary on the subject, which is easy to find. Just launch your browser and search "world's scariest drug."

Reading Group Guide

1. When we first meet Jake, he is struggling to come to terms with his responsibility for the car accident that wounded his daughter. How is he dealing with the guilt he feels? How much responsibility do you think he bears for the accident? Have you ever been in a situation where you felt responsible for hurting someone close to you?

2. *The Dead Girl in 2A* is a book about memory and how the things we remember or forget shape our lives. How do you think Jake's life would have been different if he had never forgotten the things that happened to him as a child? How might his life have been different if he never sat down next to Clara on the flight to Denver? Are there things from your own past that you wish you could forget, or do you feel that all your experiences have made you the person you are today?

3. When Clara announces to Jake that she intends to kill herself, he feels a deep sense of responsibility to stop her from doing it. How do you think you would react if you were put in the same

situation? Would you do anything to try to prevent the death of a stranger? If so, what?

4. Jake and Clara both agree to participate in Landis's trial. What do you see as their motivations for doing so?

5. *The Dead Girl in 2A* is written in multiple points of view. Did you feel more connected to the story through one point of view versus another? How do you think having access to the internal thoughts of multiple characters affected your understanding of the story?

6. Many of the characters in *The Dead Girl in 2A* have faced trauma in their pasts. How do you think each character has coped with the events they lived through? How do their coping mechanisms line up with what you know or have experienced regarding the aftermath of traumatic events?

7. Part of the narrative is closely tied to the Maroon Bells, a significant place to several of the characters. Do you have a place in the world that feels significant to you or that you are drawn to time and again? If so, why do you think that is?

A Conversation
with the Author

The Dead Girl in 2A has a very clear theme: memory. Why did you decide to tackle the idea of memory and how it shapes us in this book?

A lot of my books deal with memory in one way or another. I think a large part of this stems from my father's death at the age of sixty-nine from Alzheimer's-related issues. One of my greatest fears is losing my memory, and I think somehow it's therapeutic for me to write about it. Beyond that, memory is simply fascinating. It's this intangible, weightless, disembodied thing that makes up so much of who we are, guides so many of our decisions, and forms our opinions about emotions ranging from happiness to terror. We are our memories, and we don't even really understand them.

Why did you choose the Maroon Bells as a significant place in this story?

Though I live in Colorado, I don't set many scenes here. In general, I like to write about places I'm not all that familiar with, because then I get to discover a new world. But in crafting this story, I knew I wanted a secluded mountain area as the setting for the school, and I wanted a location that plausibly had an air of the fantastic about it (like the Oceanic survivors' island in *Lost*). The Maroon Bells has that kind of mystique, and I thought it would provide the kind of setting necessary to imprint so strongly on my characters.

You have published several previous novels. Does it get easier to write the longer you have been doing it? Was there anything particularly challenging about writing this novel?

Some things get easier the more you write: setting the scene, establishing the flow, driving the pace. The part that doesn't get easier is the most enjoyable aspect of writing for me: figuring out what the hell the story is all about. I don't outline, so I tend to write a series of events that I find interesting without a whole lot of idea as to where the story is going. About halfway through a novel, I'll start to take a look at the book's trajectory and make some decisions about direction, but even those decisions are subject to change as I continue on. It's not uncommon that a major plot point occurs to me 75 percent in, and that realization often changes much of what I've already written.

The Dead Girl in 2A is very much a book that, in the process of its creation, had several threads I needed to tie together but wasn't sure how. In that regard, it was probably the most difficult book I've written to date. But I loved finding new ways to evolve the plot, close open loops, and (hopefully) keep the reader guessing. Every story line is a problem to be solved, and I love solving problems.

Did you do any research to bring this novel to life?

I did. I researched locations, covert government programs, the effects of scopolamine on the human brain, memory loss, among other things. Definitely more research than normal for me, and I have to say it was a lot of fun. I just wouldn't want anyone looking at my internet cache.

What does your writing process look like? Do you always write in the same place at the same time every day?

I write in the mornings and/or evenings. It's important for me to be consistent in location and time when I write, because writing is a job and it should be treated that way. If I wrote only when I "felt the muse," I'd never get anything done. I need to sit down and type regardless of my mood, and that's most easily achieved with a firm schedule. In the mornings, it's a coffee shop; in the evenings, it's in a leather chair at home, or perhaps sipping a margarita in a bar.

If you could have lunch with any writer, dead or alive, who would you choose, and what would you talk with him or her about?

I'd dine with the late Douglas Adams (*The Hitchhiker's Guide to the Galaxy*). I don't know what I'd ask him specifically, but I imagine he has some hysterical stories to tell. I'd just sit back and listen.

What is the best piece of writing advice you have ever received? How about the worst?

It's a cliché, but the best advice is *put your ass in the chair and write*. Seriously, it doesn't get any simpler than that, but somehow the actual act of writing is the biggest obstacle for aspiring writers. Everyone has an idea, but it's hard work writing the idea out. Like anything else, it takes practice and repetition. If you write every day, you will eventually write a book. It might suck, but, hey, you wrote a book! The more you write, the better you will become at it.

I think the worst advice (at least for me) is to read as much as possible within your own genre. I say read what you like to read, and write what you like to write. Maybe those two realms intersect; maybe they don't. I love to read memoirs, historical nonfiction, literary fiction, short stories, essays, a bit of horror, and, of course, thrillers. I find that writers who read obsessively within a genre in order to "crack the code" are the least likely to come up with an original story.

(and roughest) version of anything I write, and God bless your savage honesty.

I'm always grateful for permission to use lyrics from my favorite band, James, so thank you, Tim Booth and the rest of the gang. It's been too long since I've caught one of your shows, so I need to make that a priority.

Dad, I think you would have liked this one.

To all readers, thank you for picking up (or downloading) this book. None of this works without you.

Carter Wilson
Erie, Colorado
February 2019

Acknowledgments

Jessica, this book is dedicated to you. I cannot express how truly grateful I am for your love, support, and guidance. We are on a wonderful journey together.

To Pam Ahearn, my longtime agent, thank you for navigating this book (and all my others) along the road to publication, and for all the wisdom you've imparted along the way. To Anna Michels, sleepless editor extraordinaire, a special thanks for putting this book on shelves and keeping me grounded through all the edits. You truly made this a better story. And, of course, to the entire Sourcebooks/ Poisoned Pen team, I am in continuous awe at your capabilities, creativity, and enthusiasm. *Thank you.*

Mom, thanks for your feedback and editorial finesse. Ili and Sawyer, you continue to make me proud, crack me up, and freak me out... What more could a dad want? Henry, I love watching you become your own storyteller. Sole, I value our friendship over all the years. Of course, a huge thank-you to my Old Possum critique-group friends: Dirk, Linda, Sean, Abe, and Sam. You always see the first

About the Author

ELKE HOPE PHOTOGRAPHY

USA Today and #1 *Denver Post* bestselling author Carter Wilson has written six psychological thrillers as well as numerous short stories. He is a two-time winner of the Colorado Book Award, and his critically acclaimed novels have received multiple starred reviews from *Publishers Weekly*, *Booklist*, and *Library Journal*. Carter lives in Erie, Colorado, in a Victorian house that is spooky but isn't haunted… yet.

To check Carter's appearance calendar, subscribe to his irreverent monthly newsletter, or to inquire about his availability for speaking events, book clubs, or media requests, please visit carterwilson.com.